ALSO BY THOMAS MCCALL

A Wide and Capable Revenge

BEYOND ICE,
BEYOND DEATH

BEYOND ICE,
BEYOND
DEATH

THOMAS McCALL

NEW YORK

LIBRARY OF CONGRESS CATALOGING-IN-PUBLICATION DATA

McCall, Thomas
Beyond Ice, Beyond Death / Thomas McCall.
p. cm.
ISBN 0-7868-6022-7
1. Policewoman—Chicago—Fiction. 2. Woman amputees—
Illinois—Chicago—Fiction. 3. Chicago (Ill.)—Fiction.
I. Title
PS3563.C3342B49 1994
813' .54—dc20   94-12713
CIP

Designed by Holly McNeely

FIRST EDITION

10   9   8   7   6   5   4   3   2   1

FOR MY MOTHER
&
IN MEMORY OF MY FATHER

BEYOND ICE,
BEYOND DEATH

ONE

FEBRUARY 1989

The Phobos case began early on a day shift. Twenty minutes after the call hit Area Six, our station house, we started north on Lake Shore Drive. Dawn had cracked the horizon an hour before, and a low, orange sun glared across Lake Michigan. A radio call-in show said the temperature was ten below zero.

In my Plymouth Fury, I led our pilgrims past the bleak winter emptiness of Belmont Harbor and into Lincoln Park. My partner, fifty-five-year-old Art Campbell, shivered in the passenger seat. Behind us were an ambulance—it ferried a clean-sheeted, empty litter—and two trailing squads. For murder, we come in caravan.

By way of introduction, my name is Nora Callum. I am a Chicago homicide detective, divorced and thirty-four years old. I'm a tall and plain-looking woman with a left peg leg, a plastic and metal prosthesis I've used for walking since losing my leg at mid-thigh during a drug shoot-out. In spite of my appearance, Meg, my eight-year-old daughter, will often beam at me with wide eyes, and tell me I'm beautiful and smooth-gaited. On good days, I choose to believe her.

"Where's the heat in this buggy?" Art said.

I flipped the heater switch to HIGH. A blast of frigid air shocked our lower halves.

"Oh, shit!" he yipped. "Turn it off!"

"But, Arthur—"

"I wasn't meant to live in this goddamned icebox of a city."

I looked over at him: the grin across his heavy black face disarmed me, even at seven-thirty in the morning. "Forget your longies today?" I chided. Art sheathed himself in woolen long underwear from October to May, unwrapping only for rare trips home to his roots in Alabama.

"Don't act the comedian," he said. "Who's out there waiting?"

"Ann Reilly."

"The redhead who works the lobby on p.m.'s? The one with the half-crossed eye?"

"She's been moved to a squad car," I said.

"Poor thing can't weigh a hundred pounds. They've got her on the street?"

"She's very good, Arthur. She's got fine judgment and a big revolver."

"She find the body?"

"No, a call-in to nine-one-one. A jogger spotted it."

"Someone running in this weather? Must have shit for brains."

We turned off the Drive at the Waveland Golf Club, a lake-hugging course run by the city. The exit road twisted along the edge of the golf course to our left. Pristine snow shrouded Waveland's bumps and flats, the snow's crust sparkling in the sun like sugared pastry. On our right, we saw a fenced stand of trees, their branches bare, their northern sides pasted white with snow. A clutch of small buildings—equipment sheds and workshops used in summer when the golf course was open—stood at the end of the road, close to the lake. Reilly's squad was parked alongside one of the buildings.

Reilly stepped from her squad; a man in the passenger seat turned to watch. Art and I left the Fury to stand with Reilly in a tight circle, all of us bundled against the lake's sneaky wind.

"Welcome to life on the beat," Art said to Reilly. "And you left the station house for this?"

"It got me to the day shift," she said, "plus an extra fifty bucks a week."

The freezing air pinked Reilly's cheeks, and the wind man-handled her short red hair. Her eyes were as Art had remembered, just the tiniest bit out of sync with each other.

"What gives, Ann?" I said.

She pointed toward the fenced trees. "He's over there, at least I think it's a he. My guy in the car found him while cross-country skiing."

I motioned the man out of Reilly's car. He wore nylon ski pants and a jacket and hat, everything stark yellow and red. "I'm Lieutenant Callum, from Homicide," I said as he approached, "and this is Lieutenant Campbell."

"Bill Hamlick," the man said. His face was round, his eyes bulbous. I put him in his early twenties.

"You ski around here often?"

"Usually I jog, but last week's snow messed up the running path."

Art said, "This is your same route every day?"

"Yes, but today's the first day I've been off the running path. If I'd been there, I wouldn't have seen anything. Too far away."

Art waved the others out of the warmth of their squads, then briefed them. Dennis Baker, the photographer, went ahead before we did any more damage to the scene. Baker moved toward the trees, aiming, clicking, rewinding his camera furiously. When he stopped at the strip of beat-up snow that I assumed was the running path, he called, "Nora, you want to look here before I go in closer?"

"I'm coming." I started toward him carefully, my prosthetic leg always unsure of itself on snow and ice.

The running path was a frozen jumble of gravel and footprints, a hard, lumpy channel trampled through the snow by crazed joggers. A chain-link fence with a central gate stood ten yards beyond the path. The fence defined the grove of trees we had seen on the way in, trees that clustered around areas of scattered openness. The snow showed a pair of ski tracks paralleling the fence, and two sets of footprints between the running path and the fence.

"Ann," I said, "these footprints—"

"Mine and Hamlick's," she said. "There were no tracks off the path when I came, just Hamlick's ski markings. When you get closer, you can see where he stopped at the fence to look, then started up again."

"Okay, Dennis," I said, "shoot the ski tracks, then move to the fence and start on the body. I want some shots before we go through the gate."

Behind me, Art was directing the others. Cold as it was, everybody worked methodically, no one complaining.

Mute, our pilgrims stood along the fence and peered through, breathing cones of steam. A half-dozen sparrows flitted in nearby branches. These sentinels chirped gaily, but none of us were able to speak. Seeing was enough.

The blue-gray face lay at the edge of a flat of ice just inside the fence. A swaddle of snow allowed only chin, mouth, nose, and closed eyes to be seen. The rest of the body seemed lost and unimportant.

Next to me, Art whispered, "Where is he? Is there any more of him?"

I shivered and clung harder to the fence. "Has to be, don't you think? Under the ice?"

Reilly turned away and walked a few feet back toward the path.

I placed a gloved hand over my mouth and nose; the stump of my left thigh ached in its freezing socket. Water gathered at the corners of my eyes.

Art playfully flicked his elbow into my side. "My go, partner." He turned to Alice Adams, our evidence woman. "Alice!" he hollered. "I need that little shovel you carry!"

Shovel in hand, Art moved to the hinged gate and pushed it open. He stepped onto the ice with one foot, carefully testing its strength. Nothing cracked, so he walked the several feet to the face and looked back toward us. "Any volunteers?" he asked, with a quirky laugh. "Or does the old guy get all the shit jobs?"

Our laughter scared the sparrows away. Art chipped at the ice on the side of the face opposite us; ice chinking like glass under his shovel, he moved away from the chin, toward where the neck and torso would begin. Diligently he worked away, sometimes kneeling, every minute or two bending close enough to the ice to kiss it, his breath pouring out fast and looking hot enough to melt the ice.

Finally, he stood and faced us, the shovel slack in his hand, sweat glistening on his black temples and in his mustache. With pilgrims at full attention, he said, "The body's clothed and fat and under the ice. He's all here, I guess, except for the side of his head that you guys can't see. That whole side's gone, blown all to hell."

We cordoned off the area from the running path to the fence. While Art and the ambulance men hacked at the ice, I divided the scene into grids that the rest of us walked sequentially, looking for clues. This first hour after discovery would be the most productive one. I was determined not to botch it; crime scenes don't lie.

The choppers found the ice to be several inches thick, with a three-foot depth of dark, brackish water under that. Muck made the bottom of the shallow pit a stinking swamp in summer, the Parks Department would tell us later that day.

The front half of the body was as hard as the ice that encased it. The rump and back, in water only, were softer, but not rotten. He had been lying in a north-south direction, with the exploded back and right side of his head on the bank and hidden in the mounded snow. Underneath his head there was no snow, only what seemed to be brain tissue on a bed of pale, bloodied, flattened grass. Our man had been in residence here for some time, at least since before the winter's first snowfall.

As Art had said, he was fully clothed: dark trousers, plain white dress shirt, white socks, black shoes, a heavy woolen jacket. None of the clothes even verged on any fashion of the previous quarter-century. He wore a muddy gold signet ring on his right fourth finger. An equally filthy gold watch clutched his left wrist. I had no guess as to his age: he could have been twenty or fifty. He was too cold to smell.

The men lifted the huge, dark, dripping body onto a solid

portion of ice. I said, "Hold my arm, Art." I went to kneel next
to the watery black crater in the ice.

"What are you doing, girl?"

"Just hang on to me."

As Art held my left hand, I pulled up my coat sleeve and
reached my ungloved right hand into the freezing water. My icy
fingers bumped something in the muck. I pulled up a leather
wallet the body had been lying on. "Bingo," I said and stood.

But bingo it wasn't. The wallet was empty, not a dollar bill or
credit card or scrap of identification. I looked at Art quizzically.
"Robbery?"

"Lots of damage for a lousy robbery. And would you leave
behind the ring and watch?"

I saw them moving in, three of them, each with a videocamera. I
turned back toward the litter that now held the body. "How'd
they find out so fast?" I said to Art.

He shook his head. "Somebody must be tipping them at the
station."

It was the film crew from Channel 6. Already through the
fence gate, they now glided their cameras around the gruesome
remains. Karl Kramer had the lead, pointing his camera, directing the shots of the others. Kramer was the Channel 6 news edi-
tor and the blight of Chicago's television journalism.

I despised Karl Kramer. A gore-monger, he wasn't satisfied
with the tasteful reporting of the city's violence that other editors
strove for. Kramer lusted for blood, and the bloodier the better,
with never a consideration for victims or families. The *Tribune*'s
television critic has written the most fitting depiction of Karl
Kramer's newscasts: "If it doesn't bleed, it isn't the lead."

My first exposure to Kramer was at my own expense, as I lay
on an ambulance cart, most of my left leg shotgunned away during the raid that changed my life. As Kramer circled me that
night, filming, filming, I used the last of my strength to swing a
fist at his camera, screaming, "Get away from me! Stop it! Stop
it, goddammit!"

But Kramer didn't. Without the audio, he showed me to the

city that night at six and ten and midnight with half a leg, showed me in my torn and bloody underwear to all who cared to watch. I never forgave him for his numbing breach of my privacy. It wasn't in me to forgive him. It won't ever be in me.

Now I yelled, "Kramer! Out of here!"

"Freedom of the press, Lieutenant!" he shouted back. A big, blond fifty-year-old, he was dressed in a puffy ski jacket with an extravagant "6" sewn onto its front.

Art stepped out ahead of me.

"You crossed the tapes," I said. "This is a restricted area."

"Some tape was down," Kramer said.

I looked through the fence to my team. Several shook their heads in denial of Kramer's claim. "That's bullshit, Kramer," I said.

"We can film," he said. "First Amendment rights."

"You can't cross the tapes," I said. "You know that."

Kramer smirked while his flunkies taped away. Incensed, I removed my coat, then laid it over the half-frozen remains, at least covering the face and the wrecked skull. When Kramer reached to remove the coat, Art darted toward Kramer and grabbed his forearm. Squeezing the arm, Art glared at the two other cameramen, who dropped their cameras to their sides. Finally, Art released Kramer. "You've got your pictures," he told Kramer. "Now it's time to leave. Out."

Unmoving, Kramer smiled stupidly.

"Look," Art said, "thirty seconds and we're charging you with obstruction. Thirty seconds and you're busted!"

Kramer and company slithered away. Freezing, I hurried back into my coat.

As the others finished, I explored the perimeter of the fence. Except for the gate we used, there was no access to the enclosed square. We found no gun, no empty cartridges, no footprints, nothing of note. Not surprising for a scene under half a foot of snow.

I walked back to the lake where a thin, icy mist hung over the water. There was no beach here: this part of the shore was covered by huge concrete blocks mortared together to keep storm waves off the land. It was a tall step up to the top of the blocks, but I made it with effort. From that height, the view seemed one of great consequence: south to the Michigan Avenue skyscrapers that doted over the lake; north to Montrose Harbor where, when I was a child, my family and I netted spawning smelt every spring.

Standing in the wind, I wondered if the killer had tried to dump the body into the lake but found him too heavy to lift. It surely would have been easier to drag him to the trees than maneuver him over the boulders. Also, if the murder had occurred the previous autumn, there still would have been leafy trees and ground cover at the edge of the swamp, better camouflage than the lakeshore offered.

Our caravan was now in reverse, with the body first off the scene, tagged and on its way to the Cook County morgue. Art was already in the Fury when I entered. I revved the engine. Before pulling away, I thought of the victim's face haloed by snow, and that vision tightened my throat. I looked to Art. "Thanks."

"For what?" he said.

"For taking the lead back there, when it was time to dig out the face."

"I was cold. I needed the exercise."

"Horseshit."

"C'mon, girl, let's get outa here. Put the pedal to the metal."

TWO

"I'm thinking about the heat," Art said.

"What heat?" I said.

"The heat from Smilin' Ray for a quick arrest."

Raymond Melchior was our Deputy Chief of Detectives at Area Six. "Smilin' Ray" was the moniker Melchior honored in the fullest breach; none of us could recall even a slit of a smile ever brightening his great, sad, walrus-like face.

"You mean because of the neighborhood?" I asked.

"Sure," Art said. "It's all got-buckers who live up there. You think they want brain tissue in the park where they exercise their skinny little asses? Hell, no. Shakes everybody up."

We were driving on Michigan Avenue in the south Loop, ready to head west on Congress on the way to the morgue.

"You're right about Melchior," I said. "Remember the Peterson sisters?"

"The two kids butchered and dumped into Montrose Harbor in waste drums?"

"The same."

"You and Jack Flaherty, right?" Art asked. Jack Flaherty, my partner who'd died of a brain aneurysm, was my co-worker on that case, one of the first big murder cases I helped crack.

"Yeah, Jack and me. Melchior was all over us like a blanket on that one. But Jimmy O'Donnell, the alderman from the Forty-third Ward, was the big problem."

"O'Donnell—the white guy with red glasses?" Art said. "The one who wears thousand-dollar suits to City Council meetings?"

"That's him." I took the turn at Congress. "So when the

Petersons' body parts started floating up to the water's surface—"

"In among the fancy boats in the harbor?" Art interrupted with sham concern smeared across his face. "How dare those arms and legs do that."

"You got it. Well, O'Donnell had gone directly to the Big Maamoo."

"The Commissioner?"

"Worse—the mayor. Everyone demanded an arrest in hours, not days or weeks. They said the city couldn't tolerate that kind of savagery in the Lincoln Park area."

"Okay in the housing projects—the savagery, I mean—but not along the lakefront, right?"

I nodded as I cleared the last stoplight before merging onto the Eisenhower Expressway. I leaned on the Fury's throttle and said, "Anyway, Melchior was ready to fry somebody—anybody— for those Peterson killings. I think Jack and I got the right guy, I really do, but it wouldn't have mattered to Melchior. He just needed someone in the can. To shut up O'Donnell."

"Hey," Art said, "what ward were we just in? The park and golf course?"

"Forty-third."

"Like I said, girl, prepare yourself."

He lay supine on one of the morgue's steel tables, water seeping from his muddy clothes, dripping off the round mountain of his thawing body.

His unwounded face was repugnant. Lips thick and ugly. Nose a bulbous tip beneath a flattened bridge. Eyes puffy and close-set. Skin alternately cratered with pockmarks and humped with hairy moles.

As his face warmed, it lost the pale gray cast of the ice and turned dark and blotchy. The left side of his neck, just under the jawbone, showed two wounds of entry. The right half of his skull was no longer there—blown all to hell, as Art had so aptly reported in the field. The enormity of this crime, the appalling arrogance of the killer, didn't hit me until I saw the wide-open half-skull leaking a thin gruel of brain onto the table.

We stood in circumference and observed a kind of reverential quiet. I stayed a step or two farther from the body than the others, my stomach churning; I suffered from the anxiety that being this close to the unburied dead always incites in me. An irrational fear, but one with the unshakable clench of a mad dog.

After some minutes, Dennis Baker announced, "He's starting to reek."

"Couldn't you leave it unsaid, Dennis?" Alice Adams retorted. "Out of respect maybe? Do you think it's obvious only to you?"

"Don't be so pious, Alice," Luis Jiminez, the ambulance driver, said. "Take a whiff. The guy stinks. Okay?"

This, I knew, was the wrangle of sensitive people who were forced to deal with the debris of excessive violence. It's noble to be outraged by murder, like the residents of the Forty-third Ward who would be so properly scandalized, but let them try physically touching, lifting, and undressing the mangled dead. Let them try that and then return home to their family to act warm and loving.

I sucked a deep breath to settle my stomach, then stepped ahead. "Okay, guys, c'mon," I said. "Chill, chill."

Dennis and Alice and Luis all looked at one another across their triangle. They smiled faintly in apology. Art said, "Got enough photos, Dennis?"

"Yes."

"Okay," I said, "let's print the watch and ring, then get him out of his things so Dorner can do the preliminary."

We checked the man's jewelry for latent fingerprints and, as expected, found nothing. Next, we undressed the body, everybody helping to lift its huge mass. He was cold and soft and wet. I stayed as long as I could stand it, then retreated, my pretext that I would go through his pockets.

His pants yielded a soaked handkerchief and a wad of bills, nearly one hundred dollars in all. In his jacket I found a chain with two keys, both undistinguished, neither looking like a car key. I placed his clothes and shoes in plastic bags that would be taken back to Area Six where everything would be hung up to dry, then re-examined later. Finished with the clothes, I washed the jewelry in a nearby sink and set it aside.

"You might be right about this not being a robbery," I called to Art, who was working with the others.

"What do you mean?" he said.

"I just found a hundred bucks in his pocket. Who leaves cash plus jewelry behind?"

"This may not be Einstein we're dealing with," Art said.

I dried the jewelry, then picked it up for a closer look. The gold signet ring showed the initials E. B. imprinted across its face. Engraved around the ring's inside was the inscription *With love, I. The Golden Swan, 1/88.*

The watch face was ornate but the bounty was on its underside. At the top of the gold backing, printed in a semicircle to follow the curve of the watch, were the words *To E. B. from I.* The bottom curve of the circle read *Thank you, Phobos I.* Between the two inscriptions, taking most of the space of the watch's back, was an abstract drawing showing intersecting ellipses and arcs etched around a small, centrally placed circle.

"Anything?" Art said.

"Something, I guess. The man you're undressing is probably Mr. E. B. and he is probably loved by someone named *I.* And, oh . . . *I.* has Phobos I to thank."

"Spell it."

"P - h - o - b - o - s. Phobos. Phobos I."

"Hot shit. What is it?"

Ignoring his question, I slipped the jewelry into my purse. "And then there's the Chagall drawing on the back of the watch. Circles and arcs and ellipses."

"Is *I.* male or female?" Art asked.

"Take your pick."

"I rate this a shade less than we need to issue a warrant."

"Yes, Arthur, but anybody can solve the easy ones."

Dressed in a starched shirt, yellow knit tie, and an immaculate lab coat, Vincent Dorner stood close to the autopsy table, his hands buried in the front pockets of his coat. Dorner was a square, dense man with the appearance of a career marine officer. The parts of his face—craggy nose, thin hard lips, deep-set eyes—fought to come together smoothly but never would. This, plus his severe gray crew cut, proclaimed him a man who suffered no bullshit. He was the county's chief forensic pathologist, one of those physicians who preferred the already dead to the still vital.

All had backed away from the table in deference; only Tommy Banks, an immense black man and Dorner's assistant, stood behind him, a towering acolyte. Dorner began a slow, thoughtful procession around the naked body, bending slightly at times, alternately peering through, then over his half-frame glasses, stopping longest to study the deceased's abdomen and half-head.

At the end of his excursion, when he had come full circle, Dorner turned to me. "This yours, Callum?"

Nervous, though I had worked with Dorner before, I tugged stupidly at my skirt, feeling my stump where it entered its prosthesis. "Mine."

"Yours, too, then, Campbell?"

Art nodded.

"Good," Dorner said. "Then I trust we have half a chance to find the son-of-a-bitch who did this."

Art and I said nothing.

"I can't get at him until tomorrow," Dorner said. "I have court in an hour—a child abuse murder."

"Could we start the preliminaries," I asked, "the dentals and the prints?"

"Sure," Dorner said. "Tommy can do that for you now. Any identity here?"

"He's a blank," Art said.

"Then it'll be good to get prints today, to get the ball rolling." Dorner said. "If he's as blank as you say, he won't get high priority on the ID checks."

Dorner turned back toward the body and the victim's left hand. Staring down, he said, "These fingers are shriveled like a floater's. That fit, Callum?"

"Sort of, but he wasn't completely underwater. He was in a shallow pit, on his back, his front half in ice, his bottom in water. His hands were low enough to be in water."

"Tommy," Dorner said, "do him like a floater."

"All right, boss," Tommy piped.

"I'll post him first tomorrow morning," Dorner said. "About eight. Come by then, Callum."

"Yes, I'd like that," I lied.

Tommy rolled in a portable x-ray machine—a clunky, dark-green monster that was no match for his strength. The x-ray tube itself, the business end of the machine, moved on a collapsible metal neck that Tommy positioned next to the body's jawbone. He snapped several x-rays.

For prints, Tommy used a scalpel to slice away the thin cup of tip-skin from each finger. After he removed a segment of skin, he placed it over his own fingertip to give the victim's skin a solid base. Then he delicately rolled his covered tip over an ink pad, imprinting the image onto a standard fingerprint card. He did this ten times, a print for each digit. In an hour, we had a start: a full set of dental x-rays and quality fingerprints.

Outside, the air was clear and cold. On the way back to the station, Art convinced me to detour to Ashkenaz's, the North Side's best take-out deli. Double-parked on Cedar Street, we ate corned-beef sandwiches in the car; Art talked about his hopes for the White Sox that year, while I pretended to listen, but thought only of Meg at school. I hoped she'd found the chocolate surprise I had tucked into her lunchbox early that morning.

After lunch, we drove to Area Six at Belmont and Western Avenues. Our station house is a twenty-year-old, dark-brick two-story born out of betrayal. Although it anchors the diverse West Lake View neighborhood, the building squats on land earlier occupied by a Chicago landmark, Riverview Park, a huge amusement complex. On warm summer nights, Riverview's twisting midway and convulsive roller coasters hustled generations of us Chicagoans through our childhood and teens: the lights and smells and heat and sweat of the park worked on us like magic, like romance. When Riverview's owners dismantled the park in the nineteen-sixties, dismay was great. Some wrongs take an era to be forgiven.

Fueled with corned beef, Art and I entered the Area Six lobby from the Belmont Avenue entrance. Things were unusually quiet that afternoon—the weather, no doubt. Street crime takes a relative holiday on the coldest days; perps and victims alike are content to stay warm inside.

Frankie Luchinski, the day-shift desk sergeant, was on duty. Frankie was a tall, muscular, sometimes genial Pole in his thirties. Art went ahead while I slowed at the desk.

"Hey, Nora," Frankie said, grinning, "I heard you guys went ice fishing in Lincoln Park this morning."

"We hooked one all right. Melchior know yet?"

"Shit, yes. It's all over the noon news."

"TV?" I asked.

"Channel 6."

"Videotape?"

"Complete. Man, some head shots, eh?"

"Asshole," I mumbled, thinking of Karl Kramer.

"What?" Frankie said.

"Nothing. Just talking to myself."

Frankie leaned forward on the countertop, coming close to me. I smelled his cheap cologne, then stepped back. Frankie fancied himself as Area Six's special gift to its female staff, and nothing put me off quicker than that kind of presumption, to say nothing of his smell. Frankie: a reminder that celibacy wasn't all bad.

Frankie said, "Quite a fat-ass, eh, Nora? The stiff, I mean."

"Yeah, quite a fat-ass," I mimicked sardonically, but Frankie was too insensitive to feel the knife's edge. "Smilin' Ray been looking for me yet?"

"He checked once."

When I turned and started away, Frankie said, "By the way, you got a little surprise waiting in the twenty-four-hour hold. Says she won't talk to anybody but you."

I stopped. "Who?"

"Paris."

"They bust her?"

"Early this morning. Too late for night court. But she claims there's no charge that can be made anyway." He snickered, and said, "They gave her the courtesy a real veteran deserves. Said they wouldn't book her till you came in."

"A raid?" I asked.

"Sort of. Not organized. A couple of rookies on Vice—Mather and Schurz."

"They just free-lanced it? Nothing better to do?"

"Something like that." He grinned again.

"Their hormones must be running high," I said. I spun on my prosthetic foot and left.

Her eyebrows, dark and highly arched, always drew my attention first. I suppose it was their nobility, or maybe the way they safe-guarded her vulnerable, pale eyes. I could have been talked out of a year's salary for Paris Viveka's eyes and brows.

She was dressed in jeans and a fuzzy, red-and-black woolen sweater. Her night without sleep had made her look every minute of her thirty-five years. We sat across from each other at a bare metal table in a room on Area Six's second floor. The only window looked out on the parking lot that held our district's crashed police squads.

"You don't need an ashtray?" I said.

"I quit," Paris said. "Since Michael Furey, three weeks ago. He hates it. The stink, I mean."

"Jesus. Must be quite the guy. A bartender you said?"

"At Juliet's. On Cedar, just off Rush."

I nodded.

"So I quit. That's it, kiddo."

"C'mon, Paris."

She smiled widely with her lips closed, her cheeks dimpling and her eyes luminous. It was the purest look of joy I had seen her wear in the eight years I'd known her. It was this Michael Furey.

"Cigarettes are killers," she said. "You know that, kiddo. Cancer, heart attacks, and who knows . . . probably hemorrhoids. I mean, the works!"

I laughed, glancing toward the windowed door—Melchior's detectives weren't to frolic with each other, let alone with prostitutes. But Paris and I had been good friends ever since we met as chance hospital roommates following delivery of our daughters eight years before.

Earlier in my career, while working Vice out of the Eighteenth District on Chicago Avenue, I had busted the Rush Street whores regularly, Paris included. Then, as now, the girls were in and out of night court in a few hours, since most of the judges did not regard prostitution as much of a crime. But on Vice we had our job, and a certain quota of arrests to make, perfunctory as they might be.

"Paris, what happened last night?"

"False arrest," she said. "Look, it's three in the morning and Michael's closing at Juliet's. Okay? So we're going out for breakfast afterwards, but while he's tallying the register, I decide to walk over and see the girls on Astor. You know the place."

"Sure, sure."

She spoke of a third-story apartment on Astor Street, the top floor of an elegant brownstone that would sell easily for a million dollars. The place had been an exclusive brothel for twenty-five years or more. All of Vice knew about it, but no one ever raided it. It was as discreet a whorehouse as the city had ever known—never a complaint, never a john robbed, no drugs dealt or used, the girls as clean as they came. The take was simple: they didn't bother us, we didn't bother them. And besides, you never knew who from the City Council or the mayor's office or the Police or Fire Department's staff might be found there. No sense shooting yourself in the foot.

"So," Paris went on, "I'm sitting alone in the living room there, waitin' for one of the girls to finish up. Alone, Nora, got it? No man with me, no money in my hand, I'm alone and I'm dressed. Anyway, in storms these two little coppers—"

"Mather and Schurz."

"Probably had hard-ons just walking in the place."

I laughed out loud, covering my mouth and looking again at the door. Mather and Schurz were the two of the youngest and most diminutive officers at Area Six, maybe on the whole Force.

"They flash their badges," Paris said, "all the while yippin',

'Vice team! Vice! Don't move!' Next thing I know I'm sitting here in the tank."

"And the other girls?"

"Down here, too. All charged and sent before the magistrate. I'm sure they're back on the street already. I said I wouldn't go without you looking at my charges first. I didn't wanna be booked for nothing. I didn't wanna give them the satisfaction."

"I'll look at the sheet," I said.

Paris suddenly leaned toward me, bumping her woolly breasts into the tabletop. "I want those guys up for harassment."

"Forget it, Paris. That's our job, to harass a little now and then."

"By coming into that place? By acting like that?"

"Relax," I said. "Their brains are still in their shorts. What's up with this Michael?"

"It's real," she said. "And don't you laugh at how corny stupid that sounds. Fifteen years of selling my ass should have made me too hard to feel this, but it hasn't. You realize how lucky that is for me, Nora?"

I nodded, staying quiet. She flicked her thumbnail at her top teeth.

My chin in my hands, I asked as casually as I knew how, "Michael realizes what you do for a living?"

She stared at the blank wall behind me. Not looking at me, she said, "Don't do it anymore. Haven't done anything for three weeks, not a single lay since I met the guy." Her eyes came back to me. "I'm looking for work."

"Three weeks? How you getting by?"

"What?"

"Money, I mean."

"No problem, kiddo. Rent's paid for another month. Icebox full. Neptune clothed." Neptune was her daughter, born the same day as Meg. "I figure I've got enough cash for another month."

"Another month? How do you do it?"

She smirked. "'Cause I had a better-paying job than you, Lieutenant."

"No kidding."

"Now, will you get me outa here?"

I touched her hand and stood.

At the desk, I found that Mather and Schurz hadn't made any charge, nor could they have. To charge a prostitute requires a witness to an act of solicitation, or evidence that money had been transferred for sex. As Paris knew, Mather and Schurz had nothing but their own pomp. Paris was out of the station in thirty minutes, but only after promising to go to lunch with me later that week, and to have Michael Furey in tow. I couldn't wait to meet him. In the meantime, I intended to run a check on him.

THREE

Art's and my Area Six office is second-floor, facing south. Our view is out to the long concrete overpass that takes Western Avenue thru-traffic above the crowded Western-Belmont intersection. Margie's Grill, West Lake View's nineteen-forties answer to fast food, nests in the shade of the overpass, and north of Margie's, a used-car lot advertises "suburban driven" specials for three hundred dollars; with luck, the heaps might last through a return trip to the 'burbs.

Our office itself is a study in claustrophobia. With our desks pushed to face each other, we gain a perimeter of floor space to navigate in, a track to pace like caged tigers when we require incessant motion as therapy. Each desktop sports a picture, mine a school photo of Meg, Art's a family pose with his wife, Helen, and their three daughters. A large pot of fake flowers—five bucks' worth of highway robbery from the Maxwell Street flea market—straddles the union of the desks.

Steve Schwartz walked in through a shaft of winter sunlight. Art and I sat at our desks.

"C'mon, c'mon, let's go over what you've got," Schwartz said with characteristic utility as he played circling feline.

I wasn't surprised to see Schwartz in our office—Melchior had no doubt transferred him in. Thirty years old and darkly handsome, Schwartz worked in Missing Persons, floating out when certain cases needed extra manpower.

I pulled a manila envelope from my baggy purse and dumped the contents onto the desktop. E. B.'s ring and watch rattled to a stop; Tommy Banks's dental x-rays and fingerprint card fluttered to softer landings. Schwartz began scavenging through things.

"That's all of it," I said, "except for what's drying out."

"Clothes?" Schwartz asked.

"Them, plus a soaked wallet I found in the water hole. Oh, and a wad of bills from his pants. A hundred bucks or so."

Schwartz began another sweep around the desks, his hand gripping the can of Coke he regularly carried. "Nothing in the wallet, you said, Nora? The bills weren't in the wallet? No IDs?"

"Nothing in the wallet, she told you," Art countered, "not birdshit. You got ears, Steve?"

Dear Art: protective father sheltering teen-aged daughter against World. An unnecessary effort, but I was flattered by it anyway.

"We figure the killer was stupid," I said. "What mugger leaves jewelry like this behind on a dead man?"

Art loosened his tie and opened his collar button. "What's Missing Persons going to do for us?" he challenged Schwartz.

"Tough without an ID," Schwartz said. He swigged his Coke, then sat on the edge of my desk. His smell was him, not all cologne like Frankie.

"So go with the prints and dentals," I said.

"Don't worry, I will," Schwartz said. "Yeah, they're decent enough." Another swig. "Tell me when he died. Narrow the search for me."

"We're not sure," I said. "No post till tomorrow morning. Dorner's in court."

"But we can guess a little," Art said. He lifted his feet up onto his desk. "The guy's probably been there since the beginning of winter."

"Because he comes encased in ice?" Schwartz said.

"And because it was just leaves under his head, no snow."

"Anybody remember the first snow last year?" Schwartz asked.

"Seems like Thanksgiving sometime," I said.

"Yep, that's it," Art said, "for sure. It was a deep one, too. Deep enough to keep me from driving halfway to hell for the family's annual Thanksgiving dinner." In baritone, he chortled, "Man, what a break that was."

I started to laugh but caught myself. It was the flash of darkness to my right: Raymond Melchior.

He loomed at the door, his girth plugging exit or entry. His suit was three-piece gloomy; his tie undertaker black. His forehead sloped to a sagging, flabby face.

We all quieted. The man had that same, conversation-stopping effect on everybody at Area Six. Art brought his feet deckward. Dutiful, Schwartz rose.

Melchior scooted his eyes over us. "I've already had a call from the ward office," he snarled.

"Forty-third?" I asked.

"You got it."

Art said, "Talk about fast."

"Anybody see the noon news?" Melchior said.

"I heard about it from Frankie," I said.

Art looked to me. "Kramer's videotape on it?"

I nodded.

"That son-of-a-bitch," Art said.

Melchior scratched the thinning gray hair over his right ear. "What's this guy doing frozen in a swamp? Most of 'em float up from the lake."

"It's hard to get to the lake from there," I said. "Big boulders to cross, and this guy's a lug. It would've taken Superman—"

"I want something fast on this, Callum," Melchior interrupted. "Fuckin' Jimmy O'Donnell's not gonna let up."

"Might be tough," I said. "The guy's been dead for a while."

"Wrong!" Melchior barked. "He's eight hours and still warm. The meter didn't start running till you found him. It's goddamn fresh to the people watching TV."

"We figure it happened sometime last fall," Art said, "when there was still some vegetation—"

"This is all because some assholes want to jog through the park in peace," Melchior interrupted again, already bored with the case details. "I mean, what the fuck? Isn't anybody ever supposed to be murdered in their ward?"

He lumbered into the hallway, then turned back. "You can

have Schwartz for a day or two, Callum." He waved a menacing finger at me. "And remember, I want some quick fuckin' results. Before those cocksuckers from the Forty-third go fuckin' off to the Commissioner downtown."

A lovely way with words, that Melchior.

Clear of Smilin' Ray, Art and I began on the jewelry inscriptions. Schwartz was off to start Missing Persons checks on the finger-prints and x-rays.

The Golden Swan of the signet ring fell easily into place. A listing in the Yellow Pages showed it to be a banquet hall on Milwaukee Avenue in the northwestern quadrant of the city. Art's telephone call caught an answering machine with a woman's long-winded instructions on making an appointment. He didn't leave a message.

The Phobos reference from the back of the watch was more problematical. No listing appeared in either the White Pages or the Yellow Pages, and no one with that name had ever been logged in the police data base or even in the Illinois driver's reg-istration records. The small pocket dictionary in my desk didn't list Phobos either, not even in the name-your-baby section. Strike out.

By the time I left the station, the sun had surrendered to the gar-ish orange of the city's streetlights. The cold seemed even more intense than early that morning at the lakefront.

I headed south to Grand Avenue. The Fury ran rough for the first few blocks, its frigid guts balking at the fierceness of the winter. I thought of E. B., his ugly face and his exploded skull, and I switched my radio station from rock to classical.

Grand to Wabash, then south again across the frozen Chicago River and into the Loop's frenzy. Headlights came at me like paired stars, BMWs and junkers alike, some drivers relaxing in deep leather for their long run to the posh North Shore, others praying their machines would last the two miles to the Cabrini-Green housing project.

At Wabash and Monroe, under the ceiling of elevated tracks,

I wheeled into a parking spot and killed the Fury's engine. Outside the car, the Loop's noise—blaring taxi horns and screeching el trains—whacked me, the kind of racket that sends tourists packing but always makes me feel alive.

David Gottlieb's shop was an elevator ride away: fourth floor, up off the high-rent district of the building's street level. Gottlieb, an eighty-year-old, had been a jeweler on this street since the Depression. I first met him when I came with Richard, my ex-husband, to buy an engagement ring; then there were a few trips to find small gifts for Meg. But most of my visits were more official than personal—the Police Department retained Gottlieb to identify and appraise jewelry involved in felony cases.

He came from his office, his diminutive form moving as slickly as an old greyhound's. His right hand took mine across the counter. "Well, Lieutenant, why am I so lucky this late in the day? Ooo, your hand is cold!"

"Been outside lately?" I said.

"Not since morning." His eyes were lively, and wrinkles complicated his face. He released my hand. "Tell me you're here to see diamonds." Everybody, I mean everybody, needed to be married in Mr. Gottlieb's world.

"Of course," I said. "Prince Charming has told me to pick out the biggest and brightest you have."

"Can he afford three carats?"

"At least. 'Nothing but a chunk of the finest ice for dear Nora,' he said."

A pause, a narrowing of his smile. "Not the day for that, is it?"

"No."

"Well—"

"I'd like you to look at a ring and a watch for me," I said. I pulled the jewelry from my purse and handed it to him. "We found these on a body in Lincoln Park this morning."

He took a small magnifying lens from his shirt pocket. He examined the signet ring first. "This is a very nice piece, nothing cheap here. You've seen the inscription?" He looked up briefly.

"Yes."

"Odd manufacturer's mark," he said, "next to the carat number."

"I wondered about that."

"It's foreign, probably. I've never seen a mark like this in the States."

"Where would you guess?"

"No idea. Sorry."

He traded the ring for the watch. Inquisitively, he moved his hands rapidly over the band and the face. Next, he brought it close to his lens.

"It's Swiss," he said, "and relatively new, by the looks of it. Could have been bought in this country, but I doubt it. Not mainstream enough."

He turned the watch over and around again. "Ah," he remarked, "same type of inscription as the ring. Etched by the same person. Again E. B. and I. are involved. Lovers?"

"I dunno."

"E. B. the dead one?" he asked.

"Yes, looks like."

"A man?"

"Yes."

After a pause, he said, "This drawing, Nora, the ellipses and circles. Beautifully done, just beautifully. Very intricate. Nothing like this is done around here, no, uh-uh. This is the kind of thing you only see from the old countries."

"Any idea what the drawing means?"

He shook his head. "And what is Phobos?"

I shrugged.

He grinned. "Sounds like a wonderful dessert from Greek town."

I headed home on Lake Shore Drive, me the model driver doing only what was necessary to defend my lane against intruders. Mr. Gottlieb's kidding about the diamonds had picked at some old scabs. Richard was on my mind.

I thought back four years to my amputation, to my first days home from the hospital. I was still on crutches, not yet fitted for a prosthesis. As usual, Richard was then "between jobs," a pleasant euphemism for too lazy to look for work. He had been moping around our apartment, acting more affected by my injury than even I was. One evening, after Meg was asleep, we sat opposite each other, the room's light stretching across our silence. Finally, out of nowhere, Richard began to speak in a monologue: a whining Hamlet.

In litany, he tallied his complaints about his life with me, what accommodations he had made because of my job and now my injury. His final remarks concerned what he called his recent lack of "quality sexual fulfillment." It seemed, he said, that my one-leggedness had become a distraction for him when we made love. He wasn't sure why—maybe, he thought, because he was such a nut for symmetry. Anyway, he had decided that he needed a change, and he now saw his future in the California wine country. If my tears hadn't been so close, I would have laughed hysterically.

But laugh I couldn't. Hurt and embarrassed, I sat mute. I had just lost a leg to the shotgun of a drunken vermin, and now this. But quickly, after the first burst of silence had passed, something ignited in me. I may have been defenseless against the shotgun, but not against the man I lived with. I moved forward in my chair, my face growing warm and flushed. My eyes honed in on Richard. My rage came in a firestorm.

"You're a no-good, Richard," I said viciously, my left hand going to my bandaged stump. "To dish out shit like that just now."

I paused; already, I needed a breath. Richard's face was so docile that I could see he didn't have an ounce of real interest in what was happening to us. It didn't matter what I said now, and my mouth felt as foul as my soul.

"I have some advice for you," I began again, my hands now locking tightly in my lap. "You'd be better off spending more time looking for a job and less time reading the garbage in *Cosmopolitan*. And then there's that crap you watch on the afternoon talk shows. I know that's where you get that stuff on *sexual fulfillment*. Well, it's bullshit, Richard, and you're buying it. Jesus, sometimes I think you must have air for brains."

I couldn't seem to stop. "And I'll tell you something else," I continued arrogantly, "consider yourself lucky if you ever find someone who's half as good to you in bed as I've been." Of course, I had no idea if there was any truth to my claim, but I fired it out anyway. "Now, get your dead ass out of this apartment and my life."

With this final broadside shot from me, Richard stood from his chair and started toward me. I smelled a whiff of reconciliation in the air, and I was having none of it. He wouldn't touch my cheek before he left.

As he closed in on me, I grabbed one of my crutches from the floor. Near enough to reach for me, he lifted his hand, but I struck quickly, shoving a crutch-tip hard and deep into his groin. He buckled and retreated. He was gone in an hour, never even looking into Meg's room before he left.

The divorce proceeded long-distance, Chicago to California, manila envelopes and rows of stamps doing most of the work. Love had been a little bit hard on me.

The smell had reached the stairwell. Sauerkraut and sausage penetrate like that.

Anna opened the door to my apartment before I finished turning the key. She stood in front of me—steely blue eyes wide open; gray hair wild—her smile carving all the age from her face. "Hungry, dearie?" she asked.

"Starved," I said.

"Guess what we're—"

"Sausage! Kraut! Practically smelled it on Lake Shore Drive."

Anna Skrabina had become my full-time baby-sitter when Richard left me to pick grapes in the Napa Valley. Her apartment was on the third floor, one floor above mine. Anna was a seventy-six-year-old Russian widow whose husband had died a year before mine quit me. She was a survivor of the German siege of Leningrad during World War II, a horror during which she lost her two young children to starvation. As cheated from her motherhood as she had been, she somehow held no bitterness. She handled Meg with a careful balance of tenderness and discipline, an example I wasn't too proud to learn from. And Meg's affection for Anna was deep and genuine; she was thrilled that Anna was willing to join her in everything from homework to rap music. Even I couldn't suffer the rap.

In the kitchen, Anna and I dished up the plates while Meg went for silverware. Carrying the fragrant, steaming plates, we trailed Meg into our dining room. Lanky Meg: her length was all mine, but her beautiful, sharply defined face all Richard's. I thought, Thank you, Richard, thank you for that, at least.

At the table, Meg said, "I think I'll get a can of soda, Mom."

"Oh, you do?"

Quiet Anna knew when to observe.

"Sure, Mom," Meg said, her words launched on a smile of reassurance. I couldn't wait to hear the logic that I knew was next. Her expression changed to an eight-year-old's mock seriousness. "You know, soda with hot sausage like this. You know, to cool it off and wash it down better."

Anna and I glanced at each other. Our vow not to laugh passed between us in silence.

"It's milk, Meg," I said. "Milk also cools sausage and washes it down. A kid your age needs milk. What about your bones?"

"They feel really good already—my bones. No kidding."

"Milk," I said. "That's it."

With a small scowl for face-saving, she trudged back to the kitchen for milk. Anna and I labored to smother our laughter.

At eight o'clock, Anna returned to her apartment. Meg read me a school assignment while we lay on her bed. After the homework, we rolled around wildly for five minutes, a sham cat-fight that she was always allowed to win. Then, both winded, we kissed good night. Her clenching hug was the briefest but warmest activity of my day.

In the living room, I plunked into the stuffed chair I kept next to the row of streetside windows. My street is Fargo Avenue and my neighborhood is East Rogers Park. It's a community of great amalgamation. We have people who drive Mercedes cars, we have people on food stamps. We have a wonderful university, Loyola, and we have illiteracy. We have the widowed and the divorced, large families and lonely gays, blacks and whites and

Hispanics, police and ex-convicts, Catholics and Jews, and everything in between.

It's my habit to sit in my chair till Meg falls asleep. I'm gone from her enough, and I want her to know that I'm there if she has difficulty with sleep. She never abuses this indulgence, only coming out for an occasional bloody nose or a question about school. She doesn't need me so close, so attentive, but I do it selfishly, for myself.

Settled in my chair, I switched off the lamp next to me and joined the dark, my view northeast, just a hundred yards from Lake Michigan. The cold had etched abstract patterns of frost across the window glass. As always at night, the lake was like pitch, its beachless edge marked only by the tall mercury lights planted to deter muggings.

I wasn't thinking of Meg or of motherhood that night. It was the dead man from Lincoln Park that I shivered to recall—the image of his face sticking out from the snow. What had he felt—anything?—when that first shell blew through his brain? And what could possibly have been in the mind of the person on the trigger?

And then there was "I.," the inscriber of ring and watch. Instinctively, I felt it was a woman, his lover. I think I wanted it that way, for E. B.'s sake. Anyone murdered so brutally deserved a love before death.

When the thought of "I." as killer occurred to me, I dismissed it out of hand.

By ten o'clock, my eyes stung with fatigue. Get up, I told myself. Haul ass to bed, Callum.

FOUR

Except for the dead, I was alone.

The room was large and L-shaped. The air smelled of disinfectant, the kind of chlorinated water a janitor would have slopped around at quitting time the evening before.

I stood near a row of six rectangular steel tables, each with a shiny, grooved surface that gently funneled toward a central drain. The four nearest tables were empty; the two far ones showed lumpy human features pushing up into the sheets that covered them. Noses and chins and male genitals defined the midlines. Shoulders, knees and feet poked off to the sides.

I was dressed formally—black suit, white silk blouse, low heels. I had purposely arrived a half hour early; I wanted the time to harden myself to the room again, even though I had been there just the day before. If, irrationally, I decided I couldn't stand it, I would have time to escape without notice. Once, my first time in the room, I ran out and heaved a stomachful of food into a hallway drinking fountain. I didn't expect that to happen again, but this time I had been shrewd enough to skip breakfast.

The door near me opened, and Tommy Banks walked through. He was clad in green surgical scrubs, the pants comically short on his long legs. He pulled a wheeled cart after him. "Morning, Lieutenant," he said, in a voice so soft I couldn't imagine it emerging from a man so large.

"Hi, Tommy." He moved past me. "How'd the x-rays and prints work out?" I asked.

"Nothing yet. Maybe later today or tomorrow."

He passed the turn of the L and disappeared from sight. In a moment, I heard a body drawer squeal open. "Dr. Dorner should be here in a minute," he called. "I saw him in the hallway."

"Will mine be first, or the two guys already out here?"

"Yours."

He came around the corner, his cart supporting a massive, sheeted body whose feet stuck out to the air. He slowed at the occupied tables. "These two had a gang problem last night. Looks like they got a life problem now, don't it?" He made a disdainful, snorting noise. "They'll wait," he said. "We didn't have room in the drawers. We're full, even the bridal suite. But today's pick-up day, so at least we'll clear out the unidentified."

At the first empty table, Tommy maneuvered E. B. off the cart and over the rolled edge of the table, then moved to the wall and flipped a switch. A ceiling lamp lit brightly, the powerful cylinder of light charging the whiteness of the sheet. I stepped backward against the wall.

The door opened again, and Vincent Dorner entered. Like Tommy, he was dressed in scrubs, but a pair that fit. He carried a mug of steaming coffee. A surgical gown and a pair of rubber gloves were draped over his left forearm. "Ah, Callum," he said, "you've come."

Dorner always called me Callum, but never out of disrespect. In fact, he was one of those men whose courtesy was consistent, never an accidental bump into your breasts or rear end, never an embarrassing double entendre. And even better, he wouldn't have considered a patronizing remark about my leg.

"Good morning," I said.

Dorner walked over to E. B. and set the mug of coffee on the next empty table. He slipped into his surgical gown and gloves, snapping the rubber of the gloves as he brought them over the gown cuffs. Hands covered, he picked up his coffee and drank some, then placed the mug at the end of E. B.'s table. The coffee steam rose grotesquely between E. B.'s long feet.

"Coffee?" Dorner asked me. "Need a jolt?"

"Thank you, no."

"Expecting much from me today?"

"One never knows," I said. "My mother taught me to always be hopeful."

"Good, I like that." Dorner smiled. "Especially down here, I like that."

Cordial as always, Dorner was making me feel more comfortable. He motioned to the two gangbangers. "I haven't seen them yet, but I'll bet you this week's pay their combined ages don't total thirty-five."

The next half hour passed swiftly. Dorner and Tommy uncovered the body, snapped their own photographs, then recorded precise measurements of E. B.'s body, most having to do with the entry and exit wounds. When the measuring was over, Dorner circled the body as he had the day before, but this time he pushed here and there with his fingers, even widening his nostrils like a horse to sniff at E. B. As he worked, he spoke to Tommy in rapid fire. Tommy jotted certain things onto a legal pad and ignored others.

His inspection done, and with the mound of E. B.'s belly now between us, Dorner said, "Before opening him, I can say a few things." He reached for his coffee and downed what was left. "He's obviously very obese, and it's all him, not the bloat of decomposition. No putrefaction, really, although he's been dead for weeks at least. The greenish tint of his belly tells us that, and the darkened skin of his dependent parts, his back and his buttocks."

I bent to see that the body's back and buttocks showed the deep color of mashed blueberries.

"But you thought he's been dead for a while, didn't you, Callum?"

"Before Thanksgiving," I said. "That was the last time we had any bare ground in Lincoln Park. He had leaves and grass, not snow, under his head. The half-skull was the only part of him out of the water and ice."

"A still-warm skull could melt an inch or two of snow, before the body went cold," Dorner objected gently.

"Yes, I suppose."

"But I still think you're probably right," he reassured.

Confused, I said, "Why?"

Dorner rested his hands on the pregnant-looking belly that stuck up between us. He was as comfortable with the dead as he was with the living.

"It goes like this," he said. "The color changes tell us he's been dead for weeks. And yet, when thawed out, he barely smells, so he never rotted. Since he was killed, the temperatures must've been at freezing or below. So when's the last day this city gave us a decent day? Tommy?"

Tommy, at the head end of the table, said, "Shit, boss, I dunno. Way before Christmas."

"Before Thanksgiving," I added, "before the Thanksgiving Day storm. I called the *Sun-Times* yesterday afternoon. They confirmed it."

"Now the wounds," Dorner said. He pulled E. B.'s chin up to show the wounds of entry under the jaw. "Not much here for you, Callum, not much you don't already know."

"Close range?" I asked.

"Very close, lots of damage and tattooing of the skin edges at entry. Barrel of the gun probably pushed right up under the mandible for both shots." Despondently, he said, "Can you imagine doing that?"

I shook my head.

"The exit wound is solitary because it's so huge. It's confluent, you see, the two shots."

"Yes."

"It's hard to say much about the caliber of the gun because you've got the exploding bone of the skull doing so much damage. If it were just soft tissue involved, then a big exit wound means a high velocity, big caliber. But it doesn't mean as much here, not with the havoc in this skull."

"Could he have died first, of something else, and then been shot?" I asked.

Dorner wrinkled his lips. "Yes, always a possibility. A way to really screw up a murder investigation by a creative killer. I've probably seen it twice—and no solution to either crime, by the way. Very inventive when it happens, but the odds in a victim like this are long. We'll know more when we split him."

• • •

A razorlike knife blade had done the belly, a motorized saw the chest. Both cavities stood open, their secret darkness penetrated by the overhead light. The belly had cleaved apart like too ripe fruit, everything inside rushing to get out. The chest contents were more complacent, satisfied to lie quietly and wait. I could smell E. B.'s early rot, but it was tolerable.

Before he began his deeper excavation, Dorner poked a needle into E. B.'s bladder and withdrew straw-colored urine into a syringe. "Routine drug screen," he said as he handed the specimen to Tommy. "Anything here to suggest a drug problem, Callum?"

"Not on the surface," I said.

Dorner stuck a different needle into E. B.'s heart. "For a serum level drug screen and his HIV status," he explained.

"You're thinking about AIDS?"

"His bulk is certainly not characteristic, but he could be antibody positive and not clinically sick yet. Just another piece of information."

Dorner fell quiet for the next twenty minutes. Working busily, he hacked organs from the belly and chest, and Tommy weighed them on a scale before making a slice of each to place in its own labeled jar of formalin. Then Tommy used his saw to open that part of the skull not already shot away. Dorner left the chest and bent over the brain, spending only a few minutes there.

Straightening, he said, "That's it for the gross, Callum. I can have the drug and HIV tests for you by tomorrow morning, the microscopic reports on all the organs by afternoon."

"Can you say much?" I asked.

"Oh, he died by gunshot all right. The damage to the brain is overwhelming. No sign of anything else inside. The drug screens may show something—we'll see."

"Of course. Well, thank you, Dr. Dorner . . . for inviting me to watch."

He said, "I think you appreciate the enormity of these murders if you see a victim a second time. Down here, I mean. A little incentive to try harder for the killer. Not that you need it, Callum. Not you and Campbell."

I smiled. "Besides our own initiative, we have the prod of our boss, Chief Melchior."

"Melchior? My regrets, Callum, and to Campbell, too. I know Melchior from his detective days. He's been down here a time or two. And I've done other cases with him, through the years."

"Oh . . ."

Dorner rolled his eyes toward the ceiling. "A perfect asshole, Callum. Melchior, I mean."

I drove northwest on angular Milwaukee Avenue, my window opened a crack for cold fresh air, the sun warm on the back of my neck. I parked a block north of the Jefferson Park rapid transit station.

The building was old and flat-roofed, its front made of variegated brown brick, the kind of insipid façade that took businesses by storm in Chicago's blue-collar neighborhoods during the sixties. A large, round, gaudy sign painted yellow and black hung out over the sidewalk : "The Golden Swan."

I walked from the street brightness into gloom. When The Swan's door snapped closed behind me, bells jingled. The waiting room, small and claustrophobic, was meagerly lit by a corner floor lamp. My eyes struggled to accommodate. The air smelled of stale cigarette smoke.

She appeared suddenly, a sequined presence spit magically from the darkness. Her words registered before I could see her clearly. "Did you wish to schedule something, Miss?" Her mouth opened to lipstick-stained front teeth.

"No, I'd like to speak to the manager," I said.

"That's me." She took a step closer. The sequins in her shawl shone like dim stars. Her gray hair, piled high like dollops of ice cream, made her as tall as me. Big, ornate glasses distorted the whites of her eyes. Age and gravity and heavyweight makeup sagged her cheeks.

"Your name, please?" I asked.

"Mrs. Bukowski."

"I'm Lieutenant Nora Callum. I'm with the police. I have some questions. It'll just take a few minutes."

"Well—"

"This ring," I interrupted, and pulled the signet ring from my purse. "Would you recognize it?" I held it toward her.

"Miss, I think another time."

"No, Mrs. Bukowski, now's the time. This has to do with a murder. We can do this here or at a police station, your choice. The Gale Street station is walkable from here."

She sighed dramatically. "We can sit in my office."

I followed Mrs. Bukowski to the back of the building and into a tiny office lit by a bare fluorescent ceiling fixture. She sat at her desk; I was relegated to a card-table chair whose edge pushed hard against my prosthesis. I handed her the ring after explaining where we had found it. She looked at *The Golden Swan* inscription, claiming it meant nothing to her.

"What sort of business do you have here?" I asked.

"A reception hall. It's for weddings and funerals mostly. Sometimes we have a club meeting."

"Where do these events take place?"

"In two rooms off the waiting area, where you came in."

"You handle things alone?"

"My husband helps." She shoved her glasses farther up onto the bridge of her nose.

"Where is he?" I asked.

"At home. Sleeping."

"You had a reception late last night?"

"No," she said.

"Then why—"

"Maybe he's tired. You ever get tired, Lieutenant?"

I didn't feel like sparring, not after an hour in the autopsy room. Calmly, I said, "You noticed the date on the ring?"

"Of course," she said. "January '88. A little over a year ago."

"Maybe we could look through your records and see if you had any affairs that involved E. B. or I."

Mrs. Bukowski opened a drawer and pulled out a black book filled with loose-leaf pages. I scooted my chair near the desk and watched her work her way through the neatly kept log. We first scanned the entries for January, 1988, then went a couple of months before and after in time. It wasn't difficult—no month

ever totaled more than five events. No function had been scheduled for or by anyone with either initials.

By the time we finished with the records, Mrs. Bukowski and
I had forged a mutual feeling of civility. I felt sorry that The
Swan's business seemed as anemic as it did, although it wasn't
something she was prepared to admit.

On my way out we toured The Swan's two reception rooms,
each a dark, scantily furnished area with stained carpet and dirty
acoustical ceiling tiles. I wondered what the divorce rate was for
couples kicking off their marriages in blank despondency at The
Golden Swan. As though I had anything to brag about.

Lunch at The Hard Rock on West Ontario. Schwartz's idea.

I arrived first, before noon, ahead of both Art and Schwartz.
It was a big, tiered room encircling a lower-level, central bar.
Rock memorabilia littered the walls. The steady thump of rock
and roll boomed from a brigade of ceiling speakers. Spacious as
the room was, I felt hemmed in by the music, music that didn't
seem to realize it was still morning.

After a few minutes, Art, bundled in his Arctic gear, walked
alone over to my table. If he'd been holding a flag, he could have
passed for the first black man to reach the North Pole.

"You're inside, Arthur," I said loudly, over a clamorous run of
bass guitar. "And this building is heated—city ordinance. The
gloves and hat can come off now."

"Shit, no," Art said, "not yet." He sat down across from me.
"I parked a mile away, then walked."

"In this weather?"

"For reasons of health," he said, with feigned indignation.
"Helen's on a exercise kick. I agreed to try it—so I'll live longer."

"If you don't die of exposure first." I tapped a passing waitress. "Emergency hot chocolate for this man, please."

Art pulled off his gloves and cap. "Tonight, Helen'll ask about
my progress. I want to tell her I walked to lunch."

"Congratulations. By the way, the Fury's around the corner. If
I drive you back to your car, you can still tell her you walked to
lunch."

"Very funny."

"Where's Schwartz?"

"Melchior grabbed him as we were leaving, told him to go to the streets in the Forty-third. So far, Ray's not impressed with our results."

"Shit."

"What'd you come up with at the morgue?"

"Nothing," I said. "Some tests due tomorrow, but nothing expected. Dorner was nice to me, though. He's a prince. And Tommy."

Art undid the zipper of his coat. The waitress brought his cocoa. We opened the menus she handed us, and ordered quickly. When she left, I said, "What's with Ray today?"

"Borderline pissed. The media's itchy. You find anything at The Golden Swan?"

"Zippo. It's a mom-and-pop operation as old as the Capone days. I don't see how they pay the taxes."

"They don't," Art said. "I ran a check at City Hall. The Bukowskis, right?"

"Right."

"Haven't paid property taxes in two years." He sipped cocoa. "Another year and the city can sell the business out from under them."

"Assuming someone would buy it. Huge conjecture, Art, huge. Anything else?"

"Mr. Bukowski has a problem with the hooch. Three arrests for driving under the influence in the past eighteen months."

"Mrs. B. did mention that hubby was sleeping in this morning. You heard from Schwartz, from Missing Persons?"

"He came up with two missing males who would resemble the age and body build of our guy. Both have dental records on file from their family dentists. Neither match Tommy's x-rays."

The waitress arrived with our orders. I loaded several swallows of cheeseburger into my belly, then said, "What about the prints?"

Art wiped his lips with his napkin. "They went through the state and FBI computer screens and came up blank. Hey, have you seen that funny new message tagging the end of the print reports now?"

"No. What?"

"It says the prints have been through full field—you know, everybody in and out of government, except for the CIA and NASA files. Apparently, those prints are now in a separate system to be accessed independently. Security or something. Anyway, I resubmitted to that data base."

"You think our guy looks like CIA? Or an astronaut? Get serious, Arthur."

"You don't like that? Okay, try this. We hit on something with the guy's pants and shoes. A tarlike substance smeared on them. It's going through Chemistry today. Should have an answer by tomorrow."

"By tomorrow? If we don't have something by tomorrow, we'll both be back in traffic division. You any good at blowing whistles?"

Blood pressure and serum cholesterol on his mind, Art chose to walk back to his car. I headed west on Ontario toward the Fury.

The sun was as high and bright as it knows how to be in Chicago in February. A few clouds dotted the sky: puffs of white smoke, too small and sporadic to joust with the sun in any serious way. I walked slowly, careful of the patchy ice. Near Dearborn, I came upon a parked pickup truck, its open back end made up into a traveling sandwich shop. A man in a ski jacket was selling lunch to construction workers from a nearby skyscraper project. My belly was full, but the smell of the steaming coffee drew me close. I was in no rush because I had no real idea about where to go next.

I paid my dollar, thanked the man, and walked away with coffee laced with sugar and cream. At the corner of Dearborn and Ontario, I sat on a wooden bench. With the wind down and the coffee hot in my hand, the cold air felt invigorating. Traffic whizzed by on Ontario, most drivers itching to crank it up on the Kennedy Expressway just half a mile ahead. But I was content to be still, to let the coffee's warmth and the city's hum comfort me. I thought about Meg, and I wondered if the nuns had judged the weather decent enough to let the children onto the playground after lunch.

From Meg, my thoughts drifted to Art. I had been too flip with him at lunch, too quick with the witless remark. But my nonchalance was a ruse, and I hoped Art realized it. At the heart of things, I felt desperation. And I knew it was Melchior.

Melchior had been my antagonist since my rookie assignment to the Eighteenth District on West Chicago Avenue, a time when he was the station Commander. When I made detective, he said, scowling, "Why, for crissake, does the Force need women detectives?" When my leg was blown off, he saw his chance—he petitioned a review board to have me sacked. The board made the obvious decision: grant full pension, but unload the poor one-legged thing.

A fire-eater in those days, I fought the decree from the hour it came down. And I wasn't above involving certain women's groups in my cause—after all, a woman has a basic right to work, hasn't she? On appeal, the board granted me two months before finalizing their decision. If I could run and shoot, I would be reinstated.

I hit the cadet fitness course as though possessed, working till my new, ill-fitting prosthesis had chafed my scars raw. Those hours I wasn't soaking my beaten stump, I spent at the target range. Within six weeks, I could shoot Lincoln's ear off a five-dollar bill.

I rested a week, watching soap operas and healing my stump. When I retested for the board, my fitness scores matched those I had eight years before with two real legs, and the best news was yet to come. At the target range, it was bingo! bingo! bingo! from my first pull of the trigger. With the targets looking as big as elephants to me, I shot the run of my life; I graded higher than anyone had in the previous year. Deliriously happy, I drove from the range to Holy Name Cathedral on North State, where I spent an hour sitting alone in a darkened rear pew.

When the review board returned me to duty, Melchior fumed his distemper. We renewed our regular combat, until his fury came to a head one midnight in his office when he placed his uninvited ham hands on my breasts. I reacted immediately and wildly, first brandishing a loaded .38 at his crotch, then in his terrified face. He hadn't come near touching me since, and I still waited in vain for his apology. In my confusion over the assault, I never brought charges.

Although I didn't hold a whit of respect for the man, I still wasn't blithe enough to ignore the pressures he perpetually applied. Like now, when he squeezed me for an arrest in the Lincoln Park murder, but my brain was empty of ideas; I felt lost, no clear path ahead to E. B.'s killer, not even a battered signpost in sight.

FIVE

Subdued activity surrounded me: an occasional industrious scholar, a glut of teen-agers on the make, a few napping drunks escaping the cold. Our wooden tabletop sported knife carvings of obscenities and cupid's hearts mingling freely with each other. This was a reading room of the downtown public library. I was here because I needed to be doing, not talking; I needed something to prime the pump. And of all the resources available to detectives, none required less prior insight into a case than a reference dictionary.

The entry on page 1455 read:

Phobos (fo'bes, -bos), n. 1. Also, Pho-bus (fo'bes). Class. Myth. a son and attendant of Ares and the personification of fear held to possess armies and cause their defeat. 2. Astron. one of the two moons of Mars. Cf. Deimos.

My only experience with classical mythology had been brief: a college course I dropped after two weeks. We'd read from a dense, convoluted text named *Bulfinch's Mythology*. If either Phobos or Ares had been mentioned before I decamped, I hadn't a chance of remembering.

Now I combed the library's copy of *Bulfinch's* and learned nothing of any value. Although I felt mildly vindicated about dropping the mythology course years before, I was still no closer to E. B.'s killer.

Dictionary definition No. 2 left me with Phobos as one of the two moons of Mars, a brother moon of Deimos—a lead as vacant and improbable as any I had ever unearthed in a murder case. And me with Melchior's hot breath on the back of my neck.

Dead-ended, I could think of nothing else to work on. It was too early to go home, and I wouldn't risk returning to Area Six and seeing Melchior. Then a ridiculous idea struck me: Halsey.

Talk about shots in the dark.

Outside, the sun had disappeared, and snow flurries, delicate and aimless, softened an otherwise somber afternoon. The cold stung my face and froze the fine hair inside my nostrils. The ache in my stump was a given in this kind of weather.

I drove Lake Shore Drive to the level of the Field Museum, then turned east onto the narrow strip of city that poked boldly into Lake Michigan. The tip of this finger held the Adler Planetarium, a squat, gracious building made of dark marble.

A staircase took me from sidewalk level into the Adler's starkly modern new addition. In the underground lobby, I found the information desk manned by a volunteer.

"I wish to see Dr. Daniel Halsey," I said to the woman. Younger than me, she had a smooth, unmarked face; her sharp cheekbones boasted of her privileged class, and a beige cashmere dress hugged her thinness. Meg and I could have done Disney World for what she had dropped on the dress.

"Quite impossible," she said, her eyelids dramatically closing and opening, like a doll's.

Her inflection was Gold Coast phony, and I was having none of it, not that late in a day when I had made all the progress of a slug in a fish tank. I opened my purse. Reaching for my detective shield, I made sure the barrel of my .38 Special came into her view. A forefinger jumped to her lips.

"It's important that I see Halsey," I said firmly. "Now."

Her finger came away from her mouth. "I understand."

"I knew you would." I smiled stiffly. "Thank you."

She directed me down a curving hallway painted flat black. Huge photographs of fiery supernovae graced the walls, the spotlit red-and-yellow images brilliant in the dimness. At the end of the hall, double doors opened to the Adler's administrative offices.

• • •

I dated Dan Halsey while we were in high school. He was a tall, lean, maypole of a boy who warmed the pines of the basketball team's bench, rarely playing, his larger talents unfurling in the classroom. Our relationship was sporadic. Never able to hold the long note, Dan migrated from girl to girl to girl then back round again. When he left Chicago for college, he escaped without the fetters of a hometown honey.

Dan disappeared from my life until a Saturday afternoon a year after my divorce when I brought Meg to an Adler children's program. A staffer announced that the program leader was ill, but we would have a special substitute, Dr. Daniel Halsey, the chief of Adler astronomy. I hoped nobody but Meg saw my jaw drop.

I went up to Dan afterward. We quickly dispatched the fifteen years since we'd seen each other, then decided to have lunch the next week. Several breezy dates followed, always during daylight. As I began looking forward more ardently to his company, I felt anxiety about my missing leg. I knew I took a chance if I opened myself to Dan Halsey—the only non-medical man to see and touch my scarred monster was Richard, and he had left.

One day, Dan asked me to accompany him to a weekend conference at the Yerkes Observatory in southern Wisconsin. I asked for a few days to consider the offer. I sensed a powerful new locomotive gathering momentum in my life; if I decided to release the brake and make myself and my disability so vulnerable, then I needed to be very sure.

My decision came easier than I could have imagined—the day following Dan's invitation, I ran into a friend, Sharon, in the grocery store. I had known her since high school; she now also lived in Rogers Park. Naturally, I was anxious to tell her about finding Dan Halsey back in Chicago. She wasn't surprised, she said, she'd known Dan was at the Adler for the past five years. "How'd you know that?" I asked.

"It's the kind of news that circulates through families," she said.

"I don't get you."

"See, Dan's married to my cousin."

"What?" I managed.

"And, Nora, you should see their lovely young children."

I left Sharon, abandoning my cart in the beans-and-rice aisle. Not thinking clearly, I sped and lane-changed the Fury to the Adler, somehow making it in twenty minutes. I double-parked and flipped down my POLICE visor.

I stood in front of Dan Halsey at his desk. It wasn't the first time I had shouted to a man's face that he was a dirty no-good son-of-a-bitch for how he had diminished me.

He sat expressionless through my fiery diatribe, his features reflecting neither shock nor nonchalance. The rest of my visit was a blur, except when I laid my left forearm on Dan's desk and swept its surface clean, my heart wickedly jubilant as papers and books and small, lunar memorabilia crashed resoundingly to the floor.

Dan stood when I entered. His suit looked ill-fitting. He still wore a luxuriant ponytail that took his brown hair down onto his upper back.

I led off: "I always seem to be barging in here."

He smiled tentatively. "Just stay clear of the desk."

"I need help on a murder case," I said, "astronomical help. To tell the truth, I'm a little desperate."

"Sit down."

I took a chair near his desk. The window behind him looked out to the flat, raw expanse of Burnham Harbor. I noticed he still wore no ring. His eyes were gray-green, his jaw narrow and square.

I said, "We found a body in Lincoln Park yesterday, under ice. He was wearing some jewelry." I dug E. B.'s watch from my purse and handed it to Dan. "If you look at the underside, you'll see an inscription with the words 'Phobos I.'"

He studied the watch.

"I've learned that Phobos is a mythological figure," I said, "and also a moon of Mars."

He lifted his eyes and said, "You know, what I did to you was—"

4 5

"Stop with that, Dan," I interrupted. "I've come about the watch, that's it. If you can't help, then fine—tell me and I'm gone."

He gave a hurt twist to his lips that disappeared in a second. He looked back to his hands.

"One of the moons of Mars, right?" I pushed.

"What about the initials?"

"We think E. B. is the murdered man. I. is his friend, his lover, whoever."

He frowned. "The circles and ellipses here are remarkable."

"They're not random?"

"No. Too accurate for that. Come here."

Reluctantly, I slid my chair closer to his desk. His suit smelled faintly of moth balls. He handed me the watch to study. "The small circle etched in the center," he said.

"Yes?"

"The Sun," he said.

"The Sun?"

"Now, the ellipse at the edge of the metal marks the path of Mars around the Sun, around the central circle."

I glanced up in confusion.

"Look back," he said. "The smaller ellipse defines the Earth's motion around the Sun." He settled against his chair back. "These aren't idle doodlings."

"What about the third line?" I said. "The one that links the two ellipses."

"That's what makes the case." He leaned toward me. "See, the watch doesn't say 'Phobos,' it says 'Phobos I.' That's the tip. Phobos I is a Russian space probe."

"What?" I said incredulously.

"Last summer the Russians launched two probes, Phobos I and II, toward Mars."

My brain felt as empty as a paper sack. "And?"

"And the intersecting line on this watch precisely draws the flight path of the probes from Earth to Mars."

"Dan, this is a wagonload of information from the back of a lousy watch. Farfetched and far-flung. Wouldn't you say?"

For a moment, I regretted challenging him, as though I had a better explanation for the drawings. As though I had any explanation.

"The solar system is my job," he said, in a voice full of confidence. "I'll wager your murder victim knew as much about all of this as I do—maybe more."

"Do the initials mean anything to you?"

"Nothing," he answered quickly.

"What kind of people would know the Phobos flight paths?" I asked.

"A serious space hobbyist would know them. And, of course, all of NASA knows them."

"NASA." The word throttled the rhythm of my brain. The fingerprints. The computers required separate access, Art had said.

I said, "Tell me why NASA knows so much about the Russian probes? Aren't we competing?"

"NASA knows because NASA has been involved in these probes."

"Oh."

"Look, Nora, I don't know the project's details, but I do know someone who does, a Phobos expert. A man who's actually worked on Phobos."

"Who and where?"

"Valery Kuzov. He's a visiting professor at IIT this year." The Illinois Institute of Technology is a prominent engineering school, its campus on the South Side near Sox Park. "I've talked with him at several scientific meetings, and he's a friendly guy. I'm sure he'd be willing to help. I can try to locate him and call ahead for you."

"Please," I said. "See if you can set something up for tomorrow morning. I'll phone you later today, or early tomorrow." I stood from my chair. "Thanks for everything, Dan."

When I started away, he said, "I'm not beyond apologies, Nora."

"Forget it. Doesn't matter anymore. So how's the family?"

"Broken." I could have turned away during his pause but I didn't. "You weren't the only problem," he said quietly.

"I'm sorry. Really, I am. It's more complicated than when we ran around as kids, isn't it?"

• • •

In the Adler lobby, I dialed Art at Area Six. "Arthur, those prints back yet? The second run?" I felt the electricity of finally closing in on something.

"Not yet," he said. "They just went back out. I told you. Tomorrow."

"Dammit," I moaned, my left hand rooting in my hair.

"Relax, girl," Art said. "Where you calling from?"

"The Planetarium."

"The Adler?"

"Yep."

"You shittin' me, Nora?"

"As you say, Scouts' honor." I held three fingers in the air. A woman walking past me looked puzzled. "Our guy E. B. may have had something to do with space. You know a better place to go than the Adler?"

She slipped into her flannel Watch-plaid nightshirt; then I tucked her inside a sheet so worn it had grown as smooth as her skin. A spray of light broke from the closet lamp she asked to me turn on every night. A benign request I always complied with.

"Can you sleep, Meg?"

"Yeah, Mom. I think I'm bummed."

"You're what?"

"Bummed."

"What's bummed?"

Her face brightened. "You're asking me what that means?"

"Yes."

"It means bummed. You know, like . . . plenty tired."

"You picked up that word at school?"

"Sure." She answered as if it went without saying.

A last kiss and I moved off her bed toward the hallway.

"Mom," she said when I was at the door, "when will I grow hair under my arms?"

I smiled. With mock sternness I said, "When you start to do some work around this apartment!"

She giggled.

I blew a kiss. "Good night, Meg. I love you."

• • •

My companion was a mountainous chocolate sundae, a week's worth of fat piled into a single bowl. My rationalization came from Art's adage: "Never limit oneself unnecessarily."

I dug deep into the ice cream with a soup spoon. The ten-o'clock news began. By chance, the set was tuned to Channel 6, Karl Kramer's lair. Kramer was at anchor, sitting opposite a winsome young blonde who smiled excessively and hadn't a clue about hard-news reporting.

That night's lead rehashed the Lincoln Park murder. In ponderous tones, Kramer narrated the camera's exploitation of half-frozen E. B. as he lay on the stretcher, his body lit by the slant of sun rising over the lake. It must have been the same footage I had been lucky enough to miss the day before. For a moment, the camera stopped on my stern face—Kramer mentioned my name—then the image switched to a quick close-up of E. B.'s wounds.

I tossed my spoon back in the bowl, my stomach sick. I stood and walked to the television. To his audience, Kramer said, "And why haven't the police released any information during the two days since this heinous crime was discovered?"

I punched hard at the TV's on-off button. The screen fizzled dark. I carried the sundae to the kitchen and dumped it into the sink, then spat into the heap of melting ice cream.

In the shower, I soaked in the hottest water I could stand. As the water tumbled over me, my rage swelled. I dried my hair while sitting naked in the dark on the edge of my bed. Outside, the lake was so densely black that it frightened me. E. B.'s image was in front of me, in the dark.

SIX

The cigar smoke spewed from Melchior's mouth in blue-white cones that fanned through the room. We had no choice but to breathe it. Sitting in his office was like following a fuming bus during rush hour: with no place to hide, your lungs just suck the filth, your nose the stench.

"What about the autopsy report?" Melchior said between puffs.

"Back later today," I said.

It was eight in the morning. Art sat in front of Melchior's desk, but I had chosen to stand.

"You said something about the pants, Callum?" Melchior said.

I moved toward the window, aiming to stand in the sun. I wore a wool sweater, but still felt cold enough to be drawn to the sunlight. "They were streaked with some sort of black stuff," I said, "like tar maybe. It's also on his shoes. Chemistry said later today or tomorrow for the final."

Melchior jammed his cigar between his side teeth. "You got anything, Campbell?"

"A phone call from the County Hospital lab this morning," Art said. "The drug and alcohol screens are negative. Oh, and the HIV—"

"The guy had AIDS?" Melchior yelped.

"The HIV test is negative, I was about to say," Art countered.

Melchior inhaled deeply, then mumbled, "Fuckin' queers are taking over the city."

A tap on the door and Schwartz walked in.

"Good morning," Melchior said politely, the kind of greeting neither Art nor I ever heard from Melchior. Schwartz was white and male, basic requirements for all members of Melchior's dream team, but none of Melchior's prejudice was Schwartz's fault, and Art and I never held it against him.

Schwartz sat in a chair next to Art.

"What about the frozen guy?" Melchior said to Schwartz. "Who is he?"

"Like I told Art yesterday, I've got nothing," Schwartz said. "The only possibilities both had dental x-rays that didn't match the victim's."

"C'mon, Steve," I said. "You're telling us there are only two guys his age missing in a city this size?"

Schwartz looked over to me, squinting. "Hell, yes, there are more, but Missing Persons files are haphazard. There's no central file, no decent cross-referencing from district to district. A report might have come in from anywhere in the city, and I wouldn't be able to track it."

I shook my head.

"Look, Nora," Schwartz said, "if you're missing and over age nineteen and aren't newsworthy and don't have a criminal record, then not much attention is going to be paid to you. People abandon families and jobs. They wander off. There's no criminal activity involved, and nobody gives a shit."

"What about the woman who inscribed the guy's watch and ring?" I said. "She cared. She spent a load on the jewelry."

"So now you know it's a she?" Schwartz said.

"Gotta be."

"Nothing's gotta be," Melchior reprimanded.

I turned to stare directly into the sun, wanting the light to hurt my eyes. When I looked back, Art shot me a small warm smile.

Melchior dismissed Schwartz, telling him to get back to the Forty-third Ward. To Art and me, he said, "You're two days into this and you don't have birdshit. Am I right?"

"Partly right," Art said, "but . . . let's say we're not discouraged. We're waiting on some prints."

I came back to Schwartz's chair, leaned forward on the arms.

"I've got something else for you," I said to Melchior, as though bequeathing a gift. "From the inscriptions on the back of the watch."

"Fine, let's have it." His cigar had mercifully gone out, but now he rekindled it.

I straightened, my hands on my hips. "The etchings on the backside—you know, the ellipses?"

He lifted his eyebrows and the skin of his forehead gathered into thick wrinkles. I had shown him the jewelry the previous afternoon, and presumed he remembered the inscriptions.

"The etchings don't seem to be accidental," I said. "They make a drawing of the paths of the planets Mars and Earth around the Sun."

Melchior stiffed me: "What the fuck are you talking about, Callum?"

Art turned to me. "The Adler?"

"Yes," I said. Then, to Melchior: "I went to the Planetarium yesterday to follow up on the Phobos thing inscribed on the watch. Turns out that Phobos is the name of one of the moons of Mars and also of two Russian space probes shot off last summer."

"Who gives a shit?" Melchior barked.

Undeterred, I said, "And one of the lines on the watch draws the flight path of the probes from Earth to Mars. Look, this guy was involved with the Phobos project somehow. Who else would have that on the back of his watch?"

Smoke breaking from his mouth, Melchior said, "This is such a load of horseshit that it's laughable, Callum. Laughable if it weren't for Jimmy O'Donnell. Who told you all this?"

"An astronomer from the Planetarium."

"Crissake," Melchior whined, "now I got some freakhead astronomer trying to solve this murder?" He looked to Art for sympathy. "And with O'Donnell calling me three times a day from the Forty-third. I mean, calling me like he goddamn owns me! Wants to know about our progress, he always says." He held his cigar up into the air and studied it as though it had a life of its own. "Our progress . . . son-of-a-bitch."

Art jumped into the breach. "There's another lead, Chief. We're working with a banquet hall on the Northwest Side called

The Golden Swan, the same name inside the guy's ring. There may be a payoff with this Swan thing."

Melchior's forehead softened, his mood slightly appeased. With his tiny black eyes glancing sharply from Art to me, he said, "You two got another twenty-four hours to come up with something. Get in here later today, or tomorrow morning at the latest."

Art and I left the office. Outside, down the hallway, I said, "Why you telling him that shit about The Golden Swan?"

"Got us outa the office, didn't it?" Art said.

"When you gonna tell him the Swan's a zero?"

"Soon as we come up with something better."

"And when's that?"

"Ten minutes from now, an hour from now, I don't know. Today anyway."

"You read the future, Arthur?"

He didn't answer, just puffed his chest and cracked a huge, sparkling smile.

I made Thirty-fifth Street and the Dan Ryan Expressway by eight-fifty-five. Halsey had called me the evening before to say that Valery Kuzov could meet with me when his first class ended at eight-fifty.

The buildings of the IIT campus—the black, square, "less is more" designs of Mies van der Rohe—rose austerely into a bright February sky. Small bands of backpacking, red-cheeked students moved along the cold walkways as steadfastly as warriors.

A lounge occupied a front corner of the IIT library, a stark, one-story building walled in glass. End tables sloppy with magazines stood among overstuffed chairs and couches. A man, the only other person in the lounge, sat with his back to me. I half-circled his chair and stopped in front of him. "Hello," I said. "I'm Lieutenant Nora Callum."

Standing, he was just shorter than me. His corduroy jacket hung casually open; he wore a neat blue shirt and no tie. "Valery Kuzov," he said, in a voice edged with a distinct but refined accent.

We shook hands, then sat. I took a chair bathed in sunlight

and at a right angle to his. It wasn't an interview room, but the setting was quiet and acceptable. "Dan was helpful to lead me to you," I said.

He smiled sincerely. "I'm always glad to talk about Phobos."

"You know about the murder in Lincoln Park?"

He tipped his head in acknowledgment. I handed him the watch from my purse. While he concentrated on the watch's backside, I considered his monkish face. His graying, close-cropped beard was the same length as the hair on his head, as though he was used to mowing the whole field at once, on the same days. Sad eyebrows declined over his dark eyes. His nose was sharp and prominent. I guessed he was in his fifties.

He looked up. "Daniel mentioned these etchings."

"And you agree?" I said.

"There is no question."

"Tell me why."

"The accuracy of the two orbital drawings," he said, "and the relationship of the intersecting flight path. The Phobos I inscription couldn't be here by accident." He returned the watch to me, then folded his hands in his lap.

"Dan said there were two Phobos probes."

"Both launched last July," he said, "from Baikonur in central Russia. Phobos I flew seven weeks, then disappeared in late August. The second probe is now close to Mars and its Phobos moon."

"You worked on these projects?"

"On Phobos I," he said, his eyes prideful, "until it vanished. The loss was a great blow to the Soviet space agency."

"I would imagine," I agreed, to keep him up-tempo. I thought about bringing out my notepad, but decided my writing might intimidate him.

"The Phobos I team was disbanded early last September," he continued. "I was sent here to teach and do research—on cooperative exchange." He lifted a hand in explanation. "Our governments do it all the time, with scientists and engineers. I will be here until summer."

"Mr. Kuzov, or is it—?"

"Dr. Kuzov," he said shyly.

"You've seen the initials on the watch, the E. B. and the I.?"

"Which are the victim's?" he asked.

"E. B. He wore a signet ring with the same initials."

A puzzled look crossed Kuzov's face. "Is the man obese?" he asked gently, as if not to give offense.

His question surprised me. "Quite. Yes."

"Edward Boyes?" he said slowly. He touched the sharp tip of his nose. Then, in a half whisper, "My God, maybe it's Edward."

I moved forward in my seat. "Wait, how do you—"

"He worked for NASA."

"An American?"

He nodded. "We were on Phobos I together until last March—or maybe April—when he was sent back to the States."

"Sent back? From where?"

"Tallinn," he said matter-of-factly.

"Where?"

"In Estonia."

I needed an atlas. Kuzov noticed the bafflement on my face.

"In eastern Europe," he offered. "We have a software laboratory in Tallinn. Most of the Phobos programs were done there. NASA helped."

"And Edward Boyes visited?"

"He lived there a while. Two months, I would say. Yes, at least."

"You worked on Phobos together?" I asked.

"With many others, of course." A pause. "Actually, Edward was sent home early. But, Lieutenant, what would this have to do with your dead man?"

I didn't know, but it was a lead. It was something. I said, "Where would Boyes be now?"

A smile brightened Kuzov's face. "Here, in Chicago. On faculty at Loyola."

Loyola, the university in my backyard, the site of my forsaken English major. "When did you last see him?"

"Oh, some time ago now. I know I saw him last fall, at a conference we both attended."

"In the city?"

"The Ambassador West Hotel."

"And you haven't seen him since?"

He shook his head. "You could ask Daniel. We're all usually at these same conferences. Maybe Daniel remembers seeing Edward since then."

I made a mental note to phone Halsey, then moved ahead. I was making good progress with the kind of witness you could milk all day. "Would it be unusual for you or Dan not to see Boyes for several months?" I asked.

"Not really," Kuzov said. "Edward's a cranky man, without many friends. I think Daniel would agree with me."

I settled more deeply into my chair. "Dr. Kuzov, who is the I. on the watch?"

"If E. B. is for Edward Boyes, then I. would have to be Irina Varonyev."

"A co-worker."

He nodded. "A programmer. Russian. They met during Phobos."

"The jewelry makes me think they were lovers."

A faint chuckle. "No one ever doubted that, Lieutenant."

I tipped my chin to ask for more.

"Their trouble was flaunting it in public," he said.

"You mean their love affair?"

"They acted things out in public places, like restaurants. Then, in Tallinn, they chose to live together." His eyes widened in emphasis. "This was their big mistake."

"Explain, please," I said. "I don't have a sense for what you're saying."

He put a forefinger to his chin. "You see, the Americans and Russians have had an uneasy truce in space. We scientists work together, but some of our superiors, both NASA and Soviet, are still very conservative. They thought team members living together at The Swan was overdoing things."

"At the where?"

"The Golden Swan. A hotel in Tallinn where many of us stayed while working at the lab."

"I see." So much for Mrs. Bukowski. I saw no reason to mention the Swan inscription inside the signet ring.

A student walked into the lounge and flopped on a couch well away from us, her feet up on the cushions. She adjusted the headset of her Walkman, then closed her eyes.

"Dr. Kuzov," I said, "would you be willing to come with me to the morgue to identify the body as Boyes?"

"You would drive me?"

"Sure."

"Okay, yes. I'm free."

We started out of the lounge. On the way, Kuzov said, "Did Daniel recognize the initials as Edward Boyes?"

"No. No, he didn't."

SEVEN

Dan Ryan Expressway to the Eisenhower would have been quicker, but I wanted more time with Kuzov before reaching County Hospital. I decided on Thirty-fifth Street west through the Armour Square neighborhood.

Kuzov stayed close to the Fury's passenger door, his eyes darting like bats, his nose even more prominent in profile than it looked head-on. Hatless and bundled into a worn mackintosh, he seemed woefully underdressed for this kind of cold. He remained quiet for the first half of the ride, only occasionally lobbing me a question about citizens we saw on the streets, people who navigated daily life at the edges of oblivion.

By Ashland Avenue, he began talking more freely, as he had at the library, now recounting details about the Phobos probes. I regarded the material as mostly mumbo jumbo, but I did glean a few interesting facts. It seemed that the first Phobos had disappeared because of a single bad command sent up by a flight controller. That controller was Irina Varonyev, Edward Boyes's lover. And the Russians knew hard-ball: Varonyev's mistake earned her a jail sentence in Moscow's Lefortova Prison.

I wondered if the Sovs had arranged to chastise Edward Boyes by sending two slugs through his brain at the speed of sound.

Kuzov stood on one side of Tommy Banks, me on the other, each of us several feet away. Tommy's powerful forearms slid the tray out of its crypt in the wall. The body had been loaded feet first, so its head came first into light. A surgical towel covered half his face and, mercifully, the dark canyon where the right side of his brain had once resided.

"Dr. Kuzov?" I said, my eyes riveted to the green nap of the towel. The smell of formalin drifted into my nose and sickened me.

"What?" Kuzov said, as if he didn't know what I wanted.

"Is it Boyes?"

He didn't answer, just stepped past Tommy closer to the tray. Leaning forward while holding his coat from touching Boyes's left arm, he perused the body. He pointed at the surgical towel and said to Tommy, "Could you—?"

Tommy said, "Sure," and lifted the towel by a corner.

Kuzov stared at the face and the demolished skull before him. He put a veined hand to his cheek and with his lips barely moving he murmured, "God in heaven."

"Is it Boyes?" I repeated more firmly.

"Yes."

"No question?"

"None."

Tommy replaced the towel.

I said, "Is he as you last remember him, Dr. Kuzov?"

Kuzov stared at me. "He has no brain, Lieutenant."

"I mean, otherwise . . . his bulk, is that greater or less than when you knew him?" It was a ridiculous question that I asked only to be saying something, anything to kill time until Tommy shoved the drawer closed and I could escape from the room.

"He looks the same," Kuzov said. "Edward has always been a heavy man."

"Would you be willing to testify to your identification?"

"Of course." He paused. "Those facial moles—I remember telling him in Tallinn he should have those removed. Some can turn to cancer."

Our return to IIT was as quiet as the first half of the trip to County. I tried some Phobos questions whose answers I didn't care about, but Kuzov replied only in monosyllables, never trying to engage me when he did answer. He had quit talking since seeing Boyes. I stopped my questions; I would leave him alone in his grief.

In the Area Six coffee room, I briefed Art on my morning with Kuzov. We still needed verification of Edward Boyes's identity, the kind that comes with fingerprint records, before we made our run to assemble Boyes's legend. We hoped to see the prints come in later that day, but if they didn't, we'd start anyway. We agreed to meet in the early afternoon.

Tired of thinking about the Lincoln Park case, I returned to our office. There, on a hunch, I scanned the Department's data bases and turned up nothing. Looking in corners and crannies made me feel like a meddler, but at least I felt more satisfied. And if I hadn't had another empty ten minutes before lunch with Paris, I wouldn't have gone a whit further.

Time-kill: access the FBI's index, the National Crime Information Center. Search him in one more place. What the hell.

Whining agreeably, my computer brought up the NCIC menu. At the screen's prompt, I typed FUREY, MICHAEL. When the blinking cursor mutated to a small, spinning ball, I knew that somewhere a mainframe toiled doggedly in my behalf. I waited, fiddling with a hangnail on my thumb.

The screen popped to life; my head jerked upward. Text appeared, amber letters streaming as silently as liquid onto the black background, filling in left to right, top to bottom. I read as fast as words surfaced:

02/21/89—11:48 AM
FLORIDA; COLLIER COUNTY; CITY OF NAPLES
FUREY, MICHAEL JAMES
SS#: 372-34-7628   DOB: 4/18/53   POB: Evanston, IL
Race: Caucasian   Ht: 5'7"   Wt: 149   Hair: blond   Eyes: brw
Occupation: bartender; auto-wash worker
    Arrested 4/23/87 for copying keys of luxury autos; member

of 20-man steal-to-order car theft ring. 15 collaborators booked in simultaneous raids. Pled guilty to larceny.

Sentence by plea: 3 yrs. 1 yr. Collier Cty Jail; 2 yrs. parole

Date of parole: 7/14/88. In violation since 9/27/88, date of last Florida contact. Present whereabouts unknown.

END

EXIT?

My lips came apart, unstuck. I breathed in and felt warm air flood my mouth.

The sweet smells of beer and frying hamburgers rushed me. I was in Mammy's, a low-ceilinged, windowless den on Rush Street that the lunch crowd had already filled. I spotted Paris sitting in a booth, and next to her, close enough that they touched, was the man I knew would be Michael Furey, parole violator. Neptune, Paris's daughter, sat across from them.

Furey stood as I approached. His eyes were narrow; his straight, light hair had gone sparse in front.

"Nora, Michael Furey," Paris said, a grin set in her lips, her eyes gleaming. "Michael, this is my friend Nora Callum."

"Hello," I said. I shook the fine-boned hand Furey put forward. Like Paris and Neptune, he was dressed in a heavy sweater.

"Pleased to meet you," he said, his voice thin and dry.

We extended tentative smiles to each other. I bowed slightly, then slid in next to Neptune. "What are you doing out of school, Miss Viveka?" I elbowed her playfully. "Are you truant?"

Neptune giggled. Even at age eight, she already had Paris's lovely round face in miniature, especially the eyes. In another ten years, she would realize all the privileges and hazards that accrue to young women of unusual beauty.

"She's got strep throat," Paris said, "so she's on penicillin. Doctor said no school for three more days."

"Oh, great, Paris, and you drag her out in ten-degree weather?"

"I wouldn't make her walk here—Michael drove us."

I looked at Furey and wondered in what stolen car he had

chauffeured Paris and Neptune. "Thank God for you," I said, grateful that he had been too stupid to bring an alias with him to Chicago. "Are you from the city, Michael?"

He broke a phony smile. "Originally."

"And lately?"

"Texas."

"Texas?" To Paris, I feigned a joke. "Why would anyone leave there for these winters?"

"When oil's cheap, Texas jobs dry up," Furey said. "So back to the Rust Belt."

"When?"

"A couple of months ago."

I had all I could do not to cuff him and drag him to the nearby Eighteenth District station house. One phone call to Florida would settle his job worries. But anxious as I was to bring him in, I knew I had time—he seemed comfortable enough; he wasn't going anywhere soon. I needed to decide how to break this news to Paris. Buffaloed completely by Furey, she had, I honestly believed, quit prostitution for him. Life with Furey might be the lesser of two evils.

"Paris tells me you're tending bar at Juliet's," I said to Furey, unable to grant him the common courtesy of using his name.

"You know the place?" he said.

"It's been a few years."

"Come by for a drink."

"I will. You can book that."

All of our orders were Mammy's specialty: oliveburgers with Cajun fries. While we waited for the food, we talked about nothing in particular, Furey alert to everything. Paris mentioned that she had two job interviews scheduled for the next day, one as a guard at the Art Institute, another selling hosiery at Marshall Field's. When the food came, we ate quietly.

The meal ended and Furey went for the check. I wasn't about to stop him—lunch on a felon delighted me. When the waitress left with Furey's money, Paris said, "You got the guy from the ice in Lincoln Park? The one's been on TV lately?"

"Yes," I said.

"Gettin' close?'"

"Not really. A couple of long shots to check."

"Your boss breathin' real hard?" Paris asked. She knew Melchior's temperament.

"Like a dragon."

"Look, I'll ask around. The girls. Surprising what they sometimes hear."

"I'd be glad for anything."

"I'll listen at Juliet's," Furey said. "The drink brings out some great surprises."

I thought, not anything like the surprise I'll be arranging for you, dear Michael.

We sat at our desks, each of us logy with lunch, each with a report in hand. Art's tie was down and his collar open. Our office baseboard radiator clanged with a charge of fresh hot water. Low afternoon sunlight sparkled in our window's frost.

"You first," Art said, "and do me a favor. Don't wade me through the heavy horseshit."

I pulled Dorner's report from its envelope. Ignoring the dozen or so pages of anatomic detail, I went straight to Dorner's abstracted summary. I said, "Dorner writes, 'No evidence of toxic substance levels, including alcohol. No serologic evidence of acquired immune deficiency syndrome, viral hepatitis, or other infectious disease. No evidence of degenerative or neoplastic disease, or of coronary artery or peripheral vascular disease. Suicide felt to have been impossible. Death of the victim ascribed to two massive gunshot injuries to the frontal half of the brain and its right cerebral hemisphere. The estimated time of death—November, 1988—is based in part on the conditions where the body had lain.'"

"No surprises," Art said.

I slid the papers back into their envelope, then tossed it a few inches into the air. The envelope landed on the desk with a slap. I suppressed a belch of oliveburger. "Your turn."

Art held a single sheet folded in half and stapled shut. Its outside face was stamped CHEMISTRY.

"Now, pay attention, girl," he ordered theatrically.

Reading, he said, "Dark, somewhat sticky material on victim's left trouser leg and the soles of both shoes is a highly viscous bitumen derived from liquid petroleum. The material is soluble in carbon disulfide. It most likely represents an asphalt used in paving materials." He looked up from the page.

"So?" I said.

"So Boyes had been on fresh blacktop."

"Remember any new paving around the park?" I said. "I mean paving done last November?"

"You kidding?" Art said. "When's the last time the city put ten lousy bucks into Lake Shore Drive?"

"Doesn't matter. The Drive's concrete, not blacktop."

"What about the golf-course parking lot?" he asked. "The one we used the other day."

"It's buried under snow," I answered. "Might be blacktop, might be gravel."

"If it's blacktop, could you tell when it was laid by looking at it?"

"No, but let's get off our asses and try to make something happen."

I picked up my phone and dialed Public Works. I identified myself, but was immediately placed on hold. Itchy, I drummed the desktop with my fingernails.

"Take a hike, loosen up," Art said. "Let me sit with it." He reached for my phone.

"Thanks."

I stood and walked into the hall to settle my stump more firmly into its socket—a habit I have, like cracking one's knuckles. I did a few laps around the second floor, then returned to the office.

"A little something here," Art said, "in the Public Works records. Very detailed. Amazing, isn't it?"

"That they keep voluminous records?" I shut the door and leaned against its frame. "Amazing, you say? When Public Works has four or five guys standing around to fill one crummy pothole with a few shovelfuls of some black shit? It means they'll do anything to burn time. What's better than keeping useless records?"

"Christ Almighty, what'd you have for lunch, Nora? Something got you in the stomach?"

"Mammy's, on Rush. Oliveburger."

"Okay, that explains it. You're forgiven."

I snickered and pointed at the scribble on his notepad. "Whatcha got?"

"The parking lot for the Waveland Golf Course was repaved last fall—November 22nd and 23rd to be exact. The job was prepared on the 22nd, and the new stuff went down on the 23rd. They worked all day and finished late in the afternoon."

I moved to my chair. "Anything else?"

"Yes," he said. "I called the National Weather Service yesterday afternoon, while you were at the Adler. This winter's first snow began on November 23rd, before midnight."

"And we haven't seen the ground since."

"Right."

"So E. B. was probably in that parking lot on the fresh asphalt on the 23rd, either killed in the lot or dragged across the lot dead."

"He must have been alive in the lot," Art said. "Standing, I mean."

"The tar was on the soles of his shoes, wasn't it?"

He nodded.

I shoved my chair close to my desk. "He was standing in that lot between the time the paving crew left and enough snow fell to cover the blacktop. He was there, alive, sometime between, say, six P.M. and midnight."

It could have been lying on our floor for twenty minutes and we wouldn't have noticed, so caught up were we in talking about E. B. and the parking lot. Was he shot in the lot, or at the swamp, or on the grassy lawn in between? Might joggers have been around that late at night to witness? Would it pay to look for empty bullet casings on the pavement when the snow melted? Should we melt the hard-packed snow now, with torches, to check if the tar matched the material on E. B.'s pants and shoes?

In a moment of rumination, Art turned toward the door.

"What's on the floor?" He pointed to a sheet of computer paper that had been quietly slipped under our door. Probably by Charley, the station's runner.

"I dunno." I started out of my chair.

"No, sit." He motioned me back and walked the few paces to the paper. Reading it, he said, "Sweet Jesus, we've got a make!"

"Boyes?" I asked.

"Kuzov was right."

He tossed the sheet in front of me. The report was the second run of prints, the request made of the CIA/NASA data base. In faint, barely readable dot-matrix print, it said:

Edward G. Boyes
DOB: 09/11/48
NASA; civilian
Assign: JPL, Pasadena
Base: Johnson Space Center, Houston
Termination: April, 1988

I said, "What a job Tommy Banks did for us, skinning those fingertips. Okay, let's start on this guy, Art. Let's detect."

"He's a teacher at Loyola?" Art said.

"That's what Kuzov told me."

"He say where Boyes lived?"

"I never asked."

With the city phone book already in my hand, I tossed a suburban directory over to Art. Neither of us found any listing for Edward Boyes. I typed the name into my desk terminal. After a few seconds, Downtown told me that Edward Boyes had no police or traffic record, and he had never been reported to the police as missing. Finally, I struck out on NCIC.

As I worked, Art used his terminal to send Boyes's name and birth date into the Illinois driver's registration bureau. He found no license recorded for Edward Boyes in the state for the past ten years. The files didn't go back any earlier.

We had worked furiously for five minutes, looked in the simple places where data on ninety-nine percent of the population resides, and we had nothing.

"What now?" I said.

"Let's get better organized," Art said. "We think he taught at Loyola; we know he worked for NASA. Which one do you want?"

"Loyola."

"I'll start on NASA. Meet you back here in a couple of hours?"

"Fine."

EIGHT

Thirty minutes later, I turned off Sheridan Road at the main gate of Loyola's lakeside campus, then double-parked at a security hut. I went in for directions. My lucky day—Russ Conlon, a retired patrolman from Area Six, manned the desk. His red face brightened at seeing an old comrade, and he assured me he would take care of the Fury. He sent me to the building nearest the lake, the Crown Administration Building, Room 422.

Crown's windowed lobby looked out to heaving water the color of blue-gray metal. Room 422 was an elevator ride away, and there I met Amanda Loomquist, the head of faculty personnel. She greeted me with the icy hand that all police come to expect.

We stood in her anteroom while we spoke, Loomquist not offering me one of the available cushy chairs. "Yes," she said, in a grandiloquent voice, "of course I recall Edward Boyes. He was brought in to teach computer sciences." She was a big-boned middle-aged woman whose sheer size overpowered her delicate facial features and soft brown eyes. She wore a navy woolen suit, severe but expensive.

"When was Boyes hired?" I asked.

"Last spring, maybe early summer."

"Which department?"

"Computer Sciences. You must realize, Lieutenant, that it's difficult to hire in that discipline," she said more humbly. "There's so much more money in industry than in academics. But we were desperate, so we jumped the gun and hired Boyes on the strength of his NASA recommendations. They didn't tell us he was a nut case."

"Meaning?"

"Lieutenant, why are you here?" Loomquist said, with a hint of exasperation.

Time to push to the point of my visit. "Edward Boyes is dead," I said. "Murdered by two gunshots to his head."

Loomquist's shoulders hunched forward and she put her hand to her lips. From outside came the sounds of the lake slamming the boulders below.

"He's been identified as the man found two days ago in a Lincoln Park swamp," I said.

Now she stepped back, as though in some danger. "I heard that story on the news yesterday." Looking unsteady, she saved herself: "Let's sit."

We moved to facing chairs with a table between. I was feeling more welcome.

"I didn't know Boyes well," she said, as though in excuse. "Not at all, really."

"It doesn't matter," I said. "What I need first is the date Boyes was last on campus. Then a copy of his personnel records."

The strain in her face eased. She turned her head toward an adjoining office and surprised me with a crass shout: "Maria! I need the minutes of the special session on Edward Boyes. It would be late November or early December."

I heard unseen file drawers clicking open and shut. In a minute, a young Hispanic woman brought a manila folder, and Loomquist set about reading through its unbound pages. I didn't interrupt.

Finally, nodding, she said, "It's coming clear again. Boyes's leaving was coincident with the computer conference. The university called this special meeting to decide whether to sanction him, but then he made the issue moot by disappearing."

I recalled Valery Kuzov telling me he had last seen Boyes at a scientific meeting a few months before. "Miss Loomquist, you've lost me."

She crossed her legs. Her shoes—smooth maroon leather with gold piping—couldn't have cost a penny under two hundred dollars. She said, "Do you remember an item on the news about a disturbance at a computer conference? It would have been last fall."

"No."

She puckered her lips and indulged me: "You must be very busy with your work."

"I am."

"Well, Loyola sponsors a periodic conference on computer science," she said. "It attracts mathematicians and computer people from around the country, even some from overseas. The programs are highly respected. We're very proud of it here."

"What's it got to do with Boyes?"

"Boyes presented a paper at last fall's meeting, original work of his, software or something. The problem wasn't his research—Loyola certainly had no quarrel with that. But after he delivered the paper, he used his time at the podium to spout off about a woman being held prisoner in Russia."

"What woman?" It had to be Irina Varonyev.

"Some scientist or engineer," Loomquist said. "I don't know any more about her."

"What was the big deal about Boyes speaking out? Who cared?"

"Lieutenant, this was a scientific meeting, not a political forum. The highest-level people participate. That kind of outburst undermines the whole credibility of the conferences."

"But if—"

"It's not a circus, you know," she said, her head tilting as though in reprimand. "Boyes was out of line. His actions were an embarrassment to the university. He would have been officially censured."

"How many attended the conference?"

"A couple of hundred or so."

"Reporters are usually there?" I asked.

"No—the conferences aren't media events. A certain decorum is demanded of the host institution," she said. "It's a question of trust within the scientific community."

"How did the media know to come?"

"Boyes had called them, told them there would be a story worth covering."

"I don't remember ever reading or seeing a thing about it."

She said, "A small item appeared in the *Tribune* and another in the *Sun-Times*. Two of the television stations ran a minute or two of videotape. It was all more than we wanted."

"How long before Boyes's disappearance did it occur?"

"The weekend before."

"Do you think the incident had anything to do with his disappearance?" I asked.

"I haven't the foggiest."

"Do your records tell you the last day Boyes was on campus?"

She turned a page. "November 23rd."

Asphalt day at Waveland Golf Club. I nodded for Loomquist to continue.

"He met a scheduled three-o'clock class that afternoon, and so far as I know, we never heard from him again."

"Never collected a final paycheck?"

"No. No trace."

"What did the university do about his absence?"

"We telephoned him, sent somebody to his apartment—he didn't live far from here. When we came up with nothing, we juggled schedules to replace him. He missed three more classes on the 28th, the Monday after Thanksgiving, and two the day after that. Never called us, never wrote."

"Did the university report Boyes missing to the police?"

Lips set, she trudged the question through her memory. "Not that I recall."

"Do you think that strange?"

"In retrospect, I think it lazy." She looked down in embarrassment. "It may even have been negligent."

At Area Six just after five, my first stop was the coffee room. The urn held end of the day-shift stuff, a solution nearly as dark and turbid as the asphalt on Edward Boyes's shoes. I should have sent a sample to Chemistry to see if it was soluble in carbon disulfide. Instead, I poured two cups and walked to the office. When Art swigged, he wrinkled his lips in displeasure. "The Bible says save the best for last."

"That's wine, Arthur." I sat at my desk.

"How'd it go?"

I filled him in on my interview with Amanda Loomquist. I finished with "She said she'd get his personnel data together by tomorrow and fax it. What's with NASA? By the way, where is NASA?"

"Houston." His eyebrows climbed his forehead. "And oooo, girl!—aren't they hot shit down there?" With his face now squeezed into a frown, he said, "Took me thirty minutes to get clearance past an operator before I end up with Doris somebody, Souchak, I think. Says she won't talk to me on a line I'd opened from this end. She hangs up, then routes her own call through Headquarters downtown, then here to me. All to prove to herself I was a Chicago cop."

"What's the big deal?"

"My first question—at the risk of pissing her off. She says it's because Boyes was involved with the Phobos project."

"The probe's lost," I said, "a goner since last August. Who cares now?"

"You're forgetting something."

I shrugged.

"Phobos II. She's still up there."

"Oh, yeah . . . that's right."

Art shuffled his notes together. "Boyes had been with NASA since the mid-seventies doing software programming. When he left school, NASA was his first job."

"Where'd he train?"

"I didn't ask, but it should be in the file Doris is sending."

"He a bachelor?"

"Yes."

"Okay, sorry. Go on."

"Boyes worked on unmanned spacecraft—that's why he was assigned to JPL, which means Jet Propulsion Laboratory, at Cal Tech in Pasadena."

"The fingerprint sheet said his base was Johnson Space Center in Houston."

"An administrative ploy. Doris says Houston's budget is bigger, so NASA hides some salaries that way. Seems to be common practice."

"Back to JPL," I said. "Why is it involved in Phobos, a Soviet mission?"

"The Russians contracted with NASA to do software for Phobos. A cooperative thing."

I took a long draft of the cooling coffee and decided to stop barging in. Without my interruptions, Art moved smoothly through his extensive notes, keeping his usual attention to detail, only occasionally breaking to look up at me. He told me the story of Edward Boyes's breakneck ascent through NASA, from gofer to software honcho. No one in the agency could recall such an innovative employee; project directors fought to corral him for their teams. Finally, NASA assigned him to troubleshoot—he was a man who could plunge into an ocean of indecision and bad planning and rescue the software side of a drowning mission.

Boyes may have been brilliant, but his genius came with a stiff tariff. Chronically irascible and idiosyncratic—Kuzov was prophetic again—he left a prickly trail behind him, and these NASA casualties eventually destroyed him. When he was brought back to the States because of his affair with a Russian programmer, he was summarily fired. Had he been able to cash the currency of past friendship, Doris noted, he might have survived his Tallinn faux pas. As it was, his brilliance could not persuade his superiors to persevere any longer. Few were sorry to see him fall; he was out the door to Loyola without farewell cake and champagne.

We stood in a loose circle in Melchior's office. Art and I had entered as Smilin' Ray was leaving for home. While he buttoned his overcoat, I flew through our news about Kuzov, the autopsy report, the make on the fingerprints, how we dated the murder, and my interview with Amanda Loomquist. Art skimmed over the NASA material. Melchior seemed as pleased as his sour face would ever permit him to appear.

"What's next?" Melchior said.

"I'll go through Boyes's personnel file from Loyola tomorrow morning," I said. "There might be some help there."

"And you, Campbell?" Melchior said. "What about the NASA file?"

"The lady didn't say when I would get it."

"She's not faxing it?"

"No," Art said. "I'm not sure how it'll come, or how soon."

"Who'd you talk to?"

"Her name is Doris Souchak."

Melchior lifted his collar. "And you identified yourself?"

"Of course."

"That bitch," Melchior growled. "I'll get on the phone with her."

"Won't matter," Art said. "Edward Boyes was fired while working on a mission, Souchak said, so no details—none—go over the wires. The woman was unyielding about that."

"But Boyes is fucking dead!" Melchior screeched.

"I told her that twice," Art said. "She didn't budge."

"Okay, for crissake, okay," Melchior relented. "Let me know when you have more."

Melchior started out the door, then turned back. "And remember, Callum, that bastard Jimmy O'Donnell's still crowding me, crowding me worse than ever. I need an arrest here. You got that?"

Meg was asleep by nine, and the apartment turned quiet. Tired, I plunked in front of the television just ahead of the news. It wasn't Karl Kramer's depravity that I had tuned in, it was Channel 5—strictly mainstream. Before a run of ads, the newscast's promo said stay tuned for tonight's lead, the Lincoln Park murder. This surprised me—why rehash the story? The city must have endured a half-dozen fresher killings since Boyes's face emerged from the mounded snow two days before.

The screen changed and the perfectly made up anchor appeared. She wasted no time: her first sentence announced that police had established the identity of the Lincoln Park victim. "Edward Boyes," the woman said, the name hanging in my living room, boosting my body upright. She already knew what I had just found out myself.

And then, as if the disclosure of Boyes's name weren't disheartening enough, she went on to mention every place and entity we had found relating to Boyes. The Phobos project. NASA.

Johnson Space Center. Tallinn. The Golden Swan. There they were, the whole string of known particulars budding on the television like morning glories on a dewy trellis. The segment ended with another shot of my personnel photograph behind the anchor's shoulder as she noted that Lieutenant Nora Callum would be broadening the investigation.

I sat through the rest of the program stunned, not stirring until a blaring piece on rock videos sliced through my inertia. I walked to the kitchen and phoned Art. He answered on the second ring: "I knew it would be you."

"Would be who?" I said.

"My podner," he clowned. "Ms. Nora Joyce Callum."

"Then you saw it, too. What channel?"

"I loved your mug shot from the files."

"Stop it, Art! What channel did you watch?"

"Seven."

Seething, I set my head back hard against the wall. "Shit, mine was Channel Five. That means everybody had it."

"Can't play favorites."

"Melchior's got diarrhea of the mouth," I said. "Why'd he give it out?"

"'Cause he's in a media pressure cooker. 'Cause large dogs are snappin' at his ass. You know, I'm actually starting to feel sorry for the guy."

"You don't air information like that," I said. "Not yet anyway."

"And how often does it really matter?"

"He was wrong to do it."

Art paused, then said, "I agree, okay? Hey, look, Nora, the guy's . . . the guy's done worse to you."

"Don't remind me."

We had a date for the murder. We had some names. It was time to start checking alibis.

The morning broke bright and cold—we'd been having a nice run of sunshine for February. Moving along Lake Shore Drive, I saw a bundled jogger hunched into the wind, running through the lakefront's stark winter tranquillity. In a few weeks, with a little luck, Meg and I could dust off our bikes and ride the same paths.

Not bothering to stop at Area Six, I went straight to IIT. I hadn't called ahead to Valery Kuzov, because I didn't think he'd be hard to find, and he wasn't. I bumped into him as he exited the building where he taught his early-morning class. He was headed for his office, and he invited me to come. On the way, he stopped to encourage a couple of students who verged on panic at an upcoming exam in Kuzov's Physics 102 course.

Kuzov's office was spacious and well organized. Double windows looked toward Comiskey Park, the venerable concrete-and-steel ball yard, then in its last years. We sat in chairs in front of a desk. Kuzov wore a crew-neck sweater.

"You were right about Boyes," I said. "Fingerprints confirm that the body is his. And NASA agrees with your feelings about his personality."

"Edward was a difficult man, Lieutenant. Shortcomings that undermine brilliance."

"I'm here because we've been able to date the murder. Boyes was killed the evening of November 23rd, a Wednesday."

With a timid smile, Kuzov said, "We need your kind of technical expertise in our space program."

"Dr. Kuzov, I want you to think about when you last saw Boyes alive. Yesterday you mentioned something about a conference?"

"It must have been the Loyola computer conference."

"And that was when?"

He ran his hand across his cropped beard. "I need my calendar for last year."

He walked to a bookshelf and returned with a small, squarish book that he searched for a few seconds. "Saturday, November 19th. The conference was all day Saturday."

"And you remember Boyes being there?"

"I'm sure of it. I think we talked during a coffee break."

"Did Boyes seem agitated?"

"I don't recall." He paused, then said, "In retrospect, if he wasn't, I'd be surprised."

"Why?"

"He was very bold later that day. The way he ended his formal presentation."

"Tell me."

Kuzov went on to relate the story of Boyes's outburst to the audience and the media, the identical story given me by Amanda Loomquist. But, unlike Loomquist, Kuzov knew that the woman Boyes ranted about was Irina Varonyev. When Kuzov finished, I said, "Did you see or talk to Boyes during the next four days? At a lecture? Anywhere?"

He looked back to his calendar. "Those kinds of things are always scheduled. I don't have anything here."

"He wouldn't have called you?" I asked. "As a result of the media coverage of the conference?"

"Oh, no," he said firmly. "Edward wasn't given to asking for advice, or solace. He would have regarded that as personal weakness."

I asked, "Dr. Kuzov, can you tell me where you were on the evening of November 23rd?"

"I wouldn't know, but thank God for this calendar." He lifted it slightly from his lap. "It was exam week here on campus."

"And?"

"Exams are scheduled on the same days and times that the classes meet. I had two evening classes on Wednesdays last semester, one at six and another at eight. Teachers must proctor their own exams here at IIT—tiresome, but I do as told. I would have finished about ten or so."

I went on to question Kuzov about Boyes's scientific presentation at the Loyola conference. Kuzov remembered it well, and described it to me in numbing detail. Although I was thoroughly confused about the subject matter, I didn't think it could have anything to do with Boyes's death. I thanked Kuzov and left.

Before leaving the campus, I stopped at the Administration Building. My detective shield gained me admission to a vice-chancellor's office, a man who knew Kuzov and his work on campus. Kuzov was a respected member of the visiting faculty, the man was quick to say, as good an exchange professor as the institution had ever had. And, although a taskmaster, Kuzov seemed to be a student favorite.

When the vice-chancellor finished, he took me to a basement room where old exams were kept on file for a full semester after being taken. In a society where even students have become litigious, IIT had learned to retain its documentation for teachers' grading decisions. A woman showed me the previous semester's syllabus that listed Kuzov as teaching two Wednesday evening courses in the adult education program. When she hunted the exams for those courses, she found them on the expected shelf and all exams dated November 23rd.

I felt some relief that Kuzov had been cleared. Intuition told me that the Phobos probes would somehow figure strongly in the mix as the Boyes case played out. This wasn't material that would be easily understood by library work, and the thought of soliciting answers from Dan Halsey didn't enchant me. I was glad for a willing helper.

NINE

"Front desk. Special delivery for you." He stopped to giggle. "From our guys at the airport."

It was Frankie Luchinski phoning from the Area Six lobby. I was upstairs in my office. It was three in the afternoon. I said, "Keep talking. . . . Look, I'm not gonna beg. . . . Frankie—"

"It's a lady, she's not bad. I think she's from the old country."

"Yeah?"

"She gets off a plane and goes to our station at O'Hare. Says she's come to find a missing person. Edward Boyes. Flying in, can you beat that? The guys out there recognize the name, Boyes. Okay, they don't say a thing, just send her to you."

"A squad bring her?" I asked.

"What, they got nothing better to do than chauffeur? You been off a beat how long, Nora?"

"Then she drove?"

"Shit, no. Taxi."

"I'll be down."

I came up to the Belmont Avenue side of the lobby desk, a big, square affair with an open center where two or three officers stood duty to greet the public. I leaned against the waist-high stone counter. "What gives, Frankie?"

"Behind me, east wall."

I saw a woman in a drab green coat sitting on the bench ahead of me and to my right. "Taxi leave?"

"You see a cabby waiting? You got eyes?"

I looked out the glass doors to Belmont Avenue, then to the north entrance and the parking lot. "No cab."

"Then she's all yours, Lieutenant."

I shook my head. "I'm gonna bake you chocolate chip cookies, Frankie. Yep, I'm gonna bring you a batch—to see if stuffing chocolate down your gullet will sweeten your sour ass."

I slapped the stone and walked away. When I approached the bench, the woman turned toward me. She was a big woman with a lovely round face, gray eyes, and short, light hair. Her eyebrows were as thick as Paris Viveka's. She was my age, no older. She wore small earphones attached to a cassette player in her lap.

I stopped a few feet from her. "My name is Nora Callum," I said. "I am a lieutenant here. May I sit?"

She nodded and slid the earphones behind her ears. I chose a non-threatening spot a few feet from her. "What's your name?" I asked.

"Olga Berggolts." Her English was stiff but serviceable.

"I'm pleased to meet you. May I call you Olga?"

"Yes."

"You traveled to Chicago today?"

"From Boston. I return tonight." Her lips and tongue formed each word with mechanical precision.

"You came from the East Coast, but you are from—?"

"Russia. I visit America, as part of my work."

I nodded.

"Physics," she said. "I am a physicist. From Moscow. I work on a project in cooperation with MIT, in Boston. You know that school?"

"Sure. Yes."

"I come there, usually once per month."

The north doors opened and a blast of fresh cold air swooshed in and chilled my foot and ankle. A woman and her child went to the desk to do business.

"Olga, why did you go to the police at the airport?"

"To find information. We are looking for a man, Mr. Boyes, Edward. We are afraid we have lost him."

"You say 'we'?"

"Myself and my friend."

"Who's that?"

"Irina Varonyev."

Startled, I swallowed to gain a second. I heard music leaking faintly from the earphones in her hair. "Where is she now?"

"In Moscow. She could not come."

"I see." I twisted my head and called back to Frankie, "Sergeant Luchinski, would you see if there is an interview room open on second?"

Frankie sneered at me and picked up a phone. In a moment, he barked, "Open. All yours. Take your pick."

The interview room's south-facing window gathered the slanted, burnt-orange light of the dying sun. There was a table, four metal chairs, and recording equipment that I decided not to use. I told Olga Berggolts that the privacy here was better than in the lobby. I wasn't sure if we needed seclusion. I did know that this woman was forlornly looking for a dead man.

We each took a chair. Berggolts placed the cassette player on the table between us, the earphones still stuck in her hair. A barely perceptible sound emanated from around her scalp. She slipped from her coat and laid it across the table. She wore a dark suit and a white blouse topped by a delicate lace collar. A piece of jewelry, a small, striking gold medal tied to a ribbon, hung from her lapel.

I needed openers. "Your medal is beautiful," I said. "Can I ask what it is?"

"An award in astrophysics," she said, "from Leningrad State University. I won it some years ago. My brain was more supple then." The precise motion of her lips made her mouth unattractive when she spoke.

"You must be very proud."

She straightened. Her chin twitched with embarrassment. "These days I wear it as an ornament."

I smiled slightly.

Looking dead at me, the warmth in her face already in jeopardy, she knifed ahead: "The police at the airport promised you could help me to find Edward Boyes."

"Why are you looking?"

"Because the letters have stopped coming. Over two months now."

"The letters?"

"Edward's letters to Irina, the woman I said to you downstairs."

"Why didn't Irina come herself?" I knew the answer from conversation with Valery Kuzov, but I wanted to test her.

"She is in jail," Berggolts said flatly. "In Lefortova Prison in Moscow."

"I see." I stared at the metal desktop, as gray and hard as a clouded sky before an evening of rain. I felt I needed to withhold the news of Boyes's murder until I had more, in case she bolted upon hearing it. I said, "Tell me about the letters. Their purpose."

"Purpose? They are the letters of lovers. Is that purpose?"

"Yes, sure," I fumbled. "Irina is allowed letters in her jail?"

"No, but I smuggle them when I visit. In Boston, I mail Irina's and pick up Edward's. I am a courier. Very simple."

"Where do you pick up Edward's?"

"At a post-office box," she said. "We have arranged for it. But the box has been empty for too long. He is not answering."

"Did you think to call Edward before traveling this far?"

"Yes. His phone has been disconnected."

To buy time, I tried a throwaway, expecting nothing. "Any of Edward's friends you might have called?"

"I had one telephone number," she said, "for Stevens."

"Stevens?"

"Robert Stevens," she said. "A teacher at Edward's university. Loyola."

"Ahh." I nodded slowly, enlivened. "And what did Robert Stevens have to say?"

"I phoned last month, in January. Robert said Edward has been missing, that is all he knows. Now, when I called last night, no one is home at Robert's, so I decided to come to Chicago actually. Enough for waiting. We are fearful."

Thinking, I stared at the cassette player on the table, watching its tiny mechanism rotate slowly inside its clear plastic door. I felt rudderless. After three days of nothing, suddenly, in the fifteen minutes since Frankie's call to my office, I had a physicist who knew Boyes and his Irina, and I had a Loyola teacher who knew of letters being carried in and out of a Moscow prison. I didn't know where to take this woman next. But I did know that being a detective means not acting fussy. You take what leads you get and you massage them, hoping they evolve into something worthwhile.

Berggolts screeched her chair against the floor and stood, the thin yellow wire stretched from under her chin to the cassette player still on the table. "Enough, Lieutenant," she said. "I will try at Edward's university."

"Olga, no."

"My plane leaves in five hours. I have no time to waste here."

"Please sit. I can tell you what we know."

"Edward is in trouble with the police?"

"No. None."

She sat. Her voice a tone lower, she said, "He doesn't write because he's gone to another woman?"

"God, no! Nothing like that. Please let me talk."

Though afraid of what lay ahead, I was tired of circling. I didn't have the heart to lie to Berggolts, even if it meant she might refuse to help me find Boyes's killer. I took in a full chest of air and on the exhale, I said, "Olga, something dreadful has happened to Edward. Last November, when you noticed his letters stop."

Her large white hands became rigid in her lap.

I said, "Edward's been murdered—found in a city park—this past Monday. I'm very sorry."

Eyes shut, Berggolts sat sphinxlike while the force of my words settled into her. Two interminable minutes passed before she opened her eyes and said, "November to February—three months. This interval makes no sense to me." It was as though dissecting details of time might deflect horror.

I said, "We can tell by forensics. His death occurred in November, before the winter's first snow. We have placed the date very accurately. It fits when he disappeared."

"Edward was not located for three months?"

"That's right."

"His body was outside?"

"Yes. Frozen under ice."

"Who killed him?" she demanded.

"We don't know yet. I was hoping you might be of help."

"And the cause of his death?" Her questions were coming like rounds from a machine gun.

"Gunshots."

"Where?" she said rudely. "Precisely where, Lieutenant?"

I understood the fury my news was creating for her. Elbows on the table, I folded my hands at my chin. Softly, I said, "Two shots through his brain. He was dead instantly."

"You give words, not proof," she said. "You could be fabricating. Edward could be imprisoned now himself. By NASA maybe. How would I know?"

I remembered Tommy Banks's photographs from the morgue —by chance I had several of them in my skirt pocket. I pulled them out and handed them across the table.

Berggolts's fingers shook as she started through the gruesome prints. In the absolute stillness of the room, I now realized that the music from her earphones was a solo piano. I twisted away to give her privacy.

I turned back. Finished, Berggolts stacked the photos neatly. Tears streamed down her round cheeks. She pointed a forefinger toward an earphone and said, "This is Bach." She broke a thin, ironic smile. "From the French Suites."

"I didn't know."

She wiped the flat of a hand across her cheeks. "Do you have any idea what this will do to Irina?"

"No . . . I mean, yes . . . I mean—"

"They beat her, Lieutenant. She is quite thin now, not good." She stopped there.

Olga Berggolts had pulled her earphones off and laid her head on the table, inside the circle made by her arms. I knew I had to move quickly. Two phone calls should do it, maybe ten or fifteen minutes out of the room.

I turned to the wall phone behind me. I found Art in our office. "Art," I whispered, "a tray of coffee and sweet rolls. Now, please. Our floor, south interview room."

Art was there in minutes. He carried a tray piled with rolls—I don't know where in the station he found them that time of day—and a pot of coffee with cups. Berggolts lifted her head when he arrived. I said I needed to use the bathroom and would be back shortly. Art smiled at Berggolts and poured coffee.

I hurried down the corridor to our office. It was four-thirty— I hoped they were still at work. Kuzov would be first, NASA second.

Luckily, Kuzov was in his office, the only number I had for him. "Dr. Kuzov," I said, "a woman named Olga Berggolts has come to see me. She flew in from Boston and leaves tonight. She claims she is a Russian scientist who does cooperative work at MIT. Do you know her?"

"Blond? A little stocky?"

"Yes."

"She is an engineer," Kuzov said, "no, a physicist. She never worked on Phobos, but I've met her. I think the project with MIT is observation of Jupiter's Great Red Spot."

"She claims to know the Varonyev woman you spoke about."

"She could. I wouldn't know that."

I went on to explain the transfer of letters in and out of Lefortova Prison. Kuzov said Edward had never told him about that, but there was no reason why he should have. When I asked about the likelihood of letters getting in and out of Lefortova, Kuzov said he could see that happening—security for a prisoner like Varonyev would not be overly tight. Finally, Kuzov said that he knew Robert Stevens. He had met Stevens a few times since being in Chicago—again, at scientific meetings like the Loyola conference. He thought Stevens once worked as a NASA programmer, but never on Phobos. I thanked Kuzov and hung up.

* * *

I found Doris Souchak's number on Art's notepad. When she answered, she dragged me through the same routine she had required of Art. I hung up and waited for her return call routed through Headquarters downtown. Satisfied I was police, she was willing to talk.

Souchak had not personally heard of Olga Berggolts, but she found the name on a roster of foreign scientists cleared for American space research. Irina Varonyev was more familiar: yes, Varonyev was Boyes's Tallinn lover, the woman who became the official reason he was fired. NASA knew of Varonyev's imprisonment from Boyes's outburst at the Loyola conference. When I told Souchak about the letters passing between Varonyev and Boyes, she reacted with mild surprise.

"Have you heard of Robert Stevens?" I asked.

"One of the whiz kids," Souchak said. "We wish we still had him."

"Whiz kids?"

"Three. Boyes and Stevens and a man named Jack Percot. They came to NASA together, ran together. Boyes was brilliant, but the other two were very keen."

"They all worked on Phobos?"

"Two of them."

"Explain, please. This is important, but I'm in a rush. What can you thumbnail for me?"

"Here goes," she said. "In 1987, the Soviets approached us, practically begged us, for help with the Phobos guidance systems. We jumped at the chance. We decided to commit our very best."

As the tempo of Souchak's delivery speeded, I straightened up in my chair. This woman seemed genuinely interested in helping me.

"We needed a small team," Souchak said, "maybe a half-dozen, to go to Tallinn for several months. The choice of director came down to two—Boyes or Stevens. If anyone but Boyes had been the competition, Stevens would have coasted into the job. But when the position was offered to Boyes, Stevens quit NASA."

"Because he had lost out?" I said.

8 6

"Not according to Stevens," she replied. "He claimed he had been considering moving back to Chicago for months, and that the timing was pure coincidence."

"Did Boyes and Stevens get along?"

"Far as I know," she said. "Boyes asked Stevens to accompany him to Tallinn, but was turned down. Stevens separated from NASA before Boyes ever left the States."

"Who's this other guy again, Doris?"

"Jack Percot?"

"Yes."

"A near-genius, but with troubles."

"Namely?"

"The drink," she said cynically.

"Friends with Boyes and Stevens?"

"Oh, yes. As I said, they all came to NASA together."

"Percot involved with Phobos?" I asked.

"Eventually. See, when Stevens refused to go to Tallinn, Boyes leaned on Percot to request reassignment to Phobos, and he did. We thought Boyes could pull the project through, and Percot would likely be an asset. But Percot was drunk half the time, so he and Boyes had a big falling-out. Boyes demanded that Percot be sent back to the States."

"And he was?"

"Yes," she said, "and then fired when he stepped off the plane in Houston. NASA had had enough of Jack Percot."

"Percot blame Boyes for being canned?"

"Jack was resentful to everybody. Wacko, really. We negotiated a settlement with him—he left without filing litigation, and, in exchange, we granted him full pension rights."

I looked at my watch. "Back to Boyes," I said. "If he was such a hotshot, why was he fired?"

"Because he went over the line with this Russian woman," Souchak said. "Now, admittedly, it was a line drawn by ultraconservative NASA and Soviet brass, but NASA had to ax him if the Soviets were going to keep us onboard."

I scribbled some notes. "Doris, did Stevens come directly to teach in Chicago after leaving NASA?"

"I wouldn't know," she said.

"And Percot?" I asked. "Where's he now?"

"Last I heard, University of Illinois. And his snoot is deeper than ever into the bottle."

"What? Main campus? In Urbana?"

"I think so," she replied. "Is that close to Chicago?"

"Couple of hours. Close enough."

TEN

I returned to the interview room just before five o'clock. Berggolts and Art had coffee in front of them, but the pile of sweet rolls hadn't been touched. I wasn't sure either had spoken a word since I left. I perched at the edge of the table. "What time does your flight leave, Olga?"

"Eight-thirty."

"Would you like a ride? To the airport?"

She looked up at me in surprise. "You could?"

"We'll get some supper, then leave." I said to Art, "Wanna come? Margie's?"

"No, thanks. I'll head home." He walked toward the door.

I followed him. "Oh, Art, will you run a check on a guy named Percot? Jack. Could be John. Currently in Urbana, at the U of I."

He turned back. "Nora, you know what I love about how you're running this case?"

"No, what?"

"The way you're surrounding yourself with brainpower. I mean, people from the Adler, Loyola, NASA, IIT, MIT, now the U of I. Who's next?"

As he pushed the door open, I said, in mock anger, "Arthur. . ."

"Yes?"

"Take a flying leap at a rolling doughnut."

With Art gone, I telephoned Anna to tell her I wouldn't be home till late, and to please put Meg to bed for me. When I finished,

Berggolts asked if she could try again to reach Robert Stevens. I dialed her an outside line. I had no qualms about listening in.

Berggolts spoke to someone she called Eileen, the woman I assumed was Stevens's wife. It was soon obvious that two people had come on at the other end, the other person being Robert Stevens. Berggolts spoke of Boyes's disappearance and death, but I made out nothing beyond simple commiseration. She mentioned Irina Varonyev's name once. When Berggolts said she had to catch a plane to Boston that evening, the Stevenses must have asked her the airline—Delta, she said—then offered her a ride to O'Hare. She refused politely, saying I would be driving her.

At Margie's, we looked out and up to the ribbed concrete underbelly of the Western Avenue overpass. Unseen trucks whined through their lower gears to climb the grade. The sun was long gone, the city now lit by streetlamps and cold starry headlights. We were warm inside Margie's, even hot; the smells were of baked and frying meat and potatoes.

I had meat loaf, Berggolts eggs and toast. She seemed more comfortable with me now, telling me about her husband and two daughters in Russia. When I asked how long she had been friends with Varonyev, she said, "Since primary school."

"You mentioned Irina has been beaten in jail," I said. "Could you elaborate?"

"No."

"But I wonder—"

"Irina is a small but a tough woman," Berggolts cut in, "and she has endured much in her jail. I leave it at that, Lieutenant."

I waited a cooling minute before asking, "Does Irina have children?"

Berggolts shook her head. "She has never married; Edward was her first lover. She relied too much on science before him."

"How will she react to Boyes's death?"

She shrugged but didn't answer. Her eyes filled.

"Olga, do you know where Irina's letters to Edward would be?"

"No."

"You don't have copies?"

"Of course not." She tipped her chin up defiantly and shoveled a spoonful of egg into her mouth. She swallowed, then said, "If I did, I would never give them to you. Not something so personal."

Embarrassed, I turned to the window and stared blankly into the night. "Do you think it was Irina's fault that the first Phobos was lost?" I finally asked. I looked back.

Berggolts squinted and said, "Irina sent a proper command. Something was defective with the probe."

The trip to O'Hare was a river of flashing brake lights all along the Kennedy Expressway. I pushed and shoved a bit, and we made the airport forty minutes ahead of Berggolts' departure time. I shut the Fury down at curbside, outside the Delta Airlines drop-off.

We passed the next twenty minutes talking about children, the universal language of motherhood. I don't make friends quickly, so I was surprised to find how easily I had come to relate to Berggolts. Though it was early in the case, she seemed to me a heroine who braved much for her friend Irina Varonyev, and I was saddened to think we would probably never meet again.

Before she left the car, we exchanged phone numbers, mine for home and office, hers for Boston and Moscow. When I cranked the Fury, it coughed a time or two, balking at the cold. I drove away and onto the ramp that merged with I-190, the bypass back to the Kennedy. The Fury was quickly warm enough to accelerate smoothly; I wasn't expecting much from the heater anyway.

Ironic, my rescue being granted by the road I had missed so many times before. I mean, that damned turnoff I never seemed to find the first time around when circling, circling in the car, waiting to pick up someone from an arriving flight. RECIRCULATION ROUTE, the sign called it, the road that brings one back to the terminals, after first passing by them to deposit or retrieve passengers. An appropriate name, I guess, but it didn't make the road any less of a pisser to me every time I missed it and had to drive clear out to the Mannheim exit to re-enter the airport.

Thwack: the first shot's sound. Dull enough to be a blown tire —until I saw the gap and shatter cracks in my window, and felt the icy night air rush through the bullet hole.

I jerked to full attention. My foot came off the gas. When I realized I wasn't hit, I looked left for the shooter. Frost covered the window, only the black bullet hole sharp and clear. I made out the silhouette of a car in the lane next to me. My fist scraped the inside frost and made a small porthole to see through.

I hunkered down to lower my head, then slammed the accelerator to the floorboard. The Fury swallowed the huge load of gas and roared and powered forward without a lurch.

Headlights flashed in my side mirror, telling me I was running ahead of the car. I would try to outrun it. My foot strained on the gas pedal, and the speedometer blew through the seventies and into the eighties. The glare in the mirror lessened for a moment, then flared again. The car was closing in: it had the steam to keep up with the Fury.

Now a second shot pierced the rear window. Another miss. Either the frost was obscuring me, or someone was firing wildly. But two misses had stretched my luck. I wasn't outdistancing the car; I needed a new tactic. It came to me instinctively.

Still ahead of the chasing car, I suddenly jerked the Fury left, serpentining into the adjoining lane and the other car's path. When the shooter's brakes screamed, I whipped back into my lane and flattened the gas pedal to the floor. The headlights receded; I had regained a lead. I only needed a few more seconds.

There, the sign appeared. RECIRCULATION ROUTE—1/2 MILE.

I stayed hard on the gas but ready to come off quickly, hoping not to hear the boom of a third shot in the meantime. When headlights again brightened my mirror, I knew the car was catching up. I backed off a hair, and at first the reflected lights intensified, then disappeared altogether as they passed the mirror—the cars were neck and neck. I sucked in a chestful of air. I was ready to maneuver.

Now I put the Fury up past ninety with one more smack of

gas that the other car matched. Then, just thirty yards short of Recirculation Road, my foot jumped off the gas and hammered the brakes, my knee going stiff-straight with the effort. The screech of the Fury's locked wheels was deafening, and her rear end fishtailed wildly at the sudden deceleration. With the car barely under control, I fought to execute a hard right onto Recirc Road, just making it, sliding sideways in the gravel along the shoulder. When I got hold of things, I looked left. The other car was weaving, trying to brake, but had already flown by the exit. I was safe.

I slowed to a crawl. Recirc Road brought me back to the terminals, and I pulled to a curb and stopped. I unclenched my fists from the steering wheel, then laid my head on the seat back and closed my eyes. I breathed deeply, the air in the Fury surging fresh and clean-smelling through the bullet hole a few inches from my face.

The apartment was quiet; Meg had gone to bed long ago and Anna was half-asleep in a chair, the *Sun-Times* crumpled in her lap. After Anna left, I checked Meg and found her angular in her bed, sleeping soundly. I touched her shoulder and kissed her. When she stirred, I left quietly.

In my own bedroom, I undressed and removed my prosthesis. I crutched my way to the shower. Holding my grab bars for support, I aimed the spray at my shoulders and let it run wide open. I stood there until the steam swirled thick and the hot water beat my chest crimson and I couldn't tell my tears from sweat.

I dried off in my bedroom. As I did, I discovered a note from Anna on the bedside table. The note said Art had telephoned early that evening and wanted me to call back. It was now near eleven; I decided he and Helen were already in bed. Whatever it was could wait till morning.

Shivering inside my towel, I turned back the bedcovers, then let the towel drop to the floor. I slid naked between the cold sheets and waited for my body to warm them. I was asleep before it mattered.

• • •

At seven in the morning, southbound Lake Shore Drive was still duck soup, most of the white-collar Loop workers just rousing from bed. I aimed the Fury for Area Six, a thirty-minute trip, but I cut it to twenty-five by speeding and lane changing. To my left, the sun was hoisting itself over the lake.

On Belmont, I stopped at Rudy's Bagels and picked up three dozen still-warm ones; I had remembered it was my day to stock the coffee room. At Area Six, I parked near the station garage. Randy Jackson, the garage manager, came over to meet me as I climbed out of the car. He looked at the punctured rear window, then walked to the driver's window and stuck a finger though that hole. "Been cruising Division Street, Lieutenant?"

"I'm not hurt. You think they'd miss twice on Division?"

"Shit, no." His smile showed a missing bicuspid. "I'll have to make a call for the glass. How fast you talkin'?"

"By noon?"

"What's in your bag?"

I brought out a couple of bagels that he took in his thick hand. "Deal, Lieutenant. By noon. Okay, now get some paperwork out to me."

The lobby was relatively calm. When Frankie Luchinski saw me passing, he reached a long arm across his counter and into the bagel bag.

"Your mother ever teach you any manners?" I said.

He grabbed one of the pumpernickels. "Guess you wasted an afternoon with that Russian babe."

"What?"

"Didn't Art tell you?"

"Tell me what?" I asked.

"They arrested a guy in the Lincoln Park murder. Got him last evening." Frankie bit off a chunk of bagel.

I was stunned. "Who brought him in? Art?"

"Schwartz."

"Schwartz?" Puzzled at first, I remembered Melchior had sent him to prowl the Forty-third. "Who is he, Frankie?"

"I got no idea. I just saw him cuffed and hauled past here, and with a shitload of reporters all around. It's a black kid."

I started away, and he said, "Hey, can you bring me some coffee out here?"

"You've got two legs, Frankie. Just like me. I'm not your goddamned waitress."

I delivered the bagels to the coffee room, saving out a couple of cinnamon-raisins for Art. I siphoned two cups of coffee from the urn and headed to our office. Art was already there, working, his blocky upper body hunched over his desk. When he spotted me, he stood to help with the coffees.

"For you." I handed him the bagels. "Sorry I didn't return your call last night. It was eleven when I saw the note."

"You didn't see the nightly news?" Art asked.

"No, but Frankie just told me Schwartz nabbed a black kid in the Boyes murder."

"Melchior's practically orgasmic."

"I can imagine. What do you know?"

"Only what I've heard around the station," Art said while chewing. "He's a twenty-year-old punk from the streets. I wasn't there for the interrogation, but I heard Schwartz got a confession."

"Does he have a record?" I asked.

"A few misdemeanors as a juvenile, a couple of muggings in the past year, both occurring in the Lincoln Park area. He's done time for those. Out on parole since October."

I carried my coffee to the window. Across the street, a man washed windows at Margie's, the water glistening in the glare of morning sun. He finished, and limped away slowly.

I sat on the sill, facing Art, my back against the glass. "Did this kid—what's his name?"

"Eugene Easter."

"How'd Schwartz find him?"

Art shrugged ignorance.

"Do you buy all of this, Art?"

"The kid killing Boyes?"

"Yes."

"Why not?" he said. "Easter confessed. You're not buying it?"

"No, no . . . I mean . . . I don't know. It just surprises me a little, Boyes's cash and jewelry left behind."

The windowpane chilled my back, so I meandered over to my desk. Art drained his coffee cup and said, "Any skepticism isn't going to make a helluva lot of difference anyway."

"Why not? We can at least talk to the kid."

"It's moot," he said. "Melchior's closed the case. Told me to clean up on the thing, then come in for a new assignment."

Silent, I played moronically with the pot of fake flowers on the desk.

Art tried, "How many times do I have to say that the guy confessed? You got a problem here?"

"Only Melchior. He'd do anything to get Jimmy O'Donnell off his back. Remember what I told you about those butchered sisters, the Petersons? Jack Flaherty and I knew Melchior would have settled for any bum we brought in. That case had the same media ruckus this one does."

"So?"

"So Melchior's looking to put anybody with a pulse in the slammer. And if he can squeeze a confession—"

"You don't just squeeze a murder confession out of someone," Art interrupted.

"Let me finish. Look, if Melchior's got something for the TV boys, then O'Donnell shuts up." The timbre of my voice rising, I half hollered, "You think Melchior gives two shits if he's got the real killer or not?"

"Pipe down," Art warned. He motioned to the open door and the back and forth traffic in the hall.

More quietly I said, "If Easter didn't do it, it's no skin off Melchior's nose. Even if the kid was found innocent, the process would take weeks. By then, everybody's forgotten about the murder, Melchior's off the hook. Except for that hook, Smilin' Ray doesn't care."

I twirled strands of my hair—I was wearing it down that day—into a wisp. "Jesus," I moaned, "even my hair looks like shit today."

ELEVEN

Restless, I was back at the window, looking out. I had scratched a fingernail down the glass and made a haphazard path through the membrane of frost. I was thinking about my father. On Saturdays, as a child, I would often walk down Higgins Avenue to his garage, a cluttered, barn-like building smelling of oil and sweat and gasoline fumes. I'd sit on a greasy wooden stool and watch him do brake jobs and front-end alignments, fighting at times with frozen bolts, broken parts, and balky tools, but never giving up on a job until he was satisfied. His relentlessness was not lost on me now as I considered the Boyes murder case.

"Oh," Art said to my back, "I checked on the Percot guy. He's been in Urbana for six months. Two arrests for DUI since hitting town. Both on a Texas license."

"NASA said he was a sponge." I circled back to my desk.

"Relax, will you?" he said. "You're wearing grooves in the floorboards."

I plunked into my chair. "So what are we supposed to do, Art? Just say, 'Fuck it. Fuck Eugene Easter.' Do we just go on to the next case?"

"I forgot to tell you, I drove to the golf-course parking yesterday afternoon," he said. "I blowtorched a hole in the ice—it's blacktop underneath. Pretty new stuff, at that."

"Don't change the subject, Art."

"What subject?"

"Easter! Dammit, Art, talk about Easter!"

His palms came up in self-defense. "Okay, okay. I will."

Hands back down, he said, "Why you so friggin' skeptical? Tell me why Eugene Easter didn't murder Boyes."

"I don't know, he probably did. But you said a couple of days ago that even a mugging gone wrong doesn't usually end up with half a skull blown away."

His chin in his hands, Art sighed. "Some days you just stretch my ass to the limit, Nora. Do you know that?"

I didn't answer.

"Do you know that?"

"There's more," I said.

"More what?"

"A bigger reason I'm skeptical."

He lifted his eyebrows. "Yeah?"

"Last night, on the bypass out of O'Hare, someone shot at me."

Art sat bolt upright in his chair. "What?"

"Aerated the Fury, times two, but missed me. Randy's putting new glass in now."

"Who's the shooter?"

"Oh," I said curtly, "you don't think it was someone sent by the punk, by Easter? He did confess, you know."

"Off your high horse, girl," Art snapped. He settled back into his chair. "Doesn't become you, not one little bit."

I looked into his dark eyes. Softly, I said, "Sorry, Art, bad night. I don't know who it was—lots of frost."

"You fire back?"

"We were doing ninety on the bypass. That was all I could handle."

I went on to tell Art how I outmaneuvered the shooter with the Fury, then spun out on Recirc Road. He asked me who knew I was taking Olga Berggolts to the airport.

"From here, just you and Frankie," I said. "Then there's that Stevens couple that Berggolts phoned from the interview room after you left. They offered her a ride to the airport and she refused."

"Anyone else? Think."

"Valery Kuzov, maybe. When I called him to confirm the information Berggolts was giving me, I told him Berggolts was

going back to Boston last night. But I don't remember telling
him I was taking her. Anyway, Kuzov doesn't drive."

"Anyone else?"

I shook my head.

"Back to the Stevens couple," Art said. "What's with them?"

"Berggolts mentioned them to me. Robert, the husband,
teaches at Loyola. He knew Boyes."

"That's it?"

"No. Doris Souchak told me that Stevens left NASA when
Boyes was promoted over him for the Phobos project."

"Stevens that bitter?"

"Maybe. Or coincidence."

"You've spoken to Stevens?"

"Haven't had time. If we go on with our investigation, of
course."

Art stood and walked over to close the door. "You'll help?" I
asked him.

"We'll talk to Easter," he said. "If we really think we've got
something, we can work it behind Melchior's back. Not full time,
just. . . I'm willing to do that."

My face opened in a huge smile. I stood and crowed,
"Gimme five, Arthur!"

The door bolted from the outside, so that in a pinch of over-
crowding, the room could be used as a cell. Light dropped from
a ceiling fixture. There were no windows. A rectangular table
and four metal chairs took up most of the room.

Eugene Easter sat across from us at the table. He wore short-
sleeved, fluorescent orange coveralls—high fashion for the incar-
cerated. The arms that disappeared up into his sleeves were like
sticks. His skin was more intensely black than Art's. His big,
round eyes would have been beautiful on a fuller face. He stank
like a musty rug.

"Tell us about killing that man, Eugene," Art said. I had asked
Art to take the lead in this interview.

Easter's stare fell into the empty space between Art and me.
He only blinked in response to Art's question.

"Eugene!" Art barked.

Easter slid his eyes over to Art. A jumbo effort. His words riding on a belch, Easter slurred, "Read the paper I signed, motherfucker."

"I know what the paper says," Art said. "I wanna hear it from you."

Easter made no response. After an interminably long minute, Art repeated, "Tell us about the killing, Eugene."

Easter stood. He looked like a bright orange bean pole, suddenly articulated.

"Sit down!" Art said.

Easter started for the door and Art popped to his feet, moving his body, like a boulder, into Easter's path. "Get your ass back into that chair!" Art hollered.

Easter stopped and glared. Mock toughness, but he couldn't hide the fear that tightened his face. He sat without further cajoling. He resumed staring into the void between Art and me.

Art sat and folded his hands on the table in front of him. Smiling faintly, he said, "I'm going to do you a favor, Eugene. Yeah, I'm going to do you a big favor, one black man to another. I'm going to give you a feeling for where you stand right now. Get me?"

Easter didn't answer. His great lips twisted like an infuriated pre-schooler's.

"That's all right," Art said. "Don't talk. Just listen." He paused—for effect, I thought—then said, "Now, I'm tellin' you, Eugene, that you are in shit up to your fuckin' eyeballs. You hear me?" No stop for an answer. "And if you don't smell that shit, Eugene, then, I'm tellin' you, you are one dumb fuckin' nigger."

Easter sucked in a long deep breath of boredom.

"Now, that paper you signed," Art continued, "that paper says you admit to blowing half of a man's head off. But, hey, this'll save the prosecutors some time, Eugene. They'll all say, 'We got no trouble from Eugene Easter. No, that man, he just sat down real calm in the electric chair and had his balls fried off. What a brother!'"

Easter jerked his chin up. "Ain't gonna be no chair," he said. "It's a promise."

"Promise?" Art said. "Promise? Who you shittin', Eugene? No promises come with a confession like that."

"Sign, and I do some time, then go parole," Easter said. "The man say so."

I jumped in. "What man?"

Head down, Easter ignored my question, so I asked him again. Again, no response—he was twenty and immortal. Or else his life had been so pathetic that death would be no comedown.

Art said, "Eugene, this white girl sittin' here across from you—hey! Look at her!"

Easter lifted his sad eyes to my face.

Pointing his thumb at me, Art said, "This whitey is the only person in this whole goddamned station who's had the balls to say out loud that maybe Eugene Easter didn't kill the man in the park. She says that maybe we should check further into Eugene Easter's story, especially if he was so dumb to sign a confession."

For a minute, everything was quiet, Easter alternately glancing between Art and me, then looking more reflective. Art said, "You dig, man? You fuckin' dig?"

Easter turned to me, the faintest hint of water collecting at the bottoms of his eyes. "Which man made the promise, Eugene?" I asked.

"The fat-ass," Easter said. "I never heard a name."

"Older and bald?" Art asked.

"Fuckin' eh," Easter said.

Art looked to me. "Melchior?"

The fine black skin of his cheeks glistened with tears, but his speech, its cadence and tone, gave no hint that he was crying.

"They come to my apartment yesterday afternoon," Easter said, "Schwartz and two fuzzballs. I dunno what the shit's goin' on. They say, 'You arrested, boy. For murder. Now, get your black ass outa that chair!'"

Finally grasping his predicament, Easter had turned as compliant as a four-year-old begging for candy. He rushed to tell us that he had been fingered by one Rodney Truman, a minor gang chieftain and drug dealer with a score to settle.

How Steve Schwartz had found Truman remained a mystery to Easter—I thought it had probably been blind luck. Regardless, even Easter knew the police were on the streets that day, drumming up suspects for the Boyes murder wherever they might find them. That kind of news spreads quickly through a neighborhood, and it sometimes yields the odd tip, an entry point of information. The risk, of course, is that an opportunistic tipster might see it as a chance to smear blame on an innocent victim.

"Why'd Schwartz think it was you?" Art asked Easter. "What did Truman tell him?"

"That two girls said they saw me slug Boyes and drag him into my car," Easter said. "Last November." He sighed deeply and groaned, "Shit, last November I ain't even got a fuckin' car."

"Where did the girls say this happened?" I asked.

"Uptown," Easter said.

Uptown: the neighborhood just north of the stretch of Lincoln Park where Boyes's body had been found. A neighborhood where you can spend hundreds of thousands for an "architecturally significant" old mansion on the same block where you can order a twenty-dollar bag of coke. A neighborhood where you put your life in your hands when you walk certain streets during the day, while at night, on those same streets, you simply trust your life to God.

"Who are the girls, Eugene?" I asked.

Easter tilted his head far left, then right, as if to stretch out his neck's tightness. Bringing his head back to center, he swiped at his wet cheek. "Truman's bitches, maybe. 'Cept for that, I dunno."

"Truman runs girls?"

"Some," Easter said, "if you wanna call 'em that. Scummiest prossies you ever seen. Just fuckholes, that's all."

We spent the next ten minutes grilling Easter about why Truman might have set him up. Easter's speculations seemed half moonshine, but in the tit-for-tat world that he and Truman inhabited, redress rarely depended on logic—or even good sense, for that matter. Frankly, I didn't much care. It was enough for me to know the murder charge against Eugene Easter might have been trumped up. And that would leave Edward Boyes's killer still on the streets.

"Who questioned you back here, Eugene?" Art asked.

"Schwartz," Easter said.

Art and I ping-ponging, I asked, "Alone?"

"At first," Easter said, "then later there were a motherfucker called Frankie. Schwartz brought in Mr. Frankie for—for *consultation* he called it."

I thought of Frankie Luchinski.

"Brown hair, big arms?" Art asked.

"Yeah," Easter said, "and smelled like a French whore."

Easter's description of Frankie's odor was the most telling indictment of all.

"What do you mean, Frankie was in for *consultation*?" Art asked.

"It was for whackin' me," Easter said. "For the rough shit."

"Turn your face side to side," Art ordered. "Slowly."

Easter obeyed, while Art surveyed his face.

"You're clean," Art said.

"Mr. Frankie Shitfuck be sure he don't touch the face," Easter said. "He don't kick there."

"Where, then, Eugene?" I asked.

"In the nuts," Easter growled, "three, four times."

"You call for a doctor?" Art asked. "Did a doctor check you?"

"Fuck off," Easter said.

I said, "I take it you had no lawyer."

"What you think?" Easter answered. "Later, a court reporter come in to type the confession."

"Why'd you sign it with no lawyer?" I asked.

"'Cause Mr. Frankie was kickin' me in the nuts," Easter said stridently. "And 'cause the man said it would get me parole."

"Who we talking about now?" Art asked.

"The lard-ass motherfucker."

Melchior. "When did he come in?" I asked.

"At the end."

"Why'd you give him a confession?" Art asked.

"The man was takin' my side," Easter said. "He says he knew I weren't no hard killer, so maybe the murder was half accident."

"Accident?" I said. I shook my head and sniffed in disdain for Melchior, then leaned forward on the table, closer to Easter. "Eugene," I said, "Edward Boyes was killed by two point-blank gunshots under his jawbone. Believe me, it was no accident. No jury in the world would ever think it was."

"You can book that," Art echoed.

Easter slumped against the back of his chair. His eyes pleading, he said, "Lard-ass promised me it would be manslaughter if I confessed. If I didn't, the charge were murder."

"It was all bullshit, Eugene," Art said. "You should've shut up." In a low voice, he added, "If you're tellin' us the truth, then your mouth got you in more shit than your pecker ever could've."

The surprise of Melchior's betrayal washed across Easter's face.

"What else did Melchior tell you?" Art said.

"The man said I would be shit outa luck with a murder trial. He said they would send me to the electric chair and—"

"And you figured you were fucked either way," Art interrupted. "With the cops having Truman and his lying girls. Better to confess and stay off death row. That what you thought?"

"Well, ain't you the fuckin' genius?" Easter said.

"Watch your goddamn mouth!" Art shot back, his forefinger lunging toward Easter, his stomach bumping the table. "Look, Eugene, you only got two people in this place who haven't got you tried and convicted. You got this lady here and me. Be a smart-ass and we're done. We're not gonna take shit from you. We've got plenty else to work on. Just don't be a dumb fucker about this, Eugene."

Eugene Easter's story about his beating was impossible to verify. Easter had not asked to see a physician, and if his assertions were true, it was inconceivable that Frankie, Schwartz, or Melchior would admit to the abuse. Or about as likely as the lost

Phobos probe phoning home to planet Earth. And yet, fabricated as Easter's claim of innocence might be, his story did fit with other elements of the case, especially the O'Hare shooting. It made no sense to me that anyone associated with Eugene Easter had any interest in shooting me or Olga Berggolts.

TWELVE

Randy had the Fury ready by noon, even washed and vacuumed of the glass fragments on the seats. I left Area Six with the two keys I had recovered from Boyes's soaked pants pocket four mornings before. I saw no need to bring Boyes's watch and signet ring to Loyola.

Under clouds swollen with a threatening storm, I headed north on Lake Shore Drive. To my right, Lake Michigan mercilessly pounded the beaches and parks. These would probably be the last of the lake's antics that winter. In another month the water would calm and begin to warm, and the smelt would start their spring run to spawn in the city's protected harbors.

I passed Montrose Harbor thinking years back of March and April nights spent there netting smelt with my parents and my younger sister, Caitlin. As children, Cait and I knew that if we came home from school to an early supper of cold cuts and hard rolls, then we were going smelting, and from that point on the course of the night was nothing if not predictable.

After eating quickly, we would drive six miles east from our Jefferson Park bungalow; those trips to the lake were sometimes the farthest ventures from home my parents made all year. At Montrose, fishermen had marked the long concrete pier with lanterns, magical yellow lights that stretched farther into the black water than a child's eyes could see or her brain dared think about.

We'd walk the pier in single file, smelling the mix of water and fish and kerosene and burning charcoal. When my father divined our post for that night, we'd bivouac. Our maneuvers were practiced and immutable: my father and I would unfold the great dip nets and set their stanchions; my mother and Cait would open lawn chairs and blankets, then fire the charcoal stove to cook the smelt we ate while on station.

If only catching fish had been as inevitable as the cut of wind off the lake. On slack nights, Cait and I played with children around us while our parents made conversation with strangers, their familiarity seeming as easy to achieve on the pier as it was difficult in the city itself. Now occasionally, mind you, the smelt *were* running, and our nets would bulge with fat, silvery fish that we'd haul up, strip of their sticky eggs, then gut and wash for freezing. What didn't go home, we cooked on the pier, our stove smoking with the grilling fish. Somehow I was convinced that the taste of the fish in the cold night air was singularly better than anything ever served at our own kitchen table.

Now, reflecting as I drove, I realized that for me the pleasure of those nights at Montrose never turned on appetite, or the luck of the catch, or agreeable weather. Rather, it rode on more subtle waves: my satisfaction at managing the chores my father assigned to me; the look of my patient, selfless mother bundled into a lawn chair, not caring whether the fish showed up or not; and Cait's and my explorations of the pier's eastern stretch into a blackness as profound and forbidding as any fiction we had ever imagined.

By the time I turned off Sheridan Road into Loyola, snow was falling hard. Russ Conlon parked my car for me. I walked to the Crown Building and was admitted to Amanda Loomquist's office without waiting. I stood in front of the desk where she sat.

When I asked why I hadn't received Boyes's personnel records that she had promised the day before, Loomquist fumbled over an excuse, then said I could take them with me today. I requested the whereabouts of Robert Stevens on campus that afternoon. Loomquist said, "You know him?"

"I've heard he was a friend of Boyes."

"Who told you that?" she asked.

"A woman named Olga Berggolts. Has she phoned you?"

"No. Who is she?"

"Doesn't matter," I said. "When did Stevens come to the Loyola faculty?"

"When he left NASA, maybe a year and a half ago."

"Computer Sciences department?"

"Yes." She shifted in her chair.

"He and Boyes got along?" I asked.

"He recommended Boyes be hired."

"Any problems with Stevens?"

She puckered her lips as though annoyed. "Lieutenant, why all the interest in one of our faculty?"

I undid the top button of my coat and sat in the chair next to me. Impertinently, I said, "Miss Loomquist, I work for the detective division. That means I find pieces and put them together. Sometimes things fit good and are easy, but sometimes I'm waiting for lightning to strike. Stevens is a piece. Now, tell me, have you had any trouble with him, like what Boyes did at the software conference?"

Loomquist slipped slightly down in her chair and shook her head. "Stevens has better sense."

"Where is he now?" I asked.

"We can check the class schedules."

Course #C321: Introduction to FORTRAN. Dumbach Hall, Rm. 106. Mon., Wed., Fri. 2:00—2:50PM. R. Stevens.

It was a mid-level course for computer majors, Loomquist said. My watch told me the Friday session would be letting out in ten minutes. Loomquist handed me Boyes's personnel file and I left.

Outside, wet snow accumulated. With my collar pulled up, I trudged the fifty yards to Dumbach.

Dumbach Hall was a hulk of rough, red brick that sat on the crest of the land's first gentle rise away from the lake. I climbed the steps at the north entrance. Inside, students spilled from first-floor classrooms. I walked to Room 106 and watched a dozen students file out in various states of lassitude. I asked a redhead if her past hour's teacher had been Robert Stevens. She nodded and said, "In there, but watch out. Like, he's on the rag."

Uneasy, I peered into the high-ceilinged room. Stevens bent over a desk while he stuffed a sheaf of papers into a briefcase. His blond hair was short and frizzy. In profile, the back of his head appeared flattened, as though his mother had laid her soft-skulled infant on his back and forgotten him for a month or two. He wore a plaid shirt, a black tie, and glasses with frames the color of butterscotch.

Two students came up to the desk—Stevens waved them away, his right hand dusting them off as it might an irritating insect. The students looked at each other with bewilderment, then turned and walked past me into the hallway.

I entered the room. If he had heard me, he ignored me. I stopped in front of the desk. "Dr. Stevens," I said politely, "I would like to talk with you for a minute."

He looked up and focused his chilling blue eyes on me.

"My name is Nora Callum. I'd—"

"I'm busy. Maybe next week, if you get an appointment."

He averted his eyes and shut his briefcase, then grabbed the overcoat lying across the desk chair. He started for the door.

I followed. "Dr. Stevens . . ."

No answer.

In the hall, he turned for the south entrance, about a hundred feet away. I walked after him, keeping up. I called his name again, but he merely speeded ahead. I began losing ground, even as I pushed myself. When he was halfway to the door, I said loudly, "Please stop, Dr. Stevens!"

My voice must have surprised him because he slowed, but only momentarily. When he accelerated again, I knew he would be gone in seconds. In desperation, I shouted to his backside, "Edward Boyes! Edward Boyes!"

He stopped, dead in his tracks. His head was bowed. I moved in from behind.

I stood facing him, close enough to touch him if I wished. "I'm a police lieutenant," I said. "Homicide."

Students streamed past us like river water around broken trees. His head still down, the man seemed oblivious to the traffic.

"Dr. Stevens?"

He lifted his chin. His glasses had slipped a ridiculous inch down his nose. Arched eyebrows made the top of his face, a small jaw the bottom. The smear of hostility I had seen minutes before was less intense.

"We should go to my office," he said, "in Damen." He adjusted his glasses.

"Where?"

He pointed to the exit ahead of him. He slipped into his overcoat.

We left Dumbach and took a winding sidewalk busy with students tramping through the weather. The wind was pouring in off the lake now, the snow coming in sheets to pile deeper on the ground.

A tall cream-colored box standing on end, Damen Hall was as utilitarian looking as Dumbach was traditional. I followed Stevens into an elevator that took us to the fifth floor. Neither of us had spoken a word since Dumbach. Halfway down a gloomy corridor, he gestured toward a door with the name "W. Serena, Ph.D.," printed across its middle. "That used to be his office," he said.

"Boyes's?"

"Yes."

"Wait up," I said.

I dug into my purse for Boyes's keys. I knocked on the door, and when no one answered, I slipped the first key I had grabbed into the lock. The doorknob turned easily.

"Where'd you get that?" Stevens asked.

"From his pants pocket."

"Off his body?"

"Yes."

Expressionless, he turned and walked ahead another four offices. He led me through a door with his name on it.

The office was small enough to make me grateful for what Art and I had at Area Six. Metal shelves overstuffed with books and journals lined the walls; a desk and two chairs occupied the floor space. In redemption, a window opened the room out onto the lake where Madonna della Strada, the university's starkly beautiful stone chapel, stood in the foreground at the edge of the water. Snow swirled around Madonna's spire.

"Please sit," Stevens said. He shut the door behind us.

I went to the chair facing the desk. Stevens dumped his brief-case on the desktop, then removed his coat and dropped it in a heap on the floor. He sat. "Want your coat off?"

"I'm still cold." I drew my purse tightly to me. Through its leather I felt my revolver.

Stevens inhaled deeply. On the outflow, he said, "On Monday, I heard about the body from Lincoln Park. At first, I wondered . . ."

"Whether it was Boyes?"

He nodded. "But I've wondered that for all the bodies that have turned up on all the newscasts since November."

"You expected him to be killed?"

"God, no," he said, his eyes locking momentarily on mine, then releasing to wander again. "It's just something you think about. Living in the city. The dead bodies every day." He cleared his throat. "Why are you here, Lieutenant?"

"To talk about Boyes. You were his friend."

"Who told you that?"

"Doris Souchak. Johnson Space Center."

He tilted his head. Wryly, he said, "Don't believe everything Souchak says. Not because she's lying, just because . . . what's she now, NASA personnel or public relations or something?"

"I think so."

"A job for bullshitters. It's not equations the woman deals with. The job's mostly bullshit."

As he spoke about Souchak, I remembered the phone call Olga Berggolts had made to the Stevenses the afternoon before. I wondered again if it had anything to do with my welcoming party at O'Hare last night.

"Boyes was a friend of yours?" I asked.

"We knew each other a long time."

Stevens slid closer to the desk and rested his elbows on his briefcase. He was being almost courteous now, but I still found his pale blue eyes unnerving.

"Do you know where Boyes disappeared to last fall?" I asked.

"No."

"Did you bother to report him missing?"

He surprised me: "Twice."

"Twice? To the police?"

"Yes."

"And the police did nothing?"

"You tell me."

I needed to check this claim with Schwartz. Stevens's answers were coming too rapidly for me to formulate questions. Struggling, I tossed out a powder puff: "Souchak told me Boyes was quite a bright man."

"That's grievous understatement," Stevens said. "The man wasn't bright, he was brilliant."

I was beginning to feel the uncomfortable smallness of the room. My right hand tightened on my purse. My left went reflexly to my prosthesis. All I could smell was stale air.

"Do you know Jack Percot?" I said.

"Yes."

"From where?"

He grinned stiffly. "You imply that you don't know all of this already, Lieutenant."

"Answer the question, please."

Looking above my head, he said, "I met Jack at college, same as Edward."

Stevens went on to tell me how the three of them had gone to the University of Illinois together, then reunited at NASA. In between, for graduate school, Percot had stayed at the U of I, while Stevens attended the University of Wisconsin. "What about Boyes?" I said.

"University of Chicago," Stevens said, "but he left halfway through his Ph.D. program."

"Why?"

He broke a skimpy smile. "He was doing original work on game theory. His faculty adviser wanted something more mainstream. Edward didn't bow to that. He wouldn't kiss ass, even when he was that young."

I nodded, only half-listening, working instead on changing directions. "Did Percot and Boyes get along?"

"For the most part."

"What about Tallinn?" I asked.

His eyes narrowed at a question he hadn't seemed to think I'd ask. "Maybe Jack was too fond of Baltic brandy. He and Edward had some differences of opinion."

"Big enough for Boyes to send Percot back to the States to be fired."

"Phobos was at risk!" Stevens snapped. He jerked his elbows off his briefcase, stretched his neck, then settled back into his chair. When he continued he was calmer. "And you'll notice I said difference of opinion. A far cry from murder, Lieutenant."

"Why did you quit NASA, Dr. Stevens?"

"I was tired of it. You ever tire of anything?"

"I tire of interviewing in the field," I countered. "I can ask these questions at Area Six, Belmont and Western, in a room with steel chairs and no windows. Would you prefer that?"

He shook his head. After a moment's silence to save face, he said, "My wife and I decided to manage an apartment building here in Rogers Park. It was owned by her parents—they were getting too old to handle it. We had been considering the move for some time."

I jabbed, "You didn't leave NASA because Boyes was promoted over you in the Phobos project?"

"You get that from Souchak?"

I said nothing, my body still. I would wait for him.

"I had no desire to spend months on remote duty in Tallinn," he said. "What does Phobos have to do with this?"

"Phobos has become a part of the murder investigation."

"Why?"

"Because it seems to have a lot to do with Edward Boyes," I said.

"The news said the police had a confessed killer."

"There are inconsistencies. The case goes on."

Stevens stood and walked to the window. Facing me, he leaned against a bookcase. In the light, his forehead shone with the melting snow that had leaked from his hair. He used an index finger like a wiper blade, drawing it through the moisture. Behind him, outside, snow fell in a curtain. Beyond that, the sky was nearly black.

He touched his glasses. "I want Edward's killer found," he said with resolution, either felt or contrived.

"Good," I said, "then that brings me to the date of Boyes's death. We've placed it on November 23rd, a Wednesday evening. Where were you then?"

"That's four months ago."

"You keep a calendar? Would your wife—"

"Wait a minute." He came back to his desk and opened a drawer. He pulled out a small booklet and thumbed through it. "November 23rd is blank. You can look at last semester's schedule and know where I was during the day. I never miss a class."

"And the evening?"

"Who knows? Where were you that evening?"

"Would anyone—"

"Hold it," he interrupted to look back at his booklet. "The 23rd was the fourth Wednesday of the month. That means the monthly departmental meeting. It's an evening meeting that Computer Sciences holds religiously. Administration will have minutes for the session."

"And an attendance list?"

"Of course. By the way, I never miss those meetings either."

I stalled for a moment, then said, "I want to know about Irina Varonyev."

Stevens looked perplexed, as though not sure what to do with me now that I had mentioned the woman. He said, "I wouldn't know more than Olga already has told you. She called me from your police station yesterday—right?"

"I want you to corroborate," I said. Berggolts had refused to tell me anything personal about Varonyev—whatever I got from Stevens would be gravy.

"Irina is native Russian," he said. "She and Edward met in early 1988, soon after the Soviets asked for help with Phobos."

"Where?"

"Jet Propulsion Lab, where the early cooperative planning was done."

"You knew her then?" I asked.

"Before we left for Loyola, Eileen, my wife, and I were with her several times. Dinners, picnics . . ."

"I heard Irina was the controller on duty when the probe disappeared."

"Where'd you come up with that?" Stevens said.

"Valery Kuzov. IIT."

"Christ, you've been everywhere," he said, deadpan.

"You know Kuzov?"

"Sure. From conferences, things like that."

"Back to Irina," I said. "Why do you think she was jailed for her mistake?"

Stevens straightened in his chair. "Irina would not have made a command error like that," he said forcefully, "Believe me, something else is up."

"Meaning?"

"Meaning the probe was probably doomed before it left Earth's atmosphere." Bending toward me for emphasis, and with his voice full of anger, he said, "Frankly, Lieutenant, I believe the Russians fucked up, and royally. I'll bet it's a wonder the probe lasted the seven weeks it did."

THIRTEEN

It would be an easy first check on Stevens's alibi.

I stopped at a campus phone in the Damen Hall lobby, and I called Maria, Amanda Loomquist's secretary. I asked her to dig out the minutes of the November Computer Science departmental meeting. While Maria searched, I stared through the glass doors to the outside, to the beautiful, steadily falling snow and the smudged colors of students who lowered their heads like bulls to push through it.

Maria came back on line. "There was no November meeting for Computer Sciences."

"I thought the meetings are the fourth Wednesday of every month," I said.

"They are, I do the minutes. But I remember that meeting being scratched."

"Any reason?"

"The next day was Thanksgiving," she said. "Wednesday was the last day of classes before break, and a lot of faculty and staff were trying to get out of town. November's a month when the meeting is often canceled."

"Thank you, Maria."

I hung up. So much for Robert Stevens attending the evening meeting of November 23rd.

I crossed the campus toward the parking lot. The snow—already six or eight inches deep—swirled crazily in my face, driven by shifts of wind off the lake. I saw the Fury buried in a white quilt, only the antenna clearly visible. I waved to Russ Conlon, dry and warm in his security hut. "Help!" I called.

Russ waved back, then slid open his window. "We got a problem with your vehicle, Nora."

"No kidding."

"Haven't had a vehicle get out of this lot for the past half-hour." He pointed to a tangle of three cars trapped in rutted snow at the parking-lot gate. "Those guys are real stuck."

"It's okay. I live pretty close. I can walk it."

"Hey, Art Campbell get ahold of you?"

"No. Why?"

"He called about an hour ago, looking for you."

"Dial Area Six, will you?"

Russ slammed the window shut. I stood in place, my thin leather flats buried in snow. I stomped my half-frozen foot to keep it warm. My eyes narrowed against the cold and the stinging flakes.

Russ opened the window and handed me the phone. It was Frankie Luchinski at the other end. "Where the hell you been, Nora?"

"Shut up," I said, tired already of Frankie's shit. "Find Art for me."

In a minute, Art was on. "Nora?" he said.

"Arthur. What's up?"

"It's snowing like hell down here."

"I'm standing in it past my ankles," I said. "That's what you called Russ about?"

"Afraid not." A pause, then, "Tell me, you know a man named Michael Furey?"

"Yeah, Paris Viveka's new guy. He's a convicted felon who's busted his Florida parole. We should meet with him very soon."

"Too late."

"Huh?"

"Furey—he's dead."

"What?" I screeched.

Russ Conlon whirled toward me.

"Shotgunned a couple of hours ago," Art said, "near Oak and

State. Close range. Practically blew his heart right out of his rib cage."

I tried, but couldn't say anything.

"Something happened in the blizzard," Art said. "I think maybe a drug deal gone wrong, but maybe . . . I dunno. Anyway, if Furey was clean, then he was sure in the wrong place at the wrong time."

"Does Paris know?"

"She was with him."

"Jesus," I moaned.

"She was whacked on the head but she's all right."

"Where's she now?"

"In our office."

"I'm on the way. Hold on to her, Art. Don't let her leave."

"It's done."

It was five in the afternoon. The CTA would be the surest thing running during a rush-hour storm like this. With a lucky transfer to a Belmont Avenue bus, I might make Area Six in an hour. I plodded to the Loyola el stop, a quarter-mile away. The silvery flakes kept coming, choking out the sky, while the city's shrill racket languished under its padding of snow

At the el station, I flashed my shield at the pay window, then walked upstairs to the boarding platform. I stood in slush with a crowd of commuters. In a minute, I had a southbounder with an empty seat in the last car. We started up. I looked out the rear window and down the distance of merging steel track that shone with melted snow in the city's evening light. Inconspicuously, I crossed myself for Paris.

Unnoticed at the doorway, I peered into the office. The dim ceiling lamp lit my friends in sepia, transfixed them in time as figures sitting for an antique photograph. Somehow, absurdly, the burnt yellow light and the room's darker colors reminded me of a summer evening. Imagine, to think of summer when buried so deeply in winter's marrow.

Paris was bent forward in my chair, her arms looped on my desk, her forehead resting on her hands. Art, across from her at his desk, shuffled through the paperwork of his report.

Art looked up to me and nodded his hello. I walked straight to Paris. She seemed not to have heard me, so when, from behind, I took her shoulders in my hands, she jumped a little, startled at first. Then she sat up and turned to see me. "Nora," she said.

I couldn't answer, torn between heartache for her and relief that Michael Furey was now out of her life. She stood and we embraced. Art twisted away from us in his chair, granting us a semblance of privacy. After a minute, I broke away, sniffing.

Paris insisted that I use my chair while she slid up onto the desk to face me. She wore a bulky, white woolen sweater. Blood that I could smell crusted the sweater's front.

"Thanks for coming in," she said.

"You weren't hurt?" I asked. I slipped my coat off.

"Just knocked down."

"What happened?"

She mumbled, "We had just left Juliet's. We'd gone there to pick up Michael's paycheck. We were walking to have supper at the Oak Tree Grill. It was freezing and the snow was blowing hard. I told Michael I knew a shortcut through an alley. We went for a ways when—"

She stopped there, plugged up. For diversion, she pinched her nose. Her headshake meant, *No more, no more.*

I looked across the desk to Art. Slowly, in his softest baritone, he began to recount what Paris had already told him.

"Two men are standing behind a dumpster, halfway down the alley," Art said, "doing business. Okay, Paris and Furey turn in to the alley and come toward the dumpster, no idea that somebody's behind it. They must've gotten too close to the men without being noticed, probably 'cause of the quiet of the snow. Anyway, Paris and Furey are nearly on top of them before the men notice. When they do, one of them panics and pulls a small shotgun from under his coat. He fires at Furey. Maybe six feet away, from the looks of it. Shit, point-blank."

Paris's cupped hand now blocked her eyes from me. I said to Art, "And what about Paris?"

"They knock her down and run."

"Why don't they shoot her?"

"I'm not sure," he answered. "Maybe because they didn't mean to shoot Furey in the first place."

"Paris," I said, "were they dealing?"

She took her hand from her eyes and shrugged her ignorance.

I followed with a question I had to ask: "Was Michael involved? I mean drugs, or any other crime? Even a little?"

"No, goddammit!" she shrieked, her fist pounding pugnaciously at her lap.

My eyes moved from hers and focused on her sweater. The blood horrified me once again. I thought of telling her about Furey's conviction and parole evasion: I decided there was no point in hurting her any more right now. To Art I said, "Any idea who they were?"

"Zero on the guy who didn't shoot, but bingo on the killer. Paris recognized him."

"And?"

"Vincent Cruzado," Art said. "He's got a record, mostly drug-related offenses. A thirty-year-old who's moved from street-punk to minor drug honcho in the past ten years."

"How do you know him?" I asked Paris.

She wiped at her cheek. "At times, he's been a regular of a friend of mine. I've seen him around."

"He uses prostitutes?"

"Obviously," she said cynically.

"No wife or girlfriend?"

"Who knows?" she said. "That doesn't mean shit to them anyway."

"Did you ever—?"

"No, I didn't fuck him!" Paris interrupted. "I told you it was a girlfriend of mine, not me. I didn't work the lower classes."

"Did he know it was you in the alley?"

"I doubt it," she said. "No."

"Did he hit you?"

"No." She motioned to Art. "Like he said, the other guy knocked me down as he ran by."

From his papers Art pulled the sheet on Vincent Cruzado and flipped it over to me. The top half of the page showed black-and-white reproductions of Cruzado's two file photographs, one a side view of his face and the other straight on. A laundry list of offenses filled the bottom half of the page. I concentrated on the photos. He had dark eyes and a handsome, resolute jaw.

"Paris confirmed him from these photographs," Art said.

"This address current?" I asked Paris. The sheet listed Cruzado as living on May Street at a number just north of Grand Avenue.

"Who knows?" she said. "They come to us. No house calls for that kind of scum. Too dangerous."

House call.

I picked up the phone and dialed the extension for the Area Six garage. "This is Nora Callum," I said. "I need a squad to get home."

Tony, the garage's second-shift supervisor, said, "Where's your Fury, Lieutenant? Randy told me he just patched you up."

"Buried in a parking lot. Way north. No hope for tonight, Tony, unless you want to dig me out."

"Bum back, Lieutenant. No lifting—orders from my quack."

"Then I'll be down."

"I'll have one ready."

I hung up and said to Art, "I'm tired and hungry and I want to see Meg. How about we pack it in?"

"Sure."

"I'll drive Paris home."

An anguished smile showed Paris's gratitude. I stood and got back into my coat. Behind me, Art said, "Say, what happened at Loyola?"

I turned back. "It's preliminary."

"Is this Stevens guy a suspect?"

"He'd have to be, I think."

"So you figure it's not Eugene Easter?"

"I don't know. The shit's awful deep around Edward Boyes and all the Phobos stuff."

● ● ●

Before we left Area Six, I called home. Meg and Anna had already eaten dinner, Anna said, and Meg was waiting for me to help her build a snowman on our front terrace. It hurt me to say it would have to hold till morning. Anna promised she would stay with Meg until I got home.

Paris and I piled into the squad, then headed east on Belmont toward Clark Street. The snow seemed less intense now, the flakes smaller and harder as they struck the windshield. The city was as busy as an ant farm. Trucks in brigade plowed streets to the curbsides, walling off parked cars behind bulwarks of snow and ice. On the backs of the trucks, rotating gadgets spat salt to the pavement, salt that would dissolve ice and automobiles indiscriminately.

Paris's apartment complex, Sandburg Village, was two miles away. We crawled south on Clark, both of us uncomfortably quiet. The robotic chatter of the scanner and the swoosh of the tires through the slush outside was all we heard.

I pulled into a semicircular driveway near Paris's lobby. I threw the car into Park and set my forehead on the steering wheel. Staring vacuously into the green lights of the dash, I said, "I'll try to bring him in, Paris."

We turned toward each other. A slice of orange streetlight lit her face. She frowned.

"Cruzado," I said.

Her mouth formed a courageous smile as tears seemed to bud on her cheeks. She looked away from me to the front window. "I don't have anything of Michael's, not even a photograph."

"We can get something from his apartment."

"There's nothing like that there."

"Let me think about what I can do," I said softly. I bit my tongue not to say that we could always go to his Collier County mug shot.

Paris rubbed her chin on the nap of her coat, then opened the door and slid out. A few snowflakes spun into the car with a rush of wind. "Are you all right?" I called to her.

She leaned back into the car and smiled. "We were having a great time in the snow, I mean laughing and throwing snowballs and . . ."

"Paris—"

"You know," she interrupted, "I have one great regret."

"Yes?"

"I didn't get to fuck him."

"What?"

"A career of fucking, and not once for Michael. Can you imagine such a mistake, Nora?"

I didn't answer.

She said, "I'm going upstairs and feed Neptune. Thanks for everything."

"I'll call in the morning."

She walked toward her lobby. I watched her backside for a moment; then I dropped the gearshift into Drive. Skidding out of the driveway, I knew my jobs for the evening would now be two. And in my head the words buzzed: *A career of fucking, and not once for Michael. Can you imagine . . .*

The Eighteenth was the closest station; I stopped there for a camera, then drove south on Clark to Grand, and west from there. I entered an area half given over to residences, and half to declining light industry and forgotten warehouses. It was a neighborhood that had been ruinously violated by the construction of the Kennedy Expressway thirty years before. When the eight-lane chasm of concrete tore through the district, anybody with a bank account hightailed it, while those without stayed in the houses and small apartment buildings.

May Street had not been plowed of snow, nor would it be. Chicago's mayors don't order the side streets cleared unless Election Day is imminent and the outcome remains in question. Used to the handling of my Fury and not the squad I was driving, I nearly got stuck in the first block off Grand. But with wheels spinning and rear end swerving, I nosed ahead, stopping near what I decided would be the Cruzado address, a frame two-flat with shingled walls.

I called Area Six on the radio, my hand at once cold and sweaty on the handpiece. Art had not yet left for home. "I'm sitting in front of Cruzado's place," I said, and described the building.

"You alone?" Art said.

"Yes."

"Nora, keep your ass in that car!"

"Furey was killed at Oak and State. That's our jurisdiction, Art, Area Six. Smilin' Ray would want somebody here."

"But he didn't assign you, and Cruzado's never going to be home anyway."

"He might be," I said. "A guy like this might have bravado enough to come here after the shooting."

"You say two-flat?"

"Yep."

"Alone, there's nothing going for you," he said. "You go in the front, he goes out the back."

"Maybe he'll ask me up for tea, Arthur. It's very cold out here. Hot tea would be wonderful."

I spoke blithely, but I was feeling a mixture of enmity and confusion at Furey's death. My sympathy was not with Furey but with Paris's suffering.

Art said, "Nora—"

"Do you know what Paris said to me? Art?"

"Shit! Who? What?"

"She said, 'A career of fucking, and not once—'"

"Goddammit, Nora!"

"Forget it. I'll call back in a few minutes."

FOURTEEN

Now and then, events compress themselves in time, all the ornament stripped away by the weight and urgency of a situation, of a moment. It seemed it would be that way that night on May Street.

I sat in the squad for twenty empty minutes, noticing only a light go on in a second-floor window in Vincent Cruzado's building. When I left the squad, the clean smell of night air was my first sensation. I smiled to myself at how the storm had perfumed the city. I stood in a streetlamp's cone of light and let snow gather in my hair and on my eyebrows. Behind me, cars streamed along Grand Avenue. May Street was devoid of life.

I walked across the street, my prosthesis working stubbornly in the ever-deepening snow. I opened the front door of the building and stepped into a tiny vestibule smelling of must. A staircase opened up directly ahead of me. Two brass mailboxes, one marked "V. C.," occupied the left-hand wall.

Still having no clear idea about how I would proceed, I pulled my gun from my handbag, and slung the bag over my left shoulder. I held the gun slackly in my right hand, hiding it behind a fold of coat, then pushed the bell under the Cruzado mailbox. In a few moments, a male voice hissed from a speaker beneath the box. "Who's there?"

"Nora Callum."

A pause, then, "Never heard of you. Get the hell outa here."

"I need to talk with you."

"Tough shit. Leave."

Instinctively, I decided to engage him on a more elemental

level. I bent and brought my mouth close to the speaker. I whispered, "But, Vincent, I've spoken to a friend of yours on Rush Street, a lady friend."

"Yeah?"

"She says you're a man with a big cock who loves to fuck." I stopped with that test of his ambition.

"I didn't put in a call," he said, more cordially.

"Of course you didn't. I'm just here with a question or two."

"Wait." The crackle from the speaker went dead.

Preposterous as our exchange had been, and although he had just killed a man, Cruzado was ignoring good judgment and yielding to the hankerings he carried around in his shorts.

Light broke from a door at the top of the stairs. A male figure, backlit from the apartment, walked onto the landing and took three steps toward me. The light was bright behind him, its contrast making his face and form implacably black against the background.

My forefinger entered the trigger guard of my gun. Outside, the wind played on the door behind me. I wondered if I had left the squad running.

"Vincent Cruzado?" I looked up and called, my knee trembling.

"How the fuck old are you, lady?" he sniggered.

"Come closer and see for yourself." I felt my breath coming in small gulps. I made early finger-pressure on my .38's trigger.

"Eat me, bitch!" he said venomously.

I went to the first step. When he began to turn away, I yelled, "Police, Cruzado!"

He reversed his turn. As he did, my brain flashed an image of Michael Furey's body being blown backward by a shotgun's smoking load. Cruzado may have surprised Furey, but he wouldn't me.

My attention riveted on Cruzado, I watched his right arm suddenly separate from the blackness of his torso. His hand held a long, dark object—the shotgun. He lifted it swiftly toward me. I dropped to a crouch and opened fire.

Before he could shoot, I boomed off two rounds, the revolver pounding my palm. My first hit him in his left shoulder and spun him like a top. When the back of his head came into view, I fired again. This time I struck him high in the midline between his shoulders. He thudded to the top stair. The noise of his fall blended with the sound of the door opening behind me. I whirled and pointed. It was Art.

"Jesus!" I said.

Art squatted next to me. "He dead?"

"I'm not sure," I said. "I think my second one's in at his neck."

"He get anything off?"

"No. When his shotgun came up, I fired."

"We'd better—"

Now Cruzado interrupted, his body moving from its perch and beginning to roll noisily down the staircase, accelerating as he came. Art and I backed up and aimed our guns at the tumbling mass. Cruzado stopped at the last step, his body wedging itself between the banister and the wall, a few feet away from us. Facedown, he didn't move.

Art approached first. "You're right about your second shot," he said. With his gun pointed at Cruzado's head, he grabbed an arm and pulled. The body rotated face-up, and I saw a ragged exit wound near Cruzado's Adam's apple. Blood seeped down his neck and under his shirt.

Now I looked down Cruzado's torso to his right hand. My stomach fell out from under me.

In death, his right hand clutched not a shotgun but a police nightstick, a billy club.

"My God!" I wailed. "I thought . . ."

Art said nothing, just glanced from the body to my face. Behind us, officers were arriving, opening the door, starting into the lobby. They looked at Cruzado, each officer grimacing in turn. A young one stared at the dead man's neck and stupidly exclaimed, "Wow! Instant tracheotomy!"

An ambulance and several squads, their roof lamps spinning out blue and red light, littered the street. I leaned against my squad's fender, trying to relieve the pressure of my stump in its socket.

My cheeks seared under the hard-as-buckshot snowflakes that rained down on me.

"I was wrong," I said to Art, "but I can't tell you how sure I thought I was. In that instant, I mean. How Christ Almighty sure I was."

Art stood in front of the squad, his foot up on the bumper. The others were not disturbing us. It happens that way, when someone is killed by police the way Vincent Cruzado had just been.

"You ever come close to doing that?" I asked.

"Worse than close."

"When?"

"Twenty years ago."

"Tell me." I hungered for solace.

"I was on a beat in the Woodlawn district," he started, his words coming on white, shrinking breath. "I went in to eat at a mom-and-pop joint on Sixty-third. Instead of getting supper, I walked into a goddamn stickup — a kid waving a big silver gun in the air, screaming at everybody like he'd gone bugs."

Art stopped talking and momentarily shifted his eyes away from my face. Looking over my shoulder, he formed a small, obscure smile on his lips, a smile without a trace of joy that lasted only as long as a blink.

"Anyway," he resumed, "when I saw the kid, I dropped to the floor and went for my weapon. He spotted me and froze up. But then, in the next second, he charged me, hootin' and whippin' his gun at me. It was like he'd fuckin' taken leave of his senses."

"He fire?"

Art didn't answer.

"Art?"

He gathered snow from the squad's hood into his bare hands, packing it into a snowball. He said, "I was a fine shooter in those days, Nora."

I nodded.

"I mean, take me to the target range and I could—not now, but for a while I was that good."

"Did the kid fire on you?" I asked again.

"I rolled behind a table," he said as his hands worked the icy sphere like a pitcher rubbing a new baseball. "I was scared shitless. When he kept comin', training his gun on me, I had to take a shot. Just one—middle of his forehead."

"Oh."

"He was fourteen. The gun turned out to be a toy. Something from the Lone Ranger department at Marshall Field's."

"I'm sorry."

"Don't be," he said. "Downtown ran me through the suspension formalities and cleared me, but I felt rotten for the kid and myself for the next couple of years. That long. You know, walking around the house like Mr. Melancholy."

"How'd you change?"

"Something Helen said to me one day. She said, sure, it was true I had killed a kid carrying a cap gun, but that any asshole, young or old, who sticks up a restaurant is taking a big risk. Especially if he acts like he's gonna shoot a cop."

He took his foot from the bumper, straightened, and fired the snowball far down May Street, then buried his hands in his coat pockets. His skin glistened under the snow melting on his cheeks.

"This here's the same, Nora. When Cruzado blasted a hole into Paris's guy, he took a big risk that it wouldn't work out for him. Look, if Cruzado had been holding a shotgun tonight, then the ambulance is here for you, not him. His ass or yours. The equation's simple. Simpler than what you studied your first day of algebra."

Art started away, then stopped and tipped his chin toward my prosthetic leg. "You oughta know that better than anybody."

I said, "You've never told me that story before."

"You think you're gonna go around telling everybody about what just happened in there tonight?"

I shook my head.

"I'm going up to Cruzado's apartment to look for the shotgun," he said. "We need to find the gun that killed Furey, especially now. Why don't you wait in the squad. I'll drive you back. This is going to take a shitload of paperwork with Internal Affairs and the State's Attorney's Office."

• • •

I waited till Art disappeared into Cruzado's building, then I climbed into the squad. I cranked the engine and wheeled left. The squad's tires bit into the snow, and I was back on Grand Avenue in a few seconds. I drove west toward the Ogden Avenue entrance to the expressway. At the corner of Grand and Ogden, I stopped at a phone booth—I figured it would save me time.

The County Hospital operator put me through to the morgue, but, as I expected, no one answered. I asked the lady for Tommy Banks's home number. Tommy must've been sitting on top of his phone because he answered halfway through the first ring.

"We stayed late and grossed the guy before Dr. Dorner went home," Tommy said. He was speaking about Michael Furey. "The tissue work, the microscopic stuff will take a couple of days."

"Why'd you post him so fast?" I asked.

"Dorner's off tomorrow. He didn't want to leave the gross behind for his partner. He's that way."

"Where's the body going next?"

"Maybe to Homewood Memorial Gardens. If there's no family, that's where they go."

"When will he be taken away?"

"I dunno," Tommy said, "maybe Monday, maybe early tomorrow morning."

"Tomorrow morning? He was only shot today, for crissake!"

"I don't know any more than that, Lieutenant," he said. He wanted me off the line.

"I need to see the body, Tommy. Tonight for sure, if he could leave tomorrow."

"Not fun to look at. The guy took a huge load at close range. Big hole in his chest."

"It means a lot to me. It wouldn't take long. Can you meet me there?"

Tommy thought before saying, "Okay, if it's that important. The path lab'll be locked up. Meet me in the emergency room. Twenty minutes."

It was ten o'clock. I rested against a wall of the barnlike waiting room. Dozens of people, many of them exhausted long-suffering mothers holding crying children, filled the chairs. The County ER always gave quickest attention to major vehicular trauma and to the freshly bloodied members of what the docs called the Knife and Gun Club. The city's indigent who complained of earaches and sore throats and belly cramps would have to wait, sometimes for hours. But they understood. They, like us cops, knew if ever they came in mangled or shot or stabbed, their care would not only be immediate but superb. The street had it that if the County trauma team couldn't save you, then you had received a Higher Calling.

Huge Tommy surprised me with a tap on my shoulder. I jumped.

"Wow!" he said. "What's wrong, Lieutenant?"

"Long day. My tank's on empty."

"You okay for the morgue?"

"Let's go," I said. "I'm fine."

We took a staircase to the basement, then wound through the hospital's underground network of corridors. Sewer and water and heat pipes popped and sweated above us. The air was dank, the human traffic surprisingly heavy for the time of night.

Tommy unlocked the door to the morgue and we entered. When the door clicked shut behind me, I felt the irrational fear that always seized me in that place. Tommy flipped on a light switch. The sharp smell of disinfectant saturated the air.

"He's in the cooler around the corner," Tommy said. "What do you want? To look at him in the drawer?"

"I need him out. Under the lights, I think."

"On a gurney?"

"Yes, that would be all right, yes. Please, Tommy."

I waited for Tommy to return. In a few minutes, he rolled a squeaking gurney around the corner. He stopped several feet from me. A yellow sheet covered the corpse. The central portion of the sheet, wet with a mixture of blood and water, stuck to the body's chest.

"What is it you want with the body?" Tommy said.

"Would you please uncover the face?"

He did and I saw Michael Furey's thin, sallow features. His straight hair was mussed, some falling onto his forehead. His eyes, narrow in life, were now closed. His lips were parted slightly.

I took a step closer. "He wasn't wounded at all in the face."

"Nope," Tommy said, "just one shot in the chest. Wanna see it?"

"Oh, no," I nearly jumped to say. "No, I don't believe so, thanks."

I closed in with another few steps. Tommy moved back. My attention stayed on the thin face so awash in calm. Paris said she hadn't fucked him, but, I wondered, had she ever held this face in her hands?

Tommy broke my musing. "Is that it, Lieutenant? Can I put him back now?"

"Not just yet. I need a pillow, Tommy. Do you have a pillow?"

"Not down here. Never a need for one."

"Do you have a clean sheet to cover his chest?"

Looking perplexed, Tommy walked away. I slid from my coat, then folded it into quarters. Tommy was back in a minute, standing across the gurney from me.

"You getting too hot, Lieutenant?"

"Would you lift his head for me?"

When Tommy placed his hands over the body's ears and lifted, I slid my coat between the head and the steel table. I touched the chilled head to adjust it on the coat. I asked Tommy to arrange the fresh sheet over the body's trunk.

I reached into my bag for my comb, then took it through Furey's fallen hair, careful to arrange the hair in a flattering manner. Next, I brought out the camera I had taken from the Eighteenth and focused on the face.

"We got plenty of pictures," Tommy said, "especially of his wound. You shouldn't need any more."

I brought the camera down. "These aren't for evidence."

"What then?"

"Personal. For a friend of his."

"They got no better pictures of him?"

"I'm afraid not."

Tommy pursed his lips in a gesture of disapproval. I refocused the camera and quickly shot half a dozen photographs, the flash suffusing the face with light. Finished, I dropped the camera back into my bag.

"That's all I need," I said. "He can go back."

Tommy retrieved my coat, covered the face, then rolled the gurney away. In the corridor, he said, "What's with this guy?"

"Convicted of auto theft in Florida, a parole jumper," I said. "But he may have saved the life of a woman I know. A friend of mine."

Lake Shore Drive was a bitch, not because of traffic or snow but because my eyes burned as if someone had jammed the lit ends of cigarettes into them. With disdain, I blew past the Belmont Avenue exit for Area Six—I wasn't setting another foot in that shithole till morning when I knew everyone would be lined up for the lady cop who had killed an unarmed man. Farther north, when I passed the Loyola campus, I thought briefly of Robert Stevens. It seemed as if I had first talked to the man ten weeks before. Not ten hours and two deaths before.

Anna made us midnight sandwiches while I brewed coffee. We sat together at the kitchen table, me quiet at first. When I did open up to Anna about Furey's death, she professed no explanation for such random violence, and no, she didn't see any point in telling Paris of Furey's crimes.

As for my shooting Vincent Cruzado, Anna said, of course I should have shot first! I wasn't protecting only myself, but also the eight-year-old who slept down the hall from us. Finally, when I told her about the morgue, she winced a little. She, like Tommy, wondered why the photographs—were they really better than nothing? Then, after thinking a moment, she said she supposed I was just being sentimental, and that was all right. She said my heart would be pumping sand and not blood if such sentiment was beneath me. Dear Anna.

When Anna left, I poured a couple of ounces of brandy, then filled the glass with tepid milk. I ran two long swallows down my throat, taking comfort in the warmth. I carried the glass to the living room. Seated in my easy chair, I stared out onto Fargo Avenue, my thoughts aimless with exhaustion.

Thirty minutes later, I crept into Meg's room. The closet light was burning, and I was able to see her in the shadows. A curled ball, she had migrated to the far edge of her bed.

I set the brandy glass on a nightstand, then slid under the covers and reached for her gently, so as not to scare her. My arms brought her tucked, animal form close to me. When I brushed hair off her cheek, she snorted and roused. "Hi, sweetie," I whispered.

She turned and looked at me, her eyes confused and blinking. "Mom?"

"It's me."

"Is it still nighttime?"

"Yes."

"Gosh, Mom, you're late."

"Yeah."

More alert, she said, "You wanna make a snowman tomorrow? There's tons of it out there."

"You're on, kiddo. Tomorrow."

"Great. Say, what's on your breath, Mom?"

"Brandy? I guess it's the brandy."

She wiggled her nose like a rabbit. "Stinks."

I giggled. "Oh, Miss Perfect, how do you think your breath smells after four hours of sleep?"

"Pretty rotten?"

"Pretty rotten." I squeezed her.

I sat in the dark, dressed in a gown, my prosthesis off. I finished the brandy and milk, then crawled into bed. Outside, the immense city rested, quiet in its wrap of new snow, no sirens or honking horns ravaging the night's simple peace. I lay back and thought about Paris until the brandy climbed up and pushed me into a sleep as deep as any I would remember.

FIFTEEN

"Mom," she urged, "it's Art. Wake up, Mom."

It was Meg jerking my arm, dragging me from coma to the dazzle of sunlight on my sheets. Groggy, I managed, "Where? What?"

"On the phone, in the kitchen. C'mon, Mom."

Lying on my belly, I grabbed for my bedside phone. Dead. I had unhooked the line before my last swig of brandy the night before.

Meg found and plugged in the phone wire, then left. I picked up the receiver. "Where are you, Arthur, and what the hell time is it?"

"Eight o'clock and I'm at the office," he answered. "You puttin' in some heavy beauty sleep?"

"Yeah, and when I look in the mirror, I'll know it wasn't nearly enough."

"Where'd you disappear to last night?"

"The morgue at County. I met Tommy Banks."

"Why?"

I summoned all my reserves to sit up on the edge of the bed. "I had to see Furey one more time," I said. "Tell you about it later. Don't hassle me now. You find a shotgun in Cruzado's apartment?"

"An Ithaca Mag-10. Short-barreled, easy to conceal. I dropped it off at Ballistics last night."

"What good is Ballistics? Wasn't it a buckshot load with no casings left behind?"

"I think this shotgun is a self-loader that ejects its spent casings."

"We need—"

"*You* need that casing to prove it was Cruzado's gun that erased Michael Furey. Anything less and you shot an unarmed punk hophead, not a murderer."

Art was right. Evidence that I was stalking a legitimate murder suspect would boost my claim of self-defense. Paris's identification of Cruzado may have put me at ease, but it wouldn't pass muster with the Internal Affairs investigation that follows every shooting by a police officer.

"God, I hope the damn casing's still in the alley," I said, "under the snow. We need a sweep with a metal detector."

"I've already sent a couple of guys out," Art said. "When you comin' down?"

"Soon as I build a snowman."

"What?"

"You heard me."

"By the way, gather your strength," Art said. "Frankie said Melchior's coming in this morning. He wants to see you before the IA boys get a crack."

"Lucky me. Anyone else expected at the party?"

"Since Cruzado's dead, the State's Attorney's Office needs a statement—to help decide if a bill of indictment should be filed against you."

"You mean this could go to a grand jury?"

"Possibly. Look, just get down here and get Melchior out of the way."

After a pause, I said deliberately, "Arthur, I'll bring sweet rolls to the meeting. But watch out. Don't eat any of the jelly bismarcks, Lover Boy's favorites."

"Why?"

"'Cause of the cyanide inside."

We ate waffles and bacon, and I drank half a quart of coffee to bring myself up to speed. Meg piled the dishes into the sink while I wrote a note that I taped to the water faucet. My message warned Anna that if she dared to wash dishes, I would arrest her for disorderly conduct. As for what awaited me at Area Six, I was in full denial. Nobody was going to stop me from spending a couple of hours with Meg.

Outside, the sun was blinding on the new snow. The wind had quieted, the temperature now settled in the twenties. Meg and I rolled a fat snowman out of the ground's quilt, and Meg named him Jake—what else? And our Jake wasn't Fargo Avenue's only creation. Up and down the street, a dozen of his kinsmen rose from the terraces to stand at attention: a gang of lumpy irregulars with no taste for battle.

After finishing Jake, we walked down Fargo toward Sheridan Road. We stopped and greeted neighbors as we went, neighbors we barely knew, the adults marveling at the muscle and beauty of the storm, the kids firing snowballs at tree trunks with comical inaccuracy.

We stopped at a camera shop on Sheridan, and I left the film from the morgue. I could have the pictures developed by afternoon if I paid an extra charge. At the grocery store, I blew a quarter of my paycheck in an hour. We lugged the bulging plastic bags back home, Meg a low-set trooper clutching bags that scraped in the snow. After we unloaded the groceries, Anna came downstairs and I left for Area Six.

I went to crank the Fury, then remembered it was buried in the Loyola parking lot. I didn't have time to dig it out now; I decided on the el. As I walked the few blocks from Fargo to the Loyola station, my thoughts returned to the violence of the day and night before.

The station's white tile floor was gritty underfoot with grime and the melting snow tracked in by riders. At a wall phone, I dialed Paris. Neptune answered and went for her mother.

"Hello," Paris said. "Nora?"

"Yeah. How you doing?"

"Not bad. Thanks for calling."

"Say, I found out late last night that Michael will be taken from the County morgue, either today or Monday."

"Where to?" she asked.

"Homewood Memorial Gardens. Way south."

"What gives?"

"You know, I'll bet it's Monday," I said, "with the weekend and all. I can find out and call you later today."

"I'm going to it, Nora."

"Good." Overhead, a thundering train sounded as if it might crash through the ceiling.

"Mind coming with me?" Paris said. "Could you get off for a while on Monday?"

I knew I might have a lot more days off than Monday if Melchior had anything to say about it. "I'll go," I said. "Work won't be a problem."

"Thanks."

Ready to hang up, I said, "Oh, I forget to tell you—Michael's murder case is nearly closed."

"Cruzado arrested?"

"He's dead."

"Killed?" she asked. "Another drugger?"

"No. Me."

"Holy shit, Nora! What—"

"We'll talk about it later. Okay?"

She said nothing.

"I'll get back to you, Paris. So long."

I climbed the long staircase to the el tracks. I waited patiently with others for the next southbound train. A college-aged girl and her boyfriend snuggled on a bench, glad for the excuse of the cold, oblivious to everyone around them. When they laughed, their icy, intertwined breaths made me feel acutely lonely.

Rather than watch the couple, I stepped past them, farther down the platform. Beyond the tracks, the flat roofs of business and apartment buildings sported their fresh white raiment of snow. I looked down past the roofs and saw my half-buried Fury in the Loyola parking lot. A hundred yards east of the car, the lake was a smooth blue-green jewel. I watched the sun flash on the water, all the while thinking of the couple on the bench and feeling vaguely sorry for myself. Soon a train growling on the tracks rescued me.

• • •

Each man leaned over his side of the counter toward the other; their faces were so close together that I thought they might kiss. It was Frankie Luchinski and Karl Kramer. Instead of blowing past them as I should have, I stopped. "What, no videocam, Kramer?"

He turned toward me.

"No interest unless there's blood running?" I said. "Huh?"

Kramer smirked, probably because he knew I had just descended to his level. "I heard Steve Schwartz brought in the killer in the Lincoln Park murder," Kramer said. "I thought you were in charge of that case, Callum."

Frankie backed away. I ransacked my brain for a jeer. Petty, but Kramer always managed to bring out the juvenile in me.

"I also heard you got a little feisty with your revolver last night," Kramer added, grinning. "Frankie, I think Chicago's citizens might be in more danger from the police than from the criminals."

Inanely, out of thin air, I said, "And I heard from a woman friend of yours, Kramer, that you got rotten breath. Like maybe a tuna has been sitting dead in your mouth for a month or so."

Not proud of myself, I spun and made the staircase before Kramer finished muttering something unintelligible. Upstairs, in our office, Art worked on the report for the May Street incident. I told him about my exchange with Kramer. "That man does something to me," I said, "makes me feel subhuman."

"Never get into a pissing contest with a skunk," Art said. "It's no win."

"I'll settle for break even."

"You're letting the guy wreck your coronaries."

I plunked into the chair, my coat still on. I opened the coat wide—I was wearing pink sweats: very baggy, very unflattering. Pulling at the shirt, I said, "What do you think?"

"Wonderful. Special for the meeting?"

"I came right from the snowman—Jake's his name."

"No doubt."

"I forgot to change."

"Maybe Ray's soft on pink," Art said. "Now, some good news—we found a casing in the alley. Looks decent enough. I sent it over to John Dover." Dover was head of Ballistics. "Said he'd do the test firings on Monday."

"Thank you, Arthur."

"Anytime. Hey, where are the rolls?"

"Already in Lover Boy's office, my first stop. Who knows, he could be dead before we get there." Smiling, I touched my right hand to my ear. "Listen for the crash."

"You fucked up, Callum," Melchior said with his usual savoir faire. "It's that goddamn simple."

The shades were pulled tightly down against the sun, but even they couldn't keep out all of the day's brightness. We sat at a conference table, Art and I across from each other, Melchior at one end. My opened box of sweet rolls was at the table's center.

Melchior was dressed in a black, double-chin-clutching turtleneck shirt. Sweat dotted his sloped forehead. In his right hand he held a cigar, its chewed tip wet and repulsive. His left hand reached for a roll.

Embarrassed at my sweats, I pulled my coat tightly closed and looked down at the table. Art watched Melchior's hand rooting in the box.

"You usually drill a guy for holding a billy club?" Melchior asked me derisively. "I mean, right through the fuckin' spinal cord?"

"Self-defense," I said. I looked up.

"What's the guy gonna do," Melchior said, "throw the stick at you? From a staircase away? Shit." He pulled out a jelly bismark.

"The club looked like a shotgun," I said. "It was dark on the landing where Cruzado stood. I was thinking shotgun all the way."

Melchior bit into the bismark and a puff of powdered sugar jumped from the roll's surface. With a piece of dough hanging from his lip, he said, "So now any spic asshole standing in the dark is armed and dangerous?"

"Cruzado had just killed a man with a shotgun," I said.

"You knew that for sure?"

"The ID on Cruzado was as positive as you could get at that stage," Art said.

"And how positive is it now that the bastard's dead?" Melchior asked.

"We have a shell casing from the alley where Furey was killed," Art said. "It'll probably match the shotgun we found in Cruzado's apartment."

Melchior bit off more bismark and red jelly collected at a corner of his mouth. "These are good," he said almost amiably. "You bring them, Callum?"

"Yes."

He swallowed. "I hear this Michael Furey was a friend of yours. That right?"

"Wrong. His girl's a friend. And so what?"

"So maybe you popped Cruzado a little too fast. You know, getting even for a friend."

My neck tightened in anger. "I was chasing a murderer. When he aimed what I thought was a shotgun at me, I shot first. Nothing else has a thing to do with it."

Melchior wiped his lip with the back of his cigar hand. "Tell me, Callum, what the hell's your supposed killer doing on a staircase talking to a copper?"

"He didn't know I was police at that point."

"Who'd he think you were? A Merry Christmas piece of ass?" He giggled luridly. "A piece come right up to his doorstep?"

"Precisely," I said.

Art hiked his body up and yelped, "What?"

"I called Cruzado on the intercom in his lobby," I said. "I asked for him by name, and he didn't deny he was Vincent Cruzado."

I paused for a moment, deciding whether to continue. Art whirled his index finger at me as if to say, *Go on, go on.*

"I told Cruzado I had talked to a girl from Rush Street . . . I told him the woman had said he was a guy who would always be interested in a good fuck."

Art plunked his forehead onto the tabletop. "Oh, Jesus Christ, Nora," he moaned, "Jesus H. Christ."

Melchior seemed to brighten, now enticed by the story. "Entrapment?" he said stupidly.

"I told Cruzado I was police as soon as he came to the landing."

"What next?" Melchior said. "He hears you're a cop and sticks his hose back inside his shorts?"

I ignored him. "When Cruzado knew I was police, he made a move with his right hand. To me, it was a shotgun without question . . . so I fired."

Melchior belched. "You must've been awful ready to shoot."

"You wouldn't have been?"

The last of the bismark went into Melchior's mouth. He swallowed audibly, then jammed his cigar back between his lips, near a bit of still-flowing jelly. Biting down, he said, "There's a ton of media pressure here, Callum. I mean, you killing a guy holding a lousy billy club. They're gonna drag that shit back and forth across the TV till hell won't have it."

Melchior looked for a response that I didn't give him.

"I'm calling it inappropriate violence," he said. "You should have been sure of the spic's weapon before you waxed him. You used unwarranted deadly force."

"*Bullshit!*" I cried. "I don't buy *inappropriate*."

"You're off the street, Callum. Turn your weapon in to Frankie, and your car."

"You can't—"

"I can't suspend you, only IA can do that. But I can stick you behind a desk and make you play telephone." His smile mocked me. "Like you did when you were a cute little girl in fancy dresses."

Melchior plucked another jelly bismark from the box. I stood and started away. Turning back, I said, "Don't forget that last bismark, Chief. I brought three."

With Melchior's next bite, Art looked noticeably more worried, his glance moving from me to Melchior.

Outside the office, Art said, "Crazy. I had the awfulest feeling that he was gonna topple out of his chair any minute, dead of cyanide."

"He hasn't eaten the right bismark yet," I said casually.

"Huh?"

"You heard me."

Eyes bugging, Art said, "There's really poison in one of them, Nora?"

I smiled. "Shit, no. Relax."

Three waited for me in my office: two men, one from Internal Affairs, the other an assistant state's attorney; and one female staffer from the Department's psychology section. They introduced themselves in turn, but playing the lead on this particular stage had put my head spinning and I didn't remember a single name.

I sat in sunshine on the edge of my desk chair. Arms crossed tightly over my chest, I never opened my coat. I delivered my statement into a tape recorder, all the while making eye contact from one person to another. When my mouth dried, I sipped the coffee Art had handed me before I went into the office.

I finished my monologue, then answered a couple of dozen questions. Like prurient Melchior, the man from IA seemed especially taken by my method of drawing Cruzado out from his apartment. Twice IA delighted in asking me if "cock" and "fuck" were *really* the words I had spoken into the lobby intercom. If he had asked a third time, I would have spat in his face. I assumed the man's wife—he wore a wedding ring—lived in the same conjugal rapture as Mrs. Smilin' Ray.

IA left after assigning my case a Complaint Registration, or CR, number. The assistant state's attorney, a big, friendly man with flushed cheeks, delayed leaving by packing his briefcase more slowly than he needed to. He answered my questions willingly.

Yes, he said, Melchior, my commander, could summarily confiscate my gun and confine me to menial work at the station while the investigation proceeded, but my paychecks would continue at lieutenant's level. He said he expected the IA report would be finished in several days. His boss, the State's Attorney, would then decide if the case merited review by a grand jury for a possible bill of indictment against me. Off the record, he ventured that political heat was often a fudge factor in whether a case made it to a grand jury. How the shooting was treated in the media could matter.

• • •

The assistant state's attorney closed the door behind him. "Again, my name is Dr. Susan Lauer," the psychologist, who looked my age, said. She sat in Art's chair. "Maybe you didn't get it through the barrage."

"I didn't," I said. "Dr. Lauer. Thanks."

"Do you want your coat off?"

"Oh, no," I said. I wasn't going further behind the eight ball by exposing my sweatshirt to someone whose gray pin striped suit and crisp blouse were worth a month's rent. "I'm still cold," I lied.

"Do you know why I'm here?"

Defensive, I fired an answer without a trace of humor. "To see if I'm a public menace. A madwoman who needs to be bound up in chains."

Her already narrow eyes crimped at my arrogance. When she lifted a hand to take hair back behind an ear, I noticed her faint scent: she smelled like roses.

"Lieutenant," she said after a reflective pause, "the men are gone now. I think we can make sense to each other. Swagger doesn't get us anywhere."

"I'm sorry." I looked away for a moment.

"My job is to see if you need help through the shooting. Whether it was clean or suspect is determined by Internal Affairs."

"Too bad. You listen to the IA guy's questions about what I said into Cruzado's intercom?"

Lauer slid her chair closer to Art's desk; she folded her hands on his blotter. She had more grace in her fingernails than I have in my whole body. "I've been with him before," she said. "His sexuality has not developed past the seventh grade. Like a twelve-year-old boy, he finds certain words quite daring."

"Then he shouldn't be on the IA team."

"He's connected, Lieutenant. He'll have his job as long as he wants it. Now, to you."

"I've never . . . I've been in a couple of shoot-outs—"

"I know," she said. "I've been through your personnel file."

"—but I've never killed anyone before. I'm not proud."

"What do you think happened?"

I looked from her face to the ceiling, then back again. I was unsure whether to open to her, and to myself.

"What you tell me is privileged," she said sincerely. "I report on whether you're anxious or despondent enough to need time off. That's it. Everything else is evaluated by IA."

I thought another moment then blurted, "Paris Viveka is a best friend. Maybe I chased Cruzado hard because of that, but it was only to question him. I knew there wasn't a warrant on him yet."

"You felt vengeful?"

"Yes, sure, I suppose. Cruzado blew a big hole in Michael Furey's chest."

She nodded to move past what she'd already heard me recite into the tape recorder. "Do you think about it often?" she asked.

"What?"

"The drug shoot-out you were in once."

I wet my lips. "On the street I'm more ready now," I admitted.

"Because of your amputation?"

"Yes." I leaned back in my chair. "Last night, I had my gun drawn before Cruzado opened the door. Obviously, I was too quick. I suppose I didn't want to be hurt again. And I have a daughter who depends on me."

She smiled.

"You've listened to me for an hour, Dr. Lauer. What do you think?"

"I think you're very natural."

SIXTEEN

Gunless and squadless—I had turned my police special in to Frankie, and the Fury was still under a foot of snow—I took the 77 Belmont bus and the Howard Street el to State and Chicago. I hiked east on Chicago to the First National Bank, Michigan Avenue branch.

Weekend customers jammed the teller lines, but the safe-deposit area was deserted. A stout young woman welcomed me pleasantly. I signed her logbook and then she walked me into the vault. Together, our keys opened the door to my safe-deposit box. When the woman slid the box from its steel compartment, it rattled deep inside. "Gee, this is a noisy one," she said innocently.

I smiled. "Yes."

"Would you like a few minutes alone?"

"Please."

She handed me the box and pointed to a row of cubicles, none bigger than a broom closet. I walked into the nearest one and shut the door. The air in the room reeked of new carpeting. I placed the box on a counter and opened the lid.

My hand rustled through a rat's nest of insurance papers, old tax returns, and a couple of different wills—as though I had anything worth leaving. At the bottom of the box, my fingers touched cold metal. I fished up the dark, snub-nosed .38 Colt Special.

This gun didn't pack the Magnum load I was used to with my police .38, but what it surrendered in stopping power it made up for in portability. My old partner, Jack Flaherty, had given me the revolver several years before, after we raided a house full of firearms. "Take this one for a rainy day," Jack had said, "it won't be missed. Smart cops don't rely only on the Department for protection."

I checked to see the gun was fully loaded; then, feeling better already, I dropped it into my purse.

An IA investigation didn't mean vacation—there was still the matter of Eugene Easter. I wasn't prepared to let Melchior stop me.

I chose a window seat, lakeside. The 151 Sheridan was easier than going back to the train, to say nothing about the agreeability of the ride itself. The half-empty bus cleared the shopping mayhem of North Michigan Avenue, then moved into traffic on Lake Shore Drive. The lake glinted with the hardness of undulating, tarnished silver. Overhead, the sun bleached the sky to the palest blue imaginable.

I stepped off the bus at Sheridan and Albion, a few blocks south of Fargo. The camera store at the corner had finished my photographs of Michael Furey. I paid the bill, wondering if the developer had given any attention to my portraits of a dead man.

Outside, I backed against the blackened window of the saloon next door while I flipped through the photos; they'd come out better than I'd expected. Furey's complexion somehow looked less ghostly in snapshots than it had in person. I was still undecided whether or not to tell Paris about Furey's record.

I stuffed the photos into my purse and headed west on Albion. It was only a block to the address I had copied from the Edward Boyes personnel file, the file given to me yesterday by Amanda Loomquist. The police had scoured the Forty-third Ward and come up with Eugene Easter, so I doubted anyone had bothered to check Boyes's address.

The brown brick three-flat was as fat and solid as a bomb shelter, but a gentle, Chippendale-like crest topped its façade. The sidewalk to the front door was neatly shoveled, the snow piled right and left into symmetric dunes. A dusting of salt sparkled on the concrete. Before turning in to the walkway, I

glanced up to the third-floor apartment. I saw closed white curtains. I wondered if it had been Edward Boyes's bedroom.

The west wall of the lobby held the mailboxes. The third floor
box no longer listed Edward Boyes as occupant—the name taped
to the metal said "G. Bell." I pushed the call button and was
buzzed in; no one asked me for my name. Opening the inside
door, my eye caught the nameplate on the mailbox for the first-
floor apartment. It read "Robert and Eileen Stevens." Surprised,
I entered the stairwell and climbed the half-flight to the Stevens
apartment. I took a moment to stand still and think, then
climbed further. I would do the third floor first.

He answered on my fourth knock, opening the door halfway.
Dark stubble sullied his otherwise pallid face. Wads of black hair
flopped on his scalp. I wondered why flies weren't circling.

"Mr. Bell," I said, "my name is Lieutenant Callum." I presented my detective shield that Frankie hadn't collected. "I'm
from the police."

"Later," Bell said. Blank-faced, he was dressed in jeans and a
mangy sweatshirt. He looked twenty-five or thirty.

"Have the police been by in the past couple of days?"

"No."

"The man who lived here last fall has been murdered," I said.
"I'd like to talk with you and look around if I could."

"Tough shit," he snarled. "Get a warrant."

I stepped forward. "Mr. Bell, I sense a communication failure
here. See, I can get a warrant"—an untruth: off the street, I
couldn't get free coffee, let alone a warrant—"or I can get ten
goddamned warrants if you want."

"I repeat," Bell said, "get a warrant. Now fuck off, lady." He
slammed the door.

A woman, tall and bony and fortyish, answered my knock. She
held a small child in her arms. "My name is Nora Callum," I said.
"I'm from the police. Are you Mrs. Stevens?"

"Eileen," she said, "and this is Jerry." She smiled engagingly, one side of her upper lip rising higher on her teeth than the other. A fine lace of acne scars marred her cheeks. A yellow cotton sweater hung limply on her frame. "Robert told me you spoke with him yesterday at school."

"I did. I wondered—"

"Come in. Let's not talk out in the hall."

She led me into the apartment. Jerry's hands gripped his mother's shoulder as he fixed his eyes on me, the intruder. I smiled at him, but he wasn't nearly ready to return the favor.

We walked through a two-stride foyer, then into a living room painted in eggshell. The room faced south; its floor was creaking hardwood. Groupings of posters and modern prints graced the walls. Like the piles of snow outside, the room's furniture and artifacts were arranged with unmistakable balance. I thought about my own apartment: I felt lucky if I managed to collect a few pieces that even belonged in the same room with each other.

"Would you like to sit over there?" Eileen asked. She gestured to a couch centered under windows filled with the afternoon light. "If you look for sun, that is."

I walked to the couch and sat. When I opened my coat, I realized I still wore my pink sweats. "Please excuse my clothes," I said. "We were building a snowman. I didn't think to change."

She laughed politely, then sat in a chair opposite me. She placed Jerry on the floor. "Everybody's out but Jerry and me. My daughters are at a movie, and Robert's at school."

"On Saturday?"

"Not class," she said. "He's working on a presentation he has to give a week from today. It's a Loyola conference on software."

"I've heard of it because of Edward Boyes," I said. "He was at last November's conference the weekend before his death."

Her expression more serious, she said, "Robert told me you've placed Edward's death on the following Wednesday."

"Yes."

Stevens had no doubt talked to her about my questioning him on his whereabouts that day. I decided not to challenge her about the cancellation of the November departmental meeting.

"Since Robert's not here, Lieutenant, I'll apologize for his bad manners. He admitted he was rude to you yesterday."

"I didn't consider him rude," I said. "When I have to question someone who is handcuffed to a chair that is welded to the floor, that's when I encounter rudeness."

"Apparently, Robert still wasn't himself."

I didn't answer, trying instead to decide whether she was speaking on her own or had been put up to it by her husband.

Jerry crawled a few feet away from his mother, then stopped to pick at a joint between two floorboards. I made an effort to get my attention off him and onto business.

"Robert's not yet over the news of Edward's death," Eileen said. "And he's nervous about his lecture next weekend. He has to present the paper Edward would have. Something they started working on before Edward disappeared."

"This conference is a big deal?" I asked.

"To these software guys, gigantic."

"I heard about Edward's outburst at last fall's conference. How he spoke out about Irina Varonyev being jailed."

She lifted her eyebrows for emphasis. "That took courage . . . at a forum like that."

"I suppose," I said.

"Would you like some tea, Lieutenant?"

"It's Nora, and I'd love some."

"Let's go to the kitchen. Jerry'll follow us."

"He's very handsome," I said. "How old?"

"Nearly one."

We sat across from each other at the kitchen table. Paired windows looked out to the building's bright, snow-filled rear staircase.

I sipped tea from a bone-colored cup, then set it down and leaned forward, my chin propped in my hands. "Tell me about the lovers, Eileen," I said. "About Edward and Irina. I'm interested in a woman's view of that."

My question must have surprised her—she appeared skeptical about admitting me to that cranny of her memory. Then, after another swallow of tea, she said, "I only saw it personally in its early stages, when we were stationed at Goddard Space Center, in Maryland."

"Robert told me they met at JPL."

"Could be, but they fell in love at Goddard. That's where I met Irina."

"What did you think of her?"

"I liked her. She sparkled. Her face, I mean."

"Attractive?"

"Oh, no," she said quickly. "Homely, really, yet radiant with this Edward thing."

"Did they have trouble while at Goddard?" I asked.

"No, they were just a happy curiosity. None of the NASA families could remember anything like it happening before."

"NASA and Soviet bosses didn't care?"

"Either didn't care or weren't looking. At first, they'd just meet for ice cream or go to a movie—junior-high stuff."

"It must've heated up," I said, to lead her.

"Yes, during their weeks at Goddard." She spooned more sugar into her tea.

"What happened?" I asked.

"They would disappear—after work, I mean. No more ice-cream parlors, no meanderings around the Center. And they began showing up for work together in the mornings. Friends said they looked glazed, like they hadn't slept well."

"Why?"

"Making love, I imagine, half the night. Wouldn't you assume?"

A blush warmed my face. I felt embarrassed that I hadn't made the deduction. "Oh . . . sure," I all but stammered; both of us were now grinning. Abruptly, I said, "This tea is delicious. Where'd you get it?"

"A Thai place on Devon," she said. Then, "Are you married, Nora?"

"Divorced."

She nodded without commenting.

"I have an eight year-old daughter," I said. "A beautiful child. As for my ex, it's a dream without him. I plan to do better next time."

Eileen moved her chair back from the table and crossed her legs. I wasn't sure if it was a gesture telling me to leave. I said, "Before I go, one more thing."

"Yes?"

"Take me to Tallinn."

She reached for her teacup. "I wasn't there, of course. What I know comes from Edward and other friends."

"Tallinn's where their real trouble started?"

"Yes, January and February of last year."

Her dates pretty well matched what I had first been told by Valery Kuzov, then had heard from Doris Souchak and Olga Berggolts.

"Living together?" I asked.

"Against everybody's better judgment."

"At The Golden Swan?"

"Yes." She seemed puzzled that I knew.

"How did their affair cause Edward's firing?"

"It wasn't normal," she said, "the way they carried on. Both off the deep end—way off."

"Meaning?"

"They shouldn't have been so public about it, not with their jobs." She bobbed her head. "So damn little discretion."

"When you say public—"

"They were kissing on the job, kissing in front of a room full of engineers trying to work out software problems for Phobos. They were fondling each other in public—on the street, in restaurants."

I nodded to keep her moving.

She said, "I mean, when locked in their room, nobody cared if they made love till their brains fell out. More power to them. Bravo!"

"But—"

"But their public display rubbed their bosses' noses in it. That was their mistake. The partnership between their two countries was fragile, the kind of thing some politicians would rather see die."

"Why their stupidity?" I asked. "They were supposed to be bright people."

"My theory?"

"Yes."

She slid a hand through her short hair. "Imagine two people, each in their forties, each given up on the opposite sex. I mean, given up completely, and having to settle for science as your mate. How does that sound as a life-style?"

"Sad."

"See, this thing hit them as if they were babes. They made all the bright decisions of adolescents."

Expressionless, I said nothing.

"Nora, I didn't know Irina well, but she seemed normal in every way. Now, I did know Edward. He wasn't an attractive man, he didn't meet women easily. Between his brains and his dedication to work, he was a little nutty, I admit. But in spite of this, he wanted a wife and family. Why not?"

I nodded.

She said, "At NASA, Edward never fit into a comfortable slot. He was cantankerous. NASA would have canned him years ago if it hadn't been for his brilliance. But apart from that, he was a kind and generous man. A woman could do a lot worse than Edward Boyes."

"Don't remind me," I said. "I think I did."

As I started to get up, I heard footsteps on the outside rear stairs. I looked out the window and saw a man's form whisk past on the landing, then head down to the backyard.

"Who's that?" I asked Eileen.

"Bell. He lives in Edward's old apartment on three. Robert rented it to him after Edward disappeared."

"Do you own this building?"

"My parents do," she replied. "We manage it for them. Robert said we couldn't just let Edward's place sit empty—we needed the money. I don't know where he found Mr. Bell."

Maybe under a wet rock, I thought.

Eileen went on: "After Edward was missing for a while, I did his dishes, then dusted once, but that's all. When Mr. Bell came in January we pushed Edward's things into a bedroom and closed it off. That was a condition of rental for Bell."

"Then you expected Edward back?"

Her face hard, she said, "We never thought he wouldn't be."

"Have the police been here to go through Edward's apartment?"

"Not that I know of."

I thanked Eileen and left, going out the kitchen door and down the back staircase.

I circled back to the front of the building and re-entered the lobby. With luck I had the right key, and a little time. I was taking a chance, but sometimes, like in late afternoon at the racetrack, you need to plop a twenty-dollar bill on a long-shot trifecta and try to redeem what has been a lousy day.

I found the second of Edward Boyes's keys in the bottom of my purse. I slid the key into the lobby's inner door: the lock turned easily. I climbed past the Stevens apartment as quietly as I could. On the third floor, the same key opened Bell's apartment. It was no more than ten minutes since I had seen Bell pass by on the rear steps. I hoped for fifteen or twenty clear minutes.

Cold permeated the living room as sunlight struggled against the closed curtains. I walked deeper into the room, onto a braided rug, and from there down a hallway. The sunless, northern kitchen was redolent of cigarettes and unemptied garbage. Filthy, jumbled dishes littered the sink and counters. I took heart: a Rogers Park kitchen looking worse than mine.

I returned to the hallway and found a bedroom as smelly and lived-in as the kitchen—this had to be Bell's. The door to another room was closed, and I figured this as Boyes's bedroom that Eileen had mentioned. I opened the door and saw a room that looked like a storage locker. Eyes wide open, I walked in.

A bed, stripped of its sheets, stood between a desk and a squat wooden bookcase. Piles of folded clothes covered the mattress. A closed shoe box, a computer, and assorted clutter littered the desk. The bookcase held a television, a VCR machine, a few books, and several rows of videotapes in their covers.

Starting at the desk, I opened the shoe box and found a row of neatly packed envelopes. I pulled one out. It was unstamped and barefaced, except for the handwritten words "To Edward" in the middle of the envelope and an August date in the upper right-hand corner. The script was distinctly feminine.

I examined two more envelopes and found only the dates different. I decided these had to be Varonyev's letters to Boyes, the letters smuggled out of Lefortova Prison by Olga Berggolts. I replaced the letters and the top of the box.

The videotapes, fifty or more, were each neatly labeled with names I recognized as a mix of classic and more modern movies. I found only two to be curious, one labeled "Baikonur," and the other, "Tallinn." I remembered Valery Kuzov telling me that Baikonur was the space center in central Russia where Varonyev was assigned after leaving Tallinn. And it was from Baikonur that the Phobos probes were launched.

I checked my watch—I had been in the apartment ten minutes. Bell might be gone for hours, or might only have walked to the corner grocery on Sheridan. I needed to leave. One Internal Affairs investigation was enough.

Quickly, I searched the desk drawers and the nearby wastebasket. Not feeling I had time to scour thoroughly, I dumped an assortment of papers from the drawers and debris from the wastebasket, along with the two tapes, into an empty grocery bag I found under the bed. I grabbed the shoe box and the bag and left the bedroom.

On my way through the living room, I stopped at a table with a few of Bell's things scattered about. Among the junk I saw a Loyola University student ID card with Bell's photograph and full name, Norman J. Bell. I noted his date of birth, December 25th. Dear Norman, a Christmas baby. How poignant.

I left. The Fury was next. I wasn't going another day without a car.

SEVENTEEN

I walked into the parking lot and stopped when I saw snow flying. Twenty yards ahead of me, clump after white clump broke skyward, then fell back to earth like spilled talcum. Somebody digging out. Maybe I could borrow a shovel.

I came upon the Fury. The mad shoveler worked next to it. "Sir?" I said.

A man straightened. The failing sun scalded his black face. It was Art.

"What are you doing here?" I asked.

"I remembered your heap was probably still buried," he said, his breath all vapor, his forehead wet with sweat. "Figured you might need help. So you can turn it in. Like Snakeface ordered you to."

"Turn it in, my ass."

"Don't be so tough, Nora. What's in the grocery bag?"

"Clues. Tons of clues."

"Yeah, great. Got a key?"

Art grabbed the bag while I fished through my pockets for car keys. I opened a door and set the shoe box on the seat, then slammed the door shut. "Gimme the shovel for a while. I worry about your age, Arthur. Heart attack, stroke—anything. Look at you, the sweat pouring off you like that."

"Meanness leaking outa my pores. Get in the car and crank her."

I obeyed. The Fury's engine grumbled, then smoothed out after I gunned her. Art walked around the front of the car and slid in the passenger side. He held his shovel awkwardly between his legs. Inside, the car was dark, its windows occluded by thick snow.

"I spent the afternoon at the Stevens apartment building," I said.

"You walked here?"

"It's close, over on Albion. The junk in the bag is from Boyes's place."

"Same building?"

"Yes, the Stevenses manage it. After Boyes disappeared, they shoved his stuff into his bedroom and rented out the rest of the apartment."

Art peeled off his gloves. "Who'd you talk to?"

"Eileen. Mrs. Robert."

"She or her old man kill Boyes?" he asked.

"No comment. Give me a couple of days."

"Who's the new renter?"

"A guy named Bell," I said. "You'd need sheep-dip to de-lice him."

"He let you take stuff from the apartment?"

"No." I grinned to smooth my passage. "I went in after he left."

"Shit, Nora!" He whacked the dash with the shovel handle. "You're not in enough trouble?"

"The clues aren't going to come to me, Art. I was just using my wits."

"But—"

"Relax, I had Boyes's key. There's not a mark on the door."

He pulled his stocking cap lower on his ears. "Where's the heat in this buggy?" he bellyached.

I flipped on the defroster switch: freezing air roared against the window. Above the noise, Art bellowed, "You're a lieutenant now, Nora, put in for a decent machine, will you? Dump this shitbucket!"

"A chariot, to me, Arthur, a veritable chariot." I leaned forward and kissed the Fury's steering wheel.

Art tried not to smile.

"Anything happen with Internal Affairs after I left the station?" I said.

"No, but Melchior's decided—"

"Don't call him Melchior from now on," I interrupted. "To me, he's Chief A-hole."

"Sure, wonderful." He wiped a swath through the steam our breath had made on the window glass. The defroster was finally warming, the snow on the window outside turning patchy as it melted. "As I was saying, Chief A-hole's decided you should stay home, forget about answering the station's telephones. He told me to tell you he doesn't wanna see your face."

"I need a paycheck!"

"Don't worry. He can't stop that—the union would raise holy hell. Consider your time off a vacation." He rapped his hands together to warm them. "Consider Hawaii, you dog."

"Get serious, Arthur. And do you think Brother Easter wants me on vacation?"

"No—you're probably all Eugene's got going for him right now. Oh, by the way, Peggy Miksis has been assigned to defend him. I told her I'd let you know."

"Easter's first break," I said. "I'll call her."

Peggy Miksis was a friend of mine, as good a friend as Paris. Ten years out of law school, Peggy still knocked around the Public Defender's Office at an age when most lawyers had forsaken the place for a living wage. I had worked with her on a dozen cases through the years. Honesty and toughness: she shined with those traits I admired most. She wasn't a castrater, but she feared no male.

Peggy and her husband, Ted, lived in Wrigleyville—natch, Ted was a PR man for the Chicago Cubs. The Miksises were childless in spite of a million-dollar try at conception by one of the city's best medical schools. Tests, graphs, hormones, in-vitro this and that till hell wouldn't have it. I had recently written a character reference for them to an adoption agency.

"Need any help with the stuff in the bags?" Art asked.

"I'll sort it out and let you know by Monday."

"Oh, yeah, Monday. Tommy Banks called, said Furey's body won't be picked up till early Monday morning. Funeral, if you want to call it that, about ten."

"I'll call Paris. Say, wanna do me a favor? Look up some names, see if anyone has a sheet? And maybe get some phone logs, too?"

"Sure," he said.

"It's Robert Stevens, and Licehead from Boyes's apartment. His name is Bell. Norman J."

"Okay, it's done. Which windows did Randy replace?"

I elbowed my driver's window. "This one and the rear."

"Ooo, close. Any sign of your friend since last night?"

"No, and I've been looking."

Art slapped his hand on the dashboard. "Okay, she's warm. Now let's get this sucker outa here. I'm getting out and push. You alternate goosing the pedal and letting off, goose and let off. We'll rock this mother right out."

"Gotcha."

"And don't drop the thing into reverse or you'll run over my ass."

"Confidence, Arthur, confidence."

He opened his door, his left hand seeking for leverage to push out. His hand found my purse on the car seat, and he stopped moving, then looked over to me, his black eyes wide. "I feel steel."

"A small .38."

"I saw you turn in your gun to Frankie this morning."

"Well, I had this one in reserve," I said, "from Jack Flaherty. The last raid we did before his aneurysm blew. Jack said we had plenty to bring in that day. Nobody would miss this one."

"You need it off-duty?"

"You denying a woman protection, sir? In a city like this?"

We ate at La Cosina de Ada, a Mexican place close enough to walk to. Once I had wedged the Fury into a spot on Fargo, I wasn't moving her again for food.

Ordering our meals went as it usually did at La Cosina, Meg never considering anything but nachos grandes, and Anna asking me fifty questions about the menu. "No, Anna, I don't remember the exact differences between chimichangas and quesadillas, but who cares because it's all Mexican and that means delicious."

When, as always, we survived the order-placing, I felt guilty about my impatience with Anna. She was one of humanity's kindest, and for me to forget that was criminal. Besides, I felt immensely better after downing a basket of tortilla chips and a couple of Corona beers.

We walked back home through the hush of the snow-filled city, me half buzzed on the beer. Outside our building, we all patted Jake the Snowman on his cold white ass, Meg and Anna giggling uncontrollably. When Meg and I walked Anna up to her apartment, Anna shyly thanked me for including her in our evening. I was touched that she would mention what seemed to happen so naturally.

Back in our place, exhausted Meg undressed and fell into bed, a goner in minutes. I went to the kitchen and made coffee. It was ten o'clock. Late as it was, I decided to make a run at Varonyev's letters.

In my bedroom, I removed my leg and massaged my tired stump. I showered and dressed in a flannel gown, then crutched my way to the living room where I switched on the room's four lamps: squelching the darkness made me feel less alone. To read lovers' letters, I needed music, and it came down to Juice Newton's Greatest Hits or Mozart piano sonatas. I went with Wolfie.

I sat on the floor like an Indian squaw, then dumped the shoe box of letters into a heap on the carpet. The pile was daunting, dozens of envelopes in a scramble. I saw many already opened, but some still sealed. When I studied a few of the sealed ones, I couldn't tell if they'd been tampered with or not.

None of the envelopes had been stamped—Olga Berggolts must have mailed them in outer envelopes, which had been thrown away by Boyes or Stevens. Every envelope had the "To Edward" greeting, and many bore dates weeks after Boyes had been killed.

I arranged things chronologically, stacking one month's letters in one pile, the next in another, and so on. I ended with eleven piles, from April, 1988, to February, 1989, the month just ended.

There were sixty-five in number. All those before November 23rd, the date of Boyes's death, had been opened. Every letter dated thereafter remained sealed.

I was intrigued by how the letters had been sent at an ever-diminishing pace. Early on and for most of the summer, Varonyev averaged three letters per week. Then, at the beginning of September, a two-week hiatus occurred; no letters arrived at all. When she resumed writing, she slowed to one or two letters in a week. By January, the flow dwindled again, single-letter weeks now interspersed with blank weeks.

I was baffled by the steady decline in Varonyev's output until I recalled the chronology of the Phobos events. Varonyev must have written the spring and summer letters from Baikonur, during the months before and after the Phobos launches in July. It would have been a time when things went well for both the probes and for Varonyev. Letter writing would have been easy and natural.

I decided the September hiatus coincided with the days immediately after Phobos I was lost. When Varonyev was jailed, it may have become impossible for her to write. Why the letters then resumed, even at a declining rate, was unclear. But resume they did, continuing steadily until the time when Varonyev would have learned that Boyes was missing. After that, the letters only dribbled in. I blamed simple despondency—and never a return letter from Boyes—for Varonyev's failure to persevere.

As anxious as I was to discover Varonyev, I felt like a voyeur: her letters had been private. Apprehensive, I picked up the envelope marked April 15th, the earliest date I could find. I removed the single folded sheet inside. The letter was written on coarse cream-colored paper. Varonyev's script was compact, her characters small and tightly drawn: she didn't give her thoughts up easily. Pushing my hair off my forehead and noticing a Mozart adagio behind me, I began to read:

Edward,

After you left Tallinn yesterday, I was flown to Moscow. There I sat in the airport for a very long time before they sent me to Baikonur. A military flight. It took most of the night.

I am assigned to a dormitory here. I am the only programmer on the floor. So small my room, like the university. Only my textbooks stay out. Poetry and philosophy stay hidden with your photograph.

Tonight, in bed, I will close my eyes tight enough to see yellow flashes on the insides of my lids. In that light, I will hold you. I can smell the perfume of our rooms at The Swan.

I love you, Edward.

Irina

PS—Olga B. talked to me before I left Tallinn. I understand the system. I pray to St. Jude it works.

I folded the letter and returned it to its envelope, then started into the rest of the April pile, reading each letter in turn, soon finding myself in May. These early letters were consistently girlish and romantic. From Varonyev's responses, I assumed Boyes's letters had a similar style.

Although affecting in its way, this kind of material wasn't helping me find Boyes's murderer. After a dozen letters, I began breezing through the amorous passages, searching instead for information about Phobos. I held out letters that spoke about anything factual. In an hour, I had hustled my way into late August, the week Phobos I disappeared. This marked the start of the two-week lapse when no letters arrived.

I stopped to reread the letters I had set aside. I rescued certain, more doctrinal passages from the slush of romance. I copied these excerpts onto a legal pad. They were dated and written as follows:

April 23:
There is confusion in Guidance since you left. Your V-hawk has been put in charge again. If programmers could vote, we would choose Orbeli or Navoi. Who do you think is better?

● ● ●

May 14:

Turmoil over the pre-flights. Your idea to remove the programs from the probe's computers is being delayed. Some (my Avis, and Navoi) favor keeping them on board. Maybe because we still have empty disc space. A minority (mainly Kuznetzov, but Vera T. also) favor dumping. Tributs is coming from Moscow to resolve this. A committee is scheduled.

May 29:

The pre-flights will be removed. The committee decided under pressure from Tributs. Your V-hawk is calmer than I would imagine. He wants to meet with me tomorrow about the deletions. Wish me luck.

June 16:

Your checking programs will not be finished. No time, Tributs says. It will be my Avis and me purging the pre-flights. Odd, that we are alone in the job. We begin tomorrow. He told the committee the system will be ready for July launch. I don't know how.

June 30:

The pre-flights question is settled. Someday, when we are together, I will tell you the details, but I cannot write them now.

Launch of P-1 is next week. Press and others from Europe and the States have started to arrive in Baikonur. Today, I thought I saw a man we worked with at Goddard. I've forgotten his name.

July 8:

P-1 launched last night. Perfect weather. A magnificent sight, Edward. Your V-hawk was most excited of all. The probe is up twenty hours and doing beautiful. Tell Robert he owns a piece of the success. Hello to Eileen and the children. I am grateful to know the people you see every day.

July 15:

P-2 is up several days now. No problems here. Except for Baikonur's summer heat.

August 1:

P-1 is five million miles from Earth. P-2 four million. Everything nominal. I am told NASA is already making setups for orbital insertions. I do a daily shift at the P-1 controller panel. Boring, boring.

August 30:

Disaster last night. P-1 is gone, Edward!

By time you receive this, you will already know. That is, if Moscow releases the news. Everybody is sick. It was an hour before I could even speak.

Two days ago, I sent a command to verify one from the Crimea station. Routine. Somehow, the thruster rockets fired and P-1 lost its lock on the Sun. No contact since. The thrusters' firing makes no sense.

Investigation is in progress. I will have to testify. I am frightened. My Avis says he will defend me. We are sorting out the command sequences I sent up.

P-2 is fine.

It was 1 a.m, but I felt strong. Meg wandered into the living room, her eyes squinting at the light, her brain bundled in sleep. I hugged her, then aimed her back toward her bedroom. I didn't hear a crash—I assumed she landed safely.

Although I still had several piles to go, the bunches were

becoming smaller in size. The autumn hiatus ended with
Varonyev's September 16th letter. The letter's paper was thinner
than what she had used in Baikonur, and now she wrote in pencil, not ballpoint. The letter said:

Edward,

I write this from jail: Lefortova. My cell is above
ground. Torlova, a large, powerful woman, is my guard. She
threatens more questioning about the probe. They accuse
me of sabotage with you. Can you imagine?

Olga is with me as I write. She has brought paper and
an envelope. It is still sweaty warm in Moscow.

I love you and I miss you, Edward.

Irina

The next half-dozen letters were the most fact-filled of the
entire collection. Varonyev detailed a variety of issues I didn't
come close to understanding: misaddressed code sequence, the
chance opening of the pre-flight programs, and so on. I ground
through this material, taking notes that I could discuss with
Valery Kuzov.

By this time, Varonyev had mentioned a dozen and a half different names, most of them once or twice, but four—Orbeli,
Navoi, Avis and V-hawk—most frequently. Avis and V-hawk were
referred to a good bit more than the other two. I had no idea of
the derivation of the V-hawk name.

In late October, the letters again changed in content. Varonyev
stopped mentioning the probes altogether—she must have covered all the Phobos facts she felt compelled to report. Also, the
hard edge of her rage eased noticeably. She seemed more submis-
sive, as though unwilling or unable to battle her jailers any longer.

A letter dated October 31st said:

Edward,

Last night I dreamed of Tallinn: walking down Vene
Street, past the old Dominican Monastery. It was snowing.

We turned at Narva Shausee and walked to Kadriorg Park.

We sat together on a bench that looked out to the Baltic. We held each other to keep ourselves against the wind. The sea was swollen with waves. A fat winter squirrel came up to us to beg for food. He would not leave, and we were embarrassed to kiss in front of him. Can you imagine?

It seemed just a dream. We didn't ever do that, did we? Write me what you think.

I love you now as I loved you in Kadriorg, Edward.

Irina

Devoid of the tedium of Phobos facts, these letters were becoming easier for me to read—until I came to the letter of November 16th, Varonyev's longest letter, the last letter opened by Boyes. I started in, unaware.

Edward,

They still question me about sabotage, but now in a different place and way. Torlova takes me from my cell to a brightly lit room. The room is underground, so there are no windows. An inch of cold water covers the stone floor. I sit in a straight-backed chair. I am told to remove my shoes and to keep my feet in the water. I have only my dress and sweater to wear.

When Torlova leaves, the inquisitors, a man and a woman, come into the room. I don't know their names. They dress in heavy coats and rubber boots. They question me for three or four hours. Most of the questions are irrelevant, but always there are some about Phobos. I refuse to admit to sabotage I didn't commit. I am very stubborn about that.

Two or three times during the session, the man leaves the room while the woman beats me. I would say the beatings last ten minutes. She uses a green rubber hose against my back and flanks. My urine is always bloody the next days after an interrogation.

Yesterday, I had a session. When Torlova brought me back to my cell, she mentioned you—she knows your name. She said, "You go through all of this instead of admitting your crime? Just because you had a few fucks with him?" Then she pushed me to the floor and said, "Varonyev, I would have fucked you right here in Moscow."

I tell you these things not to make you sad, Edward, but because I need to share them with you. So I don't say good-bye to reason and life. Thank God for Olga.

I love you so much, Edward. Torlova has no idea.

Irina

Trembling, I set the letter on the carpet, inside the space made by my leg and my thighs. I stared at the paper, but the words only blurred. The inside of my nose seared. Tears rolled down my cheeks and dropped off my chin onto the letter. At my back, Mozart sounded shrill.

It was five or ten minutes before I could think clearly. When I did, I began to sense how desperate and powerless Boyes must have felt when he received this letter. It struck me that the Loyola conference would have occurred just a few days later. Anything, even an embarrassing public outburst in Varonyev's behalf, must have seemed necessary to Boyes.

I carried the pack of unopened letters under my arm while I crutched my way to the kitchen. I poured milk and brandy, then sat at the kitchen table where I emptied the glass in one long noisy chug, thinking all the time about green rubber hoses and bloody urine. And Varonyev—was she being beaten just then?

I slit each unopened envelope and read their letters in sequence. These letters were brief and mostly nonsensical. Varonyev now knew Boyes was missing, and she alternated between despair and crazy exhilaration. One letter fantasized Boyes breaking into her cell and delivering her back to Tallinn. Nowhere did she mention if her beatings continued.

The totality of the letters—the accretion of Varonyev's pain and fantasy mixed with streaks of her profound courage—was beginning to run through me. I felt Varonyev coming apart in small bits and pieces. Half a planet away, my outrage kindled. I wished to send Frankie Luchinski in against Varonyev's inquisitors. I would pistol-whip Torlova myself.

Sighing deeply, I picked up the last letter Varonyev had written. It was done in mid-February, about the time Boyes's body was found. It was the least loony and most poignant of these final letters. It simply said:

Edward,
 I fear you will never read this, but I send it for consolation. Yours and mine.
 It's from Nietzsche, Edward. He says:

"Our life, our happiness,
is beyond the North,
beyond ice, beyond death."

I love you forever, Edward. You know that.

Irina

I read this letter ten, maybe fifteen times, running it through my brain in every different way I could think of. I read it quickly and casually, then slowly and carefully. I read it trying to think of nothing. I read it picturing poor huge Boyes in the morgue, the sweat of decomposition on his face, his brain leaking like gruel onto the table. I read it with the overwhelming desire to punish the person who had annihilated Varonyev and Boyes's love.

After thirty still minutes, the energy went out of me, as fast as air from a pricked balloon. Immersed in vindictiveness, I shoved the letters together on the table, and took myself to my bedroom.

EIGHTEEN

Sleep wouldn't let itself be trapped. When I approached, it ran like a stray cat down another alley. My brain churned with images of Boyes and Varonyev. After an hour of disorder, I tossed off the blankets.

The tapes. I needed to watch the videotapes from Boyes's apartment.

I tightened my robe against the living-room's chill. Lighting no lamps, I flipped on the television and used its gray light. The tape labeled "Baikonur" slipped easily into the VCR. Power on, the motor hummed for half a minute before the screen's fuzz turned to a display written in Russian. Background music boomed, plenty of horns and timpani. I turned down the volume so Meg wouldn't waken.

Several screensful of credits zipped by. First picture now up: a huge, white-lighted rocket, fuselage venting steam, nose pointed at an ebony sky. When the music faded, the rocket's engines wound themselves into a primal, deep-throated scream, then poured fire from its holes. The brilliant white obelisk lifted into the night, its red-and-yellow tail blazing and shrinking as it ascended.

Was it a Phobos probe going off? Was Varonyev pushing buttons somewhere?

The launch completed, the tape proceeded to a tour of the Baikonur facility. I stood and watched attentively, but the twenty minutes of narration—more Russian—left me empty. The people and machines I saw were mildly interesting, yet gave up nothing of value. The ascent sequence had provided the tape's only thunder.

Discouraged, I ejected the cassette, then hesitated before reaching for the second tape, the one labeled, "Tallinn." If it was a damned travelogue, then I'd go back to bed. I popped the tape in and the machine whirred again.

No credits this time. Two people, a man and a woman, snapped onto the screen. Standing very still, they faced me, side by side, eyes wide: "American Gothic." When they seemed to realize the camera was live, they hammed with each other, embarrassment on their faces.

The man was obese, with a pocked face; every feature unattractive.

I stepped backward, transfixed. I dropped into a nearby chair. My mouth opened in horror.

Shouldn't we introduce ourselves soon? the man said.

The same face I had seen mantled by snow, frozen . . . then thawing . . . fluid popping out of it like sweat on a dog's nose.

He said, *We'd better say something. Announce ourselves, at least. For posterity, for God's sake.*

Both giggled.

Edward Boyes. Alive! Before someone had blown half his skull away. My arms clutched at my stomach.

The woman looked at him, then turned to face me directly. A tiny, self-conscious nod of her head, then, *Yes. Introduce . . . my name is Irina Varonyev.*

English competent. Frame thin. Fortyish. Too prominent cheeks, full as a squirrel's. Hair dull brown and straight. A plain, light blue dress tucked around her narrow waist.

Boyes bowed extravagantly and made Varonyev giggle again.

My name is Edward Boyes. No, we aren't making this record for posterity, not really. A laugh. *It's to watch ourselves. For our own enjoyment.*

I touched my dry lips. The image of the room behind the couple was so still that I guessed the camera was unattended. On automatic, probably mounted on a tripod. Home video all the way.

The couple broke. Behind them was a small table where a

meal had been set out. They sat opposite each other, now both seen in profile. Boyes wore dark trousers and an open-collared white dress shirt. I wondered if it was the same outfit he had worn to be killed in.

We should do this more often, Varonyev said.

What?

Room service. Not go out.

Boyes didn't answer, concentrating on the food. A few swallows and he said, *Did you try the checking program I sent over?*

I didn't have time. Besides, your V-hawk was around all day. I didn't want him to see me on it.

Because I wrote it?

It's not just you. The program's not Russian. They feel there is a limit.

They? Boyes asked.

Tributs and your V-hawk.

Who gives a damn? Avis is an idiot. Would you like a sip of my beer?

The meal went on, mostly in silence, but occasionally they spoke, at times their conversation about Phobos. The references were too complex for me to understand—far more complex than those in Varonyev's letters.

Would you mind changing now? Boyes said gently.

Varonyev smiled and stood from her chair. She disappeared offscreen while Boyes continued to eat. Once, he looked toward the camera as if to check that it was still filming.

In a few minutes, Varonyev returned in a sleeveless, sand-colored nightgown. The gown hugged her thinness, but flared at the neck into a lovely scalloped pattern. Narrow panels of lace ran from top to bottom. Exquisite.

Boyes set his fork down. *Are you too cool?* he said.

Oh, no.

He leaned toward the table. His small eyeglasses clutched his head, their frames angled an inch above his ears. Varonyev sat, oblivious to the camera, her hands folded in her lap, her gaze fixed on Boyes. Homely as she was, her face broke into a smile of pure enchantment. Now I knew what Eileen Stevens had meant when she spoke of Varonyev's sparkle.

You look very lovely, Irina.

Thank you for saying it.

I'll tell you something, Boyes said.

Yes?

I've had a dream the past few years. You know, the kind that couldn't possibly happen, but one wished it could.

Yes. What?

My dream is to sit on the shoulder of the Voyager probe and be whisked past Jupiter and Saturn and Neptune. Just to see those planets in rendezvous. Imagine, riding Voyager, like a horse! The sights!

Varonyev said nothing.

Only being with you is better, Irina. Being here with you.

Thank you. I know.

Suddenly, the video clicked off. The screen went dark, but just as I started out of my chair, it lit again. This time the camera's image was bouncy, its operator moving herky-jerky. From out of the motion I deciphered a room with a large bed. Two pillows, small and side by side, lovers' pillows, were lost in the bed's great width.

Now the camera jumped from the bed, swiftly scanning the room's heavy furniture, the brocaded wallpaper. Then the screen went black again; this time the video ended.

When I went to bed, it was nearly five in the morning. Eyes wide open, I lay in the darkness and recalled the luminous faces of the lovers. My mind kept circling on their imperfect features, their clothing, their bed.

Boyes's explanation for the tape—I supposed it had been made at The Golden Swan—made perfect sense to me. I took him at his word when he told the camera that he and Varonyev had made the tape for themselves, to watch themselves together. Awkward and contrived as the occasion might seem to others, it wasn't made for others. I was sure that to Boyes and Varonyev, their simple, slice-of-life encounter was bewitching. I'd bet that Boyes had watched the scene a hundred times after he left Tallinn.

I rolled over and faced a wall of my bedroom, thinking how the tape betrayed the lovers' naïveté that Eileen Stevens had spoken about. Like teen-agers who trade rings and letter-jackets, Boyes and Varonyev were still green enough to be unsure of their common devotion. They required accidents, necessary accidents, to view and touch as proofs of their love. It wouldn't have surprised me to see them make love on the tape, their sex confirming that yes, yes, after forty years, they each now *did* have a mate, someone to hold and lie naked with in a bed.

Finally sleepy, I realized my growing obsession with Boyes and Varonyev. Whether it was envy or voyeurism, their adversity now gripped me in iron claws.

Meg dragged me through breakfast; then I dragged her through the dishes. I called Paris and set up a time I would pick her up for Michael Furey's funeral the next morning.

Outside, it was clear as a bell and cold as hell. Meg and I walked the few blocks down to the Touhy Avenue beach. We spent half an hour firing snowballs across the frozen edge of the lake, trying to land one in open water, neither of us ever coming close. On the way home, we touched up the icy skin of Jake the Snowman.

I needed time alone to sort through the bag of papers I had collected from Boyes's desk and wastebasket. I promised Meg to take her to the movies if she would let me work in peace for an hour. *Star Wars* was the matinee feature at The 400, a Sheridan Road movie house that showed old films on the cheap. Meg pounced at the bribe like a bobcat after raw meat.

I emptied the grocery bag from Boyes's apartment onto my kitchen table. Before starting in, I telephoned Peggy Miksis.

"How do you get all the good cases in the Public Defender's Office?" I asked, joking.

"I'm the oldest and dumbest," Peggy said.

"Have you talked with Easter yet?"

"Tomorrow," she said, in her deep-throated voice. "Today's the Sabbath, remember?"

"He's confessed, Peg, but I'm not convinced."

"Then you'd better invent another suspect, because I see by his mug shot that he's black. That's halfway to a conviction in this city, innocent or not—and especially if a black attorney argues his case."

"I'm working on it," I said. "Give me time."

"We may not have much. Looks like his indictment will reach the grand jury by midweek."

"Isn't that fast?" I asked.

"Fast? Try lightning. Who'd this guy shoot, the Cardinal? His Eminence?

"Don't you read the papers? Or watch TV?"

"I'm blank," Peggy said. "I got home last night from Arizona. The Cubs started spring training, and Ted has to be there till the team breaks camp. He took me along for the first week."

"I'm bleeding."

She laughed. "When I got back to my office, the assignment was on my desk. Where's the heat from?"

"The body was found in the Forty-third Ward. That help any?"

"Oooo! Not supposed to happen in the Forty-third, is it? As we say, their shit don't stink in East Lincoln Park. Jimmy O'Donnell?"

"Right. That your ward?"

"We're the next one west," Peggy said. "Compared to O'Donnell, our hack alderman looks like Thomas Jefferson."

"Listen, Peg, I'll call you tomorrow at the office. When you seeing Easter?"

"First thing in the morning. You rate him a morning person?"

"Uh . . . better take espresso."

A dapple of sunlight from the window over the sink cheered me. Meg kept her promise like a good soldier: I worked at the kitchen table without distraction. I was able to get through Boyes's desk material in less than an hour.

Most of the papers from the desk were magazine and newspaper stories describing the loss of Phobos I. Boyes had collected dozens of them, many foreign. The articles in English chewed on the political effects of the broken Phobos program and the suddenly magnified importance of Phobos II. All the stories blamed controller error for the Phobos I loss. Varonyev's name was never mentioned as the controller, and her jailing seemed unknown.

At the bottom of the pile, I found two small clippings, one from the *Sun-Times* and the other from the *Tribune*, each dated Sunday, November 20th. The clippings reported the Loyola computer conference that had occurred the day before. The stories virtually ignored the scientific content of the meeting, all column space being devoted to one Edward Boyes's outburst about a Russian woman being held in prison because of the Phobos debacle. Impartial as the reporters may have tried to be, their unmistakable tone painted Boyes as a deranged man with a microphone, a kook who needed a lesson in etiquette.

I considered the dates and thought back to Amanda Loomquist. I remembered her saying that Boyes last met a class the afternoon of November 23rd. I wondered if the proximity of his disappearance and the conference was just coincidence.

I gathered and stacked the desk material. Only the trash from Boyes's wastebasket remained to be searched. I combed the debris, most of it from a bill-paying session. I found stubs from Boyes's credit card, telephone and ComEd bills mixed in among junk mail. Before quitting, I saw a small, crumpled piece of notepaper fall out from between pages of a Marshall Field's catalogue.

I had mined a nugget I never expected, a memo that I assumed had been written by Boyes. Scribbled in pencil, the note simply said:

11/23

dinner—8
Helmand

Helmand. There was something vaguely familiar about the name. I went to a kitchen drawer for the White Pages phone book, looking for help and hoping there were less than fifty Mr. or Ms. Helmands listed. Easy—there were none.

I stood reflecting, knowing I had heard the name before. When my concentration weakened, I realized how hungry I was. The thought of food did it, shook my memory. To prove what I suspected, I went to the restaurant section of the Yellow Pages. Bingo!

There it was: The Helmand, 3201 N. Halsted.

It was an Afghan restaurant I had been to once with Richard, probably two or three years before. I went to the phone and dialed the number. A recorded message told me The Helmand was closed on Sundays, but would be open at five the next day for dinner. I would have to put The Helmand on hold, but that was all right: I needed a few hours off. *Star Wars* would do nicely for the rest of the day.

The 400: the smell of buttered popcorn hung thick in the lobby air. You felt yellow grease slipping through your lungs and into your bloodstream. But once your nose had accommodated, the place was tolerable, especially at two bucks a ticket.

Inside the auditorium, Cokes were spilling and popcorn sailing. Parentless kids ran up and down the aisles in packs, little marauders yipping and hooting in falsetto. For safety, Meg and I chose corner seats in the back row. The only danger there was having your shoes permanently bond to the city's stickiest floor.

When *Star Wars* finally started, a cheer went up and banged around the ceiling and walls for a couple of minutes. Then the theater went as silent as a tomb. I stuck with the film for a while, but ultimately the budding romance between Luke Skywalker and Princess Leia failed to move me. Feeling the effects of only three hours of sleep the night before, I opted for a siesta. Meg elbowed me a few times when Darth Vader scared her, but each time I was always able to nod off again.

After the movie, we returned home for supper. We settled for packaged macaroni and cheese, the kind of meal only an eight-year-old can appreciate. I read the nutritional information on the box and considered reporting myself to Social Services for child abuse.

We were both in bed by eight. I stalled on the edge of sleep, reflecting on the memo written for Boyes's dinner date at The Helmand.

The memo listed a day and time and place, but it implied much more. Its very existence argued that the invitation had not been spur of the moment, but rather, something needing to be written down. This meant arrangements were made in advance, at least by a day or two, maybe even the weekend before at the computer conference.

And I thought the memo gave more yet. With no name recorded, I doubted that Boyes was meeting a stranger—he knew who he dined with those few hours before he was shot. Nearly asleep now, I wondered what it felt like to have a friend shove the cold barrel of a gun tight against your jawbone.

NINETEEN

"You think I'm going whoring again, don't you?"

Paris's question dropped into the slot between the radio's business and sports reports. Goosing the Fury to change lanes, I said, "Never crossed my mind."

We were pushing south on the Dan Ryan, aimed toward suburban Homewood. Overhead, the sky was leaden. The morning rush hour had dwindled to leftovers.

Paris wore a navy-blue suit, beaver coat, and no hat. I had gone with navy also, a dress, but a cloth coat instead of mammal's fur. As Paris liked to say, I never held as good a job as she had.

"Seems logical you would think that, Nora."

I refused to look at her. Then, my eyes still trained ahead, I finally burst out, "What you said is too goddamned stupid to deserve a reply, Paris! And why are you dishing out shit like that on a day like today?"

She turned toward me. I took my gaze from the road and looked at her. The faintest pink swelling rimmed her eyes. She shrugged confusion. "Sorry. I dunno . . . my head's spinning today."

"Mine, too. Forget it."

She murmured, "It's me worrying about the whoring, not you."

I smiled. "I'm not worried. You're gonna land the job at Field's, I know it. And, hey, I expect discounts at the lingerie and perfume counters. Don't laugh about that, Paris, about the lingerie and perfume. A woman like me has to have high expectations."

A smile softened Paris's face. Her eyes lit.

Ten miles south of the city limits, we left Dangerous Dan and turned onto I-80. We arrived at Homewood Memorial Gardens at just ten o'clock. A guard directed us to a road that twisted through dense trees and tall headstones. After about a quarter of a mile, the trees quit and the road opened into a flat, snow-filled field. If there were any graves there, the markers were as hidden as the remains they identified.

We followed the road to the end where a car and a truck were parked next to each other. The truck was dark green and shaped like a bread truck. I pulled behind the car and shut off my engine. To the left, I noticed five piles of dirt in a neat row, a hole in the ground alongside each pile.

I stepped out of the Fury. A man left the car and walked over to the truck. He called up to the driver, "It's ten. Let's start."

The driver climbed from his cab and walked to the rear of the truck where he opened the delivery doors. Three men in dark coveralls filed out. The four worked swiftly together to unload five caskets, each casket set next to a dirt pile.

The man from the car came over to me, his feet crunching in the snow. He was older than the others and had a ragged, ashen mustache. He looked past me into the Fury to see Paris. Politely, he said, "Are you here for one of these?"

"Michael Furey," I answered.

"I'm Father Fondy." He pulled a folded paper from inside his black topcoat. "I'm retired, but I still do this. No one has to preside at these things, but some of us do it anyway."

"I see."

He scanned his paper. "Mr. Furey would be the middle one of the five. He Catholic?"

"I've no idea."

"Doesn't matter."

"Of course not."

"Are you Catholic, Miss?"

"Mostly."

Fondy nodded his head. "I'll be starting now," he said. "I doubt if anyone else will show up. We usually have nobody, here."

I motioned Paris from the car, and she joined me. Fondy

began the service, moving sequentially down the row of caskets, his mustache folding in the breeze now and then as he spoke. Paris and I stood closer for the minutes he intoned prayers at Furey's casket. Paris kept her eyes shut.

The whole shot didn't take more than twenty minutes—twenty sunless minutes to ship five off and on their way. Bon voyage, but hold the champagne and caviar.

When the caskets had all been prayed over, we walked away, Fondy next to me. I asked him how often he did the service.

"For the unclaimed?" he said. "Once a week."

I nodded; then it struck me what body had been found exactly a week before. I said, "Could you look at your list again, Father? Is one of the names Edward Boyes?"

Fondy took the wrinkled paper from his pocket. After skimming it, he turned back toward the graves and pointed. "Mr. Boyes is there. The last in the line. The furthest away from us."

I turned to Paris. "Would you wait for me in the car?"

"The guy from Lincoln Park?" she said.

"Yes."

I retraced my steps to the graves, careful with my prosthetic foot in the trampled snow. I stopped a few feet from Boyes's casket, hesitant to go closer. The men at the other end of the row stopped their shoveling, their chatter. In my mind, the videotape started up, Boyes and Varonyev facing me, hamming with each other, giggling.

I stood in place for the minute it took to wash the tape from my memory. When my head cleared, I went close enough to lay my ungloved hand on the casket: cheap wood, rough to the touch. I wondered what Varonyev's hand—her nails, the pads and curves of her fingers—would look like if she was feeling the wood instead of me.

I wondered why Robert and Eileen Stevens had not claimed the body and given it a proper burial. Or why, at least, they were not standing next to me at this casket.

Greektown: I needed an upper. To say nothing of the fact that I hadn't challenged my gallbladder with a plate of gyros and onions for a month or more.

When I phoned Peggy, she leaped at the invitation. We met at a small place on South Halsted, near Jackson Boulevard. Brilliant white-and-blue posters of island harbor scenes hung on the yellow walls of the room, and our simple table and chairs looked as if they'd been stolen from the County Jail's cafeteria. Speakers tucked into the ceiling corners wailed traditional Greek music: an offensive, blistering stringed instrument of some sort and a caterwauling tenor. I pined for Elvis and "Love Me Tender" at The Hard Rock.

We sipped anise-flavored ouzo, clear and fiery. To kill the heat, I alternately sucked Coke from a fat glass with a straw. "You see Easter?" I asked.

"Just finished with him," Peggy said. She was dressed in a camel suit and white silk blouse. Her lips were a kiss print, her mahogany skin as smooth and unblemished as Meg's. If I could trade my eyes for Paris's and my mouth and skin for Peggy's, then I might have something.

"Well?" I asked.

"Every other word is 'motherfucker.' He's either a moron, or his brain is hopelessly undernourished."

"Why does his brainpower matter so much?" I asked.

She closed her menu. "Makes me think twice about putting him on the stand—the guy'll kill himself up there. And the 'motherfucker' word doesn't enchant the jury, even as a single slip of the tongue."

"You'll plead him not guilty?"

"I have to for murder one in Illinois." She brushed her right hand across her close-cropped hair. "A jury trial is mandatory."

A waiter in a stained white apron came to our table. His demeanor was gruff; his eyes dark pools. When he left, Peggy said, "You guys haven't found a gun yet, have you?"

"No."

"Good. Now, what about these girls who'll testify they saw Easter grab Boyes?"

"Easter says they're Rodney Truman's whores and Truman had a score to settle. Maybe you can sort that out. I couldn't."

Peggy shook her head. "We're dealing with layers and layers of gang bullshit here. Somehow or another, whether Easter

killed Boyes or not, all of their stories will be knotted up with
gangbangers and drugs."

I leaned in closer to the table. "Peg, I think the case against
Easter is sloppy. I mean, a mugging that ends in two point-blank,
large-caliber wounds under a jawbone? And leave a gold watch
and ring and a hundred bucks behind?"

"I read Boyes's wallet had been emptied."

I settled against my chairback and flicked my hand at the air
with disdain. "Look, the body was found in a swamp in Lincoln
Park. What mugger waits for a victim in a place like that? In
November?"

Peggy swigged the last of her ouzo. The drink shone on her
lips like butter. "Fine, then explain Easter's confession."

"They promised him plea bargaining and parole if he confessed. If he didn't, then they go for the death penalty."

"He bought that?"

"They'd softened him up a bit first."

She tipped her head. "Meaning?"

"Easter claims a cop beat him."

"What?" she said, her eyes widening.

"Easter didn't tell you?"

"No. He looked fine to me."

"He said they were very careful. Nothing done to the head or
face, only his balls."

"Christ, Nora! Do you know what you're saying?" She waved
frantically to our waiter and yelled, "More ouzo!"

We said nothing for the first five minutes of the meal, each of us
content to ride on the taste of the food. My plate was a fragrant
still life: strips of dark-fired gyros meat on a bed of parsley and
sliced raw onion. It wasn't fare for the fainthearted, but the gut-
busting Polish meals of my childhood had been my boot camp.

When I took a breather, I began telling Peggy the Phobos
story: the engraved watch and ring, the love affair, the Stevenses,
Olga Berggolts. Between bites, Peggy questioned me adroitly,
detail after detail. Then, finished with Phobos, I told her about
Paris and Michael Furey and how I had killed Vincent Cruzado.

Peggy swallowed and laid her fork down. Hesitantly, she said, "The Department do anything?"

"An Internal Affairs investigation is in the works. An assistant state's attorney took my statement."

"Don't worry about that—it's mandatory if there's been a death." She pushed her plate away. "Need some cash?"

"No, thanks," I said. "My checks keep coming for now."

"You'll need counsel if the State's Attorney sends it to a grand jury. Want help with your defense?"

"You're a public defender."

"Yes, and you're not indigent. But the city has nothing to say about what I do on my own time. Does it now?"

I shook my head. She smiled and lifted her chin. The waiter cleared our plates and brought coffee that was as black and bitter as chicory root. I tamed mine with sugar and a flood of cream.

"Would you mention Easter's beating to his grand jury?" I asked.

"Probably not," Peggy said. "It won't stop the indictment, and who knows if it's a load of shit or not?"

"Would you save it for his trial?"

She twirled a diminutive forefinger round and round inside the handle of her coffee cup. Eyes back up to me, she said, "Nora, any testimony about the beating, whether it occurred or not, will bring you down at Area Six."

I didn't answer. I knew what she meant.

She continued: "People will know who helped me figure out the bogus deal offered Easter, and about his alleged beating. You will not be held in high esteem by those who run the station. Who's your boss, Chief Melchior?"

"No, new name—Deputy Chief A-hole."

"Being frivolous won't change anything, Nora." She paused for a sip of coffee, then said, "If Easter was beaten, who did it?"

"Probably Frankie Luchinski."

"Okay, then you go to the top of Luchinski's and all his friends' shit lists. Dangerous position."

"Well, fuck Frankie Luchinski!" I snapped, teeth clenched. "That's what I think, Peggy."

"Relax, will you, dammit?" She glanced to nearby tables.

"Listen, you're going to beat Internal Affairs and the State's Attorney—ninety-nine percent of cops are exonerated in these investigations. When you do win, you need something to return to at that station."

"I've got Arthur," I said. "He's all I need."

"Art wouldn't agree with that. He's not a stupid man."

I knew I was acting juvenile, and as disappointed as I was with myself, I seemed unable to stop.

"Did Easter ask to see a doctor?" Peggy said.

"No."

"Then anybody who might have been involved will deny it. So it's Easter's word against theirs. Figure it out. While they're testifying in three-piece suits and police uniforms, Easter looks the jackass in orange coveralls. Or else they let me dress him up in his piece-a-shit suit from Maxwell Street. Figure out whose story the jury buys."

I downed a mouthful of coffee. "I'm still chasing a couple of other things in the case," I said quietly.

"Well, hurry for God's sake, will you?" she said, kidding. "I need a defense that relies on what happened on the night of Boyes's death, not during Easter's interrogation three months later."

Discouraged, I pushed away from the table. "I'm looking," I said. "It's out there, and I'm going to find it."

The sun had emerged during lunch, and now it burnished the jagged downtown skyline to the color of gunmetal. Monroe Street shone dazzling white, as though its salt-stained surface might suddenly combust in winter's glare. Ahead of me, Lake Michigan, a calm, blue-green plank, ran hard and steady to the eastern horizon.

I pulled into the parking lot of the Burnham Harbor Yacht Club. At a pay phone, I called Area Six. "I need to talk to Art," I said to Frankie Luchinski. "He's not answering in our office."

"I don't see Fart," Frankie said. "I mean Art."

"Of course not, you're at the lobby desk. Try the coffee room."

"You don't need Art," he said. "You're suspended."

"For crissake, Frankie, ring the goddamned coffee room! Quit being a pain in the ass."

Art picked up the phone on the first ring. "Where are you, girl?"

"A pay phone. Monroe and the Drive."

"Hey, it's Blue Monday here. I miss you, partner."

"Thanks. You find anything when you ran those names I gave you Saturday?"

"Zero on Robert Stevens," Art said. "Now we did hit a little something with Bell."

"Yeah?"

"Norman J. is thirty and has done time in the Joliet pen. Once for beating his sister senseless during a domestic, and once for two counts of child pornography. Released last year."

"Ahh, a new and lovely Rogers Park neighbor for me. I'll have to ask him over."

"You think he's a player?"

"I dunno but his record is predictable. One look at the guy and you know he's human shit. What's Stevens doing with rabble like that in his building? Loyola must have a thousand students renting off-campus. This is all Stevens can come up with?"

"What else is up?" Art asked.

"Got the phone logs for those guys?"

"Yeah, but I haven't gone over them."

"Don't bother. I'll stop by and pick them up."

"What you looking for, girl?"

"Art, the O'Hare shooter knew that I was delivering Olga Berggolts to her flight the other night. I'm just droppin' some lines in, fishin'."

"Anything I can do here?"

"Not unless you can talk Randy into redoing the Fury in bulletproof windows."

I called Tommy Banks from the same booth. "Tommy," I said, "did anyone try to claim the body of Edward Boyes during the past week? Before it was taken to Homewood this morning?"

"Nope."

"Anybody named Stevens call about the burial of Boyes?"

"Stevens? No."

"You would know? They always check with you?"

"I sign out each body that leaves. I've been here every day for a month. It didn't happen, Lieutenant. No one wanted to bury the guy."

"So Boyes was taken—"

"Boyes'd worn out his welcome. Time's up. It's Homewood and worms' meat after a week."

TWENTY

After I had cooled from my desk-clearing blowup with Dan Halsey, his memory, like an insurgent, made occasional night raids on my common sense. I recognized the spark of my attraction—upbeat and good-looking, he was male company outside the station house. But the man had treated me so poorly that I couldn't shake my bitter distrust.

I parked in the drive that circled the Adler Planetarium like a noose. Overhead, a few slate-gray clouds gathered. I saw one shaped like a flowing, liquid trumpet. In another, a bear crept maliciously toward the downtown skyscrapers.

This time, I knew my way down that dark corridor lit by fiery supernovae. Halsey's secretary, a woman with cheeks flushed cherry-red, ushered me into his office. "Hello, Dan," I said. "Got a minute?"

I had surprised him—on his desk, a take-out sandwich and a can of soda. He swallowed a mouthful of food. "Want to share something?"

"Nope." I patted my stomach. "Just came from Greektown." I took the chair he gestured me toward. "I'm tying up loose ends in the Lincoln Park case."

"Don't you guys have the killer?"

I smiled grimly. "Say, thanks for sending me to Valery Kuzov. He's been a help."

"Sure." He took a bite of sandwich.

I said, "I came by to ask you what you know about Robert Stevens."

"Loyola?"

"Yes."

"He's computer science. Used to be with NASA."

"You see him much?" I asked.

"Meetings, lectures. The circuit."

"Such as the Loyola conference last November?"

He drained his soda can and tossed it into a wastebasket. "I'm sure Stevens was there, and I see he's on the program for the one coming up this weekend."

"What do you think of him?"

"Nothing, I don't know the guy. We've talked during coffee breaks at meetings—that's it." He sat back. His tie—ducks in flight on a mustard-yellow background—rode askew on his shirt.

"Let me run another one by you," I said. "Jack Percot."

"Spell it."

I did. "Used to be with NASA," I said. "He spent some time on Phobos, was in Tallinn for a while last spring."

"Percot," he said slowly. "In a big ruckus in Tallinn?"

I nodded.

"Then I know who you mean. I have a couple of astronomer friends at NASA who got it off the grapevine. They talked about infighting that jeopardized the launch of the first probe."

"Percot's now at U of I in Urbana."

"I've never met him and haven't heard anything since the Tallinn gossip."

"Okay, thanks." I stood. "By the way, how's it going with Phobos II?"

Halsey had started to stand, but I motioned him back down. "One of those same astronomer friends called me last week," he said. "She thinks the project's wobbly. The probe's main transmitter is down, and the mission's running on a backup system. They've been forced to push up the schedule by a couple of months."

"Meaning?"

"NASA's helping with settings for a rocket burn that would put the probe into the orbit of Phobos, the moon, next week. People are nervous."

I went toward the door. "Thanks for the info, Dan."

"Anytime. Say, Nora, lunch here at the desk—not the greatest. If you're ever downtown, come by and we'll go into the Loop and get a bite." He raised his hands, palms toward me. "Lunch with another human. That's it. Promise. What do you say?"

I smiled. "I'll see."

I picked up the Stevens and Bell phone logs from Art at Area Six, then drove home. I grabbed the newspaper and flopped onto my living-room couch, my leg unstrapped and on the floor, my right shoe off. I was asleep in minutes.

I awoke when drool itched my chin. It was two-thirty. I phoned Anna and told her I would pick Meg up from school, then run errands. Anna said she was making lamb stew—she knew how Meg loved it, and would we come for supper? My answer shot from my mouth like a Baikonur rocket: Yes, yes, yes!

Parked on Loyola Avenue across from St. Ignatius, I watched the youngest ones, the kindergartners, lead the charge through the school's double doors. These were small, low-set troopers, their bodies wrapped like fat packages, their faces lost in puffs of colorful hats and scarves. Absent any sense of direction, they plowed straight toward the street, their lives saved only by the coterie of parents and baby-sitters waiting on the sidewalk.

As more children spilled out, their ages and penchant for mischief rose concurrently: the middle-graders pulled and shoved each other, with broad smiles and high-pitched yips that split the frozen air for half a block. Finally, the school's sophisticates, the eighth graders, tagged at the rear. Coiffed like rock stars, the girls streamed languidly from dimness into sunlight, their bearings full of pretense, their expressions coolly indifferent. The hatless, open-jacketed, less mature boys were not above the spirited whacking endemic to younger children.

I smiled in my pleasure as I watched Meg hurry toward the car. Her red jacket and its furry hood hugged her. She was surprised to see me and it showed in her eyes. She climbed into the car. "Hi, Mom!" she cried, and kissed my cheek with her chilled lips. "Is Anna sick?"

"No, kiddo, I'm off work. I thought I'd come for you."

"But it's Monday," she said, puzzled. She undid her hood; a few electrified hairs stood on end.

"Let's get out of here."

We drove south on Broadway. Meg rattled on about a field trip to the Shedd Aquarium, but I only half listened, thinking instead about the boys at IA and the State's Attorney's Office. If Melchior didn't want me answering telephones, then I was going to be off more than a day or two, so I needed to be truthful with Meg. I pulled in front of a fire hydrant near Bryn Mawr and put the car into Park.

Meg said, "Are we where we're going already?"

"No. I just want to tell you that I might be taking you to school and picking you up for a few days."

She stared at me, waiting for more.

"I've been suspended from work," I said. "My days will be more free for a while."

"I don't get it, Mom. Sorry."

"I won't be going down to the station."

"Like, you're on vacation?"

"No. I'm not allowed to go in. My boss won't let me."

"Why?"

"Because I shot a man last Friday night."

"Oh," she said, pretending to understand, but her slack jaw showed she was lost at sea. A mammoth truck blew past us, its rush of wind rocking the Fury.

I said, "Remember the other night when Anna put you to bed, then I came in late and snuggled next to you?"

She nodded.

"The shooting happened that night."

Confusion still reigned in her face, but I waited; we would do this at her pace. After a moment, she hiked up a shoulder and said, "I know sometimes you might have to shoot people."

"I do, yes. But this time my boss thinks I shouldn't have."

"Do you think that?"

"No."

"Was this man trying to hurt you?"

"I thought so."

She rubbed her nose with a mittened hand. "Who was he?"

"His name doesn't matter."

"Mom, do you mind if I ask these questions? Is the stuff secret or something?"

I smiled gently. "Not at all. The man I shot had killed a person named Michael Furey. Michael was a friend of Paris's."

Meg frowned as the violence came closer to home for her. "Was he Neptune's friend, too?" she asked. She and Neptune played together when Paris and I could arrange it.

"Neptune liked Michael."

"The man you shot is dead?"

"Yes."

She looked away from me and out to the street. The sun had become lower and fatter, and Broadway's squat buildings languished in a cold, dwindling light. Self-consciously, I adjusted my rump on the seat.

Meg said, "You can drive again if you want, Mom. I don't have any more questions."

"All right."

I pulled the Fury back into traffic. A mile farther south, as we waited for a red light at Lawrence Avenue, Meg slid across the seat and brought her body over against mine. She took off her mittens and tossed them back to where she'd been sitting. Not speaking or looking up at me, she laid her warm left hand on my thigh and patted me with a rhythm as regular as her heartbeat.

I wondered if she knew how much I cherished the bias that wound through her love.

In decent weather, it would have been a pleasant, after-dinner walk from The Helmand to a stage play at one of the nearby off-Loop theaters. The restaurant occupied the street-level space of a somber, blockish brick building at Halsted and Belmont. Dark green awnings brooded over the windows, and inside the plate glass, baskets of plants hung from the trim. Past the greenery, white linen covered the room's tables, each one graced with a candle bowl that made a circle of yellow light. Two busboys busied themselves setting silverware and napkins. A third hauled an open hamper of flatbread.

We had parked a block east on Belmont, then walked hand-in-hand past a staggering drunk and into a biting west wind. Three paces inside The Helmand put us squarely in front of a desk whose high, slanted top made it look like a portable pulpit. The desk's wood glowed with remnants of daylight streaming through the windows.

Meg pulled on my hand. "I like the smell in here." It was pungent and sweet, like cooking raisins.

One of the boys noticed us—the restaurant would not open until five, he called from across the room. We knew that, I said, but could I please speak to the manager?

The boy disappeared to the murky rear of the room, and a minute later a portly man in a rough black turtleneck came toward us from among the tables. He walked with a toe-out gait and a hip waddle. A mustache shrouded his upper lip. I put him in his forties.

"My name is Lieutenant Nora Callum," I said to him. My police shield was ready.

He marked time: "Lieutenant. I see." He glanced at Meg, then back to me, as if to ask why Meg was in tow.

"This is Megan, my daughter," I explained. "I'm off-duty today."

He dipped his chin and smiled. In a clear, Indian sort of accent, he said, "I am Ahmad Durrani. Welcome to The Helmand." He offered a fleshy hand.

"There's been a killing, Mr. Durrani," I said, "and the victim may have eaten dinner here on the evening he died."

"And that would have been?"

"The Wednesday before last Thanksgiving. November 23rd."

"Some time ago."

"I wondered if anyone here has a memory of the man, or if you have a record of a reservation."

"And the name?"

"Edward Boyes."

He thought for a requisite moment. "Do you have a description?"

"About forty years old," I said. "Obese. A pockmarked face."

"A few like that come every week." He looked down and aimed a smile at Meg. "I'm going back to the kitchen, Lieutenant. To ask about your Edward Boyes. Sit if you wish." He lumbered away.

We sat at a table for four. Meg futzed with the candle bowl while I scanned the room and tried to imagine Boyes eating here just over three months before, and with whom.

Five minutes later, Durrani returned with a book and took the chair next to me. "This is the reservation book for last year," he said. "The name Edward Boyes is unknown in the kitchen. And his description, forget it. Means nothing also."

He opened the leather-covered Daily Register and flipped to November 23rd. Here, last names, perhaps two dozen, came in blocks arranged in fifteen-minute intervals. Some names were written in ink, others in pencil, and most appeared after the box marked "7 P.M." My eyes skipped to the eight-o'clock slot.

I felt a rush when I read it: ✓—*8PM: Boyes, 2.* The check mark was in red. "What does the check mean?" I asked.

"That the Boyes reservation was kept," Durrani said.

"Can you tell if he arrived on time?"

"No."

"There were two people in the party?"

"It says that, but we have changes in some reservations."

"But Boyes did come?" I pushed.

"Somebody came, Lieutenant," Durrani said. "Somebody used the reservation. Parcha and I are—"

"Parcha?"

"The woman who helps me at the desk. We are both—what do you say . . . punctilious? Yes, that's it, we are punctilious about the reservations book. Do you understand me?"

"I want to be sure about things," I said. "We've had trouble with the whereabouts of Mr. Boyes on the evening of his death. This is the first help we've had. I'm grateful to you."

As Meg and I stood to leave, Durrani waved one of the busboys to our table. The boy came carrying a small carton that he handed to Meg. Durrani said, "This is for you, Megan, but only after your supper."

Meg looked at me: I nodded that it was okay to accept the gift.

"What is it?" Meg asked.

"A sweet rice pudding," Durrani said, "and very good. There's plenty for your mother, too."

When I smiled my thanks, Durrani lifted a cupped hand into the air and held it there like a teacher. With enthusiasm he hadn't shown in his answers about Boyes, he said, "You might shake a bit of cinnamon onto it, or nutmeg. But be careful if you use nutmeg—a little goes a long way. Easy to kill a flavor as delicate as the pudding's. Now, Lieutenant, that would be murder!"

Paris's apartment: a final errand before supper, an errand to unburden myself of the load that had pestered me since I typed Michael Furey's name into the National Crime Information Center computer.

Fifteen stories up, I stared out a window to the western edge of the city. The sun had just disappeared, but its last light scorched the horizon to a ribbon of glowing red ash. My view downward was into the blue-gray canyon named Clark Street.

I came back to the couch where Paris, her legs folded under her, sat in lamplight. Dressed in a satin bathrobe, she was smoking an unfiltered cigarette. Meg and Neptune were off playing in the back of the apartment.

I sat at the opposite end of the couch. The room stank of cigarette smoke. "I thought you stopped smoking," I said. "You told me when you met Michael you quit."

Paris inhaled deeply, as if in repudiation. "I picked up a pack when you dropped me off this morning," she said. "I bought straights because I knew they'd taste so shitty that I'd be able to quit again."

I nodded clumsily and handed her the packet from the Sheridan Road camera shop. "You mentioned you didn't have any pictures of him. I forgot to give you these at the funeral."

She pulled the prints from the envelope, then started through Furey's lifeless images. She studied them carefully, the corners of her eyes as sharp as dagger points. After a few minutes, she said, "You took these at the morgue?"

"Yes."

"Thanks." She crushed the cigarette into an ashtray and blew a final tube of smoke into the air. "I'm looking at pictures of a dead man. Jesus Christ, Nora, what's wrong with me?"

"Nothing. Who cares what you look at?"

She didn't answer.

No matter how ludicrous it seemed to me, Furey's murder had torn a gash in Paris's heart. I could think of only one way to help heal it. "You know, Paris, I've been meaning—"

"I don't know what's happened to me," she cut in, "why I'm so sad. It was just three lousy weeks with the guy. To feel what I did . . . I mean, off the deep end, at my age."

I thought of Boyes and Varonyev, and their ages, and their unbridled deep ends. I breathed in and said, "Paris, Michael Furey wasn't what he seemed to be."

She grimaced. "Now, what the hell's that supposed to mean, Lieutenant?"

"I ran a search on him the morning before we met for lunch. Furey was a convicted felon—auto theft. He did time in a Florida jail and was freed last July. By September he had jumped parole. If he was still alive, I'd have to bring him in and extradite him."

She grabbed and lit another cigarette. "That's a crock, Nora. You have him mixed up with someone else."

"No. It was him."

Her eyes glistened with tears. "And even if it was true, why would you bother me with this now? The guy's dead! Why tell me now?"

"Because knowing will help you."

She jerked her cigarette through the air. Harshly, she said, "Please, save your pop-psychology bullshit for someone else. Why don't you go home now?"

I stood and started after Meg. At the edge of the living room, I turned back. "It hurts to be buffaloed, Paris — I know that from experience. I'm telling you about Michael Furey because I care about you." My voice resonant with anger, I finished with "If I can't be truthful with you, then what the hell do you think we've got for a friendship? You answer me that, goddammit!"

TWENTY-ONE

Anna's stew was good enough to be a last meal, and for dessert, we split Durrani's pudding. Stark white, cold, and sweet, it made three portions that we flecked with cinnamon. Before Meg and I told Anna about The Helmand, she had guessed the pudding was Afghan or Indian: nothing so elegant, she said, could claim origin in her northern Russia.

Just after eight o'clock, I left to see Robert Stevens. My belly was full so I decided to walk the several blocks from Fargo to Albion. I piled into my down jacket and pulled a stocking cap low over my ears.

The air outside was thin and cold, but "the hawk," Art's name for winter wind that cuts like talons, had forsaken the city. A mosaic of lit windows cheered Fargo's buildings, and on Sheridan Road the streetlamps beamed a high orange canopy of light. I walked south. Traffic was meager and courteous. The sidewalks were nearly deserted.

Stashed in my pocket was the inventory of names I had gleaned from Varonyev's letters and the Tallinn videotape. I passed The 400 theater and the camera shop, walking along slowly, thinking about Paris.

Stevens answered the door in a purple Loyola sweatshirt. "Eileen's putting Jerry to bed," he said.

The apartment smelled of roasted meat. In the living room, I took a chair. Stevens went for the couch under the row of windows looking out onto Albion Avenue. He dispensed with two minutes by discussing the weather in monologue. I was glad to see Eileen enter the room. "Jerry's finally down," she said. "Hello, Nora."

She sat at the other end of the couch and tucked her stockinged feet under her.

"I found Irina's letters in Mr. Bell's apartment," I said.

Both Stevenses looked surprised. I was grateful neither asked how I had entered the apartment.

"I've never read them," Stevens said.

"I did," I said. "Some names are mentioned. I need help."

Stevens lifted a leg and rested it on the cushion between himself and Eileen. Fidgety, he didn't look directly at me.

"Is tonight bad for you, Dr. Stevens?" I asked. "I can come back."

"No, it's just—"

"He's been working on his presentation for this weekend," Eileen interrupted, "the conference we talked about, Nora. It's monopolizing his attention."

"It's okay," he said, already more conciliatory, as though his wife's mere mention of the project had paid him his due. "The paper's nearly done."

I pulled my list of names from my jeans pocket. "The letters contain several names with some frequency. I've got these in no special order."

"Fire away," Stevens said.

"First, Orbeli and Navoi. Men or women?"

"Men," he said, "both in guidance systems, software side."

"As opposed to?"

"Hardware people who tend to be engineers, not programmers."

The distinction lost on me, I said, "Irina wrote that she hoped Orbeli or Navoi would be named head of Guidance after Edward left."

Stevens straightened from a slouch: I was gaining his interest. "Either would have been a good choice. They're both Russian, both bright."

I checked my notes. "But Irina said someone else, named Avis, was put in charge."

"Avis?" Stevens said, "Avis? Never heard of him, or her. You, Eileen?"

"No."

"It's not a Russian-sounding name," Stevens said. "That surprises me. He NASA?"

"I've no idea," I said.

"Why don't you talk to your friend Doris Souchak about that one?" Stevens said glibly.

"Here's another name," I said. "V-hawk."

"What the hell kind of a name is that? Spell it."

"Like it sounds," I said. "V-h-a-w-k."

"V-hawk," Stevens mumbled. "I don't know. Do you, Eileen?"

"No."

"The name is mentioned as many times as Avis is," I said.

"I'm blank on both of those," Stevens said.

I glanced to my paper. "Then how about Vera T.?"

"Tachinski," Stevens answered quickly. "A Pole. Blackest hair you ever saw. Like it came from a can of shoe polish. She did onboard memory systems, various hard-drive arrangements. Understand?"

"Not really," I said.

"The devices that store . . . doesn't matter." He waved his hand curtly in the air. "Vera's partner was a man named Josef Kuznetzov, a Russian. Big, angry-looking guy, like a bear. Do you have him?"

I scanned the list. "Yes. Mentioned several times."

"They were lovers," Stevens said, "don't you think, Eileen?"

Eileen put her hand through her hair. "I was at a couple of parties with them, and maybe once a picnic. They probably had something going, but they weren't like Edward and Irina. Not pawing."

I moved ahead. "There's someone named Tributs. This is a man."

"An engineer," Stevens said matter-of-factly. "Older—I think the guy might go back to Sputnik, seriously—but very capable. He turned administrator ten or fifteen years ago. I'm surprised he was at Baikonur. Did Irina write that?"

I went again to my notes. "She wrote that Tributs was called from Moscow to decide what to do with something called the pre-flight programs."

"Those programs were still on board the probe's computers at Baikonur?"

"I guess," I said. "Is that bad?" I was struggling now to keep up.

"They're for ground testing. During the probe's flight, all they could do is cause trouble. They needed to be dumped prior to liftoff."

"Irina wrote that Tributs decided that."

"Makes sense," Stevens said.

I plowed through another dozen or more names that Varonyev had mentioned only once or twice each. Stevens or Eileen recognized a few, but could make nothing of their significance. When we finished, I asked Stevens, "Weren't all of these people mentioned in the letters at Baikonur when Edward was killed?"

Stevens pushed his glasses to the bridge of his nose. "Except for this Avis and V-hawk, the names are all Russian or Eastern Bloc. They should have been on station in Baikonur when Edward was shot—because Phobos II is still flying."

"Then let me mention one who was not on station," I challenged. "Jack Percot."

"I told you the other day," Stevens said, "Edward and he had an argument in Tallinn. Not a federal case, Lieutenant."

"Percot wasn't angry?"

"He was furious. He and Edward had short fuses. It was nothing new."

"Did Boyes and Percot have any contact after Boyes left NASA?"

Stevens shrugged. "Edward never said anything to me. You'd have to ask Jack."

"When's the last time you talked with him?"

"Percot?"

"Yes."

He scratched his chin with the heel of his palm. "I don't recall. Early this winter? I don't know." Anticipating me, he said, "And, no, I don't remember what we talked about. Probably the Bears."

"Did Percot make the Loyola conference last fall?" I asked.

"He tried to but didn't. Uhh . . . he was indisposed."

"Meaning?"

"Too drunk to drive."

Eileen left the room, and returned with coffee and a plate of oatmeal cookies. I didn't wish to stay longer, but I did so out of courtesy to Eileen; she seemed a gentle, refined woman who had none of her husband's quirky manners.

As long as I was staying, I decided to test new waters. I said, "Did either of you watch the videotapes?"

"What?" Eileen said. Stevens stared at me over his mug of coffee. Both seemed baffled by my question.

"I found two tapes in Edward's apartment that weren't old movies," I said. "One was made at Baikonur—rockets going off and things like that—but the other was labeled 'Tallinn' and had Edward and Irina together on video."

"Doing what?" Stevens asked.

"Eating a meal," I said, "talking to each other casually."

"There's audio?"

"Yes."

"Where was the tape made?" Stevens asked pointedly. "And when?"

"I assume it was done at The Golden Swan, when they stayed there last winter. Looks like a homemade job."

"Why would they do it?" Eileen asked.

"They said it was for fun, and I believe them. They spoke some about Phobos, but most of what they said was fluff."

For a moment, neither responded. Stevens pushed his lower lip out, then folded it back into place.

I broke the pause. "I think the tape meant a lot to Edward, especially after he was separated from Irina. I'll wager he watched Irina every day."

Stevens came to life. "What, all they do is eat?"

"Not much more," I said. "Oh, Irina did leave and come back changed into a nightgown. Edward said some nice things to her at that part. Near the end, there's a quick tour of their bedroom."

"Christ," Stevens said. "The gall." He turned his face to the wall.

"Would you like to see it, Dr. Stevens?" I asked. "The tape?"

He didn't answer for a moment, then in a near whisper said, "Yes—maybe."

"Anyway, it made me feel better, especially after the letters," I said.

"Why do you say that?" Eileen said.

"Some of the letters weren't fun to read," I said, "but the video lifted me up."

Stevens's face turned back to mine, his eyes now softer and more pleading. Much as he seemed to want me to elaborate on the letters, he asked nothing. He would rely on Eileen to pursue me.

"I want to know what's in the letters," Eileen said firmly, her eyes fixed on me.

Through my jeans I tugged discreetly at the top of my prosthesis. "Irina was being mistreated in jail," I said, "maybe still is."

"Mistreated?" Eileen's eyebrows rode high.

"Beaten. With a rubber hose during interrogations."

Eileen exhaled a short, noisy blast of air. "Dammit!"

Stevens glared at me cruelly, as though it had been I who hurt Varonyev.

Eileen said, "Did Edward know this? Was this stuff in letters that came before he disappeared?"

"The most graphic letter was the last one Edward opened," I said. "It probably arrived here a few days before he died."

"The beatings—how do you think Irina is now?" Eileen asked.

The conversation had devolved to Eileen and myself, Stevens listening but otherwise not a factor.

I said, "Hard to know. Maybe lately she's a bit more disorganized."

"Disorganized?"

"Crazier, I guess, her thoughts. But see, it's been some time now since she's heard from Edward."

"Did Olga Berggolts say she'd tell Irina about Edward?"

"When she got back to Moscow, yes."

I set my coffee cup down and stood from my chair. "The County buried Edward today," I said. "We missed you."

Stevens stared into his lap. Eileen put a hand to her cheek, then pulled it back. She shook her head slowly. "We didn't know. Where?"

"Far South Side."

I started for the door, slipping into my jacket as I moved. Eileen walked next to me.

"We've heard about your Internal Affairs problem," she said, "on the news last night." We entered the foyer. "I hope it goes well for you. I believe in you."

I nodded, not knowing what to say.

"I mean that." She touched my elbow. "Everybody in this city isn't a shit, Nora."

A fine snow came off the lake and descended on Albion Avenue and Rogers Park. The flakes spun in the night, defying gravity, seeming too delicate and airy to land on the ground.

Back on Sheridan, I passed The 400 again, this time meeting a couple of dozen Loyola students leaving the first show. Walking in small, boisterous groups, they would return to dorms and apartments scattered throughout the neighborhood.

I had lasted two years as a Loyola student, quitting amidst a sea of poor grades. The reasons for my demise had always been perfectly clear to me: too many nights at The 400, and at Hamilton's beery saloon a few blocks south, and at the Chicago Stadium watching Black Hawks hockey while yelling my lungs out in the second balcony, the Polish grandstand.

At the time, I knew I was failing in school, but I was still too immature to see that I gained nothing by avoiding steady effort. I did eventually learn that lesson, thanks to the Chicago Police Department and mentors like Art, and Jack Flaherty before him. Now, suspended and disheartened and making little progress with the Phobos case, steady effort seemed to be the only decent card I held.

I turned off Sheridan onto Fargo. An east wind picked up, and it blew the soft flakes into my face like a cold, dry shower. My stump ached in its socket.

Walking the final block to my building, I considered my visit to the Stevenses. Varonyev's letters attached significance to the probe's pre-flight programs, but it was a problem that seemed beyond my understanding. Then there was the Avis and V-hawk thing. Stevens denied any knowledge of these people, yet they were regularly identified in Varonyev's letters. Somehow I felt that if I nailed down those two identities, I could better judge Robert Stevens's involvement in the Boyes murder. And finally, there was Jack Percot, the wildest card of all.

I needed Valery Kuzov's input.

I trudged up the back stairs to my apartment, as sure as ever that, beaten or not, Eugene Easter was innocent of murder. I sensed a break in the case would eventually come. I would find the key to the Boyes murder if I just stayed at it, stayed at it like a bulldog chewing at a leg.

In my nightgown, I sat on my bed and reviewed the phone logs Art had given me for Robert Stevens and Norman Bell. I used my bedside phone to check the numbers.

Bell's list of calls for the month prior to Boyes's murder was short and monotonous. Six calls were to the same number, a Rogers Park pizza place that delivered. The others were to six different numbers. Dialing each one in turn, I reached six North Side adult bookstores. Bell was nothing if not consistent.

The Stevenses' list was more complicated—dozens of calls. I was too tired to check through the list that night, so I concentrated only on calls outside the 312 area code. There were five.

Three of the calls were to the same number in the Houston area code, all placed after we had discovered Boyes's body. I dialed and an answering machine identified itself as the Benefits Department at Johnson Space Center. The message said that any pension and insurance questions could be answered by calling during business hours. Stevens's fresh interest in NASA's pension funds or insurance policies was a lead to be followed in daylight.

Stevens's other two long-distance calls were to the same number in Urbana, Illinois—Jack Percot country. One of the calls was made before Boyes's body was found and the other afterward.

I dialed the number. A gravelly voiced man said, "Lamp-lighter Inn." I heard loud music—piano and brass—in the background. The music sounded live.

"Is this Urbana, Illinois?" I said.

"That's right, lady." He spoke loud, above the music, but in the easy drawl of central Illinois.

"A motel?"

"Keep swingin'. You're two for two."

"The noise I hear—it doesn't sound like a motel."

"Front desk man's gone this time of night. The phone rings back here to the lounge. We're open till three. C'mon down."

"Not tonight. Can you put a call through to a room?"

"Try me."

"A Mr. Percot, or Dr. Percot. Is he registered?"

"Jack?" he said, and belly-laughed. "Sure. Been here a couple of weeks or more. Since his ol' lady kicked him out. You a friend?"

"A friend of a friend. Can you ring his room?"

"Not likely there this early. But I'll try."

The clamor of the music stopped when the call was put through. When no one answered after ten or fifteen rings, I hung up. I didn't think much of Robert Stevens's recall for his recent long-distance phone calls to friends.

I lay back and thought about Doris Souchak's whiz kids: Boyes, Stevens, Percot. Now two seemed to be back together again. While the third was newly covered with mounded dirt.

TWENTY-TWO

Tuesday morning meant Police Headquarters on South State.

I stood at the desk that guarded access to a large, open office redolent of cigarette smoke. Harsh fluorescents bathed the staff, who drifted from desk to desk with an utter lack of urgency. The receptionist said, "Callum? You say, Callum?"

This woman was a gum-chewer, young and stylishly under-nourished. Remarkably, she had found someone in the city willing to cut her hair to look like the skull-hugging cap of a Renaissance monk. A great pity, because her laughable hairdo overwhelmed her immaculate skin and light green eyes. I discreetly raised a hand to the side of my own head—I needed a touch to reassure myself that my own hair looked better. It did.

"That's right," I answered, "Callum. Lieutenant Nora."

"Spelled with a 'C' or a 'K' ?"

"'C.'"

She finished a second trip through her index cards. "I've got you as CR Number 5119."

"Anything from IA yet?"

"Nope."

"Nothing preliminary you can tell me?"

She smiled unexpectedly, then cracked her gum like a .22 pistol fired in the distance. "You got it, Lieutenant," she said, "yep, you got it." She could afford to be smart-assed with the disenfranchised.

I shrugged. "How about the State's Attorney's Office?"

"That wouldn't come to this file." She grabbed a printout and held it close to my face—my name and CR number were last on a list of several. "These are the active investigations, beat cops and detectives alike. You're at the bottom. Talk to your chief if you want things speeded up."

I transferred my weight to my prosthetic side. "Do you understand that my paychecks are to continue?"

"If your name is on this printout, your pay keeps comin'. Hey, you didn't think I would know that, did you?"

I said, "Just please make sure the checks aren't stopped. I need the money."

Another gum-snap. "Like, I'll swap you salaries, Lieutenant."

"Yes, well—"

"Of course, no one's shooting at me."

"Don't be so cocksure," I warned. Leaning toward her, I looked over her head, scanned the room behind her, then riveted my eyes to hers. I was close enough to her to smell hair rinse. "At the Academy we're taught to never expose our backsides to danger," I said. "You know, I'm not sure I'd like my location in this office if I were you. I don't envy you one bit."

She frowned, then glanced behind herself. I left her with her face twisted away from me.

In the Headquarters lobby, I walked to a pay phone to call Art. Before dropping in my quarter, I felt a tap on my shoulder. I turned and saw Karl Kramer in his Channel 6 ski jacket. He stood taller than me by a couple of inches. His thick hair had been tangled into ropes by the crazy Loop winds.

"Callum!" he said extravagantly. "And I thought you'd be vacationing today. Florida, maybe?"

"Buzz off."

I intended to use all my maturity, remembering what Art had said about pissing contests with skunks.

"Maybe you'd like to make a statement about your problems with Internal Affairs," Kramer said, with a wicked grin. "You know, a little public defense for yourself."

I blew air at him from my extended lower lip.

"I can have a crew here in five minutes. We still have a slot on the noon news."

"I'll argue my case in private, thanks."

"Don't underestimate the power of the media, Lieutenant."

I considered using my keys to put out his eyes. I slid my hands into my coat pockets.

He kept coming: "I've heard you may face more than suspension for shooting Cruzado. Maybe even a criminal charge. You know, the spics are very upset about this. In fact, I'm taking a crew into Cruzado's neighborhood this afternoon."

"You're as full of shit as a Christmas goose," I said.

"If your mother was here, she'd soap your mouth, Callum."

Seething, I turned to the telephone. When Kramer laughed out loud—it was his laugh that undid me—I made a reflexive half-turn toward him on my good right leg. He stopped laughing and said, "You friggin' dummy." He started away.

Lightning quick with my prosthetic leg, I pushed it between Kramer's striding legs. When I jerked it back, he stumbled. In an instant he was headed down, his face aimed at the floor, his torso already in mid-belly flop. He landed on the terrazzo with the thump of a watermelon.

"My God, Kramer!" I stooped down. "What happened?"

"You tripped me, goddammit!"

People walking by slowed but didn't stop. I poked my index finger at my chest. "Me? Impossible. I didn't feel a thing."

He pushed himself to the sitting position. A trickle of blood started from his nose and he swiped at it. "You tripped me with your left foot, you bitch."

"My left foot? That's it, Kramer—why I didn't feel anything. It's my fake leg! Remember? The one shot off a few years ago? The one you videotaped to show to the city? Here, look."

I hiked my skirt and extended my prosthesis. I rapped its hard plastic with my knuckles. "The leg's got no feeling. Gosh, I don't even know where the damn thing is at half the time."

He made it to his knees. I offered him no help. Starting away, I said cynically, "My leg's all form, Kramer, all form and no substance. Just like those piles of shit you whip up and call newscasts."

Outside, at a booth on State, I phoned Art and told him about Kramer. Art said don't waste energy on media piss-ants. He felt that since Peggy Miksis and I were the only things between Eugene Easter and death row, I'd be better off spending my free time on the Phobos case.

While this close to IIT, I tried to find Valery Kuzov. He didn't answer his office phone except by machine. IIT Administration told me Kuzov's class schedule; then I called his office back and put a message on his machine. I said that I needed to talk with him and would try to meet him after one of his Wednesday classes.

In sunshine, I walked aimlessly north on State Street. Melchior's sending me home had dismantled the structure of my days, and I wasn't nearly used to it. I turned east on Eleventh for no particular reason, then walked past the First District station house to South Wabash. Out of sheer indifference, I stopped at a hamburger joint near Congress.

The cigar smoke of a patron at the lunch counter defiled the air inside, but I shrugged it off and decided to stay. At a window booth, I slid onto an orange leatherette seat. I ordered a Polish sausage and a Coke.

While I waited, I thought about Jack Percot and the Boyes murder. Art had already discovered Percot's drunk-driving record, but I wanted information on his situation at the University of Illinois. I didn't wish to stir the university's suspicion—Percot could be scared off—so I hoped to find out whatever I could covertly.

On a hunch, I walked to a pay phone at the end of the lunch counter, and phoned Amanda Loomquist at Loyola. She said she had a good friend in Personnel at the Urbana campus. And yes, she might be able to find out something about Percot through unofficial channels. I told her I would stop by Loyola on my way home.

My Polish came and I started in on it. As usual at noontime, I thought about Meg. I pictured her pulling her sandwich and apple and brownie from her Chicago Bears lunch bucket that I had packed that morning. While I ate I felt the sun's warmth beat down on my cheeks.

• • •

Lake Shore Drive was a breeze, so I made Loyola by one o'clock.

"He's hanging by a thread," Amanda Loomquist said of Jack Percot.

We stood in the Crown Building lobby where I had bumped into her. The glass wall in front of me opened out to the heaving, deep azure lake; Loomquist's large physique was framed by the vista of lake behind her.

"His life?" I said. "What? His job?"

"Both."

"Who'd you talk to?" I asked.

"My friend in Personnel. Lucille." Loomquist anticipated my next question. "Don't worry, Lieutenant, Lucy can be trusted. My inquiry won't go beyond her."

Clearly enjoying her part in the investigation, Loomquist motioned for us to sit on a nearby couch. "Percot hired on last spring," she said. "When he was let go by NASA in April, he wrote a letter to his old professor in Urbana. The man is a campus patriarch and the person Percot worked under for his Ph.D."

"Did Percot apply to other places, like Loyola?"

"Not here, anyway." She pulled at the elegant silk scarf over her shoulders. Self-righteously, she said, "We never would have taken him if he had."

"Why?"

"He was a drunk! Lucy said it was explicitly mentioned in a letter from NASA. Percot's drinking had caused a huge rift with a senior NASA programmer on the Phobos project."

"That would be Boyes," I said. "Why'd the U of I ever bite?"

"There was a favor due Percot's professor by a dean of faculty." She dressed the word "favor" in a tone that begged me to ask her more.

I am usually put off by such verbal blackmail, but I was struggling with this investigation—I couldn't allow pride to stand in my way. "What sort of favor?" I asked.

"The most persuasive," she said, then tipped her head for emphasis. "A series of sexual indiscretions on the part of the dean that Lucy, Percot's professor, and just a few others were aware of. Indiscretions with an undergraduate who was still a minor."

"And the professor called in his chit. He keeps quiet if Percot is hired."

"Precisely."

"But things have fallen apart with Percot?"

"Yes," Loomquist said. "Here's the litany. Percot comes to class on occasion. The rest of the time he can be found in various Urbana taverns. And he's been evicted from his apartment for disorderly conduct. He's living in motels."

"Lucy know the latest one?"

"She said try the Lamplighter Inn."

"Percot have family?"

"A wife and three children.," she replied. "They left for Texas two weeks ago. As I said, he's hanging by a thread."

"Sounds like the U of I got stung."

"Boyes here, Percot there. We both got stung."

Though Loomquist's manner was inflated, she had done a fine job with Percot. I thanked her and she smiled broadly.

At home, I skittered around the apartment picking up odds and ends; then I scrubbed the bathroom. At three o'clock I picked up Meg from St. Ignatius. We squandered the rest of the afternoon by buying underwear and socks she didn't need. For supper, at Meg's request, we tried a Sheridan Road fried-chicken emporium where the air stank of grease spewing from an open kitchen.

We sat at a table near the windows, and we watched the sun slide into an envelope of western clouds rimmed in purple. We were back home by eight. Meg was kissed and in bed by eight-thirty.

The wind came up and howled against the windows. The living room was dark except for a feeble intrusion of light from the hallway lamp.

Once more the VCR sucked in the tape. The motor hummed gently, emitting a faint smell of burned plastic as it came up to speed. The television flickered. Usually I sat to watch, but this time I would stand close by.

The lovers, side by side, now lit in color in front of me. The script flowed on; they acted their set roles. I noticed I was becoming ever more aware of the wonderful lightness of Boyes's mood when he spoke of riding Voyager's shoulder to the outer planets. I put my fingers to the screen during the part I loved most, touching Varonyev when she appeared in her nightgown. "Be ready, Irina," I mouthed to her.

I moved my eyes to Boyes, watched him smile across the table at Varonyev. When he spoke to her, I didn't listen: I had heard it fifty times before. Instead, I studied the side of his skull that had been mercifully hidden from my vision as he lay swaddled in ice in the Lincoln Park swamp.

Enchanted, obsessed, I pushed the STOP button before the bedroom tour began. The machine thudded still, the screen doused in black. I walked to my bedroom and lay down on the bed.

A blocky, powerful woman who I assume is Torlova admits me to the cell. The door—rusted iron with only a peephole and a slot for a food tray—slams behind me. A single bulb housed in a cage on the ceiling lights the cell. The floor shines with dampness; a sheen of ice paints the walls. A wooden-plank bed is cantilevered from one wall. The air is still and acrid.

Head down, she sits in a corner, ten feet away. She looks up at me when she hears the door bolt slide home. Her expression is blank, her face gaunt except for the roundness in her squirrel-cheeks. Her hair is matted and stringy. A ragged dress and sweater adhere to her as they would a scarecrow.

"Hello," I say, my breath trailing vapor in front of me. "I am Nora. I know you."

Though nervous, I laud myself for making this visit: a corporal work of mercy.

She stares at me, says nothing.

"I've brought something," I say, and take chocolate from my pocket. I walk over and hand her the bar. She seems uninterested, but takes it anyway, then unwraps it and bites into it.

I lean against a wall: there is no chair for me. "I saw you on the video."

"At The Swan?" she asks, her voice as dry and cracked as dead leaves.

"Yes. I loved your nightgown."

"I don't remember it." She eats more chocolate.

"It has a scalloped neckline."

"Oh, yes, that one."

"I've read your letters," I say tentatively.

"You may do that. That would be all right with Edward."

"I was very moved."

Her small, dark eyes look into mine. "We have a wonderful love . . . a first love, actually. Can you tell that from the letters?"

"I thought so."

She finishes the chocolate. "Have you seen Edward's letters yet?"

"No," I say.

"Olga has them. I can't keep them." She stands and walks toward the bed. "Olga can show you, if you like."

She moves past me and I notice her dress is torn over her right flank. Her skin is discolored blue-black. At the bed, she reaches under and grabs a metal bucket.

"Wait," she says as she lifts her dress and squats. Urine colored cranberry spills from her crotch and pings into the bucket. When she's empty, she stands and dumps the urine into a floor drain. She places the bucket back under the bed, then returns to her stool in the corner.

The cold is now seeping into me. I begin shivering. "Have you been beaten recently?"

"Yesterday. The urine will clear tomorrow," she says. "Tell me about Edward."

"I haven't any news just yet." I feel myself shaking more noticeably.

"He's all right, though?"

I nod.

She says, "Have you ever had a love like that? Do you understand me?"

"I think so."

"You've had that experience?"

"No. Never."

"I'm sorry." She gazes toward the ceiling. *"The light never goes off in this room."*

"Not at night?"

She lowers her eyes. I hear the muffled sounds of two or three people tramping by in the corridor.

"I am waiting for more letters," she says, "but I am thankful he has Robert and Eileen and you as friends." Her tone seems brighter.

She stands and walks toward me, comes just in front of me. She puts her filthy open freezing hands on my cheeks and I jump—

I vaulted awake, my skin soaked with sweat. I shook my head to clear the confusion. With no covers or bedspread over me, my body felt as cold as Varonyev's hands. The dream had ended but I scanned the bedroom to make sure Varonyev wasn't in a corner. My clock said 2 A.M.

I crutched my way to Meg's bedroom. Her covers were snugged to her neck, her hair fanned across her cheek. I kissed her hair and left.

In the kitchen, I toasted English muffins and spread them thick with peanut butter. Outside, the lake was flat black and the wind no longer punished the windowpanes. I ate in silence at the table, my shoulder leaning against the wall, the image of Irina Varonyev still in my brain.

TWENTY-THREE

I waited for Valery Kuzov outside his Wednesday-morning Physics class. When the students finished dribbling out, Kuzov invited me into a lecture hall lit by ceiling lamps shaped like bowls. Blackout curtains concealed the windows.

We sat at two first-row desks, with an empty one between us. I regretted not sitting in the desk next to his—I wanted to show my alliance with him as I worked for Phobos information.

Kuzov looked professorial in his rose-colored crew-neck sweater and white lab coat. "What can I help you with?" he said.

The room was warm; I opened my coat. "Do you remember me telling you about Irina Varonyev's letters?"

"The ones Olga Berggolts carried out from Lefortova?"

I nodded. He recalled what I had told him during our phone conversation the afternoon Berggolts popped in at Area Six.

I said, "I've gone through Irina's letters, and I'd like some help."

"Of course."

I reviewed the same list of names that I had with Robert and Eileen Stevens. Kuzov's responses were similar, but more munificent. Like Stevens, he was genuinely puzzled by the Avis and V-hawk names. As to Jack Percot, Kuzov said, "A chronic drunkard. It's a shame to waste talent like that."

"Boyes felt the same as you?"

"Edward was furious for weeks in Tallinn." He smiled slightly. "Actually, I was surprised he didn't throw Percot off one of The Swan's balconies."

"Did you know Percot's teaching at the University of Illinois?"

"No."

Next, I switched to the issue of the probe's pre-flight programs. "Were these things removed from the Phobos I computers prior to liftoff?" I asked.

"As I remember, yes. Did Irina confirm?"

"One letter said Irina and Avis were to do it on order of a man named Tributs. When I spoke to Stevens, he also felt the programs needed removal."

"It's a complicated technical matter, Lieutenant. But it seems that everyone is in agreement. They should have been removed, and it sounds as if they were."

The desk was pressing hard against my back, so I was eager to leave. Before standing, I wanted corroboration of the Phobos II update Dan Halsey had given me. "I hear the second probe is in some trouble."

Kuzov's face tightened—a nerve had been jabbed. "A friend at Baikonur has written me that. The prospect is very distressing."

"I see."

"You know, we were so discouraged last August." He paused thoughtfully, his eyes focused beyond me. He said, "Losing Phobos I felt as though you were about to marry a beautiful girl, and then, after the first kiss, she was killed."

Lamentably, I managed only a shrug. To me, Phobos I was still a Russian junk pile lost in space, but my gesture was impolite.

Kuzov saw me and averted his eyes.

I waited at Ballistics' intake, the ivory-colored Formica work counter where evidence was logged into the lab. Finding John Dover meant a second consecutive morning at Headquarters, but at least I didn't have to endure the receptionist in Personnel. Across the counter from me, two seated clerks girded for their shift with coffee, doughnuts, and the *Sun-Times*.

Dover turned in from the hallway, the sharp scent of his aftershave surrounding him like a balloon of antisepsis. "Nora!"

he said, with a puckish smile. "And I thought Melchior had you on ice. How'd you get in here?"

I straightened extravagantly. "You don't support the common right of the accused to prepare her defense?"

Dover sported his standard garb: a paternal cardigan sweater with grimy cuffs, probably gunpowder; a sadly rumpled dress shirt; and a dead-dog of a tie. He was a genial man, a time warp from a fifties sitcom who spent his days soberly examining the firearms used in some of the city's most heinous crimes.

The clerks glanced up at us from their newsprint and glazed sugar, but their interest was only passing.

Dover leaned an elbow on the counter for support, then thrust his tongue out to lick down errant hairs in his mustache. His face was doughy with late middle age. He said, "I hear on the television how some guy in a dark stairway pulls a billy club on you. And then you go wacko!"

"Yeah, well—"

"Look," he waved his hand and interrupted, "don't worry." He stood upright. "Nora, I think that billy club must've looked a helluva lot like Ithaca's Mag-10 Roadblocker."

"What?"

"A 10-gauge shotgun—hear me, 10-gauge! The monster I fired here in the lab yesterday. The gun that killed somebody in an alley behind Oak Street the other day."

"Go again with me, John. I think I'm feeling better, but I'm not all with you yet. Go again for me."

Another slippery tongue-swipe at his mustache. "Righto," he said, then folded his arms over his belly and rocked slightly backward. "See, I'm betting that one very dumb son-of-a-bitch named Cruzado threatens you. You know what he's just done in the alley, so, naturally, in the dark hallway you figure his uplifted hand holds a Roadblocker, not a billy club." He reached out and patted me gently on my shoulder, as my father might have. "You don't have to convince me of a thing, Nora."

"You get a match from the alley?"

He backed against a wall, his arms now unwound at his sides and rather limp. "You can thank Art Campbell for this one."

"Huh?"

"Our intake register has Campbell logging in the Roadblocker last Friday night, 3 A.M. Now, there's an exceptional cop—that kind of respect for a piece of evidence. And then, holy shit! the next afternoon he brings in an ejected casing found buried under a foot of snow."

I said, "Dear Arthur—"

"Take that guy to Sox Park, will you? Third-base box — you owe him."

I wanted Dover back to center. "You did some firings with the gun Art brought in?"

"Yesterday," he said. "The ejection marks on the test casings were identical with the casing found in the alley. Firing-pin marks on the cartridge primers identical. Beautiful. The scope doesn't lie. No question about anything here, a perfect match. I hope it helps you."

Then, forgetting what Art had told me about the killer shotgun, I said, "Hey, John, one minute. How can Art find a casing in the alley when Cruzado shot and ran? Shotguns don't auto-eject, and Cruzado never would have stopped to empty his chamber."

"Easy," he said, his eyes twinkling. "Roadblocker is Ithaca's self-loader, their only shotgun that automatically dumps its spent casings from the receiver. Like I said, there's no question—the gun found in Cruzado's apartment was used to kill the guy in the alley. What was his name again?"

"Michael Furey."

"Yeah, Furey. I heard that on the news, too. Must've died quick, at least."

Furey's image in the morgue broke into my brain. Tentatively, I asked, "Roadblocker a big gun, John?"

"Big? Didn't I mention it's chambered for 10-gauge shells?" His face full of earnestness, he said, "You could ventilate an armored truck with it. It only holds three semi-automatic rounds, but by the time they've been fired, somebody's dead."

The case against Cruzado was nearly airtight: John Dover's ID on the shotgun, coupled with Paris's visual identification of

Cruzado, was enough proof that the man I chased and shot had killed Michael Furey four hours before. Whether or not Internal Affairs and the State's Attorney's Office would accept my plea of self-defense was a separate issue, but I was becoming more optimistic. If the investigators believed Cruzado was a murderer, they would likely concede the imminent danger I faced when I went to question him. I hoped they would judge my mistaken aggression to be justifiable.

I took the darkened Wacker Drive underground north out of the Loop. To my left, daylight broke through the network of mammoth girders that supported the street above. Beyond the rusted iron, the sun romped on the Chicago River, the angle of light uplifting the usually dirty green water to sparkling aquamarine, a new glory. I cracked my window a little and cold fresh air ran across my face.

I parked out back at Area Six and came in the garage entrance: there was no need to announce that I was still driving the Fury during my time in limbo. I found Art and Steve Schwartz in our office, Schwartz seated at my desk. His starched white shirt hugged his neck and thick shoulders. A cigarette smoked in an ashtray next to his ubiquitous can of Coke.

Art smiled when he saw me. Schwartz, looking the intruder at my desk, stood. "Here, Nora, use your chair."

"No, I'll stand. What you guys working on?"

Schwartz sat down and mashed out his cigarette. "We've got two male Latins found dead in a dumpster on Navy Pier," he said. "Side-by-side bullet holes in the backs of their heads. Gang work, execution-style."

"Suspects?"

"A couple of teen-age gangbangers out on a dare. Females, actually."

"My, aren't we making wonderful strides?" I smiled devilishly at Schwartz; I was still angry at him for Eugene Easter's arrest. "Who said it was a man's world, Steve?"

Art slapped his hand on his desktop to divert me from Schwartz. "What you been up to, girl?"

"I just saw John Dover. Cruzado's shotgun killed Michael Furey. No question."

"All right!" Art said, and beamed. "That helps."

"Thanks for getting the gun from Cruzado's apartment, partner, and the shells from the alley. I owe you. How about opening day at Sox Park?"

"Deal." He gestured to his chair. "Wanna sit?"

"No, thanks."

He lifted his feet to the desktop. "You doin' any good on Edward Boyes?"

"A little. I'm plugging." I didn't want to talk about the case with Schwartz in the room.

Schwartz sipped at his Coke, a colored dewdrop gathering on his lip. He said to me, "Art gave me your message about checking on Robert Stevens."

"You mean his claim to have reported Boyes as a missing person last November?"

Schwartz nodded. "Stevens didn't contact anyone, at least not at the Twenty-fourth District on Clark, or the Twentieth on Foster. Those'd be the nearest station houses to Rogers Park. He may have called somewhere else, but like I said the other day, we don't have a good cross-referencing from district to district."

"Can you can look further?" I said. "Beyond Stevens's neighborhood?"

"Sure, but it'll take time and a shitload of phone calls." Schwartz wiped his lips. "How bad you need it?"

"It's important. Stevens is definitely on the board, but I can't put him in his right place. If I'm sure that he lied about the Missing Persons report, then his stock goes deeper into the tank."

"Why don't you forget it anyway, Nora," Schwartz said apathetically. "The Boyes case is history."

"You're so sure you've got the right guy?" I unbuttoned my coat and took two steps closer to my desk.

Refusing to look at me, Schwartz squeezed the Coke can and it crinkled.

"You might be way off on this one, Steve," I said. "Eugene Easter may be stupid the way he got himself mixed up in it, but that's a mile away from killing Boyes."

Schwartz labored to repress a grin. "He confessed, Lieutenant."

I decided to push the hypothetical, to see if Schwartz gave
himself away. I said, "Oh, yeah, Frankie kicking Easter's testicles
like it was goddamned soccer practice, then—"

"Nora, hey!" Art interjected. "Wait up!"

"No, Art, not yet," I said sharply, never looking away from
Schwartz. "And then there's Melchior's phony promise of accidental homicide as plea bargain." In disdain I blew air noisily
through my puffed lips. "Tell me, Steve, who except Easter
would buy that accidental homicide shit? In a corpse with two
point-blank gunshots under a jawbone? As I said, Easter may be
stupid, but stupid isn't guilty."

"I repeat—Easter confessed," Schwartz said, "and he can't
take that back. As for alleged brutality, nobody's gonna believe a
guy with a sheet like Easter's. I mean, him over Sergeant
Luchinski? Over Chief Melchior?"

"Melchior," I mumbled, shaking my head in dismay, "my
Prince of Darkness. Jesus."

Art brought his feet to the floor. "Got all the vitriol out, girl?"
Sweat was popping out of his forehead.

I sighed deeply and backed up a step.

Schwartz pulled another cigarette from his shirt pocket. I
turned and started away. Behind me, I heard a match strike.
"Hey, Nora," Schwartz called, "maybe you should forget Easter
and Stevens and worry about why you put a hole through
Vincent Cruzado's spinal cord. You should know better than to
take revenge like that."

Spinning on my good foot, I glared back at him and hissed,
"Goddamn you, Steve! I hope your tongue turns into a friggin'
blister!"

That afternoon, sitting in my kitchen, I telephoned Doris
Souchak. I had called her the day before and asked if she could
look into the phone calls Robert Stevens had made to the
Benefits Department at the Johnson Space Center.

Souchak said, "The department manager verified that Boyes,

like all high-level NASA employees, had life insurance as a perk. A policy of a hundred and fifty thousand dollars, paid for by NASA."

I thought for a moment. "But, Doris, Boyes hadn't been with NASA for months before he was killed. Wasn't his policy defunct?"

"No," she said, "he paid the premiums himself after he left. Every NASA employee has that option available when they leave the agency."

"Okay, who's the beneficiary?" I asked.

"Robert Stevens, primary."

"Any secondary?"

"Eileen Stevens."

I had nothing planned until the Loyola software conference on Saturday. I was interested in hearing Robert Stevens's presentation, although I had no idea why.

The week tripped by. With nothing better to do, I spent mornings determined to enrich my ever-softening brain. I struggled like a dope through an annotated volume of e. e. cummings's poetry that my father had given me the year he died. It seemed mostly gibberish, but what I did understand was arresting. And I found myself transforming each of cummings's love poems into uncanny commentary on Boyes and Varonyev.

Afternoons meant lightening up. Between naps, I would lie on my living-room couch and listen to tapes of everything from reggae to opera. After I picked Meg up from school, we would cook together, then present our best efforts to Anna at supper— the food may have been borderline, but Anna was magnanimous. When Meg was in bed, I usually found myself with Varonyev's letters and the Tallinn video. More than ever, those written and visual images clenched me by the throat.

Usually in bed by ten, I slept like a stone, awakening the next morning with no recollections of ever dreaming. It surprised me that I slept so well, with my job and reputation as threatened as they were. I suppose it was the undercurrent of optimism that began with John Dover's identification of Cruzado's shotgun. And I had the feeling that things would begin to break right for me, that I would find a way to resolve the Boyes problem, and mine and Eugene Easter's along with it.

On Friday night, we had company: Anna, Paris and Neptune, and Peggy Miksis—her husband, Ted, was still in Arizona with the Cubs. We ordered from The Fish Keg, a tiny storefront place on Howard Street that sold deep-fried fish and shrimp for take-out. I cleared the center of the living-room floor and all of us, Anna included, kicked off our shoes and sat in a circle around greasy paper sacks bulging with fillets of lake perch and French fries. We ate and drank beer and soda till we couldn't hold any more. While we ate, Meg and Neptune took center stage, telling us stories about their classmates and teachers. We laughed so hard—even Paris joined in—that at times we couldn't swallow.

At nine, everyone but Peggy left. She stayed behind to help clean the living room; then we sat at the kitchen table to finish the last two bottles of beer. Meg, because it wasn't a school night, stayed up late to watch television.

Picking a fingernail against my bottle's wet paper label, I said, "Peggy, I heard a bad rumor that the Hispanic commnity is in uproar about my shooting Cruzado."

"Who said?"

"Karl Kramer, Channel 6."

"Nora, consider the source, will you? What you've shown about Cruzado puts you in good shape."

"Good." I swigged the beer. "How's it going with Eugene?"

"Help." She drank from her glass and a ring of white foam showed on her lips, then disappeared in an instant. "Help, I said."

"That bad?"

She bobbed her head. "I'm stuck with trying to incriminate the two women who will testify they saw Eugene load Boyes into a car Eugene says he never owned or drove. And then there's the question of whether or not to put Eugene on the stand—talk about a frightening possibility."

"Hang on. I hope to have something soon."

"Hurry."

"Do you believe Easter?" I asked.

"I have no instinctive feeling whatever. Get me some evidence, will you?"

When Peggy left, I tucked Meg in and went to bed myself, my head still a little dizzy from the beer. In the dark, I slid under the covers and curled into a ball, my knee tucked near my stomach. I formed the covers around the cold end of my stump, and fell asleep listening to sonorous horn-blowing coming from Friday-night traffic on Sheridan Road.

TWENTY-FOUR

Saturday morning on Lake Shore Drive was an amble: I was at Goethe Street by seven-thirty. I jockeyed the Fury onto rutted ice between two Mercedes on North State Parkway, then walked a block to the Ambassador West. The hotel and its sister across the street, the Ambassador East, occupied two corners in the tree-lined area of the Gold Coast given over to million-dollar brownstones and condominiums. Once, when we were first married, Richard had treated me to dinner at the Pump Room in the Ambassador West. It was summer and we sat at a table and looked out into the evening shadows that gathered under the ancient, green elms along Goethe. We were light-years from our economic universe, and intimidated enough that when a waiter dumped a glass of ice water on my lap, I acted as though I were grateful. But out of place as we were, we had a wonderful dinner, then went home and made love half the night: we were still riding the crest of young love.

A doorman in a long coat greeted me. I took the three steps up into a lobby smelling of leather and pipe smoke. A notice board announced the meeting:

Loyola University Computer Science Conference
Guild Room
Welcome to Chicago

The Guild Room was off the lobby to my right. A crowd,

mostly men but a few women, milled around the entrance where two tables held coffee urns and piled sweet rolls. I looked for Robert Stevens, but I found Dan Halsey. I walked over to where he was standing.

"You're out early," Halsey said. "And for this?"

"My flair for computers," I said jokingly.

"Promise not to leave with any secrets?"

"Promise."

The Guild Room was a spacious hall defined by yellow-painted walls and a maroon carpet. An immense, complicated chandelier spread out from the center of the ceiling like a cut-glass octopus. Its light blinked brightly in the crystal, then faded to dimness in the room's corners. A stage with a podium faced rows of upholstered straight-backed chairs divided into two sections by an aisle. Each chair held a pamphlet with the day's schedule. The air was dank and chilled.

I went directly for the inconspicuous last row where only one man was seated. When I came closer, I was surprised to see it was Valery Kuzov. Kuzov waved me next to him.

"I knew you had a love of pure science, Lieutenant," he said, in innocent banter.

I sat. "I'll stay close in case you have any software questions," I said.

Promptly at eight o'clock, a man walked to the microphone, and in a squeaky voice said he was Dr. Elias Simon, the chairman of Loyola's Computer Science department. Simon dumped a few tired jokes about Chicago's weather and politicians, then introduced the morning's first speaker, a heavy, bearded man from the Jet Propulsion Lab. In numbing monotone, the speaker launched his talk. I checked my program for his presentation's title: "Optical Character Recognition and Gray-Scale Scans." Kuzov or not, I was in for a long morning.

While Kuzov and people ahead of us took notes furiously, I flipped to the back page of my program and did my grocery list. Then I thought to look when Robert Stevens was scheduled: eleven o'clock, just after the morning coffee break. Stevens's topic, another scintillator: "Patterns of Error Messages in Decompensating Systems Software."

Two speakers later, I reached my limit and decamped for the lobby. Ahead of me I saw Robert Stevens walking with a man in an orange jacket. They stopped and spoke briefly, then the man in the orange jacket turned and left the hotel. Stevens came toward me. He looked uncharacteristically formal in a dark, beautifully tailored suit.

"Hello, Dr. Stevens," I said. His surprise at seeing me creased his face. His cheeks were pink with cold.

"Oh," he said, and stopped walking. A bellboy burdened with luggage trudged between us. "Why are you here, Lieutenant?"

"Remember Eileen telling me you'd be speaking? About the project you worked on with Boyes?"

"That's right."

"I thought I might be interested, seeing it was you and Boyes, but now I think I'm dead wrong. I've just listened to the first three papers. And I thought e. e. cummings was tough."

"What?"

"Nothing. I just can't imagine lasting for much more. I'm considering going for groceries."

"No, don't," he said earnestly. "There'll be more for you than software claptrap."

"Meaning?"

"Meaning, stick around. You'll find it worthwhile." He looked away. "See you," he said, then breezed past me toward the Guild Room.

The coffee break began and the Guild Room emptied. On the refreshment tables, trays of fresh fruit had replaced the sweet rolls, and cans of soda poked out of pots of crushed ice.

I loitered at the edge of the crowd, reading name tags as unobtrusively as I could, looking but not finding anybody from Varonyev's letters. I watched Halsey and Kuzov mingle easily with others. When the break ended, I returned to the Guild Room and my seat next to Kuzov. Halsey sat several rows ahead.

I perked up when I looked at the stage—the man in the orange jacket from the lobby was walking across it. Wearing a headset, he pointed and called to another man, who busied himself with something far right on the stage. I craned my neck and saw two other men hauling black bags through an offstage door. The bigger of them bumped along in a puffy Channel 6 jacket. It was Karl Kramer.

I squeezed my hand hard around the program I held, feeling my eyes pinch with annoyance. Stick around, Stevens had said. No shit.

Kramer spoke with the man in the headset, then, with the others, began assembling what I now recognized as video equipment. They worked for several minutes before Robert Stevens appeared to their left. He and the man in orange nodded to each other; then Stevens disappeared offstage.

"What's going on?" I whispered to Kuzov.

"Looks like local television," he said.

"Hard to imagine that error-message patterns in systems software sells on the evening news."

The men finished with their cameras, then sat near them on the stage floor. Looking confused, Dr. Simon approached the podium. He introduced Stevens as the next speaker, carefully noting that Edward Boyes was co-author of the paper Stevens would present.

The podium's small lamp illuminated the bottom half of Stevens's face, his eyes and forehead cut off in dimness. He cleared his throat nervously. His first sentences sounded choppy, but he gained confidence as he went on; his subject matter was the same sort of drivel I had listened to all morning. The only thing that kept me awake was watching the television crews, who waited patiently at the edge of the stage. Stevens spoke for thirty minutes.

When he'd finished, Stevens switched off the podium lamp and said, "Instead of using my allotted time for questions, I wish to say something in behalf of Edward Boyes." He drew in a deep, settling breath. "Many of you knew Boyes's genius from his NASA work, especially with Phobos, a project from which NASA, in its lunacy, terminated him a year ago. Nevertheless, he presented a brilliant paper at this meeting last November. But since then, he has become involved in an appalling tragedy."

A buzz lifted from the spectators; a few moved uncomfortably in their chairs. Stevens had their attention. When he glanced left, the men on the stage floor reached up and touched switches on their cameras. Red lights blinked on. Tapes rolled.

Stevens stiffened his spine. In a clear, bold voice, he said, "Edward Boyes was found murdered in a Chicago park two weeks ago."

Now all the audience noise and motion stopped. The room became so quiet I thought I heard crystal tinkling in the chandelier.

Stevens said, "You'll remember that last November, after Boyes read his paper, he made a special plea about a Russian programmer from the Phobos project."

A cameraman stood to check focus. I wanted to speak to Kuzov, but I couldn't turn my attention from Stevens. My thoughts bounced back to Amanda Loomquist and her story of Boyes's misbehavior at the last conference.

Stevens said, "Irina Varonyev, the programmer Boyes spoke to you about, is still being held, even tortured, in a Moscow prison. Varonyev's alleged offense is treason in the loss of Phobos I." With his shoulders straining forward, he shouted, "There is no truth to this charge! None!"

I jumped with his emphasis. Ahead of me I saw a head turn: a man in a maroon suit leaned and whispered to the woman next to him. I said to Kuzov, "What's going on?"

"Identical to what Boyes did, Lieutenant. I'm very surprised."

Stevens continued. "The errors that wrecked Phobos I were made by others who now blame Irina Varonyev." He lifted his hands like a preacher. "I ask you to protest the injustice of Varonyev's imprisonment. The scientific community needs to shout that publicly."

Murmurs were spreading through the audience. When a few more heads turned, I noticed embarrassment on their faces. Two people stood and walked toward the door. Stevens continued on, his voice ever louder as he detailed his plan for protest in the media. With every succeeding sentence, other people stood to leave, Halsey among them, his face angry.

Within minutes, Stevens was addressing less than half of the original crowd. Dr. Simon went to the podium and pulled the microphone in his direction. Resolutely, he said something about Stevens having gone beyond his allotted time. He nudged Stevens away from the podium. Head down, Stevens walked past the cameras and off the stage.

I looked at Kuzov. He said, "I don't know if he has a point, but this isn't the place. I am embarrassed for him."

I thought of Varonyev in jail. Confused and somehow frightened, I stood and walked briskly from the room and the hotel.

Meg and I went to bed so early that we both awoke before Sunday's dawn. We showered and dressed, sharing our bathroom and the mirror, neither interested in chatter.

Outside, in the dark, the air was cold and remarkably calm. At the end of Fargo, a streak of silver flared on the lake's horizon. I cranked the Fury; then we worked together to scrape thick whorls of frost from its windows. We drove on deserted streets to six-o'clock Mass at St. Gregory's on Paulina Street.

The church was brightly lit and smelled of heat from its clanging iron radiators. It was a beautiful church, with colorful plaster statues of Mary, Joseph, and the Saints gracing the walls and sanctuary. No liturgical storm troopers had yet made it to St. Greg's to rip out magnificent tradition in the name of Vatican reform.

A scatter of parishioners, mostly elderly loners, had also come through the dark that morning. Meg and I sat on the center aisle, and I noticed those in uniform around us: two young nurses one pew ahead, and a cop across the aisle. The priest, a tall, Lincolnesque man, moved effortlessly through the Mass's rituals, delivering a forceful sermon about the respect for our fellow men and women that was arduous but essential in urban living. Fully awake now, I listened intently.

By the time Mass had ended, a low eastern sun cheered the city. We drove south on Broadway, looking for a place for breakfast. At Foster, Meg, who had been noticeably quiet, said, "Mom, did you hear much of the guy's sermon?"

"I did. I liked it."

"You know the stuff about loving your neighbor?"

"Yes?"

She patted her mittens together. "I'm not sure about that."

"Why?"

"See, at recess the other day, Jennifer told me that Suzy said she hated my guts."

"Hated your guts?"

"Yeah, so why do I have to love Suzy?" She shrugged her shoulders in confusion. "I mean, when she says something that awful about me."

"I think Father meant you should love Suzy, but you don't have to like her."

"What? I don't get that."

"You will someday. I was pretty old before I understood it myself."

She was quiet, staring abstractly at the traffic. Then she turned to me, and with her face full of great seriousness, she said, "Mom, you know what?"

"What?"

"This last couple of minutes, I've been trying hard not to, but I really still do hate Suzy's guts."

"Meg, see—"

"That is, if she has any guts."

I bit my lip not to laugh out loud. I changed lanes without signaling, then rammed the Fury into passing gear.

TWENTY-FIVE

Winter in Chicago holds you captive for a time, and it's hard time, but never a lifer because you always reach a day when you stand up and convulse the ice that inters you, a day when you spit in Winter's face and say, "There, I made it, so bang me with another storm, go ahead, I don't care because nothing you do will last, and by income-tax day, I'll win back my lake and its beaches and my life will be in order again."

Monday's sun rose in a stark blue sky. Temperatures climbed. The sidewalks' filthy piled snow and the curbs' furrowed ice began wilting under the vigor of the light. The March thaw had begun: dirty water streamed toward the sewers, and the air smelled soft and balmy.

I parked on Belmont and walked to Donut Land in the strip mall just north of Area Six. I had half an hour. When Frankie Luchinski had called earlier that morning, he'd said Melchior wanted to see me at nine.

I stood at the counter and ordered coffee, a jelly bismark, and a chocolate doughnut. The girl who served me had ragged, bitten fingernails and stringy hair that cried for shampoo. I took my food to a seat and watched traffic climb up the long Western Avenue overpass. I polished off the bismark, but when I saw my server sneeze into a tray of doughnuts that she carried, I decided to forgo the chocolate one. The coffee would be enough.

At quarter of nine I walked over to Area Six. Frankie was

stone-faced at the lobby desk, none of his usual off-color sleaze in his hello.

"Wait," he said. "I'll tell Melchior you're here."

"What are you, Frankie, the palace guard?" I kidded. "You going to announce me to His Highness?"

"Shut up, Nora."

He walked down the hall into Melchior's office. In a moment, he was back in the corridor waving to me.

I stepped into Smilin' Ray's office, making sure I left the door open. I could be comfortable in this office when Art was with me, but never when I was alone with Melchior.

Melchior hunkered at his desk. He was dressed in a black V-neck sweater and police-issue tie, his stinking, wet-tipped cigar wedged in his right hand. Without looking up, he said, "Sit, Callum."

"No, thanks."

I didn't move because I didn't want him to think that I felt it was safe to be with him alone. Art called my attitude "hating long and hating hard." I never had the courage to tell Art, but he apparently didn't have a clue about the humiliation a woman feels over a physical assault like the one Melchior had made on me.

Melchior's walrus eyes lifted guiltily to my face: his memory was as acute as mine. "Have it your way," he said.

"Thank you."

"I tried to reach you last Saturday. I couldn't find you."

I folded my arms derisively. "I had a busy weekend."

He shifted in his chair. "It's been over a week and I still have no report from Internal Affairs."

"And the State's Attorney's Office?"

"Nothing," he said. "Most of these cases are resolved in a day or two. Yours is going on ten—that's a long time."

"So?"

"It makes me think the case could be headed for a grand jury."

I took a step closer to his desk. "Do IA and the State's Attorney know Cruzado was a murderer?" I asked. "And that his gun was ID'ed as the one that killed Michael Furey?"

"Yes. I sent out Dover's ballistics the end of last week."

Neither of us spoke for a half minute until I said, "I'm confused. You've impounded my gun, taken me off the street, and sent me home. Why drag me down here today to tell me there's no ruling yet?"

Melchior started the cigar toward his mouth, but stopped in mid-arc. "To help you, Callum," he said flatly, his eyes averted from me.

"What?"

"You heard me."

Stunned, I said nothing.

"The dice might be rolling against you," he said. "I wanted to tell—" He stopped, still not able to look at me, then, "I felt obliged to tell you . . . maybe you should get prepared."

I took a seat in the chair most distant from his desk. "Hold it, I'm not clear, I—"

"I'm talking about counsel, Callum."

"Oh."

"If a grand jury returns a bill of indictment, then you need representation. You should be thinking about that now." He stuck his cigar in his mouth. "You know anybody?"

"Um . . . actually, I've spoken to someone already."

"Who?"

"Peggy Miksis."

"Forget it —she's a public defender. You're not indigent."

"I know that. She said she'd help me off-hours."

"Shit, Callum, she's black!"

His remark, so typically Melchior, instantly returned him to predictability. His benevolent advice about counsel, that tiny olive branch, had both startled and discomforted me. Any semblance of a truce from his side demanded a response from mine, and, uncharitable as it sounds, I wasn't ready to grant an inch. Not to the man who had insulted me time after time in countless ways since the day I made detective. I felt my stubbornness pushing right up underneath my skin: *hating long and hating hard.*

I said, "If I need an attorney, it'll be Peggy. I couldn't do better."

• • •

I walked to my office. People I passed on the staircase and in the hall noticed me in an obligatory way before looking away. The most anybody could manage was an oblique "How are you, Nora?" and that came from Randy, the garage manager, who said it with his gaze focused somewhere beyond my shoulder.

The office was empty. I sat at my desk and dialed Peggy Miksis. "I've just talked with Melchior, Peg. He thinks the delay in my ruling means the grand jury may become involved."

"Could be, but maybe it's procedural. Let me check around and get back to you. Don't worry yet."

"Thanks."

"Sure. You getting anywhere on the Boyes thing?"

"I'm still at it. Don't give up on me, Peg."

I hung up and Art came into the office. He wore a Christmas-red tie knotted below his open collar.

"Hi," he said. He shut the door and walked past me, affectionately squeezing my shoulder with his powerful hand. He sat across from me at his desk. The sun highlighted the richness of his deep brown face. "You all right, girl?" he asked gently.

"No. Say, what's goin' on in this place? You're the only one that acts like I've ever worked here before. Have I got the pox or something?"

"It's Melchior. I mean, when he gets as far down on someone as he is on you, then everyone's scared."

I doodled idly with a fingertip on the desktop. I decided to forget about Melchior and mention what had been fermenting in the back of my brain for days. "I have a question, Art."

"Shoot."

"You've had over a week to think about it. So what's your take on what I did to Cruzado?"

He put a foot to the edge of his desk, slouched back in his chair, then set a forefinger on his temple. "Like I told you on May Street, if Cruzado's got a shotgun—and you felt that he did—then it's his ass or yours. I vote for yours every time."

"Revenge enter into it?" I asked. "Maybe me getting the guy for what he did to Paris?"

"Only you know that, Nora, and I'll bet it's so friggin' complicated that even you can't figure it out."

I nodded.

"Anyway, if a part of you didn't feel like avenging what happened to Paris, then you're not much of a friend, are you?"

Petulant, I didn't answer, but twisted my head away as though spurning his support.

"Look," he said forcefully, "once more and then we're finished with this goddamned thing! Got it?"

I looked back and stared straight into his black eyes.

He said, "You told me you thought Cruzado held a shotgun. Is that right?"

"Yep."

"So at that moment, in that stairwell, there was no question for you."

"None."

"Then case closed. Now go do something productive."

"Wait up," I said. "What Schwartz said the other day about me drilling Cruzado's spinal cord, that—"

"Fuck Schwartz!" Art hollered, and slapped his desktop. "Get your ulcers over something you can control, will you, Nora? Christ Almighty!"

My smile was feeble and joyless, but Art knew it told my thanks.

"Now," he said, "where are you on Boyes?"

I breathed deeply. "I was at the Loyola Computer Conference Saturday. Robert Stevens went wacko."

"I saw a clip on the news," Art said. "What do you think?"

"Maybe it was a front, maybe Stevens spoke out to someone specific in the audience. I dunno, I haven't talked to him about it yet."

We were quiet for a minute before Art said, "You have a list of names from Varonyev's letters, right?"

"Right."

"Ever think of taking that list and comparing it to the attendance lists for the two conferences? I mean, a speaker went bonkers for Varonyev at each conference."

"Go on."

"Maybe there's some connection between her letters and the attendance lists. Could you get the attendance lists?"

"Easy. Amanda Loomquist. Loyola."

"Go to it."

I pushed my chair away from the desk and walked to the door. As I reached for the knob, Art called, "Keep it shut a second."

I turned back. Art leaned forward onto his desk, both elbows spread widely for support. He said, "About the Cruzado thing . . . "

"Yeah?"

"Do you actually think I'd go out on the street with you if I didn't trust your judgment?"

I shrugged.

"We're partners, girl, meaning a part of each other—understand?"

"I do."

"Don't forget it."

I smiled. "I won't."

"You'll be back here to work—tomorrow, next week, six months, shit, I don't know when, but it doesn't matter. I'll be waiting."

"Thanks."

"Besides, Melchior has me paired with Schwartz, and I want his white ass off your desk chair. Hurry back, dammit."

Loyola. Amanda Loomquist's office.

Four floors beneath us, melting icepacks jostled each other in the cold, viscous-looking water. Loomquist might have been the mother lode of Brooks Brothers: a white cotton blouse with starched collar; a charcoal sweater-vest and straight skirt.

"I tell you, Lieutenant," she said while searching a sky rimmed with distant clouds, "the university is ready to jettison sponsorship of the whole software conference idea."

I played dumb. "Why?"

Spinning back to me, she scowled. "Because we aren't here to service faculty hell-bent on crackpot political agendas, or to provide grist for the city's scandal mills." She grinned in a self-mocking way. "And I thought Robert Stevens was one of his department's great assets."

"Any action planned against Stevens?" I said.

"Ask me tomorrow—a faculty board meets tomorrow evening. We will consider a sanction. This isn't simply an annoyance, Lieutenant."

"I understand."

I went on to ask her for lists of the conference attendees for the past two conferences. "That's easy to get," she said. "We dug them out already. Popular lists, I see."

"What do you mean?"

"Robert Stevens was here for the same thing last Friday."

"And you gave it to him?"

"It's not secret material," she said.

"Did he mention why he wanted it?"

"He said to tailor his presentation for Saturday."

"You didn't ask him for specifics?"

"I wasn't concerned."

Loomquist stepped to her desk and made a phone call. While Maria prepared the attendance records, Loomquist delivered a mean-spirited diatribe about the damage Boyes and Stevens had done to the university. She shook and bellowed, her cheeks reddening and her short brown hair dancing on end.

The Elizabeth Cudahy Library was Crown Hall's next-door neighbor. A large addition had been made to Cudahy since my student days, and its architecture was nothing to brag about. Tedium had won out over imagination, the boxy, utilitarian new building detracting mightily from the cathedral-like elegance of the original.

I sat at a table in the high-ceilinged reading room of the older section, and glanced around at the sprinkling of people, remembering time I had spent at these tables as a Loyola student. It always seemed like winter in those days, the lake gray and churning, the snow swooshing in the air outside. For every hour I spent studying, I would spend another with my head down on a book asleep.

Finished daydreaming, I opened Loomquist's two lists and compared them. The numbers were already totaled for me: 125 people attended the November meeting and 113 the one last

Saturday. Checking each list against the other, I realized that these were gatherings of regulars, names like Halsey and Kuzov and Stevens occurring on both lists. But there was no Jack Percot, and, not surprisingly, I found no record of either Avis or V-hawk attending the conferences. I'd have been shocked if I'd gained even a fragment of a make on either of those creatures.

TWENTY-SIX

On Tuesday morning I busied myself washing windows, and then, undaunted, I tackled the kitchen floor. While on my knee, I heard the radio newsman say, as indifferently as if giving weather, that a wire story had just been filed from Moscow. "Phobos II," he said, "the Russian space probe flying to a Martian moon, has been reported lost."

My hands stopped in mid-squeeze, my rag poised over the water bucket. I let loose and the rag dropped into the bucket's dirty water.

My brain circled. After a minute I climbed to a kitchen chair and the telephone. Valery Kuzov was not in his office. My next best choice would be Dan Halsey.

I was on Lake Shore Drive by noon. A stiff southern breeze washed the air clean and hustled the lake's surface into rough whitecaps.

At the Adler, I found Halsey seated at his desk, several open books piled in front of him. On a sideboard to his left, a television beamed an all-news station.

"Hello," I said.

Halsey glanced up, then invited me in. His face was pulled tight with seriousness. The blood of a shaving cut stained his shirt collar.

"I've just heard about Phobos II," I said.

"The Russians are frantic," he said glumly.

"What happened?"

He shrugged. "A friend from NASA called me an hour ago. No contact with the probe since last night."

"Didn't you tell me Phobos II was going to do a rocket burn or something?"

"Yes."

I said, "So nobody's heard overnight—big deal. They'll find it."

Halsey flicked his head and his ponytail bobbed. "Twelve hours of no contact is an eternity. The probe's lost, Nora."

I looked out to the chop on Burnham Harbor. Turning back to Halsey, I said vindictively, "Well, the Russkis can't charge Boyes and Varonyev with this one, can they?"

Halsey didn't respond.

"Any official excuse from the Russians?" I asked.

He gestured at the television. "I've been waiting for something on the news channel."

"Any predictions?"

"It's anybody's guess." Preoccupied, he fingered a page of his nearest book. With a halfhearted grin he said, "This makes the Phobos program a double bust. Can you imagine what this will cost someone over there?"

I walked Meg to school early Wednesday morning. A low sun reddened the sky, but to the west clouds had stacked themselves into menacing, high gray pillars. The sharp air on our skins told us the thaw was in peril.

After leaving Meg off, I returned by way of Glenwood Avenue. It was time to talk with Robert Stevens about his harangue at the Ambassador, and I was anxious to hear his reaction to the loss of Phobos II. With any luck, I would catch him before he left home for class. I was assuming he had weathered the Loomquist storm and, unlike me, was still fully employed.

I used the outside back stairs of the Stevens building, the way one friend calls on another in Rogers Park. At the first landing I saw Eileen Stevens in her kitchen, standing at the sink in her robe, her back to me. Jerry puttered on the floor. When I tapped on the window, Eileen jerked as though frightened, but recognized me when she turned. She motioned me in.

I leaned against the doorjamb. The air inside was warm, and thick with the smell of fried bacon. Jerry started crabbing toward me. "I'm sorry to bother you so early, Eileen. I wanted to talk with Dr. Stevens before he left for school."

"It's okay," she said, with blank eyes and a watery smile. She tightened the belt in her robe.

"I heard from Amanda Loomquist about the committee scheduled to meet last night," I said. "What did they decide?"

"I don't know."

"No resolution?"

She shook her head obscurely. When Jerry began climbing my prosthetic leg, I reached down and plucked him up, my forearm beneath his bottom. He took a slap at my face and I ducked.

Eileen stepped toward me. "Here, let me take him."

I waved her away. "No, no—he's just playing. It feels good to hold a pint-sized guy again."

"I was just thinking about calling you," she said.

"For what?"

She backed up to the support of the sink. "Robert didn't come home last night."

Surprised, I said, "Did he go to Loomquist's thing?"

"No, but Loomquist called here about nine to ask him over. She said the board was having trouble reaching a decision. They wanted to talk to Robert in person."

I put my hand into the hair that curled on the nape of Jerry's neck. "Have you slept, Eileen?"

"No," she answered softly.

"When did you last see Robert?"

"He left about seven. He had had a phone call from Jack Percot a couple of hours before, then another call a minute after the first. Do you know Jack?"

"I know of him."

"Anyway, Robert said he had to meet someone."

"Percot?" I asked.

"I don't know."

"Are you sure it was Percot who called?"

"I answered the phone," she said.

"They talk long?"

"Ten, fifteen minutes."

"You mentioned a second call—Percot again?"

"I don't know," she said. "Robert answered it. He only talked for a minute or two."

"When Robert left, did he give you a reason?"

Her sad, closed-lip smile showed her ignorance. "I should have asked him more, but he was on edge."

"Any idea where he was headed?"

"Out for dinner, he said, to East Lake View. Some place he didn't know. I didn't listen closely."

"A home or a restaurant?"

"Restaurant."

I put my nose into Jerry's cheek and whispered "Jesus" under my breath. I inhaled to slow myself, then said, "Eileen, The Helmand. Was the place Robert named The Helmand?"

"Yes." She perked up. "That's it."

I moved squirming Jerry from one arm to the other. "You ever been there?"

"Never heard of it."

"Did Robert ever talk of going there with Edward?"

Her lips pushed hard against each other, and a small tremor mounted itself in the muscle of her chin. She was done answering for now. I walked over and handed Jerry to her. "I'm going to do some checking," I said. "Will you be here?"

"Where would I go?"

I was back to Fargo and the Fury in ten minutes. I decided to cut the angle, so I took Clark Street southeast. I hadn't expected to find The Helmand open, but maybe Ahmad Durrani was doing the books, or someone was cleaning up in the kitchen. I rapped loudly on the door for a couple of minutes before giving up. I kicked the door once with my good right foot, then left.

In a phone booth across the street, an operator gave me The Helmand's number. The phone rang until a message machine said dinner would be served from five to ten o'clock, and that, beginning at noon, the phone would be answered for reservations. I left the booth knowing I would have to be content to wait.

I walked on broken sidewalk toward the Fury, wondering if it had been Robert Stevens who had eaten with Boyes at The Helmand the night of Boyes's death. And, if so, why had Stevens returned with somebody—maybe Percot—last night? It didn't figure; nothing figured.

When I got to the car and lifted the latch to the door, the idea blindsided me, making my knee so weak that I leaned on the car for a prop. When I finally fumbled my way onto my seat, I slammed the door shut and rested my head on the steering wheel.

I chased a squirrel around humps of snow and across the flattened, dormant grass. The once-frozen running path was now cold, stiff mud: nothing for the squirrel to negotiate, but rugged for me. The squirrel waited while I crossed, then he disappeared up an oak. Out of breath, I stopped a few yards from the chain-link fence that surrounded the swamp. When my breath came back, I walked to the fence gate and shoved it open. I entered, eyes down, unable to lift them from the near distance in front of me.

I moved along inside the fence, careful of the footing, a hand always on the wire for help. I walked until I saw an edge of blackened water immediately ahead. My fingers clutching the fence, I forced my eyes upward.

I knew Robert Stevens would be there. It had to be him: the dark, lumpy torso lying facedown in scrub; the legs so carelessly hidden in shallow water.

I unclamped myself from the fence and stepped closer. A hole gaped in the back of Stevens's skull. I grabbed his coat to roll him over, but he was too waterlogged and heavy. A wound of entry violated his forehead, and a second shot traversed his neck at ear level. The blood on his skin and light hair had dried blue-black.

I released him and he fell back down, his body splashing water as high as my knee. With my good leg tremulous and unable to do any more, I sat down at the edge of the swamp and hid my face in my hands. I saw Eileen at her sink and Jerry on the floor. I ached for them.

Alone with Stevens, I sat on the frigid ground, numb with confusion. Finally, using my hands on his back for push-off, I stood and walked back along the fence, out the gate, then toward the lake. At the lake's edge, I climbed up onto a boulder, swung my legs over, and sat facing the water that slapped the rocky shore.

I sat motionless for five or ten minutes, my thoughts disordered enough to be worthless. Then I pulled my .38 from my purse and capriciously fired a shot into the water. I felt the jolt, and listened to the air twang and the birds stop trilling. A short distance behind me I heard the tedious din of Lake Shore traffic. It was time to call Art at Area Six.

Art did as I asked: he discreetly took Alice Adams and Dennis Baker aside, asking them to gather their equipment and come with him. He kept Melchior, Schwartz, and Frankie out of the circle. Once on the road, he radioed his cousin at the East Chicago Avenue fire station to request an ambulance be sent to Lincoln Park, and without fanfare. From the Fury, I patched into Tommy Banks at the County morgue; Tommy would place Stevens's body with the unidentified, then ask Dr. Dorner to post it quickly.

Stifling the news of Stevens's murder might not prevent the next one, but at least it gave me a piece of quiet time to decide my next move. We were dealing with someone so deranged and atavistic as to dump dead bodies in the same hole, as an animal might dump excrement. The concealment would only last hours, perhaps a day at most, but it might help.

Pilgrims arrived thirty minutes after I called. While Dennis did the photography and Alice paced off grids, Art and I picked futilely through the brush for a weapon or empty cartridge casings. We discovered that Stevens wore no right shoe—it was found in the parking lot. His sock was torn and his heel was deeply abraded through its full thickness of skin. We decided he had probably been dragged dead from a car and thrown into the swamp.

After the paramedics loaded Stevens's remains into a body

bag, Art came over and rested his forearms on the top of the fence. Several feet away and across the fence from me, he faced the outbuildings and the lake beyond; I looked past leafless trees toward the Drive. The sun, nearly as high as it would be for the day, yielded little warmth, but the clouds and their threat had disappeared from the western sky.

While neither of us looked at the other, Art said, "Two killings, mirror images. We are dealing with one crazy fucker here—to say nothing about dumb."

"Yeah," I said sighing, "but we need to use this somehow."

"What?"

"The attraction the killer has for this shithole."

"You gonna camp out here and wait for the next body?"

I shook my head. "We should think of a way to run with this, Art."

He looked to me. "You need a hand-wash, girl."

I rubbed my palms together. "It's just mud from his coat."

"Any idea what happened?" he asked.

"Stevens went out last night and never came back home. His wife was scared. She told me this morning."

"You think he kept it in his pants all night?"

"It's nothing like that," I said.

"How'd you know to come here?"

I lifted my collar against a lake breeze running up my back. "Stevens left home to meet someone at The Helmand."

"The restaurant where Boyes went the night he died?"

"Yes. Boyes and Stevens both spouted off at the Ambassador, they both went to The Helmand. I had a hunch Stevens was here."

"Wasn't Eugene Easter this time, was it?" Art said.

We fell quiet, me watching the body bag and Art staring at the lake. Then I felt a sadness well up inside me and I coughed stupidly.

"You okay?" Art asked.

We looked down the fence at each other. "This one hurts, Art. I mean, goddamn, I was a mile off on this guy, thinking he killed Boyes."

"I'll go to his wife," he said. "Don't worry."

"No, I'm going." I started down the fence toward the parking lot.

"By the way," Art called, "who's next in the swamp? I mean, if someone's whacking everybody around here who knew anything about Phobos, who's left?"

"Only two that I know—Jack Percot and Valery Kuzov."

Noon.

I used the front entrance, and that was the element of ceremony that tipped her. Before Eileen Stevens heard a word drop from my lips, her face announced what she already knew: I would utter something that would take her life and break it forever into small pieces.

The images from that day would stick in my brain for months, then unpeel in front of me any night I battled sleep. I'm talking about the figure of Eileen's small bare feet on the carpet, her toes flexing at the edge of a step. And the robe and gown she had neglected to change out of, nightclothes that stood open and showed half-naked breasts she was too distracted to hide. And her mouth, first crimped in fear then cleaving and re-forming into a silent, round O when the news actually came from me. And her wail that rattled in the corners of the stairwell. And faithful Jerry, his arms wrapped tightly around one of his mother's calves and squeezing like hell.

Back home, I worked by telephone—Vincent Dorner first. I suspected Dorner would put Stevens's post-mortem ahead of other work that afternoon. A murder so similar to another just two weeks previous means, *Shake the dust off, partner*, because somebody who is acting on more than simple impulse is out there rampaging. It's a time when a single utterance of the word "serial" on an evening newscast can turn a city as inside out as a blouse on its way to the cleaners. And the fear of the citizenry is not lost on the police or its forensics staff: antennae go high up into the twilight.

"Dr. Dorner," I said, "Nora Callum here. Anything different about this second body from Lincoln Park?"

"We have something for Ballistics this time," he said, "a bullet found in the chest cage. Looks like a ricochet off his spine, after it split his heart."

"I never saw that, I—"

"Understandable, Callum. His heavy coat hid the entry wound."

"But he died by gunshot?"

"Any of the three shots would have killed him. I tell you, this killer has pitifully low esteem of the effects of his first salvos."

"Will you send the slug over to John Dover?"

"It went twenty minutes ago."

Peggy Miksis was next. Although baffled by Stevens's murder, she became heartened about Eugene Easter's case and decided she would petition the court for a delay in his trial. And even if it wasn't granted, she said, she now had a proposition to submit to a jury: when Robert Stevens was killed in a way almost identical to the killing of Edward Boyes, Eugene was finally in the right place at the right time—Twenty-sixth and California, Division 1 of the County Jail.

I sat at the kitchen table. Feeling pushed but knowing nothing better to do, I spent two hours rereading Varonyev's letters. I plowed line by line through each, grappling for a hidden linchpin to the murders.

No new insights burst into my brain, but I did notice a minor item related to the Avis/V-hawk confusion. Of the sixty-five letters, never once did Varonyev mention both the Avis and V-hawk names in the same letter. If one name appeared, the other never did.

And another oddity: when Varonyev mentioned Avis, he consistently wrote, "my Avis," and for V-hawk, "your V-hawk." This possessive treatment—Avis reserved for Varonyev, and V-hawk for Boyes—was puzzling because it was obvious that both Boyes and Varonyev knew both Avis and V-hawk.

Finally, I rooted in my dictionary. I found "Avis" defined as a female given name derived from the Latin word for "bird," although it was obvious from the letters that Avis was a male.

Feeling desperate, I phoned Art.

"How long you think this Stevens thing is gonna stay quiet?" he said.

"I dunno."

"Ray's gonna fry my ass when he finds out."

"Please, just take it till Melchior goes home from the station," I said. "That'll buy me the night."

"What's next?"

"I'm leaving for Urbana, to find Jack Percot."

"Why in hell—"

"Because I can't fit him in anywhere," I said, "and somehow he's involved. He phoned Stevens a couple of hours before Stevens left his apartment last night."

"Anything I can do?" Art asked.

"It would save me time if you could call the Urbana police to locate Percot. I'd have them try the university, or a motel called the Lamplighter."

"It's done," he said. "You'll call me?"

"From the highway, when I'm near Urbana."

TWENTY-SEVEN

I delivered Meg to Anna's where she would stay the night. With Varonyev's letters in my purse, I drove I-57 south into corn and soybean country. The moon rose like an ivory ball over empty winter fields. Farmhouses, their windows lit yellow, appeared sporadically along the roadside.

I drove thinking of Jack Percot, wondering why he had called Robert Stevens the afternoon of Stevens's death. I didn't have time to soft-shoe around Percot as I had with Stevens and Kuzov—the media hold on Stevens's murder was too flimsy. If there was any clue to the Lincoln Park murders in Varonyev's letters, I hoped Percot might tip it, even if he was the killer.

Thirty miles north of Urbana, I stopped at a gas station and phoned Art.

"Percot's at the Lamplighter," Art said, "on a side road off Route 45." He gave me detailed directions. "An Urbana cop will meet you there."

"Percot hard to find?"

"No, first place they tried."

"Things still quiet on the home front?"

"All I do is listen to newscasts," he said. "Not a peep on Stevens so far."

"Good. Where will you be?"

"Home. Call me. And, Nora, don't do anything dumb-ass."

The Lamplighter's gaudy neon sign blazed scarlet in the intense blackness of the rural night sky. The building was a one-story L-shaped affair made of pink stucco illuminated by a series of mercury lamps on the roof. An office and a bar occupied the crotch of the building.

I pulled into a gravel drive pocked with puddles. A man sat in a police car parked halfway down one side of the L. I stopped the Fury, got out, and walked over.

."Lieutenant Nora Callum," I said to the officer, who rolled down his window. Young, and square-shouldered as a bull, he wore a crew cut done so short that his pink scalp showed through.

"My pleasure." he said. "I'm Carl Badgely." He pointed straight ahead of his car. "Jack's there, in Room 103."

"You know him?"

"He's a regular with us lately—DUIs and disorderlies. And we had to enforce an eviction notice on him recently. That's when he moved in here."

"Family?"

"Wife and three kids. They skipped for Texas when the family was booted from their apartment."

"What's he been doing the past couple of days?"

"Mickey, the bartender in the lounge, said Jack came in last night about midnight and—"

"No, before that," I interrupted. "Where was he?"

"Been holed up here for several days, according to Mick. Last night, he drank till closing time at three, then Mick lugged him back to his room."

"He's not been to the university?"

"Hasn't made a class in a week," Badgely replied. "His job's in deep shit."

"How long you been here, Carl?"

His leather jacket squeaked as he put his forearm on the window frame. "When your partner called from Chicago, I came here first. Couple of hours ago."

"Sitting in the car?"

"Stinks too bad to wait in there," he said. "Don't worry, there's no other way out—no rear window."

"You search him?"

"He's clean. I went through the room—if he has a gun, it's not in there."

"He own a car?"

He twisted left and pointed. "Behind you."

I turned and saw a station wagon fifty feet away. A long, deep gash in the passenger-side doors led to a smashed rear fender.

"Jack's machine needs body work," Badgely chuckled. "He's lucky when he makes it out of the lot in one piece."

"Thanks for everything," I said. "I'm going in."

"You armed, Lieutenant?"

"I have a .38 in my purse."

"Want me to come with you?"

"No."

"Should I stay or leave?"

"Your call."

"I'll wait. It's a pretty night."

Percot failed to answer four knocks. I pushed on the door and it opened easily. The stench—booze, dirty socks, and cigarettes— hit me; it was like walking into a flophouse on a sweltering summer day. A television spilling light but no sound dimly lit the room.

Percot lay supine on a bed pushed into a corner. His eyes were closed and his long legs spread. He wore a stained undershirt, and jeans opened from the waist to halfway down his fly. His bare white feet stuck out of his jeans like a dead man's. An aquiline nose anchored a square, unshaven face, and his hair was as matted as a stray dog's at the end of winter. But hosed-down and razored, he would easily have been the most handsome of the three NASA whiz kids.

I shut the door and Percot roused. Hoisting himself onto an elbow, he squinted at me, then took a hand across his eyes. "Who's it?"

"My name's Nora Callum."

"Fine," he said, scowling, "and I'm Christmas Past." He flopped back down. "I'm not interested and I couldn't afford you if I were." He zipped up his pants. "See the door behind you? Come back when you can't stay so long."

"I'm a police lieutenant from Chicago."

"Hot shit." He elevated again, this time reaching for a bottle on his nightstand. He poured an inch of Wild Turkey into a tumbler, then lit a cigarette. "I don't go to Chicago—too polluted. My body's a temple. See?" He chugged the glass empty, then coughed. "Want a drink?"

"We need to talk, Mr. Percot." I pointed to a battered chair next to me. "Do you mind?"

"Go ahead."

I said, "Your friend has been killed."

"Long drive for old news, lady." He poured more whiskey but let it set. He took a bite from a partially eaten hamburger next to his tumbler. "Ed's dead all winter."

"It's not Boyes. It's Robert Stevens."

He grinned while chewing. "You're a lovely broad, but you're mixed up on the names. I phoned Robert last night."

"Eileen told me. Robert was killed a few hours after talking to you."

His lips drew back in surprise, exposing particles of food. "What?"

"Where were you last evening, after the call?" I asked. "Meeting Robert?"

He sipped his drink to wash his mouth. "You assume I could have made the drive from here to Chicago and back."

"That's right."

"Lady, I couldn't have read the friggin' road signs. Besides, my travel agent hasn't booked me off the property here for days. I go to the bar, and Mickey helps me back. I take a piss when I can stand up. I call out for food once a day. Say, how 'bout we have a pizza delivered? I binge best on pepperoni."

"Why'd you call Stevens yesterday?" I said.

"To shoot the shit. . . to learn the price of bananas. Take your pick."

"Percot, you're a suspect in two murders. I suggest you become more serious."

Pale and gaunt, he looked like a man sunlight hadn't touched for months. It was hard to imagine he had the wherewithal to make it even into Urbana, let alone to Chicago to commit murder, and then back again.

Sitting now, he set his broken hamburger into his lap and

drew deeply on a cigarette. I reached out and opened the door slightly for air.

"Robert and I talked about the loss of Phobos II," he said cautiously. "I heard about it on the TV in the lounge." He drained his drink and poured another. "Tell me about Robert's death."

I did, slowly, and he took it in. When I finished, he crushed out the cigarette, which was nearly burning his fingers. I said, "Do you know who killed Robert, or Edward?"

He shook his head.

"No idea?" I said.

"No!"

"Then what about Phobos II?" I said. "Why was it lost?"

"I'm too far away from the project to guess. Probably another Russki fuck-up."

"Any ideas on Phobos I?" I asked.

"The pre-flights. No question."

"You mean the programs on the probe's computers?"

"That's right, the programs—look, what's your name again?"

"Nora Callum."

"It's technical, Nora Callum, very complicated. I could spend the whole night and another bottle of Turkey explaining, and you still wouldn't get it. Believe me."

I didn't doubt that he was right, nor did I feel it mattered to the case. I switched gears: "Do you remember Irina Varonyev?"

A kindly smile. "Sure, a peach." He raised his glass into the air as in celebration. "We all had a riot in Tallinn." His face again going somber, he said, "Robert told me she's in the lockup."

"Do you know why?"

"Because she wouldn't say 'shit' if she had a mouthful."

"I don't get you."

"Phobos I wasn't lost because of Irina," he said.

"Then who?"

"It's anybody's guess."

"I've brought some letters Irina wrote to Edward. Maybe there's help there."

I pulled the couple of dozen letters I thought most important from my purse. I took them over to Percot, then returned to my

chair. He started in on them with an earnestness I hadn't expected. My mind reviewed the names I'd memorized from my incessant readings.

As Percot flipped pages, it struck me, smacked me in the forehead like a comet hurtling out of the deep Urbana night. My
insight: before meeting Percot, I knew one Phobos worker, only
one, and that man was never, not ever, not even goddamned
once, mentioned in any of Varonyev's letters. And he had been
sticking up in front of me all the time.

Fingers to my lips, I waited for Percot.

Finished, Percot tossed the letters into a messy pile. "What you
wanna know?" He belched a wet one, lit another cigarette, then
settled on his side. Smoke curled into his eyes.

"Do you recognize the people referred to by Irina?" I asked.

He nodded. "I worked with them every day in Tallinn."

"Is everyone of importance to the project mentioned?"

He hesitated, then, "I dunno."

"One's missing," I said, bearing down. "Isn't that right, Jack?"

Eyes closed, Percot stayed mute, his cigarette tip glowing in
dimness.

"Jack?" I hollered, shoving forward in the chair, my hands
rolled into tight fists. "Answer me, goddammit!"

Unfazed, Percot dragged reflectively on his cigarette. Finally,
when he opened his eyes to me, he said, "One's missing. Yep."

"What's his name, Jack?"

"You tell me, you're such a—"

"It's Valery Kuzov," I snapped, the name searing my throat.

"Hot shit, lady. You're a very hot-shit Chicago dickhead." He
reached to scratch the top of his foot. "Congrats."

I dropped my head back onto the smelly chairback. My thinking was mayhem. When the spinning slowed, I said, "Who are
these Avis and V-hawk people?"

"No idea."

"The Avis and V-hawk names are all through those letters," I
said.

"No shit." Another deep draw on his cigarette, then a noisy swallow of whiskey, this time from the bottle.

I looked blankly at the TV. "Do you know what Avis means?"

"Sure. A blond honey sings, 'Rent our cars—we try harder.'" He giggled stupidly.

"It means bird," I said. "Think about it—bird and V-hawk."

"Great. Big deal."

I sat higher in my chair. Now I thought out loud, talking to myself by bouncing words off Percot. "Do you think Avis and V-hawk are the same person?" I said.

He looked at me nonplussed.

"Wait, Jack, I don't mean Avis and V-hawk. I mean, *my* Avis and *your* V-hawk."

"You need a drink, Lieutenant." He slumped back on the bed. "You're nutzo."

I stood. "Was Valery Kuzov important to Phobos?"

"Oh, yeah, ol' Val was a big player." He drew his mouth down at its corners. "But he struck out, like Casey at the Bat. Then Ed goes and saves his arrogant ass."

"What? Explain."

"No. It's a load of computer shit. Really, I'm too fuckin' drunk to even start."

Suddenly, I cared nothing for Phobos details. I needed to get back to Chicago.

I thanked Percot; he barely acknowledged. When I opened the door, he called, "Hey, lady copper."

I turned back.

"Do you know how good we three once were?" Percot asked, his raw-boned face toward me, the first fire I had seen now lighting his eyes.

"What?"

"Ed and Robert and me, like goddamned wizards. Like brothers."

"No, I don't know."

He said, "I mean, there was a time—the Viking and Voyager projects—there was a time by Christ when we three had NASA/Software squeezed tight by the balls." He cupped his hands. A faint smile came and went evanescently. "Now those two fuckers are dead . . . and I might as well be."

• • •

I hustled the Fury along on I-57, through the black, frozen night,
cutting northeast across the Illinois prairie from Urbana to
Chicago. Southbound headlights streamed by in procession; I
blinked continually to ease the burning in my eyes.

Near Kankakee, I pulled off and phoned Art. I convinced him
that what I had found out from Jack Percot justified a meeting. I
didn't have to argue about waiting till morning: Art knew I
wouldn't drag him from home for nothing.

TWENTY-EIGHT

"Sort of a Boyes-Stevens-Percot triangle, isn't it?" Art said, eyebrows lifted. We sat over coffee and warm pie in a booth at the Oak Tree Grill. Outside, in this kind of weather, Rush Street had quieted. It was midnight.

He continued: "They trained together, they did NASA together, and now they're dying together. You get a gold star for persistence, girl. And off-the-street yet!"

I smiled weakly. "Cut the crap, Art. It's late."

He pulled at the throat of his heavy turtleneck, so white against his skin. "Where'd you talk to Percot?"

"In a sleaze-bag motel room, slash, ashtray that rents by the hour. I sat on a chair that stunk like a goddamned vermin infestation held it together. Percot lounged—I use the term loosely—on the bed, half in the bag."

"You're trusting a drunk?"

"Not just a drunk," I said, "but a destitute drunk. Look, he's stinking and unshaven, and dressed in filthy jeans and a dirty undershirt. The guy's too far down to bother with lying. It takes energy to lie and to murder—he doesn't have any left."

Art sipped coffee from a mug. "Repeat the Avis stuff for me. You lost me on the phone." He forked a piece of pie into his mouth.

It was the notion that had struck me while I sat in Percot's motel. I used the drive time from Urbana to Kankakee, where I stopped to phone Art, to mold my conception from mush into particulars.

Now I lifted my jaw slightly, ready to spiel what I had

rehearsed. I said, "We've got either Avis or V-hawk mentioned in fully half of Varonyev's letters, way more than anybody else. Right?"

"Right."

"And yet no one who knew Phobos—and I mean, Stevens, Percot, or Kuzov—no one admits ever hearing these two names before. People recognize every other name in the letters, but not Avis and V-hawk. Why the hell is this?"

Art, his chin in his hand, shook his head. "Keep goin'."

I pressed my elbows to the tabletop and slid forward in my seat. Suddenly, fatigue washed out of me in a wave, and I felt the best I had in days. "Okay, flip side," I said. "Consider one Valery Kuzov."

"I'm considering," Art mouthed.

"Here's Valery," I said, "a man who everyone knows is a fixture at Phobos. He works with Varonyev in Tallinn and on station at Baikonur. Here's an important, everyday Phobos guy, and somehow, some-goddamn-how, Varonyev never writes his name once in sixty-five letters! Why? When a dozen other less important people are mentioned regularly?"

"Tell me, Nora Joyce."

"Because Varonyev *does* in fact write about him—but she uses other names."

"Avis and V-hawk?"

"Gotta be, Arthur!"

He scratched his head in polite skepticism.

I said, "Avis and V-hawk are nicknames for Kuzov, belittling names that Boyes and Varonyev dreamed up while together in Tallinn."

"What's the sense of the names?" he asked.

I tugged at my prosthesis under the table. "You ever see Kuzov?"

"No."

"It goes back to his face," I said. "In profile, Kuzov's nose is striking—big and hooked. Hawklike. So . . . V-Hawk means Valery Hawk."

Art rolled his head lazily to one side. "You're stretching me, girl. What about Avis?"

"Avis is the Latin word for bird."

"Bird—hawk?" He smiled. "I love your wacky consistency."

"Here's more. Varonyev never writes the name Avis without saying 'my Avis,' and she never uses V-hawk unless it's 'your V-hawk.' I think Boyes and Varonyev each had their pet name for Kuzov."

"Anyone in on the tease but them?"

"I don't think so," I said, "not even Stevens."

Art mulled things over, his eyes flicking around the ceiling, his fingers pulling his turtleneck to loosen it. Then he said, "If we plug Kuzov into the letters every time we see Avis and V-hawk, do you think Varonyev is sending us a whole new message?"

"Yes, like how pivotal Kuzov was in the Phobos I botch," I said. "But there's a twist here. Percot claimed that Kuzov made mistakes with Phobos I, but he also said Boyes somehow saved Kuzov's ass."

"Making Kuzov grateful to Boyes?" Art said.

"Very. As though Kuzov wouldn't be a man in the mood for murder. And remember, he was busy giving exams the evening Boyes died. It's a solid alibi. I checked it out myself at IIT."

Art said, "But do you see any other cards on the table except Kuzov's?"

"No. Not with Stevens dead and Percot a chronic drunk."

"What about motive?"

Discouraged, I said, "I have no idea."

A car honked on Oak Street and Art turned. He looked back at me and said, "You tired?"

"Shit, yes."

He drank more coffee. "You tell Percot that you found Stevens dead today?"

"I had to—and it shocked the hell out of him."

"Probably figures he's next in line for dinner at The Helmand."

I said, "Maybe it's worry that's turned him so strong to Wild Turkey. For courage."

Art finished his pie and set his fork across his plate. "You're not eating."

"I forgot how sour the gooseberry is—makes my lips pucker."

"Nora," he said soberly, "what's next?"

"To try and break the alibi," I said. "We need to go to IIT tomorrow, early. There's no way we'll get through another twenty-four hours before the Stevens thing breaks apart. They're probably burying him tomorrow or the day after."

Art said, "Call me at Area Six, first thing in the morning."

Art and I parted at 2 A.M. The Drive was empty and I was home in twenty minutes. For a while I stared out my bedroom window at the black lake, thinking mostly of Eileen Stevens's torment. When no solace erupted from the pitch, I lay on my bed, still in my clothes. I would sleep fitfully for three hours.

Up at five-thirty, I showered, then dried off in the chill of my bedroom. I refitted my thigh into my prosthesis. After dressing in jeans and a sweatshirt, I walked up to Anna's to fetch Meg. I could take Meg to school, but I asked Anna if she would pick her up afterwards—I wasn't sure where'd I'd be at 3 P.M.

Back downstairs, I cooked breakfast while Meg showered. When she was dressed, she fed like a hungry tiger, clearing her plate of waffles and bacon in minutes. She poised a final forkful near her teeth and asked, "Mom, why the special breakfast?"

"Because you're a good kiddo." I was glad she was enjoying the food after I had pawned her off on Anna the night before.

She shook her head of still-damp hair tied into pigtails. "No, the truth."

"That is the truth, Meg. I have the time. Besides, you need a decent breakfast to fight the weather."

"Yeah," she said while chewing. "Probably, you mean like at recess."

"What's with recess?"

"Sister makes us go outside for a half hour, no matter even if it's the coldest."

"Exercise is good for you."

"We don't exercise, Mom, we sit on the blacktop. The boys play really stupid games, but the girls—most of us just sit there and freeze."

"So run around. Warm up. It won't kill you."

"It might," she said, tipping her head slightly, the gesture she always made when she brewed farce. "You and Sister don't know what the cold might do. You can't be sure. You can't prove it won't kill a kid, Mom. Watch the newspapers for that, will you? Huh?"

I giggled at her joke. Nervous about my trip to IIT, I was glad for the distraction of Meg's kidding.

While doing the breakfast dishes, I reflected on what it was like to chase murderers. The surprise, I mean, of realizing how close they've actually been: same city, sometimes same neighborhood, yet as undiscovered as one of those crazy galaxies hiding in a distant corner of the universe. But then one day their season ends, and they explode in all their guilt, and you can't imagine they were under your nose all the time.

I dropped Meg off at school before eight and was back home in ten minutes. I sat at the kitchen table and dialed Art at Area Six, but he was gone. I called around till I finally found him at the Eighteenth District. Before I had a chance to say more than "Hi," he barked. "Relax, I'm still going to IIT."

"Hey, easy," I said. "Inhale."

"Consider yourself lucky you're suspended."

"What are you doing at the Eighteenth?"

Art said, "The story broke at Area Six on the Stevens murder. Melchior knows. Jimmy O'Donnell knows."

"Shit. The media got it?"

"Not yet, but we'll never get through more than the next few hours."

I tried again: "So what are you doing at the Eighteenth?"

"Hiding out."

"From Melchior?" I asked.

"Brilliant."

"All right," I said, "then here's more astuteness. I'll bet that the celebrated Alderman O'Donnell has already been spotted at Area Six with flames shooting out of his ass. A walking, talking, anal solar flare."

"You were a college girl after all, weren't you?" Art snarled.

"And, thanks to O'Donnell, Melchior is now all over you. All over you because the moneyed lakefront will soon discover that the Lincoln Park killer is still loose. And worse, his sap is running again. All that with Eugene Easter now out of the picture and Area Six groping in the dark."

Art said, "Actually, Ray invited me into his office this morning before I left Six. A private conference, we had. Lovely—the silver tea service, the delicate pastries, a string quartet playing on the radio. Yes, very lovely."

"Do I hang up now, or do we talk? Your call, Art."

A long sigh, then, quietly, he mumbled, "Sorry, girl . . . here's the truth: I stand in a dark corner farthest from Melchior's desk. I remain silent—*silencio*, complete—while the no-good son-of-a-bitch raves in monologue. He threatens me, he humiliates me. Then you call, and I offend you. Nice touch, eh?"

"Melchior is driven by a black heart, Art. I learned that a long time and one leg ago. I try not to let it eat at me, because when I do, then I'm double-fucked. Once by what he actually does to me, and again by what I do to myself, by how I beat up my own coronaries with rage."

"You're right." After a pause, he said, "Did you sleep?"

"A little. Enough."

"Say, I think we're ready to break this case wide apart. How do you feel, Nora?"

"Good. I'm riding on a river of adrenaline."

When I hung up from Art, my watch said eight-ten. Moving briskly, I redid my prosthesis with a clean stump sock, then put on black slacks and a heavy wool sweater. I tied my hair back into a ponytail so it couldn't fall into my eyes.

I pulled my camel winter coat from the closet. This was the fullest-cut coat I owned, and best for hiding a gun with my arm down at my side. I slid into the coat, grabbed my purse, and started for the door. I squeezed the purse and felt my .38 in its place.

It was showtime.

• • •

I met Art at Thirty-fifth and State, the edge of the IIT campus, at nine o'clock. A cheerless sky had begun to spit flurries. We decided I would start at the Student Union—we thought Kuzov unlikely to come there and see me—while Art would go to the Science Building. We were to meet at the Union in an hour.

Eager to dig for information, I entered the Union's largest room, a sterile space populated with cafeteria-style tables and lit by recessed fluorescence. The warm, still air smelled of coffee. Thirty or forty students, most alone or in quiet pairs, sat scattered among the tables. More read newspapers than textbooks; nearly all had coffee or a can of soda in front of them.

I spoke with a half-dozen students before I found one who recognized Kuzov's name. He said he had never registered for a Kuzov course, but that he knew several people who had. He surveyed the room, then pointed to a woman and a man who sat close to each other at a far table. I walked over to them.

"My name is Nora Callum," I said. They each wore sweatshirts, neither with "IIT" emblazoned across its front. They looked about twenty years of age. I showed them my detective shield and they straightened their spines reflexively.

"Don't worry," I said. "Can I talk to you for a minute?"

I sat in a chair across from them. The woman was a round, curly blonde with her hair tied back. Her teeth were buck. Her boyfriend wore a stringy mustache and horn-rimmed glasses from the sixties. His pale face hadn't a trace of deceit in it.

"A person across the room told me you know Dr. Kuzov," I said.

"Second-semester physics," the man said, "we have it." His right hand, slightly trembling, moved to encircle his soda can.

"Did you have one of his courses last semester?" I asked.

"Physics 201," the woman said. "Mondays and Wednesdays."

"Days or evenings?" I said.

"Evenings. Seven to ten. No labs."

"Tough subject?" I asked, as filler.

"Yeah," she said, "but he's a good teacher."

"And fair," the man quickly added before taking a slug of soda.

"How do you mean?" I said.

He wiped his lips. "His grading, his tests. It's your own fault if you don't do well in Dr. Kuzov's courses."

I jumped at his lead-in. "Oh, the tests—do you remember the midterm?"

They glanced at each other, quizzical as they rummaged their memories.

I helped: "It would have been the Wednesday before Thanksgiving."

The man's face lit in recollection. "Sure," he said. "I did better than I thought I would on that one."

"I aced it," the woman blurted with unabashed pride.

"You mentioned physics was an evening course," I said. "Are tests given during regular class times?"

"Yes," she said, "unless—"

"Unless you can talk the professor out of it," the man interrupted with a roguish laugh.

"And did you?" I coaxed, smelling bounty. "Talk Dr. Kuzov out of it?" My pulse came up into my neck.

"Didn't have to," the woman said. "He gave it earlier that day, because of Thanksgiving. Getting us away for the break, I mean." Her teeth jutted from her smile. "He's a good guy."

"So it was Dr. Kuzov who offered the time change?" I asked.

"He said it would work if we didn't let Administration know," the man answered.

I said, "What time—"

"Then we went to my home together for the holiday," the woman cut in. She grinned at her boyfriend.

"What time did you take the exam?" I pushed.

"Three, maybe four o'clock that afternoon," the man said.

"Done by six?" I said.

"At the latest," he said.

"And did Administration ever know of the change in test time?" I asked, looking at both of them.

"I doubt anyone tipped it," the man said.

"Who cares?" the woman added irreverently. "Hey, why are you asking, Lieutenant?"

"Mmm . . . let's call it an immigration matter."

TWENTY-NINE

Students streamed from the Union, heading for ten-o'clock classes, slipping into their coats as they walked. Art and I had taken a corner table away from the flow. "Tell me about your guy," I said anxiously.

Art unzipped his parka. Snowflakes still clung to the thick fur of his hood. "He's an adult student, maybe thirty. Works days driving a bus for the CTA and does school in the evenings—Kuzov's physics course last semester. He's so sure about the test time because it forced him to miss work that afternoon. His supervisor had a shit-fit."

"When did he say the exam ended?"

"Between five and six."

"That confirms what my kids said. Then Kuzov could have been at The Helmand to make Boyes's reservation at eight."

"With ease," Art said, "even during rush hour."

"Wait, the guy doesn't drive. I hauled him to County to identify Boyes."

"So he hops a bus, or he splurges on a taxi. Anyway, that takes care of opportunity, but I'm asking again—what about motive?"

I ignored the question because I couldn't answer it. I stared at my hands, picking at a hangnail. Then, deliberately, I said, "It's time to move on him, Art."

Art shifted his bulk closer to the table. "Aren't there a few hoops to jump through first? Like giving Administration another whack at the exam time they told you was in the evening?"

"Waste of effort," I said. "Kuzov's alibi's dead. Administration assumed he followed the school's policy on exams, so they just spit me that information. They're ignorant about what an individual professor might actually have done." Like an evangelist, I lifted my hands into the air. "And look, how can we doubt these students?"

Art said, "We don't have a warrant, and—"

"And won't be able to get one," I broke in. "Shit, I'm supposed to be confined to home! Besides, I'm talking about flushing him, not arresting."

Art looked away from me in frustration. The snowflakes on his hood were turning to beaded water. "Yeah . . . flushing. You cut some goddamn fine lines, Nora."

I stood from my chair and pointed to a pay phone on the wall. "I'm going over there and I'm going to call him at his office, Art."

"And say what?"

"I dunno. Maybe I'll just blow smoke down his hole and see what happens."

He answered on the second ring, his voice pleasantly edged with his faint, refined accent. "Good morning. Valery Kuzov."

"Dr. Kuzov, this is Nora." I leaned backward to the cold tile wall. Twenty feet away, Art sat with his eyes stuck to me.

"Ah, Nora," Kuzov said warmly. I could picture his smile and his cropped beard. "Have you recovered from last Saturday's conference?"

"Oh, sure," I said. "Say, I wonder if we could meet—about some new developments in the Boyes case."

"What sort of developments?"

Into thin air, I floated, "Having to do with Irina Varonyev." I made a funny face and watched Art shake his head.

Kuzov's pause was long enough to tell me I had set a hook in his gullet. I heard him exhale before he said, "Where are you, Nora?"

"On the North Side," I lied, "but I can come down to IIT."

"I have to be in the Loop this morning. Could we meet there? In about an hour or so?"

"Fine."

"In front of the Art Institute?" he asked politely. "Would that be convenient for you?"

"Perfect. I'll be there."

"Good."

I sat back down. "Where are you meeting?" Art asked.

"Art Institute, in an hour."

"One of the galleries?"

"No, out front."

"Where after that?"

I shrugged ignorance.

"What makes you think he'll show?" Art asked.

"Because he's dropped fresh dung by killing Stevens, and that scares him. Maybe enough to get suckered."

"He won't know yet that we've found Stevens. You going to confront him?"

"Yep, it's time for a push," I said. "When the media starts chewing on the Stevens murder, Sweet Valery might be riding the first plane across the Atlantic."

Art wiped sweat off his forehead with both his hands. "Mind getting a little practical, as in making a plan to catch the bad guy?"

"Go ahead."

"Okay, he walks up. Then it's 'Hi, Val, how are you? Isn't this weather shitty?' That's about it for talking on the street, so where do you go next?"

"Any suggestions?"

"The Palmer House is only a block west."

"All right," I said. "You backing me up?"

"Of course—it'll be easy in that big lobby." He aimed a thumb at my purse. "You still armed?"

I nodded. "Same .38 you felt the other day in the Fury."

"Got a pocket radio?"

"No. One of the few things I *did* turn in to Frankie."

He reached inside his coat and brought out a portable police radio. "Take mine. I have another in the car."

"Thanks," I said. "Where you going to start out?"

"Under one of the Institute's lions. Very close to your ass, cowboy."

• • •

I followed Art off the campus, but lost him in traffic. The flurries were coming harder now, the clouds lower and darker as the snow thickened. I made the Loop in thirty minutes. The best I could do for the Fury was a spot at Michigan and Balbo. It was highly illegal parking, but I decided a detective under investigation by Internal Affairs and the State's Attorney's Office could cut herself some slack.

I tramped to the Art Institute through slushy snow, watching for Art. I stopped midway between the two huge, standing lion sculptures that guard the Institute's Michigan Avenue stairs. In a minute, I saw Art turn at Monroe and walk toward me. I was careful not to look directly at him as he closed. He stopped next to me, putting his back to mine so he looked up the stairs while I faced the street. "I'm parked in the Underground," he said quietly. "I'll be under the south lion."

With my eyelids lowered, I watched Art walk away. He leaned against the great concrete base that held the lion, his head barely as high as the animal's feet.

For the next fifteen minutes, I stood near the curb, distancing myself from any cluster of people that might hide me from Kuzov's notice. I couldn't guess whether he'd approach along the Michigan Avenue sidewalk or across the street from intersecting Adams. My eyes never stopped scanning. Wind and snow lashed my face. The street was sloppy with whizzing traffic and dirty, half-melted snow.

When a maroon sedan pulled up, I waved it away—I didn't want it blocking my vision across the street—but then its driver reached out and opened the passenger door. I noticed an IIT emblem on the door. "Quick," I heard him say, "get in out of this weather."

It was Kuzov. Smiling. Driving.

My brain whirred. After a few confused seconds, I entered the car. This wasn't the Palmer House, but I couldn't risk haggling with him.

I slammed the door shut, and Kuzov pulled away quickly. When I looked out the window to the side mirror, I saw Art running after us, slipping in snow, losing ground with every second. Inside, only the slap of the windshield wipers broke the quiet.

I touched the back of my hand to a water drop on the tip of my nose. "I didn't know you drove," I said.

Headed north on Michigan, he made the light at Madison. "I've been practicing," he said. "The school is kind enough to lend me this car when I wish."

"I see." I wondered how much practice it took to do ninety on the O'Hare bypass while shooting.

"Where is your car?" he asked.

"Parked back there a ways."

He turned west at Randolph. I glanced over and saw his V-hawk profile, and I shivered inside. "Where are we going, Dr. Kuzov?"

"You mentioned new developments in the Boyes matter," he said. "I have a theory about the case that I thought I would share with you. Let's go back to my office."

We passed parking lots and run-down steak palaces and pizza shops on Randolph until we turned south at Wells to head for IIT. Fog and falling snow half swallowed the ceiling of el tracks overhead. I was trying desperately to hone the plan of action that Art had begged me to make back at the Union, but my mind was as blank as white light. Outside, the new storm had driven pedestrians off the streets and sidewalks.

At Monroe we turned east, away from any reasonable route to IIT. Although we were circling back toward the Art Institute, I knew Art would never still be there. Then, not looking at me, Kuzov said, "On second thought, maybe it would be better to start where you found Edward's body."

The idea of accompanying Kuzov to Lincoln Park rattled me. I thought about the swamp and I reviewed my options. I opened my coat, telling Kuzov I was warm, but he said nothing. In the quiet, I felt my wits finally sharpen. My eyes darted continually to the buildings we were passing—I knew what I was looking for.

We crossed La Salle Street. Casually, I reached to be sure that my purse strap was firmly on my shoulder. My right hand, hidden by my coat, searched and found the cold metal of the door handle. I waited for my best chance.

• • •

At Clark, at a red light, I said, "The park is going to be full of snow by the time we get there."

Kuzov said nothing, now so arrogant that he needn't bother responding. I was jittery to the point of distraction, but his discourtesy kindled a fury in me. I stared out the windshield, imagining the wrecked heads of Boyes and Stevens suspended grotesquely in the moving white curtain falling in front of me.

We continued east on Monroe, crossing Dearborn. I was running out of time: in a few minutes we could be at high speed on Lake Shore Drive. Sidewalk traffic was minimal, virtually no one to help me, but my chances weren't going to get much better.

My hand tightened on the door handle. I made sure my prosthetic foot was not encumbered by anything on the floorboard. Just ahead, half a block before State, I saw an alley opening off of Monroe. I felt ready.

My hand jerked the door handle while my good foot pushed hard on the floorboard. I banged my shoulder against the door and it flung wide open. Blowing snow slapped my face as I jumped from the car. I smacked the street hard, then rolled clear of the car, my left hand never leaving my purse strap. The asphalt surface under the snow tore skin off the heel of my right hand.

Kuzov drove ahead another twenty yards before stopping at curbside. By this time, I had righted myself and hurried into the alley. Walled in by tall buildings, it was narrow, dark, and confining. A dozen or more dumpsters overflowing with garbage were scattered as erratically as toys in the deep-rutted snow. Ahead, a high chain-link fence closed the alley to the south. I was trapped in a dead end.

I ran farther into the alley, past the first half-dozen dumpsters, then stopped and crouched behind one, a rusted hulk with a cap of new snow and the stench of rotting garbage. My bloody right hand dived into the purse I had held so tight when I jumped from the car. I brought out Art's radio. I leaned against the brick wall of a building and peeked around the dumpster's edge, watching for Kuzov.

I clicked on the radio and called Area Six. Young Mike Jewett was the dispatcher on duty. "Mike?" I said. "Nora Callum." I tried to slow my breathing. I was freezing but I felt sweat rolling down my chest.

"Gotcha," Jewett said. "Go ahead."

"The rat's out of his hole."

"What?" the radio crackled.

I squeezed the radio hard in my hand. "Get Art for me, Mike. My need is now. You—"

"Hey, Nora, aren't you suspend—"

"Goddammit, Mike! Don't interrupt me!"

"Okay, okay."

"You tell Art I'm in an alley off Monroe, just west of State. He's close by here somewhere. Find him, Michael. You find him for me, goddammit!"

"I will."

I clicked off and shoved the radio back into my purse. The wind roiled down the alley at me, whipping my ponytail. Above, past iron fire escapes jutting from walls, the hard gray sky poured snow into the tunnel that entrapped me.

Kuzov, hatless and wearing a light trench coat, entered the mouth of the alley.

I slipped from behind my dumpster and crawled back two more, trying for distance between myself and Kuzov. I reached into my purse for my .38. Except for the wind, the alley was quiet, the traffic noise from Monroe muffled by the padding of snow.

Kuzov stopped next to the first dumpster. He kicked at something while his bare right hand grasped the dumpster's side for support. He twisted his head this way and that, looking for me. I peeked out from behind my dumpster. Nothing. Nobody. Art or no Art, it was time. I had nowhere else to go, nothing else to do.

Careful with my prosthetic foot, I stood and moved from behind the dumpster. Snow melted and ran off my cheeks. My face was cold and wet, but I was warm inside my shirt.

I opened my coat to its fullest. My arm was slack at my side, my revolver in my hand behind a fold of coat. I set my forefinger against the gun's still-dry trigger.

When he saw me, Kuzov let go of his dumpster. He straightened and took a step forward. We were forty or fifty feet apart. Into the windblown snow I yelled, "Stop right there!"

Kuzov did. He called to me, "Ahh, Nora. I hope you didn't hurt yourself coming out of the car."

I stood motionless, too outraged to speak.

"I would like to come closer," he said.

"Don't bother. Not yet."

He wiped snow from his eyebrows. "This weather makes it difficult to see well."

"Would you rather I had stayed for the ride to Lincoln Park?" I said contemptuously. "To the swamp?"

I thought of the two dead, half-frozen, waterlogged bodies I had seen and touched in that swamp. Impulsively, at my anger's bidding, I said, "You want me to talk about the men I've pulled from that shithole lately?"

He said nothing but took two steps forward, stopping before I could object. He patted his coat's left pocket, then glided a hand inside. "I received a letter today that I'd like to show you," he said calmly. "It's about Phobos and Irina Varonyev."

"I didn't meet you to read letters or talk about Varonyev. I'm here for the two men whose brains you've blown out."

His hand started from his pocket. I looked for the letter, but instead saw a gun. Before I could speak or move, two flashes of light burst brightly in the alley's dark air.

Both slugs crashed my left leg. I spun hard to the ground, face-first, my feet pointed toward Kuzov, my head toward the fence that closed off the alley's exit. I tried to stand but realized I couldn't. I felt snow jammed up my nose. The end of my stump, the flabby, boneless part, seared with pain.

I snorted the debris from my nose, then glanced down my left side. Blood oozed where my slacks were ripped open at mid-thigh. The second bullet had torn through the metal and fiber of my prosthetic knee, had harmlessly hit me where I wasn't.

From the corner of my eye I saw Kuzov. He began to lope

toward me, but on his third step he slipped in snow. Arms flailing for balance, he fell, his gun firing aimlessly when he landed; the bullet ricocheted off one dumpster then another in earsplitting clangs.

I had been granted an extra few seconds. He was now ten or fifteen yards away. I didn't have a decent shot at that distance, not with both of us down and the corner of a dumpster in the way. My advantage would have to come from surprise.

I waited, unmoving, except for my eyes looking past my leg toward the fallen Kuzov. The snow was coming so thick that I fought to keep him in focus. My right hand firmed on the .38 under my belly.

Kuzov struggled to his feet. When he saw I wasn't moving, he seemed less hurried, taking time to shake the snow from his arms. He started toward me again, now raising his gun.

I whirled up out of the snow to a sitting position, firing as I turned. Both my shots struck him in the chest, stopping him in place. His arms dropped to his sides. The delayed force of the hits now drove him a step backward. His eyebrows raised in disbelief.

I thought he would fall, but instead, he lurched forward, toward, me, his gun again coming up. I squeezed off my final round, and it punched in under his right eye. When the slug blew through the back of his braincase, a crimson hemisphere of blood sprayed into the snowflakes behind him.

He thumped into the snow next to me, dead before he hit the ground. The smell of gunpowder was all around him. An artery, a small red pumper, made a few squirts out the hole in the back of his skull. Still sitting, I dropped my gun and pressed my palms to my face. In the cold, black, smelly darkness of my hands I thought of Vincent Cruzado, and I whispered, "Jesus, God, please help me."

THIRTY

Exhausted, I stretched back on the ground, next to Kuzov but facing away from him. I rested my cheek on my forearm. At the entrance of the alley I saw gyrating red and blue lights. If they had used their sirens, I never heard them over the howling of the wind.

I lifted my face. Several dark forms, their outlines blurred, moved in front of the lights. I wiped my eyes and looked more acutely. One figure separated from the rest. Low to the ground, the leader began running toward me, between dumpsters, through the white miasma of snow. I couldn't be sure of the face because there seemed to be only snow and blackness. "Son-of-a-bitch!" he screamed. "Get an ambulance! Son-of-a-bitch!"

Familiar baritone: that's what broke me. I rolled onto my back. I began sobbing in my relief.

Art slid to a stop next to me. "Where you hit, girl?" he shrieked. "Where? Goddamn!"

"Just my stump. That's it."

He stared momentarily at the dead Kuzov, then pocketed his own drawn gun. He bent and fingered the remains of my prosthesis, which had been ripped half off my thigh. Dropping to his knees, he split open my slacks, then eased my broken socket off my stump. He found a handkerchief in his pants to put pressure on my wound.

"I'm all right," I said, choking on tears. "I'm not crying 'cause I'm hurt. It's just . . . I dunno." I shrugged inanely.

"Easy." Keeping his handkerchief pushed down with his right hand, he closed my coat with his left. "I didn't know where he was bringing you. When Jewett called, I couldn't get through the traffic to—"

"He's a southpaw," I interrupted. "That's why I wasn't ready enough."

"What you talking about?"

"He brought the gun from his left-hand pocket. He said he had a letter about Varonyev. I didn't think it would be a gun, not from that side. I thought—"

"Stop with this shit."

"No." I half sat up, propping my weight on my extended right arm. My head spun with dizziness when it left the ground. "It wasn't retribution, Art, like they said about Cruzado. Kuzov fired first, and then, when he got back up . . . "

"Nora, look—"

"The ones into his chest didn't stop him. I needed a head shot, to defend . . . he was coming at me, gun up."

Art let go of the handkerchief and wrapped both his arms around me. "Christ Almighty, Nora, shut up, please. Just shut the fuck up, will you please?"

He pulled me tight against himself. I felt his cold stubbled chin scratch my forehead.

Others reached us, and Art gently lowered me so my head was in the lap of kneeling Officer Ann Reilly. I watched Steve Schwartz walk a semicircle around Kuzov while talking into a diminutive radio. He gave me a thumbs-up sign. Alice Adams from Evidence was the last arrival from the first group. She leaned over and affectionately squeezed my calf. Grinning irreverently, she glanced at Kuzov and said, "Afternoon delight? In an alley? In the snow?"

The ambulance arrived and medics wrapped my stump in a thick cotton pressure dressing, then lifted me onto a litter. When I shivered, they covered me with a blanket. We started out of the alley, just myself and the medics, the cops staying behind to begin their work. I closed my eyes and thought of Meg.

• • •

They had stripped me naked—emergency room trick to ensure patient compliance—then covered me with a ridiculous gown that quit at waist level, with a sheet for territory beyond. I had already completed an unpleasant round-trip to X-ray. Now I hugged the side of an exam table; off the table edge, my stump hung hip-deep in a basin of dark iodine solution. The injection of Demerol I had been given on arrival made my pain easily tolerable.

Confined to a cubicle, I hadn't seen a nurse for thirty minutes. Overheard conversation told me it was shift change. I had no good reason to be irritated at the Northwestern Memorial staff, but I was anyway. All I could think of was getting home to Meg.

Dr. Charnley, a young, already-balding resident in General Surgery who had checked me on admission, slid back the curtain and re-entered. Without expression, he said, "Your films look good, Lieutenant."

"Films?"

"X-rays." He came nearer the table. He wore an azure-colored scrub suit. Hair flourished in the V-neck of his shirt, accomplishing on his chest what it couldn't on his scalp. His fingers and nails were pink and immaculate. He smelled of disinfectant soap. "No bone damage, just some small metallic fragments embedded in the soft tissues—from the slug that passed through."

"Good. Then I can get out of here."

"Oh, no. I'll have to place a drain in the wound. I can't suture it shut because it's contaminated—by definition. Sewing it up risks infection."

"I'll take my chances." I had Meg at home and a funeral tomorrow for Robert Stevens. More to the point, I felt bitchy and couldn't seem to stop myself from pushing this man.

"You'll need a day or two of IV antibiotics," he said. "That can't be done at home."

"Give me a prescription for the tablet form. I'm intelligent. I'll take as directed."

"I don't think you understand, Lieutenant."

I sat up and hoisted my stump from the basin. The fluid

iodine mixed with a track of blood from the bullet hole and ran back into the basin. I grasped this dripping half-thigh in both my hands and I said, "Look, Dr. Charnley, I've lived with this god-damned thing for some time now. I know what it is to have infection in it. I know open wounds and skin breakdown and how to change dressings. I'll do the right thing by it. See, I need it to walk."

"But, if you—"

"I have places to go, people to see," I said flippantly. "Really, I'm a big girl. Tell me when to come back for an appointment. You can count on me showing up."

He backed off a step. "It's bad practice to sign you out like this. I can't do things that way. My chief will—"

"I'm leaving, Doc."

"Then you'll be required to absolve the hospital and myself of all responsibility. You have to sign papers."

"Get them."

Lips shut tight together, he turned away.

"I'll need a pair of crutches," I said to his rear.

"I'm not the crutch man," he answered angrily without looking back. He started down the hallway.

"Then send that person in," I called after him.

I plopped my stump back into the iodine and lay down again; I wiped my wet brown hands on the gown. I had plenty of time to review my situation—my boorishness had just earned me another thirty minutes of deserved helplessness.

I had been arrogant with the resident and now felt ashamed. Whether it was an excuse or not, I realized I had finally struck bottom after thirty intense hours at the mercy of my adrenaline. Killing Kuzov had been the final, hectic spike, and now, weary and discouraged that I hadn't delivered him alive, I was lashing out at people trying to help me. I wasn't too spent to be an embarrassment to myself.

When someone finally came in, it was a student nurse in a striped uniform. She carried a pair of crutches, a handful of dressings, prescriptions for antibiotics and pain pills, and the forms Charnley had mentioned.

"So you're the sacrificial lamb," I said meekly.

"What?"

"Nothing. Could you please ask Dr. Charnley to step back in here for a minute?"

"He's left for the operating room."

"Oh. I wanted to apologize for being so rude."

She nodded her understanding. "People get crabby when they're hurt. They're not at their best."

"Let's hope not."

She dressed my wound—it would remain unsutured as Charnley had wanted—then helped me on with my clothes. I phoned the Eighteenth and asked for a squad to pick me up. I was back home before Art was the wiser. I was glad to see someone had driven the Fury back to Fargo Avenue.

The next morning's sun was higher in the sky than I had remembered it for some time: spring was really upon us. Over the lake, a few opalescent clouds skidded along the horizon from south to north. The breeze smelled sharp and fresh, and the lake lapped at the seawall that stood near the entrance to Madonna della Strada.

The procession of family, faculty, and students into the church was long—Robert Stevens had been more admired than I would have guessed. Slow because of my crutches and the ill-fitting, spare prosthesis I had unearthed in my closet, I brought up the rear. Before entering Madonna's doors, I looked up and noticed the lake side of Damen Hall. I wondered which window marked Stevens's office, the room where I had first told him about Edward Boyes's murder, news he would have been better off never having heard.

Inside, the altar occupied the center of the church, not the west end as it had during my student days. The mourners filed into the circular rows of chairs that rippled out from the altar. At the head of an aisle, Stevens's casket stood trimmed with yellow flowers. The chapel's high, stained-glass windows shone with colors fired by the sun.

I chose to sit for the service because my stump throbbed inside the leg that I wore only for looks. One of the university's

Jesuits, who apparently knew Stevens well, said the funeral Mass. Standing with his folded hands on the casket, he gave a sermon about Stevens's dedication to family and school and friends: the priest cut so close to the bone that I thought he must have known what Stevens had sacrificed for Edward and Irina. He said the Loyola community would now draw together with Eileen and the children, would console them against the great misfortune they had suffered. No tongue of fire rested on the priest's head as he spoke, but I listened intently and was touched. I suppose I was sensitive because I knew how near I had come the afternoon before to my own Rogers Park funeral.

Outside afterward, I stood respectfully near the edge of the crowd—I had known the man for little more than two weeks. While the pallbearers carried the casket toward the hearse, Eileen Stevens noticed me and came over. She tugged on my coat sleeve and took me a few feet away from the people I was near. "I heard the news," she said. "Are you hurt?" She gestured to my crutches.

"Not much." I smiled self-consciously.

Her Catholic scruples still whole and prickly, she said, "I know I shouldn't admit this, or even think it, but I'm glad about what you did. Killing him, I mean."

I didn't answer.

"He was the one who murdered Robert, wasn't he, Nora?"

"I think so. I'll find out more this afternoon."

"Let me know."

"I will," I said. "Can I call sometime?"

She nodded. "I'll be waiting. I'll have time."

She turned and walked back to Jerry and her girls. I looked at the hearse: sunlight flashed off the handles of the casket as the men lifted it for loading.

THIRTY-ONE

I decided not to follow to the cemetery; inside my socket the
dressings were saturated and needing a change. At home, Anna
drew a tub of warm, soapy water, and I soaked for half an hour.
We redressed the clean stump, but I didn't put the leg back on
because of the swelling and ache. When my phone rang several
times, I told Anna not to answer. I wasn't ready for reporters. Art
was the only person I wanted to talk to, and I had decided to see
him soon. At one o'clock, after phoning Olga Berggolts in Moscow, I left for Area Six.

I parked the Fury in front of Margie's Grill. Hungry, I went in
and bought hamburgers and French fries for Art and myself,
then crutched across the street. Cops and staff came up to me in
the busy Area Six lobby; no one treated me like a leper any
longer. People asked how I felt, congratulated me for bringing in
Kuzov. I might have luxuriated in the attention had not the pain
of Eileen's loss been so fully upon me.

I started up the stairs when behind me I heard, "Hold it,
Callum." I turned. Melchior stood in the doorway near the
stairs, one foot on the first step, a beefy hand gripping the rail.
"You're cleared," he said without emotion. "The report came in
this morning."

"You mean Cruzado's death?"

He nodded. "But round two starts this afternoon."

"Kuzov?" I asked as if I didn't know. I wondered if Internal
Affairs had ever begun a second shooting investigation on the
same day that the same cop was cleared of a first shooting.

"Two o'clock," Melchior said. "Same bunch will be in your office."

"I'll be there."

"This one'll be easier. I give it a forty-eight-hour turnaround, max. Campbell confirms the asshole practically kidnapped you at the Art Institute. And you were shot first."

He paused for what I thought might be the moment it would take him to ask about my wound, or to thank me for stopping the Lincoln Park murders. Instead, he waddled back into the corridor.

I stood in place, thinking. Melchior hadn't been warm in telling me of the Cruzado decision, but neither had he been mean. Two instances of civility toward me inside of a week: it seemed daring behavior from a man I found so easy to despise. Was he gradually, confoundedly, shifting the burden of hate onto me? If his conduct lost predictability, it meant a new confusion for me.

I resumed climbing one step at a time, my crutches always in the lead. My right hand struggled to hold the lunch bag against the crutch handle.

In our office, Art took the bulging sack from Margie's. He sat across from me, opened the sack, and divvied the food between us. He bent to the desk and sniffed. "How'd you ever make it through the lobby with this?"

"People don't mess with the wounded."

He unwrapped a burger, his face suddenly stern. "I checked at Northwestern last night," he said carefully, "after we'd finished at Kuzov's apartment. Must've been after eleven. I hoped not to wake you, just wanted to see how you were doing."

"Oh."

A stiff grin appeared on his lips, then vanished as quickly as it came. "Seems like Lieutenant Callum had already signed herself out—and against medical advice, mind you."

"They cleaned things up and bandaged me. They gave me some prescriptions."

He bit into his burger to try to stop himself from talking but he couldn't. "See, Nora, you've got this flaw, this lack of basic trust . . . "

I grabbed a handful of fries. I lifted my eyebrows in anticipation.

" . . . or is it simply a presumption that you know more than the doctors, or any other expert you don't feel like waiting around on?"

"Art, I know my leg."

"And do you know the proper treatment of a gunshot injury?"

I reached for my hamburger and held it high into the space between us. "I'm going to eat now. I'm listening only selectively."

He mumbled, "Aw, shit, Mother, I can't dance."

We sat quietly and ate for several minutes before he opened a drawer in his desk. He pulled out my purse and slid it over to me. "It's a little muddy, but I think everything's there."

"Including my spare .38?" I asked.

"Yes, and reloaded." He smiled—unable to hold a grudge, he had ended his complaining.

"Thank you, Arthur."

"Don't mention it. There wasn't enough left of your prosthesis to bring it back to life."

"What hit it?"

"Kuzov carried a .45 Colt automatic loaded with hollow points."

"That explains the holes in Stevens's and Boyes's skulls. There is a match, isn't there?"

"John Dover phoned me this morning. The gun that shot you fired the round Dr. Dorner found inside Stevens's chest."

"Tell me about Kuzov's place," I said.

Art's big hands crumpled the wrapper of his finished burger. "He lived in a development just south of the Loop, near the Headquarters Building, actually."

"Dearborn Park?"

"That's it. Nice place for a rental, neat as a pin." He pushed his chair away and crossed his legs. "Everything we needed was in or on his desk."

"Like?"

"Like practically every newspaper or journal or magazine article ever published on the Phobos probes—in English and a few other languages. Like the *Trib* and *Sun-Times* stories about the conferences where Boyes and Stevens shot off their mouths. Like news photos snapped at the swamp the day Boyes's body was brought out."

He wiped his chin clean with a napkin, then scornfully tossed it back to the desk. "Was it Kuzov who shot at you at O'Hare?"

"Had to be, wouldn't you think?"

"What kind of a hand-job was this guy, Nora?"

I set my half-eaten hamburger down—my appetite wasn't holding its own against talk about Kuzov. "I phoned Olga Berggolts in Moscow," I said. "She said she visited Irina yesterday. When Olga told her that Edward had been murdered, Irina opened up like a spigot."

"Tell me," Art said.

I leaned back into the hollow of my chair. "See, in Tallinn, Kuzov was demoted as head of Phobos Guidance in favor of Boyes. Kuzov sulked bitterly, Irina said."

"But Boyes was canned by NASA."

"Yes, so Kuzov was reinstated," I said, "but he made one bad decision after another. He reversed the good work Boyes had done."

"Where does Irina come in?" he asked.

"Higher-ups, doing what Boyes had advised, told Kuzov to dump a certain program called 'pre-flight' from the probes' computers before launch. Kuzov did not obey, yet he told his bosses he had. Only Irina knew of Kuzov's defiance. She consented to keep quiet—for a price."

"Reunion with Edward," Art said, with an insightful grin.

"You got it. Kuzov had the political clout to get her to the States."

"So how does she end up in jail?"

"She sent up an innocent command to Phobos I that turned deadly because pre-flight was still on board. It's complicated computer stuff, but it boils down to the probe being lost because Kuzov had not erased the program as ordered."

"Still, why jail for Irina?"

"Soviet brass needed a scapegoat," I said. "They didn't know Kuzov was really to blame."

Art said, "Irina has a tongue. Why didn't she speak up?"

"Because Kuzov promised her that when things blew over, he would still help her leave Russia."

"You haven't touched motive yet," Art reminded.

"Easy. At the Loyola conference, Edward went public with Irina's suffering in jail. Kuzov heard it and got itchy."

"Boyes was too close?"

"Yes," I said. "If the Soviets learned of Kuzov's non-compliance, then it's him in Lefortova instead of Irina. Boyes had to go, and quickly."

"And Stevens?"

"Same thing—he mouthed off about Irina in public. Kuzov needed damage control."

After a long pause, when I thought, hoped, we were done, Art asked, "Why'd Stevens bother anyway? Getting involved, I mean."

"He and Edward were like brothers," I said. "After Edward was found dead, all the cops could come up with was Eugene Easter." I turned my face toward the window. "Stevens was such a stubborn son-of-a-bitch. I told him —"

I stopped there, unable to go on, the words stuck in my throat. My hands clenched in my lap.

Art finished for me. "You told him that Eugene may not have murdered Boyes, and that the case was ongoing."

My face still turned away, I nodded my assent.

Softly, generously, he said, "So what the fuck?"

I jerked my head back so hard that the tear tracking down my cheek turned a right angle toward my ear. "I was shooting my mouth off to Stevens because I was so goddamned pissed at Jimmy O'Donnell, and at Schwartz and Melchior and Frankie!"

"For—"

"For arresting and beating some poor, dumb bastard who doesn't know from shinola about Phobos probes or Lefortova or anything else about this case!"

Art leaned his bulk against his desk. "Nora, you were right about Easter—get it? And you couldn't have known Stevens was going to go vigilante."

I rose higher in my chair. "Goddammit, Art! Don't you see that involving Stevens cost him two hollow points through his squash?"

Art slammed his fist onto the desk and I jumped. "You've saved Eugene Easter from the death penalty! Doesn't that mean anything to you? Isn't his shitty Uptown life just as valuable as Robert Stevens's?"

"Of course, it is. You know I believe that. It's just that Eileen Stevens and her kids . . . if you could have seen them this morning . . . "

Quieter again, he said, "There's no cop in the Department who could have done this case better. Take credit for five minutes, will you?"

Saying nothing, I stretched my neck so my head rested on the chairback. I stared at the ceiling's acoustical tiles, exhausted, my brain empty.

"You stay honest and do your best," Art said. "That's it. You can't control everything, Nora. When you gonna learn? When in Christ's name are you gonna wake up about that?"

Art stood and walked to the window that looked down onto Belmont Avenue. Staring into the luminous blue sky, he said, "So you were at the Stevens funeral?"

"Yep."

He turned and nodded to me obscurely. He came back to the desk, patting me once on my back as he passed. "Need some aspirin or something? Coffee?"

"No, thanks." I smiled, lips closed. "I feel good being back here with you."

Practice and more practice. Fifth try: *Anybody for supper?*

I mouthed those words into my kitchen phone the day after my new IA interviews. Satisfied that I had scoured the uncertainty from my voice, I punched in the Adler's number. His secretary transferred my call.

"Nora?" Halsey said.

"Hi. Umm . . . how are you?"

"Good," he said. "Say, are you—"

"Anybody for supper?"

A pause for his surprise, then, "I have to stay over—a meeting of the volunteer staff. Is seven or seven-thirty too late?"

"Gosh, no," I said.

"Any special place?"

"You pick."

"Do you know the Green Door?" he asked.

"No."

"A tavern on Orleans, near the entrance to the Kennedy."

"Okay, got it. I know the corner."

"Do you feel well enough for this, Nora? I heard on the news—your being shot, I mean."

"I'm fine. See you about seven-thirty."

Later, when Meg was settled upstairs with Anna, I showered and powdered and dressed. I chose a blue knit dress with a turtleneck collar and a belt that gathered things at my waist. I pushed the sleeves up off my wrists and tied my hair back with a ribbon. I slid my foot into a red flat.

I would have to meet Halsey on crutches; the prosthesis I had worn to Robert Stevens's funeral was still too ill-fitting to be comfortable. And besides, it was well past time for me to shake the chronic, naïve mistrust that can burden the disabled. I needed to concede to people apart from family and cops that I came with only one perfect leg. If they didn't understand, then to hell with them.

This was River North, the district shoehorned between the North Branch of the Chicago River and the Gold Coast, and bisected in the sky by the Franklin Street el tracks. The neighborhood defined capitalism at its shiniest, most of the old brick buildings lately rehabbed into a profusion of high-ceilinged art galleries, rare-map dealers, lofts for rental, eclectic restaurants, flower shops, and occasional rummage tagging along for the ride.

I parked on Erie and crutched toward the corner of Orleans.

The Green Door had the ground floor of an ancient frame building painted bottle-green, transfigured to black by the evening
darkness. The Orleans side of the tavern was undistinguished,
but the Erie flank sported a wall of uncovered windows. I moved
past slowly, watching the patrons at their tables while trying to
remain inconspicuous. Most were more fashionably dressed than
me, probably singles let out the hour before by their jailers at
LaSalle Street legal and financial houses.

I stood against a streetlight, my hands in my coat pockets; the
loss of the March sun had cost the city thirty degrees. The air
smelled of rain, or snow, but nothing was there. Down the street,
cars wound through second gear and growled up an entrance
ramp to the Kennedy Expressway. As I waited, I thought that my
invitation to Dan Halsey may have been a mistake. The man had
hurt me once by being untrustworthy in the most basic sense,
but the recent deaths of Cruzado, Stevens, and Kuzov had made
my heart hungry for company beyond Area Six.

Halsey didn't arrive till eight, and he looked shaken as he
climbed from a squealing, braking taxi that had sped through a
U-turn and nearly broadsided a crossing car. If I hadn't been on
crutches, I would have nabbed the driver. Halsey smiled thinly at
me and said, deadpan, "The Eagle has landed."

I grinned.

The noise whacked us immediately upon entry: the Green Door
was jumping. Young and middle-aged men and women, swigging
beer and laughing raucously in crescendos, filled the barstools
and circled the oilcloth-covered tables. Country music blared
from a corner jukebox, the sound of deep bass guitars hammer-
ing the air, air sweet with the smells of beer and frying onions
and hamburgers.

A hostess told us of a last empty table near the end of the bar.
We worked our way through the mob, then threw our coats over
the backs of the chairs and sat. Memorabilia heralding Chicago's
sports teams littered the walls and ceiling. A dusty moosehead
kept watch from high in a corner behind us.

"Great that you called," Halsey said above the thump of

music, "really." He wore a wool jacket and red-checked shirt that had much in common with our tablecloth. When he turned and called a waitress, I saw his ponytail hang up on his shoulder. The girl came; we each ordered draft beers.

Halsey pointed at my crutches up against the wall. "I guess I didn't know you were an amputee. When we were seeing each other, I didn't know."

I smiled. "So we each had our little secrets back then."

He shrugged and said nothing more about it. The waitress brought our beers and took our orders for food. When she left, Halsey said, "What happened to the black guy locked up for the first Lincoln Park murder?"

"Eugene Easter?" I said. "The State's Attorney's Office ordered his release yesterday. All charges against him were dropped."

I didn't say how Easter had left Cook County Jail and returned to his Uptown neighborhood without contacting Art or myself with even a shred of thanks. Staring into the flickering red candle bowl in the middle of the table, I was lost for a moment, my thoughts suddenly back to Eileen and Jerry alone on their staircase when I told them of Robert's death.

Halsey broke the trance: "Tell me about your child, Nora. I know you have a daughter."

"Her name is Megan." I tried to restrain my prideful smile. "She's eight, nearly nine . . . mmm . . . and she's very beautiful. She takes after her father."

"You don't claim contribution?"

I ran past him: "She's a second-grader—because everyone holds their children back these days. Did you do the same with yours?"

As though he had never heard me, he sipped his beer, then said, "You know, Nora, I once read a novel in which a man with a reference question goes up to a librarian, a woman, at a branch library. They're both about the same age—thirties, I think. Anyway, the woman guides the man into the stacks where they hunt through atlases and encyclopedias for a while. Then, as the woman is discussing the strategy of the search, the man abruptly interrupts her and asks, 'Are you beautiful?'"

Halsey stopped talking and stared at me. I smiled moronically; I had no idea what to say. My brain's only counsel told me I was sitting across the table from a man who two years before had lied boldfacedly to me.

"So what do you think, Nora?"

I tried to deflect him. "I want to know what the woman answered."

"She didn't. She ignored his question, yet she was intrigued and flattered by it. I don't remember much else—I didn't finish the book. That scene just came to me now when you talked of your daughter's beauty."

"I see."

"Crazy as it sounds," he said, "I wanted to ask you the same question the librarian was asked. Not to embarrass you, no, no. Just to see if you had the same impression of your beauty that others do."

I grabbed my mug and pulled a long cold swallow of beer down my throat. "I'll have to think about it."

The food arrived to save me. We ate quietly, the volume of the Green Door's music now swelling to make conversation a bigger chore. We each ordered another beer.

The music stopped completely and laughter, chatter, and banging silverware was all we heard for a minute. Then a slightly drunk young woman walked past our table to the jukebox where she bought several new selections. On her return trip she covered her ears with her hands and said to us, "My hearing's being wrecked, for God's sake! Let's slow things down a little."

She stumbled away. Her first choice began playing—a country ballad with a mournful harmonica working behind a husky female vocalist.

Halsey started into a monologue about the horrific losses sustained by the Phobos project. I pretended to listen, but instead, I daydreamed about resting my head on the scratch of heavy tweed that Halsey's jacket was made of, of seeing his ponytail in stark relief, so close I could count hairs if I chose, so near I could smell it above the wool. My reverie lifted then, but I was left with a warmth that radiated through my spine, and I sensed the gathering of sweat in the hair at the back of my neck. Behind me, Johnny Cash whooped out his music, and my heat was so great that I knew if Halsey reached out and touched me, I might blow through him like a firestorm.

We walked past the Green Door's clapboard siding toward the Fury. The sky was starless as always in the city, but a yellowish moon had risen from behind shifting clouds to the south. I walked with my coat open so I could feel the cold air against my damp dress and on the bare wet skin of my throat.

I followed Halsey's directions to his apartment near Wrigley-ville. During the drive, he jabbered about funding at the Adler, but again, I paid no attention. I pulled to the curb at his address. He opened the car door, but before he slid out he leaned over and kissed me first on my cheek, then, very lightly, on my half-opened mouth. I made an effort not to smile.

Halsey stepped out. "And don't you love their cheeseburgers?" he said.

I laughed out loud, my hand over my mouth. "I do, Dan, I really do. Maybe the best cheeseburgers I've ever eaten."

"Now, let's remember where to get those burgers. Erie and Orleans. Please help me remember, Nora."

"I dunno. But don't worry about it."

He closed the door and walked away, turning back to wave once before entering his lobby.

EPILOGUE

During the next few days, events proceeded rapidly behind closed doors. I was unaware of and didn't care about the mechanics, my interest only in outcomes.

Peggy Miksis telephoned me at home, and told me to report to duty when my leg felt well. Internal Affairs had determined that I had not acted radically in firing on Valery Kuzov. The State's Attorney's Office had shown no interest in pursuing the case, either.

A follow-up on Boyes's life-insurance policy established the innocence of Robert Stevens's phone calls to Houston. NASA confirmed that the Stevenses were listed as beneficiaries on the policy, and Eileen would be paid the proceeds. Stevens had had every reason to call Houston after Boyes's identity had been established.

Olga Berggolts called very early one morning to say that Irina had been released from Lefortova Prison. Russian officials now understood Kuzov's part in the Phobos fiasco. Olga and her family were taking Irina into their home for a time.

Two weeks after Kuzov's shooting, I managed to slide my healed stump into a new leg, an occasion that should have uplifted me, but didn't. Enigmatically, I had been crabby with Meg and Anna for several days, and now, sitting alone in the quiet of my apartment one afternoon, I was finally understanding why.

Television and newsprint—FEMALE COP BRINGS IN LINCOLN

PARK KILLER, SAVES UNDERPRIVILEGED BLACK YOUTH—had buoyed me during those early post-wounding days, and I bloomed like a winter hothouse flower. When media exaggeration inevitably withered, I folded deeply and tightly into myself. It wasn't loss of attention that collapsed me inward—at heart, I found public notice discomforting—but rather, the weight of my personal involvement with the Kuzov and Cruzado cases.

So many people I had known or come to know had been hurt: Michael Furey and Paris; all of the Stevenses; Edward and Irina. I myself had killed two men, men whose manifest guilt couldn't sweeten my memory of their tumbling, dying bodies. And in Cruzado's case, there was the disturbing notion that eagerness to see a score settled may grease one's trigger finger.

"Sentiment is a big problem for you, Nora," candid Art had said as he walked from our office one day when I dropped by Area Six to pick up my check. Then, at the door's threshold, he stopped and looked straight at me. "But, you know, I'm not so sure that isn't why I always want to be your partner."

I left the station and drove Lake Shore Drive until I found myself pulling off at the exit to the Waveland Golf Course. I parked past the outbuildings, the Fury aimed at the lake that shimmered with sunshine. I sat in the car for an hour, thinking about about Art's compliment, unwinding my confusion. I had been slogging through introspection and self-pity, and now I needed to let the air back into myself. It was time for me to stop blocking Meg's and Anna's and Art's access to me.

That night, I lay in bed thinking about the beautiful abstract drawing of the planets on the back of Edward Boyes's watch. In sleep, I dreamed for the last time about Irina Varonyev.

In my dream, we walked into a field where the air smelled of mowed grass. Fragile Irina went ahead of me, quickly to the lead, drawn to where I had pointed. As she speeded, I slowed: respect demanded a distance.

At Edward's grave, Irina stood upright for a moment, then knelt in the grass, next to the marker I had ordered installed, near enough to read it. With her head bowed, she placed her open palms on the white stone, leaning her weight forward onto her extended arms. She became rigid in this position, as if transfixed. Finally, she rose and turned to me, her wet cheeks glistening. She waved me closer, then gestured back at the marker, the marker that had been inscribed,

Our life, our happiness,
is beyond the North,
beyond ice, beyond death.

She said, "This stone—you?" I answered, "Yes," and when I did tears gathered thickly in my eyes. And when she asked why I had done the stone, I simply said because I had wanted to, but I thought, Because I know I have never felt for a man the way you felt for Edward. Because maybe if I honor what you had, Irina, I might find it, too.

Irina smiled at me shyly, and her expression made me want to shed my every trace of sarcasm. She thanked me for bringing her to the grave, then asked if we could leave. We headed back toward the Fury, she in the lead.

When I awoke from the dream, Irina was walking farther and farther away from me, through a cut of deepening afternoon sun that lit her tiny figure and shone brilliantly in the tops of the maples she approached.

The next evening, Meg and Anna and I picked up Paris and Neptune at their apartment. We drove to a small, bright Persian restaurant on North Wells where we met Peggy and her husband, Ted, who had just returned from the Cubs' Arizona camp. We ate falafel and tabouli, and pita smeared with hummus, and nobody said a word about recent events in our lives. Instead, we thoroughly analyzed the Cubs' chances for '89, only Meg successfully predicting the division championship they were to win that summer.

The next morning, I reported for duty at Area Six, and Frankie handed me my police .38 Special. Instead of taking lunch that noon, I drove to the bank at Chicago and Michigan, and asked for my safe-deposit box. Alone in the small booth, I took the extra gun from my purse and hid it in the bottom of the box. I might need it again someday.

One never knows, does she?